WITHIN THE GARDEN OF TWILIGHT

THE HOUSE OF CRIMSON & CLOVER VOLUME XI

SARAH M. CRADIT

Cover Design by Sarah M. Cradit
Editing by Emily A. Lawrence

First Edition
ISBN-10: 1545035288
ISBN-13: 978-1545035283

Publisher Contact:
sarah@sarahmcradit.com
www.sarahmcradit.com

ALSO BY SARAH M. CRADIT

KINGDOM OF THE WHITE SEA

Kingdom of the White Sea Trilogy

The Kingless Crown

The Broken Realm

The Hidden Kingdom

The Book of All Things

The Raven and the Rush

The Sylvan and the Sand

The Altruist and the Assassin

The Melody and the Master

The Claw and the Crowned

THE SAGA OF CRIMSON & CLOVER

The House of Crimson and Clover Series

The Storm and the Darkness

Shattered

The Illusions of Eventide

Bound

Midnight Dynasty

Asunder

Empire of Shadows

Myths of Midwinter

The Hinterland Veil

The Secrets Amongst the Cypress

Within the Garden of Twilight

House of Dusk, House of Dawn

Midnight Dynasty Series

A Tempest of Discovery

A Storm of Revelations

A Torrent of Deceit

The Seven Series

1970

1972

1973

1974

1975

1976

1980

Vampires of the Merovingi Series

The Island

and more

The Dusk Trilogy

St. Charles at Dusk: The Story of Oz and Adrienne

Flourish: The Story of Anne Fontaine

Banshee: The Story of Giselle Deschanel

Crimson & Clover Stories

Surrender: The Story of Oz and Ana

Shame: The Story of Jonathan St. Andrews

Fire & Ice: The Story of Remy & Fleur

Dark Blessing: The Landry Triplets

Pandora's Box: The Story of Jasper & Pandora

The Menagerie: Oriana's Den of Iniquities

A Band of Heather: The Story of Colleen and Noah

The Ephemeral: The Story of Autumn & Gabriel

Bayou's Edge: The Landry Triplets

For more information, and exciting bonus material, visit www.sarahmcradit.com

You can find a complete list of content warnings on my website: sarahmcradit.com

For Dad

THE CALM

“The man who has experienced shipwreck shudders even at a calm sea.”

Ovid

JUSTICE

1
COLLEEN

Colleen Deschanel moved with measured strides as she transported the sacred candelabra from the concealed Deschanel Magi Collective Council chambers to the extended dining hall of The Gardens. So many of her kin awaited her words there, and her words would matter. The hall had not been so overflowing since the resurgence of the Deschanel Curse, but circumstances were even more dire now. Complacency was not a response they could afford.

A warm hand pressed into her lower back. Colleen released the breath she'd been holding. "You're here. You came." She knew without turning.

"Of course I did." Her dearest sister, Evangeline, kissed the back of her head, right at the crown. She'd stayed away from New Orleans after her daughter Katja's breakdown, at Katja's request. Her presence in the most recent Council meeting, where they'd voted on several crucial issues, had come by way of video conference. One of the few pieces of technology Colleen found useful, but it wasn't the same as her physical presence.

"Thank you." Colleen choked back the swell of emotion. As Magistrate, she could not afford to lose herself to the innumerable contemplations and fears threatening invasion on her heart. She had much to do here. She required all of herself.

"Have you seen the turnout, Leena? I daresay we might not be able to fit them all!" Evangeline declared as she guided them through the long paneled hallway, one arm looped around her sister's waist.

"You daresay?" Colleen smiled. "Now you sound like me."

"Well, we are two heads on the same mad coin."

"Or hydra, depending on who in the family you ask."

Evangeline threw her head back and laughed. Her full, frizzy mane sparkled under the dim light of the crystal chandelier. She pulled her sister tight with a yank and whispered, "But, really. Have you seen how many showed tonight?"

"They'll fit," Colleen assured her, though the words were more for herself. Over the years, attendance at Collective meetings had ebbed and flowed. The tide rose when turmoil descended, and receded in periods of peace. Whenever the numbers swelled as high as they were tonight, Colleen found herself worrying over capacity issues. Her worries always proved unfounded. "And if not, we can open up the parlor as well."

"Aren't there privacy concerns? The windows aren't frosted or soundproofed."

"That's what our security detail is for. Not to mention it would be patently impossible to sneak up on a meeting of Deschanels without a score or so knowing immediately."

They stopped at the end of the hall, which fanned out into a broad marbled foyer. Clusters of Deschanels huddled together, sipping from teacups and brandy tumblers. Their cousin Luther Fontenot looked up from a conversation with his brother, Llewellyn, and nodded. The women returned the gesture. Luther was frequently Colleen's greatest ally, next to Evangeline, on the oft-divided Council of seven. A pragmatic, dry man, he was nonetheless open-minded enough to see reason. *If the cat is obviously black, then why are we arguing shades of blue?* He was known to say.

"Will the Sullivans show, do you think?" Evangeline asked as they smiled in tandem at fellow Councilwoman Imogen Broussard.

"Not tonight," Colleen said. "I have yet to meet with them." She passed her gaze around the entrance hall with a light frown. Council leaders and their families clustered together, but where were the others?

"Seated, Leena. They're all eagerly awaiting your words." Evangeline read her mind, as only she could. "While we hang about whispering, they're in there ready to know what's been happening in the family. Can you blame them?"

"We're not the only ones out here," Colleen defended.

"Yes, but *you* are the only magistrate."

LUTHER PULLED THE HEAVY OAKEN DOORS CLOSED BEHIND HIMSELF and Colleen. The room descended further into darkness, illuminated only by the sconces lining the walls between ancestral portraits, and, soon, by the candelabra Colleen held.

Imogen sat at the far end of the table, marking attendance in the red leather book. The other Council members were scattered around the oval table, as was customary. She spotted them all, one by one: her cousins, Jasper Broussard and Pansy Guidry. Her nephew, Nicolas Deschanel. Colleen, Luther, and Evangeline rounded out the attendance.

But they were few in a sea of many. Deschanels, Fontenots, Guidrys, and Broussards. Other names by marriage. Hopefully, by their next meeting, Sullivans. Cousins upon cousins sat in the grandfather velvet chairs lined around the table's circumference. Many more perched in chairs and benches on the room's perimeter, bumped up against bookshelves or corner tables.

Colleen took each face in, one by one, cataloguing them to memory. So many; more, she guessed, than any other prior meeting. The list of those *not* present would be much shorter: her insufferable sister, Maureen; Maureen's daughter, Olivia; Evangeline's girl, Katja. *I'm so sorry, Evie,* she sent quietly when she noted the absence. *I had hoped she would come. I know how much you wanted to see her.* Katja's brother, Markus, was also not present, though he was back in Washington D.C., resuming his studies. Others, such as Tristan and Harriett, were overseas in service to the family in other ways.

The absence most alarming to her was her own daughter, Amelia. Amelia never missed a Magi Collective meeting. She would have called if something urgent had come up. So where was she?

All eyes fell on Colleen. Luther and Evangeline both bowed their heads at her as they took their own seats.

She moved to the head of the table, to the magistrate's seat. With an outstretched hand, she beckoned her six fellow Council members to come forward and light one of the seven tallow candles on the candelabra.

Surprise lit their expressions, followed by solemn understanding. The candles were centuries old, heirlooms from when the Deschanels still lorded over chalets in France, and only brought forth on occasions when additional protection from their ancestors was required. Only the magistrate could summon the candelabra's presence. And as Colleen hadn't brought it out at any other time during her tenure as Magistrate, not even when they rallied to solve the Curse, the Collective held their breaths in grim fear.

As the other six lit their candles, one by one, Colleen led the room in the incantation of the Collective's sacred vows.

Her eyes went to the clock on the wall. The room seemed to stop breathing as they all, collectively, awaited the twelve chimes. At last they came, sounding one by one. The witching hour.

"Repeat after me, please," she began, both hands outstretched to signal the family to stand. "In power, obligation."

"In power, obligation," repeated over a hundred voices.

"In obligation, commitment." She paused for the echoing verse. "In commitment, solidarity." One last pause. "And in solidarity, enlightenment."

With the final words repeated back, Colleen lit her own candle. Her hand shook, barely, but enough that Luther noticed and offered a tight, reassuring smile. "And for the Council, we also live under governance, through enlightenment."

Six voices reiterated her final words. Colleen eased into her seat.

"Thank you all for coming," she began.

Jasper approached and lifted the candelabra, with careful reverence, and set it at the center of the table. The room was already growing warm with the large number of bodies. Several people used books from the shelves to fan themselves, coughing from the resultant plumes of dust.

"It has been some time since we've met. I know many of you have questions, and we will come to most of them before the night ends.

"I ask, though, that you allow us to speak upon what we know first. You may, of course, interject for clarification purposes, but it will be a long night if we get derailed down any number of rabbit holes."

Murmurs of assent passed through the room. A handful of *hallelujahs* and *amens.* Musty pages flapped as cousins continued their enthusiastic self-fanning.

"Wonderful. Imogen, will you take us through tonight's program?" Colleen felt a slow roll of sadness pass through as she asked this. Her youngest sister, Elizabeth, had held the secretarial honors for so many years. The wound of her loss ran exceptionally deep.

Imogen pushed aside the leather tome where she'd been taking attendance and pulled forth another. "We have three items for discussion this evening.

"The first and most important is The Prophecy. Champion for The Prophecy will be Evangeline, who was scheduled to join via video conference but is instead here in person, a most wonderful surprise. Second tonight will be an update on the situation with the Necromancer and the Starlight Awakening, Champion Nicolas, with special assistance from Ashley. Third and final is the subject of the Blanche Broussard and Ophelia Deschanel letters, and the Sullivan Connection. Champion Colleen, with assistance from Jasper."

"Thank you, Imogen." Colleen nodded. She turned to her family. "Any questions before we begin?"

Not one voice broke the silence, though she read plenty of questions in the sea of wide eyes. "Very good. Evangeline, you have the floor."

Evangeline gathered her flowing skirts as she pulled back from the table and moved to the lectern. She had tied her wild hair back in a ribbon, but it wouldn't last the night. Nothing could tame Evangeline's mane.

"Thank you, Colleen. The subject of The Prophecy, of course, is one most in this room are familiar with, to varying degrees. You may also know it as Morrigan's Prophecy, or The

Prophecy of the Four." Nods from around the room. "But very few know the story in its entirety."

Evangeline shifted, tucking a bang of hair behind her ear. It immediately popped back out of place. *Sister, you need not be nervous,* Colleen sent. *We know this, inside and out. It is time they all do.*

Her sister shot her a quick smile and continued. "Let me begin first by setting the stage with what we now know about ourselves, as Deschanels, as there are new faces in this room tonight and it is integral we are all working with the same information.

"Our family recently discovering our tremendous power does not come to us by chance. As many of you learned in our last big meeting, we are descended from a race of hyper-natural, human-like beings who are the creation of a single deity, the god Emyr, who forged them from the fires of the land he created for them. From that land, they are governed by a body of leaders known as the Eldre Senetat, who rule in Emyr's name. Farjhem, which lies in the outermost reaches of Norway, can be reached only by those carrying Empyrean blood, which we do. Three living members of our family have, in fact, seen it with their own eyes. Anasofiya, her husband, Finnegan, and their son, Aleksandr."

"Finn St. Andrews isn't one of us," Remy, Luther's boy, interjected. "So how did he get in?"

"He was able to enter because he was with others who did carry the blood," Evangeline explained.

Colleen relaxed at this first question; the first was often the one that set the tone for the evening. It was a reasonable one. A good one.

"And Finn is special in other ways, which we will get to," Evangeline added.

"Why aren't they here tonight? They're back in town, aren't

they?" Remy pressed. He seemed frankly curious, rather than showing off his habit of impertinence. Until he'd said the words, Colleen hadn't realized their absence.

"I can answer," Augustus, Anasofiya's father, spoke up. "They've been away too long. Now that they're home, they need time as a family. Their son requires normalcy. I am here representing them. If you have questions for them, you may pass them through me. If the question warrants an answer, I'll get one."

Colleen had a strong urge to hug her brother, though she could count on both hands the number of hugs they'd exchanged over the years. Stoic and unmovable, she would have said of Augustus. Unchanging. Yet here he was, against his better nature, listening and ready to act if called upon.

"And there you go," Evangeline said with a patient smile in Remy's direction. "As I was saying. I will not run down the many things we know about Empyreans, thanks to both our relations with them as well as our own independent research, but I will remark upon what I believe is important to this meeting. We know they are very powerful, born of fire, though they share many of our traits. The main difference appears to be, according to the late Aidrik, our benefactor, that where certain genetic markers are dormant in the human race, they are quite active in Empyreans. We also know their ruling Senetat has, along the way, grown corrupt. They created a magical tattoo of sorts called Emyr's Mark, instituted under the guise of tying the faithful to their god. In fact, we know this Mark to be something far more sinister: a tracking device and a means of control. When 'activated,' the Empyrean dies, though they are taught to believe they will 'ascend' into service to Emyr. Our Aidrik removed his Mark in proof there was no tie to Emyr at all.

"Lastly, and most important, without the tether of the

Mark, an Empyrean can enjoy a life everlasting. In fact, many do. The Senetat has a derisive slur for these rogue individuals: Runeans, named after the rebel Runa who attempted, and failed, to rise up against the Senetat. We know them by another name: The Dragon Brotherhood. These particular Empyreans are greater in number, not bound by the restrictive procreation rules put in place by the Senetat, and they are our allies. They are banished from Farjhem, their home. They are trying to get it back, and to do so, they must overthrow the Senetat once and for all and establish a new order of governance."

"Are you suggesting we join forces with them, Evangeline?" Augustus looked up from where he appeared to be taking notes. While no electronics were allowed inside, paper and pen were permitted as long as the notes were checked at the door upon leaving. Many retained what was said better through the act of writing it down. Augustus had always been an obsessive note-taker.

"We already have, to an extent," she answered. "Our Tristan and Harriett are with them. Others have expressed a strong interest in wanting to join up and help. We will be taking more volunteers at our next meeting, when we have fewer topics on the docket. For now, we await news of their next move."

"And why should we?" Llewellyn asked. "What do we gain by them re-taking Farjhem?"

"It's more what we lose if they don't," Evangeline explained. "As most of you know, the Deschanels, or any halfling Empyreans, are considered an abomination by the Senetat. They would destroy us if they could get to us. We were protected first by Aidrik's powerful ward, and later by the one Finn and Aleksandr stretched over the family. But a ward will not keep them at bay forever. While that corrupt body rules, we remain in danger. It is in our best interest to see that come to an end."

"How can we be sure they care that much?" Rex Guidry jumped in.

"They cared enough when they saw Aidrik had created Anasofiya. They may or may not know she is not the only halfling he created. We are all who we are because of Aidrik, who joined with one of our distant ancestors and began the line of Deschanels who were to inherit great powers. He is gone now, but taught us much before he passed. Foremost is we must be vigilant."

"How did Aidrik die?" little Julius Guidry, Rex's boy, asked. He couldn't have been more than twelve or thirteen, which was too young for membership, but the Council allowed for children as young as ten to attend special meetings such as this one.

"He was put to death by traitors," Nicolas slurred before Evangeline could answer. Colleen smelled the cognac on his breath from across the room. "Ana was forced to watch, and is probably fucked up for life as a result. You wanna know why she's not here? Try going through that shit, and then being held captive by the creature responsible. That's part of why we're here, to decide what to do about those traitorous fucks."

Julius' mother Sissy's eyes went wide. She clapped her hands over his ears, too late.

"Nicolas jumped ahead a little," Evangeline explained with a tight smile. "We won't take volunteers to join the resistance until the next meeting. But our time is short this evening, so allow me to press on.

"You may be wondering what this has to do with The Prophecy, our topic at hand. Or us, for that matter. I'll come to this now.

"You see, all our prior hypotheses on the matter of the

Deschanel Curse were wrong. Well-intentioned, but still incorrect. This has never been about words spoken by our ancestress, Brigitte Deschanel, nor does it have to do with a family rumor about perpetuating the blood line to protect our gifts. All ills that have befallen this family, or at least many of them, have come for a reason far deeper. Something else that ties us to the Empyreans, and a decision that was made long, long ago. Something that plagues them as well."

Evangeline drew a long sip from her water and looked out at those listening in rapt interest. "By show of hands, how many of you are familiar with the legends of the Tuatha Dé Danann?"

About half the room raised their hands in the air.

"Fairies," said Charlotte Fontenot. "Irish fae."

"Yes and no," Evangeline said with a smile. "You are drawing from the correct legend, but it is one which has been distorted over time, as things go. I will now read to you from the words of Nora Quinlan, which were passed down to her from her mother, Deirdre. I know these names mean little to many of you, but they mean a great deal to Colleen's husband, Noah. Nora is his sister, and Deirdre, his mother."

A murmur passed through the room. Colleen glanced at her husband, sitting to the left of their son, Ashley. His face was unreadable. He hadn't yet fully absorbed the information Evangeline was about to share, but he had come, and that was enough.

Evangeline slipped on her horn-rimmed glasses and read from a stack of crinkled pages. "The Tuatha were the original deities of Hibernia, or Ireland as we know it now, rulers under the Goddess Danu. Legend says they first appeared out of a great mist and burned their ships in order to force themselves to settle. This happened over four thousand years ago, and the earliest origin of the stories is from Norway, before the Tuatha settled in Ireland."

She flipped to the next page. "The Tuatha were rich in magic and storytelling, tales of regular passage between our physical realm and Tir Non Og, or the otherworld. There were four ruling tribes, each with a scryer who had bound a magic item, giving the tribe its virility and power. Be it a stone, bowl, or weapon, each item held unique importance to the success and prosperity of the Tuatha, who were revered as gods and treated all benevolently in return."

Evangeline turned another page. "The clans of Tuatha were great friends of the Farværdig, or Empyreans as they later coined themselves. The Empyreans were central to Scandinavia, and the only other divine race walking the Earth at that time. Their alliance offered mutual benefit, and they lived together in peace. Later, when the Tuatha migrated to Hibernia, they settled into being allies from afar."

Evangeline stopped for a moment. She shuffled the pages, which had seemingly come out of order. Her face was bright, flushed. Colleen debated sending her more soothing words, but all that would soothe her scientist sister was order.

"Ah, here we are. It was a perfect balance, really. The Tuatha had a special, intrinsic connection with earth and nature, while the Empyreans had fire and a spiritual connection to their god. The Tuatha taught Empyreans about connecting with the Earth, and Empyreans protected the Tuatha from the threat of the wider world. Both were gods, in their own right, but together they were peaceful and prosperous. They created a pact, bound in magic and blood, to always protect and sustain one another. Breaking such an oath came with the punishment of war and strife."

"Let me guess," Remy murmured. "Someone broke the oath."

Evangeline ignored him and went on. "Eventually, a race of men came to challenge the authority of the Tuatha. Milesians they were called then, but have become the same race of men now living in Ireland. The Tuatha, as gods, were not prolific upon the Earth and didn't have the numbers to defeat an attack of thousands. When Morrigan, a goddess of the Tuatha, called Empyreans for help, they did not come. Because of this, many of the Tuatha were killed, and the rest were driven back to Tir Na Og.

"And so this group of survivors became the Caoinlean, or Quinlans as we are known today. Legends called us many things. Aos si or faeries, seems to be the most common name given to us, though our histories bled into others, such as the stories of little people. We were none of those things, though. We were so much more."

Evangeline slipped off her glasses and looked up from the papers. "That's the end of Nora's narrative. This defection marked all involved. The Empyreans. The Quinlans. The Empyreans saw war after war, and eventually, the creation of the Senetat, which came with crippling restrictions and a divided race. As we descend from the Empyreans, we, too, have seen much pain, most strongly manifested through what we have always believed to be the Deschanel Curse.

"The Quinlans were forced into exile, their land and span much reduced from what it was. Worse, this rift has only grown over the years. Empyreans hold Quinlans responsible for their strife, and the reverse is also true. Only the Brotherhood knows the value in renewing the alliance with the Quinlans, and they have. But what is done cannot be undone."

"Then why are we here?" Fleur, Remy's twin sister, asked. "Just to tell us we're screwed and can do nothing about it?"

"No, dear," Evangeline said, leveling a hard gaze. "I'm coming to a solution."

Fleur flopped back in her seat, red-faced and contrite.

"Before the Tuatha split, they had four ruling tribes. Falias, Murias, Findias, and Gorias. All living Quinlans today descend from one of these tribes. What I'm about to tell you may come as a shock, or it may not. But it explains quite a bit.

"Noah Jameson and his children, Amelia and Ashley, descend from the Findias tribe. I have told you Finn St. Andrews is special. He descends from Falias, through his mother. Jacob Donnelly, the husband of our dear Amelia, descends from Gorias, through his own mother. And finally, Anasofiya, also through her mother, descends from Murias. As you may begin to see, there are no coincidences where our family is concerned."

A titter of whispers rippled through the room. Quinlans? Ana? Amelia? What did it mean? What did that have to do with the Curse?

Evangeline had them at the peak of their attention. She struck on. "We come at last to The Prophecy. Some of you have heard these words, from the goddess Morrigan, and others have not. She delivered them as a means to end the sundering between the races. As you hear them, think on what I have told you about our own Quinlan connections."

"Two millennia of wars and strife, which cannot be avoided, but can be stopped. One descendant from each of the four to emerge. Four become two, their offspring the peace that unites the two races again.

"From Falias, a male, draoi, pure of heart and an affinity for creatures.

"From Murias, a female, born of fire and darkness.

"From Findias, a female, reincarnated over the many moons.

"From Gorias, a male, draoi. The lover of the Findias heir.

"A son shall spring from Falias and Murias. Findias and

Gorias join after many reincarnations, bringing forth a daughter. This son and this daughter will join together, in peace, uniting the Quinlans and Empyreans once more, thus ending the long days of war."

"Reincarnated?" Lougenia Frederick-Guidry piped in. "What in the Good Lord Jesus does that mean? Amelia gone and had other lives, or what?"

"Does it mean something else in your language, Lou?" Nicolas quipped.

"Amelia and Jacob coming together in this life was no accident," Colleen spoke up. If Amelia was not here, she would speak for her. *Where are you, Mia?* "For they've come together many lives before this one, all to learn the lessons needed to fulfill their piece of The Prophecy."

No one knew what to make of that.

"But they ain't got no kids," Lougenia pressed. "Amelia, now, I remember she's said a good dozen times she don't want none, neither."

"No," Colleen said. "And they may never have them. But The Prophecy calls for their child, and the child of Anasofiya and Finn, to come together to end the suffering. Aleksandr is here, and he has grown to adulthood in a manner of months, as The Prophecy foretold. Whether he will decide to follow the goddess or not, it's his choice. He must be allowed to express his free will. And should Amelia and Jacob have a daughter, the same is true of her as well. We can't tell you what will happen. We can only convey what we know."

"So, we believe this, then?" Remy asked, looking around at his relatives for accord. "That everything is tied to some ancient words and having babies is going to fix it all?"

"You were quick to believe our problems were tied to ancient words before this, so why not?" Ashley said. Ashley, Colleen's once nonbeliever who was now one of her greatest supporters. "Hell, the whole family thought our ancestor was the cause of every damn cold or flu. Why is this such a stretch?"

"Babies," Remy repeated with a scowl. "We tried this already, when Katja and Alain decided to rut like a couple of back alley dogs. That didn't work so well, right? One of them is dead and their kids are mutants."

Evangeline stiffened. "Katja's research was sound. As scientists, we are often faced with what appears to be the most likely conclusion when all the variables line up. The variables lined up. But she was wrong, and we know that now."

"But how? How do we know that?" Remy pushed. "How is this different?"

"This goes much deeper than us. We are only a piece of a much larger picture," Evangeline said. She appeared collected, but Colleen could see her sister struggle to stay calm. "Two ancient races believe in this. Believe in us. Ana, Finn, Amelia, and Jacob are not the end game of this prophecy because of who they are as Deschanels. They are here because of who they are as Quinlans, and who they descend from. Mixed with the Empyrean blood our line carries, the union of their children is what will more than likely end this madness, not only for us, but for both races."

"Why aren't any of them here, then?" Fleur asked.

"Augustus has already explained this," Jasper said. His face was long and sallow. All three of his children were gone. Of them, he only knew where one of them was. "Ana and Finn are handling matters closer to home."

"Okay, Amelia and Jacob?" Fleur pushed.

Colleen's chest tightened. Where *were* Amelia and Jacob? She had left her phone outside the room, as was protocol, but Aria had permission to interrupt for an urgent call. Something was amiss. But what?

"Like Ana and Finn, they have also been through very trying times recently. We can't blame them if they need some normalcy," Evangeline said, then put up her hand to silence the growing chatter. "The point here is, we, as the Collective, have a duty now to protect all four heirs and their children. We will be calling another meeting soon to discuss the division of this protection for all those choosing to volunteer to assist. Should Amelia decide to have a child, and should her child and Ana's decide to come together, we have a bigger matter at hand. Until then, we will err on the side of caution and ensure Ana, Finn, Amelia, and Jacob are safe. If we are wrong about The Prophecy, there is no harm in protecting our own. If we are right, we may finally see the end of our endless strife and the beginning of a much brighter era for the family."

"Imagine being able to have kids without fear," said Pansy Guidry, who had been quiet the whole meeting.

Colleen thought it an odd statement coming from the Guidrys, who had never seemed to have a problem with procreating.

She immediately scolded herself as she remembered Pansy's son, Rene, had been one of those lost recently.

Colleen had intended to hold the open questions until the end, but the cousins fired off one after another, and waiting would only keep them from focusing on the other matters. They wanted to know more about the Quinlans, about how the Deschanels could be the savior of two entire races. Some wanted to force the issue of Amelia and Jacob having a daughter and end everything now. Others refused to believe.

Despite the dissent in opinions, Colleen felt as if the conversation had gone well. The family was informed. With this information, they could move forward.

"All right." Colleen stood and silenced the cacophony of cross-talk. "If we are to get out of here by dawn, we must move on. Nicolas and Ashley, you are up next to discuss an update about the Starlight Awakener."

Nicolas and Ashley approached the lectern. When Ashley hung to the side, Nicolas nudged him forward.

"You want me to talk?" Ashley whispered, but the microphone caught it. "Aren't you the sponsor?"

Nicolas shrugged and leaned into the musty bookcase. "This is me sponsoring."

Ashley shook his head and stepped into place. "Okay, then. Hi, all."

The room softened at the arrival of Ashley. *Such a sweet boy,* Colleen heard someone say, though Ashley was closer to thirty than twenty.

"We all know about our ancestor, Margarethe Deschanel, who has been trying to return to the living, so to speak?" Nods all over. "Right. Well, then, so..." He stumbled through his words. This was all so new to him. Colleen swelled with pride. "She had a bit of a fancy with necromancy, and had, over the years, tried to come back by possessing various Deschanels who seemed to have that trait. She never found one that worked, because none were strong enough to keep her for long. But then there's the legend of the Starlight Awakener, the necromancer powerful enough to sustain the summoner not only temporarily but forever. Eternal life and all that, except we know her intentions were pretty awful, so it would have likely been really bad news for us if it actually worked. The legend infers maybe even complete catastrophe. Not good. Unfortunately, Margarethe found her Starlight Awakener, as we know, when Katja and Alain's twins were born and began to grow at abnormal rates. She went after them both, but decided that in order to become strong enough to do what she needed to do, she had to sacrifice one for the other. She decided Sebastian would be the one to survive and become her, um, vessel, but in an odd twist of fate we're all still scratching our heads over, Stella was kidnapped by Estella Broussard and we have yet to find them."

Ashley exhaled loudly as if he'd done that entire speech in one breath. "The good news is, Sebastian is safe with Katja and Olivia. Although Stella's whereabouts aren't known, we believe she must be safe because nothing crazy has happened. Leander Broussard and Lauren Weatherly have been off in search of them, using tips we've received from both within and outside the family. They're on their way home now for a day or so, and we have more leads for them."

"And the bad news?" Rex asked.

"Well," Ashley said, running his hand along his stubbly chin. "The bad news is we still don't know for sure *where* Stella is. Quillan Sullivan also ran off, and might or might not have something to do with this. We just don't know. Really, there are a lot of unknowns."

Nicolas leaned in. "Way to instill confidence, cuz."

"Way to not help me *at all,*" Ashley shot back through clenched teeth.

"What are y'all doing about it, then, except sending them kids on some goose chase?" Lougenia asked.

"We believe we *will* find Estella and Stella. There are only so many places they can be," Colleen interjected, pulling the conversation to an end. There was nothing more to say, and she had no patience for spin. "And perhaps Quillan, when we do. That is all we have on this topic for the evening. We expect to have more when we debrief with Lauren and Leander."

She transitioned them, then, to the final topic: The Blanche and Ophelia letters, and the decision they had made on the Sullivans.

This was her subject, though Jasper was her assist. He was an eccentric fellow, her cousin, but he took a personal interest in this particular issue due to his daughter Estella being the one to first read the letters. Letters, he believed, somehow led to her kidnapping little Stella and skipping off into the sunset.

"I will keep this brief. Some of you know this already, as we've had to make decisions based on this information. We have uncovered a series of letters between our ancestress Ophelia Deschanel and her niece, Blanche Broussard. Ophelia, as we know, is the granddaughter of our first Louisiana ancestor, Charles Deschanel. Blanche was the grandmother of many sitting in this room today, and was a force in her time." Colleen left out the part about Blanche's potentially disastrous involvement in communicating with Margarethe and potentially doing her bidding. The Council knew this, but the information would be too hard for her ancestors in the broader Collective to hear. They all worshipped her. This white lie was harmless, and better for all involved.

"The letters are sealed away in the Council chambers. The contents are mostly personal notes between aunt and niece, but through them we learned something that opens up our family in a unique and important way."

Colleen looked at Jasper. She could feel him itching to speak. She nodded at him.

"Ophelia never married," Jasper said. He cleared his throat and coughed into his purple lapel. "But we know now she did in fact have a child. A *love* child."

Everyone looked around at one another with bewildered expressions.

"With Seamus Sullivan," Jasper finished with a wry smile. Colleen almost laughed at how he took pleasure in dropping the very unexpected information. If he'd had a mustachio, it would be twirling.

"Sullivan?" Many in the room uttered the word in confusion.

"Seamus and Ophelia were the parents of a one Patrick Sullivan, who is the ancestor of all present day Sullivans in New Orleans. Ophelia gave the child up for adoption, and Seamus and his wife, Claire, adopted Patrick, raising him with the secret safe. Ergo, the Sullivans are also Deschanels."

This got the room going. There wasn't a quiet mouth at the table.

"Which brings us to the point of this item," Colleen said, bringing the roar to a hush. "The Council has met and decided that, should the Sullivans be interested, we will open up two more Council spots for Sullivan members. This will keep the Council at an odd, or majority, number, and will allow us to bring more of our family into the fold. They deserve a voice. They are one of us."

"This decision has been made," Jasper intoned when the voices rose once again. "We cannot ignore who they are. They shouldn't ignore it either."

Colleen glanced at the grandfather clock in the corner. They were already over time, and they hadn't yet come to the open forum or the question and answer series.

Amelia... where are you?

With a sigh, she raised her hands once more.

"This was a lot of information for one evening, I know. We will call a second meeting to answer all questions, and also let you know the outcome of the Sullivan talks. Our current priorities are to protect the four heirs and their children as best we can, and to prevent any further trouble with Margarethe. We may find ourselves deeper entrenched with the Empyrean cause, but that's a topic for another night. For now, we must adjourn this meeting. Know that myself, and all members of the Council, are always available for anything you might need."

She rose, and the Council rose with her. "Oh! There is one

final matter I wish to convey to every single person in this room. Make no mistake, this is important. If you encounter a man calling himself Victor de Blanchefort, do *not* engage him! I can't stress this enough. And then let myself or another Council member know immediately."

Is that where you are, Amelia? Has he, at last, come to find you in the future?

Colleen blew out the candles amidst the flurry of questions.

EVANGELINE CAUGHT HER IN THE HALL AS SHE WAS RUSHING TO GET TO her office. "Any particular reason you cut the meeting early, Leena?"

"We were over time," Colleen answered, not slowing her pace.

"That's never stopped you before."

Colleen reached the doorway to her office and turned. "I don't know where Amelia is. She hasn't called. She hasn't come by. She didn't show. I'm not proud of being unable to put that behind me at the doors of a meeting, but there it is. Now, I need to find out what's happened to my daughter."

"Calm down, Leena," Evangeline said, pulling her into an embrace. "I'm the last person who would ever judge you. Come, I'll help."

"Don't you see? We are all, all of us, falling apart. The whole of us, this *midnight dynasty* as you've so aptly named us. We stand within our elaborate gardens, watching the twilight descend on all we've built, and we can do nothing to stop it."

"You're not yourself, sister."

"I'm more myself than I've ever been, sister."

Evangeline went to close the door when Nicolas stumbled

in, shoving the door open and against the back bookcase. "I just came to—"

"You!" Colleen hissed. She stormed toward him, finger wagging. "You might have fooled others, but not me. You're *drunk*, Nicolas Charles Deschanel, and I won't have it. Not in my meetings and *certainly* not on my Council! You are better than this. I am not your mother, but if I were, I would tell you that losing control every time something goes wrong in your life is a sign of cowardice. Mercy is gone, but your self-control doesn't need to depart with her. If you can't get your act together, I *will* vote to have you removed, and there are plenty of people waiting in line for your seat. Now get out of my sight!"

Nicolas gaped at her with bloodshot eyes, tottering between wasted and exquisitely confused. "I was just going to say that I'm happy to handle the debrief with Leander and Lauren..."

Evangeline tugged him lightly by the arm and guided him back toward the door. "Now may not be the best time," she said in a hushed tone.

When at last he shuffled back out, Evangeline turned to Colleen. Her face was a mask of deep concern.

"I think *you* need a drink, Leena."

2

AMELIA

"Go on," Jacob said. He squared his stance into perfect form, one Amelia recognized all too well. "Tell me why I shouldn't kill you where you stand."

"Let's take this inside. Ashley is across the street," Amelia said, glancing at Oz's house, where her brother was housesitting. She noticed both the interior and the porch gaslights were off, so maybe he was out.

Her breath caught.

The Magi Collective meeting! How had she forgotten?

She ushered them in, though Jacob moved much slower. His highly controlled and deliberate strides conjured up images of a cheetah stalking prey in the savannah. His eyes never left the intruder.

Amelia pulled her robe tighter. She thought about positioning herself between her husband and Victor de Blanchefort, but a part of her very much wanted to see Jacob lay into the man who'd dared come to *their* home, uninvited. She wanted to lay into him herself. She still might, depending on the words he chose next.

She shuddered from head to toe as her mind traveled back to the horror of the night before. As Jacob made love to her, for the first time since her brutal assault—as they came together—they opened their eyes to see Victor standing on the street below, watching.

He didn't belong here. Not at their house, and not in their *time.*

Jacob kicked the door closed. He didn't drop his gaze. His approach toward Victor was a contiguous, fluid movement. "You have some serious balls coming here. Amelia told you to leave us alone. *I* told you to leave us alone. Ophélie even told you to leave us alone."

Victor's hands went up in bemused surrender. "Are you going to lay fists on me, Jacob? Or are we going to have a discussion, like gentlemen?"

Jacob's hands turned to tight balls at his sides. Amelia sensed him fighting with himself: to fight this battle with violence or words. The competing emotions rippled off him in violent waves. His muscles tensed under his white tee, his sinewy strength on full display. Although he made no immediate move, Victor gave a subtle recoil.

"I wouldn't let my husband bloody his fists on your account," Amelia said. "There are three guns in this house and I know how to get to each one of them in less than thirty seconds."

"We parted nary two weeks ago, and my arrival incites the threat of a gun battle?" Victor shook his head with a maddening air of benignity. His hands hovered in the air, conducting his words. "Dare I ask what has changed in that period of time?"

"Nothing has changed," Amelia said. "When I saw you last, I asked you to leave us alone. Don't act like there was an open invitation. I was clear."

"But we are friends, are we not?"

"Friends?" Jacob repeated with a heavy laugh. "I don't care if you lived part of your life as Cianán or not, or what else we might have in common. I'm not okay with how you look at my wife, or the way you confused her when she was at her most vulnerable. You knew exactly what you were doing."

"I'm not confused," Amelia stated. Her eyes bore holes in Victor. "I know what I want. And I know what I don't want."

Jacob's smile in her peripheral was so fleeting only she would have recognized it. He returned his full focus back to Victor. "You may be immortal, but you're not invulnerable. You have five minutes to tell us why you're here."

"Two," Amelia countered.

"Ten," Victor said amenably. His smile was as furtive as it was apologetic. "What I have to tell you could take the remainder of the evening, but I can compromise for the sake of brevity, and perchance, my head."

Amelia thought of calling her mother. She had never missed a meeting when she was in town. Colleen would worry, especially given all Amelia had told her about her time away. She was probably already worried. Maybe even out of her mind.

More pressing was the immediate problem of getting Victor out of their home, though.

Jacob pointed at an armchair. He then dropped into a perched position on the couch across, as if he might spring to action at any moment. Amelia settled in next to him and rested a hand on his knee in what she hoped conveyed an outward sign of their unity.

"Say what you need to say and leave," Jacob said.

"Yes, well," Victor began. He relaxed into his chair and folded his legs. Amelia's anger roiled to the surface at how casual the creature acted against their growing frustration. "I must confess. I came to request your assistance in a matter that is quite vexing."

"I'm not helping you with anything," Amelia said. "Except getting out of my house."

"No? You may change your heart when I share the nature of my request." Victor pulled at the lapel of his waistcoat. How much attention did he attract in his nineteenth century garb? And why hadn't he updated his wardrobe over the years? New Orleans was an eccentric city, but this was odd even by their standards.

"Eight minutes," Jacob said.

"Then I shall come right to my point," Victor replied with a slow, charming smile. "You see, the truth of the fate of your ancestor, the most lovely Ophélie Deschanel, our beloved Cerridwen, has been steeped in many falsehoods over the years. Some stories, of course, quite true. You witnessed with your own eyes the abuses wrought upon her by her horrific mother, Brigitte. It is also true that Charles turned a blind eye during the War to what the Union soldiers did to poor Ophélie."

Amelia flipped her palms out. "Okay. We know this. And?"

Victor continued unperturbed. "It can also be said that Charles, in his guilt, lifted the knife meant to take her life and deliver her of her sorrows. Indeed, he used it on her! But, ah, Ophélie did not die." His eyes twinkled. "Can you guess, my friends, what *did* become of her?"

"What do you mean, she didn't die? Of course she died." Jacob's foot tapped in mounting impatience. He looked at Amelia. "We don't have to entertain his delusions."

"Get on with it," Amelia demanded. "Make your point and leave."

Victor brightened, growing ever more animated. "But she did *not* die, Jacob! For you see, I was forewarned of Charles' notions, courtesy of Ophélie's own visions, and had confirmation of the same from the time travelers sitting before me. I followed the man, though he did not know it. As Ophélie bled toward what would have undoubtedly been uncertain death, I leaned before her and gave her my blood."

Amelia gave him a pointed look. "So, what, she became like you? You clearly told me that a dhampir cannot make another dhampir himself. That he has to take the person to the... uh, tree or whatever."

"The Master's Tree," Victor clarified. "And so I did. But first, my blood healed sweet Ophélie. Our blood does not heal as your mother heals, Amelia, but it bought necessary time. Though, some, like my father, Marius, were healers before we took the blood of the Master. I then carried her to *Coquillage* and laid her before my father. He healed her further, but she did not immediately awaken."

Victor's time was running out, but both Amelia and Jacob listened in shocked suspension. "Come on now," Jacob said. "If you took her away, why would the family say they found her stabbed to death? That's why Brigitte threw herself from the damn gallery. If Ophélie had lived, everything would have been completely different. Everything. This doesn't make any sense."

"They did not need a body to confirm the worst when Charles confessed his crime. While the story passed down was that Ophélie's life was stolen by soldiers, the immediate family always knew it was Charles. When he noticed the body missing, he assumed those selfsame soldiers who had earlier spoiled her body took her to perform further unmentionable injustices. To spare his loved ones the grief of envisioning their sweet girl bandied about, he lied and claimed to have buried her himself, on the property. You have seen her grave marker with your own eyes, in present day. His lie allowed me to permit Ophélie new life."

"So you socked her away like a hostage?" Jacob charged.

"No, I did much more than that. I took her to the Master."

Amelia shot forward, launching to her feet. "And she consented?" No, this was not possible. She'd talked to Ophélie herself before they traveled back to the present… she was clear in what she wanted… she would never…

Victor pulled back. "She was in no presence of mind to consent or not consent. I had no means of asking her, and her wounds were too grievous for even my father's great skill. There was no choice for me, when the alternative outcome meant her death. I brought her before Childeric, our leader, and requested we find one willing to give their dhampir life for hers."

Jacob closed his eyes, processing. "So you're telling us you kidnapped Ophélie, against her will, took her to the Master's Tree, and had her turned into… whatever *you* are?"

"She had no will. She would not awaken."

"That's like saying the woman was too drunk to consent, so you raped her anyway," Amelia accused. "Please tell me you didn't really do this. Please tell me you did *not* do this to our Ophélie!"

Jacob rose to her side. His temper was a fine match to her own, two flames rising higher and higher. She sensed him restraining his, but it wouldn't be long before he was no longer able to.

Victor was taken aback. "I did not rape Ophélie."

"You raped her of her choice!" Amelia stepped forward. She leaned over where Victor sat, as relaxed as a man sitting for afternoon tea. "You don't get to make decisions for other people simply because it suits you. Ophélie *knew* she was going to die. You offered her this choice and she *turned you down.*

How much more clear does it get? You did this against her will, against her wishes." Amelia backed away from him, stumbling into the sofa. "You really are a monster. Where is she? Where is she, Victor? If you really did as you say, where is she?"

"You need to leave," Jacob said. He looped an arm around Amelia, gentle but protective. His hand burned hot at her back. He had always carried his rage most potently in his hands. "Now."

Victor ignored Jacob and focused his answer on Amelia. "That's why I'm here. I do not know where she is. As you are now, she was angry at what I had done and she abandoned me. She yet carried the child that grew in her belly at the time of her assault. I never saw her again, nor do I know what became of the child." He knelt before Amelia.

She gaped at him in horror. She went stiff. Still.

"I beseech you, Amelia. I have searched the world for my Cerridwen, and she has eluded me for over a century. I come to you, arms wide, begging for your assistance in locating her and bringing her back to me."

A burst of vibrant anger surged through Amelia. She lifted her hand and swung it at his cheek, palm open. He recoiled in shock, as did Jacob at her side. "You want me to find her for you? You took everything from her! Her right to choose her own destiny. You may have forsaken who you were born to be, but *she* did not, and you stole it from her. You unbelievable bastard. You get *out* of my house and *out of our lives,* and if I ever see you again, God help me I will use every last breath in my body to see to it that you never hurt another living being again!"

"My darling—"

Jacob lifted him from the chair with one hand. Victor stumbled as Jacob dragged him toward the door, biceps straining to control the ancient creature. "She is not your darling. We are not your friends. And if we do find Ophélie, you are the last person on earth we would ever tell." He swung the door open and released Victor with a light shove. "You're uninvited."

Victor gave him a curious, amused look from the porch as he straightened his jacket. "You read too many vampire novels, Jacob. I don't require an invitation, and so neither can you uninvite me."

"Yeah? Watch me."

Jacob kicked the door closed for the second time.

AMELIA STARED, WHITE-FACED, INTO NOTHING. SHE COULDN'T FOCUS on any specifics of her surroundings. She could hardly think coherent thoughts. What Victor had confessed could not possibly be true, but she saw no reason for him to lie, nor did she detect any deception from him.

"You okay, *Blanca*?"

Amelia breathed in deep and turned to her husband. "Yes. No. I don't know."

Jacob nodded. "Yeah. Me too. Do you think he'll stay away this time?"

She thought about it a moment and then shook her head. "No. He'll be back. And, you know, I don't think he came here for us, either."

"How do you mean?"

Amelia glanced outside. Dawn prepared to crest on the horizon. The Collective would be adjourning soon, if they hadn't already. "He knows I can't find her. I'm an empath, not a telepath or a tracker. But there are others in the family who are, and he must know that."

Jacob ran his hands across his face. When they passed over his eyes, she saw they were red and tired. "So why not just go to them? Why bother us?"

"He doesn't know them. He needed us to bridge that gap." Amelia let out an exhausted half-laugh. "He really miscalculated."

"He's insane," Jacob said. "Maybe that's what immortality does. Drives you bloody mad."

Amelia switched off the porch light, but not before checking to make sure Victor was no longer prowling around. Not that he would go far, she was sure. A man who had spent a century and a half on a single fixation wouldn't be deterred by one bad conversation. "I don't think he's lying. I wish he was, but I sense he's telling the truth about what he did to her."

Jacob nodded. "I know." He turned down the light on the chandelier to the lowest setting, then extended his hand to Amelia. "And if she is out there, we can't let him anywhere near her."

"Do you think she might be?" Amelia was shame-filled at even allowing herself to hope she might see Ophélie again, after what the poor girl had been through.

"Maybe." Jacob squeezed her hand as they made their way up the stairs. She leaned into him. "If she is, I hope she's found herself some sort of happiness. Lord knows she's earned it."

JACOB AWAITED HER IN BED, HIS FACE VISIBLE BY THE LAST OF THE night's moonlight streaming through the gap in the curtains. He'd insisted they sleep with them closed now, with the threat of Victor looming. Amelia didn't disagree.

"What did your mother say?"

She dropped her robe on the chair of her vanity. "I feel terrible. She was really worried when we didn't show up at the meeting."

"It wasn't your fault Count Nightwing showed up tonight."

"No, but I knew better than to leave her hanging." She

reached for the brush on the oak table and pulled it through her hair. It was smooth and unsnarled already, but running through her routines helped steady her. "She warned the family tonight about not talking to Victor. That's my mother, always steps ahead of danger." Amelia laughed. "I think it's inevitable he'll reach out to more of us now that we've turned him down. Hopefully they heard my mother's message."

Jacob turned back the covers on her side of the bed. "Come to bed, *Blanca*. Your hair is beautiful. You're beautiful."

She twisted her lips at him and set down the brush. When she slid in bed next to him, a great calm settled over her heart. The warmth of him, of his body, yes, but of *him* quelled the fears in her heart.

Amelia pressed her face into her husband's chest. He hummed an Irish folk song, one she had never learned the words to but always found the melody and the vibrations from his vocal chords soothing.

He abruptly stopped his tune. "If he comes back..."

She heard the end of his sentence clearly in her own head. "You don't have to worry what I think. If you don't kill him, I might step up for both of us. I'm sure it will be a bit harder to take out a vampire, but you and I are resourceful."

Jacob traced lazy circles over her bare back. "I just don't want you thinking I can't control myself. I promised I would be a better man when I married you. It's only been a few months and already I've failed."

"Stop," she whispered. She kissed his chest. "I married Jacob Donnelly, the Irish orphan boxer of the Channel, not some faint murmur of who that man thinks he should be. I want you, not a changeling."

"I know. I've been thinking something along those lines myself," Jacob confessed.

"Then no need to bring it up again," Amelia said. She

yawned into his side as the first of the morning sunlight peaked through. “You double checked the locks on the doors?”

“I did. ‘*You’ve been reading too many vampire novels, Jacob.*’ What an ass. I don’t even read vampire novels.”

Amelia slid up his torso and pressed her lips to his. “Forget about him.”

Jacob returned her kiss, grabbing lightly to her lower lip with his teeth. He cupped her bottom in his hands, lifting her higher. “I’m trying. It’s hard.”

Her hand slipped between his legs. “I found something harder.”

3
OZ

Lucia wedged the rest of the dishes in the servant just as Christian and Naomi whizzed by, knocking her off-balance, one plate balanced precariously in the air. Livia appeared hot in pursuit, chasing the little ones in a circle around the long dining table.

Lucia spun, one hand on her hip, the other waving the china. Her face was a veneer of unbridled fury, but Oz knew better. All three of the children came to an abrupt halt. "*Someone* almost broke this fancy pants heirloom plate."

"It didn't break!" Naomi cried out.

Christian kicked her ankle. "Hush, Na. You'll make it worse."

Oz hid his amusement by turning and placing the glass tumblers in the hutch on the other side of the dining room.

The two younger children dropped their faces in total contrition. Livia bit back a smile. Lucia flashed the older girl a quick wink, and then proceeded to march around the room, flapping the plate like an Oriental fan. "No, it didn't, but what have I said about intention versus outcome?"

"Um... um..." Naomi's pale face went pink. "I know this one, I do."

"Don't answer." Christian said the words from the corner of his mouth in a way that suggested he thought only his sister could hear with this technique, something he must have seen in a movie, Oz thought. "It's a trap."

"A trap would imply you didn't know this was coming," Lucia said as she paced the room, eyes twinkling with mischief. Her bleach-blonde hair was piled atop her head in a messy bun, several inches of untouched roots peeking through. She'd stopped styling her hair altogether recently. Oz read that as a sign she was growing more comfortable and no longer needed to impress him.

As far as he was concerned, she never needed to impress him to begin with. They were here for the kids, and for the house; for Nicolas. If she'd spent her days in nothing but old, mismatched pajamas that would have been quite all right.

"We didn't! It was Livia!" Naomi pointed at the reedy Empyrean halfling standing in the corner snickering. "She's the one who wanted to play tag!"

"I believe we also have rules about accountability in this house, and not blaming our choices on others," Lucia clucked. She set the plate down and knelt before the two little ones. "Now, you both tell me. I know you know. What is the punishment for misbehaving? Yes, *even* if nothing bad happened?"

Naomi and Christian exchanged looks. They both bolted in opposite directions, but not before Lucia snaked out her arms and reeled them both in, falling to the floor in a pile. "Tickles!" she declared, and that was it... all three dissolved in a fit of tangled struggle and giggles.

Oz shook his head with a grin and continued to put up the last of the remnants of dinner.

The tables turned when both children crawled out from

under Lucia and pounced, their little hands flying at her from all angles. She laughed so hard she was in tears, and finally, she raised her hand—the white flag. "That's it! I surrender!"

Naomi and Christian climbed back up to their feet with satisfied grins and hair pointing in all directions. Christian gave Livia an air high-five from across the room.

Oz reached a hand down to Lucia to help her up. She whistled as she accepted it. "Wow, Oz. I think someone replaced your kids with some wildebeests!" she teased, leveling a mock hard gaze at the guilty twosome.

"Or their babysitter is teaching them bad habits." He ruffled her bun before leaning down to kiss his children. "It's a school night, guys. Time to get ready for bed."

"Aww!" they cried in tandem.

"I've got this," Livia said, assuming the role of weary older sister. She took them by the hands. "We'll get baths drawn, teeth brushed, and stories read. Not to worry."

"Thanks, Liv," Oz said and kissed his kids again. "Night, you little squirrels. You've got a long day of math ahead of you tomorrow."

They both groaned again in unison, and then followed Livia.

"You know, for someone who has an active disregard for children, you sure seem to enjoy them," Oz remarked. He'd left two wine glasses out, and he opened a bottle of Oregon pinot noir. He poured them both a glass, then handed her one.

"Do I? Maybe I'm just an excellent actress." Lucia took a deep bow. Oz's stomach clenched as she nearly spilled the dark wine on the original cypress flooring. "A regular Hollywood starlet."

"Or a damn dirty liar who secretly loves kids and wants twenty."

Lucia laughed and gave him a light shove from behind.

"Come on, Dad. Better watch that movie before it gets too late. It's a school night, *remember*?"

At night, after the kids went to bed, was the only time of day where Oz remembered what it was like to feel like an adult. For years he'd grown used to his life at the law firm, working with a variety of unique personalities, from clients to legal peers. Most of his interactions were of the everyday type, the little moments that all added up to make a life, and he hardly remembered them now. He'd come home to his wife and kids, thinking how lucky he was to have them, how the moments playing and laughing with them were the best of his day.

Now a widower who spent his entire day with his kids and this strange, slightly wild Empyrean woman, he found he craved the bustle of practicing law. Of dry conversations and endless briefs.

Movie nights had been Lucia's idea. For weeks, their days had revolved around the kids, dawn until dusk: teaching, cleaning after them, feeding them, playing with them, bathing them, reading to them. *Livia needs something to do,* Lucia said, finally. *And so do we, frankly.*

So while Livia put the kids to bed each night, and disappeared to read in her own room, Lucia had forced Oz to slog through one Viking movie after the next. She loved to pick apart their inaccuracies, especially those that made any earnest claims at authenticity. *No shield maiden in their right mind would ever step out into the fjords half-dressed. And will you listen to that accent? Clearly British. How soon they forget William the Conqueror descended from Rollo the Viking, not the other way around!*

Once they ran out, the subject broadened to fantasy and science fiction. They started with *Star Wars* and then *Star Trek,* followed by the first few *Harry Potter* films—she was especially peeved that the others weren't out yet and resolved to write J.K. Rowling a letter titled *Write Faster, Lady*. They'd moved on last night to *The Lord of the Rings*. She found it rather tedious until the big orc battle near the end of *The Fellowship of the Ring*. When Oz informed her almost the entirety of *The Two Towers* was one long combat sequence, she perked up. That was all she talked about for the rest of the day.

There were no televisions in *Ophélie*, except in the heir's suites, where Oz had been staying while Nicolas was off and about. Oftentimes he would opt for an armchair, while Lucia propped herself on the bed. Other times they'd switch.

Tonight, she hopped in the bed beside him and put on the movie before he could think of something to say about it. If any other woman had done this, he would have pumped the brakes. But Lucia was not any other woman, nor was she actually *a* woman, though the softness of her flesh brushing against his, and the light femininity to her giggles when her guard was down assured him, woman or not, she was definitely female.

About an hour in, she turned to him. "I've been thinking a lot about Gandalf and about Aragorn."

Oz's mouth curved into a bemused smile. "Have you, now?"

"Yeah, you know, how Gandalf has all this power but is so reluctant to use it. I mean, why didn't he just use that power to get the hobbits to Mordor?"

"How do you know he doesn't? We haven't finished the movies yet."

"Please. We watched enough *Star Trek* for me to understand all these martyr heroes have their own form of the Prime Directive. He doesn't *want* to get involved, for some boring noble reason or another. There's a lesson to be learned, by our little hobbits, and if he uses magic, well, what's the point?"

"The point, I suppose, is—"

"The question was rhetorical, Oz."

"Oh..."

"And then you have Aragorn, who is really the only goddamn Child of Man in this movie who has any right wearing a crown, not to mention he's descended from the Dúnedain and whatnot, and he doesn't want it! He's the gloomiest guy ever, and for what? He needs to suck it up and do what he was born to do. Just like Gandalf could avoid so much heartache if he would zap those little assholes to Mt. Doom."

"You really have been thinking about this," Oz teased. On the screen, hundreds of orcs fought elves and men in the battle Lucia had waited all day to see, and was now oblivious to.

"Yes, I have, because I *personally* don't feel everything in life has to end in a damn lesson. So *what* if Frodo comes out a more enlightened hobbit when this is all over? In the meantime, he's a mess. All of Middle-Earth is a mess, and it doesn't need a drawn out journey to fix it."

Oz tried not to laugh. "Should we just stop watching now?"

"No, *Oz,* I'm not saying I don't enjoy the movie." Lucia huffed and flopped her head into the pillow. "I'm making a point. If you have a skill, use it. There's nothing noble about holding back who you are."

"Why am I sensing this is more personal than wizards and hobbits?"

Lucia paused the movie. The look she gave Oz was so intense, he feared for a moment she intended to kiss him or kill him. He wasn't thrilled with either possibility. "Why haven't you explored more about what you can do?"

"Me?"

Lucia wrinkled her face. "Yes, you. You might laugh at me when I say I've been around a while, but I have, and dreamwalkers are no light matter. If you can do that, there's no doubt in my mind you have other fun tricks up your sleeve."

Oz paused before answering. He'd asked himself this same question on occasion, but he never got far. When he thought about his brief stint as a dreamwalker, playing around in Amelia's head in an attempt to save her, the memories were not good ones. While she'd survived in the end, the experience left them both confused, at a time where they needed to be focused on things other than each other.

"Maybe, Luc. But, as you know, that was not a happy experience for me, or for Amelia. Adrienne was suffering, and all I could think about was..." He couldn't finish the sentence. With some distance, the reality felt even more incongruous.

"Banging Amelia? Yeah, I know. But you were new to dreamwalking. Anyone new to their abilities isn't great at them. With practice, that won't happen with the next person."

"I didn't want to *bang* her."

"Sure you did."

"You're the worst sometimes. Do you know that?"

Lucia grinned and fluttered her eyelashes in an exaggerated fashion. "You only tell me all the time, Dad."

Oz pulled himself into a seated position against the headboard. "Why do you care whether I explore this stuff or not?"

"Did I say I cared?" Lucia looked aghast at the suggestion.

"You prepared a long speech about Gandalf and life lessons to get your point across, so it sure seems that way."

Lucia shrugged and rolled onto her back. She flung her arms out and one hit Oz in the leg. He nudged it off. "Let's face it, Oz. I'm the only buddy you have right now. Sure, you have better friends, but where are they? It's just you and me and the kids in this big, lonely mansion. I'm all you've got, as far as adults go. I take that responsibility seriously."

"I'm not your responsibility, and you're not even human," Oz countered. "So you're off the hook."

"Anyway," she sighed, rolling her head toward him. Her face spread in a broad, insolent smirk. "You can turn the movie back on, Dad."

"Call me Dad one more time..."

"Daaaaaaad."

Oz moved to sock her in the arm, but she dodged the attack.

She grinned. "Sucker."

Oz awoke hours later to a dark room. The television had shut off on its own from inactivity, the movie long over. He adjusted his vision and shrugged off his sleepiness. When he tried to sit, he was weighted back into the pillow.

Lucia lay against his chest, softly snoring.

Her messy hair spread everywhere, the tie having long ago given up. She smelled faintly of cinnamon and vanilla, but also of flour and oil from the meal she'd prepared Oz and the kids. Her hand draped over his torso, and he noticed remnants of the flour on her knuckles.

Lucia was insufferable, and a brat, but she took care of them. She took care of *him*, if he was being honest with himself. There was nothing making her do it, either. She stayed for Livia, she said, but she and Livia could go anywhere. They were Empyreans, and the world for them was as big and welcoming as they desired. Livia, as a halfling, would be no more protected here than she would be with the Brotherhood, her people.

So why stay? For him?

He hoped not.

Oz tried to move his arm, which was pinned under her somehow, but he couldn't without waking her. Instead, he let his hand come to an awkward rest on her bare arm. Even this innocuous gesture felt like a betrayal to Adrienne, who was gone, and never coming back, but was still the only woman in his heart.

Lucia rolled over, settling into him further. She murmured words in her sleep, then proceeded to drool all over his shirt. Oz sighed, but his heart also fluttered faintly. The girl was a mess, but her heart was wider than the river just beyond their doors.

The truth was, he didn't want her to leave. He was glad she had stayed and helped him where he feared he would fail: at raising his children after their mother passed.

But he also couldn't risk giving her the wrong idea. Did she stay for him? Were there feelings brewing? If so, he would need to do better. He possessed just enough self-awareness on the matter to know he could offer her nothing beyond these light-hearted acts of friendship, but was selfless enough to not want to hurt her.

He'd received word Nicolas was back, and without Mercy. He stayed in his Frenchman Street apartment, but sooner or later, he'd come back to *Ophélie*, his home. His travels were more than likely done, and even if they weren't, they should be. Maybe it was time to turn the reigns back over to his old friend and return back to New Orleans with the kids. Life had to go on, and this suspended sense of limbo, where he and Lucia played a secluded, peculiar game of house, wasn't helping anyone.

Oz lay there with Lucia sleeping against him for several more minutes before he carefully slipped from bed and went to stay in one of the spare rooms.

4
FINNEGAN

"Darling, I love what you've done with the place," Barbara, Ana's stepmother, declared as she lifted her wine glass with the daintiest of gestures; pinky out, wrist bent. Her dark blond hair was pulled tight in a bun at the nape of her neck, and Finn couldn't stop wondering if she was uncomfortable, having her skin stretched like that across her face. "Don't you, Augustus?"

"Hmm?" Augustus rolled the last of his okra to the edge of his plate, as if deciding whether to eat it or slip it to Forbia.

"Magnolia Grace, dear," Barbara replied with light reprisal at his lack of attention. "Isn't it lovely?"

"Yes, of course," he replied. He folded his napkin in a neat triangle and placed it to the right of his plate. "Aleksandr, how are you finding Tulane?"

Aleksandr smiled at his grandfather, holding in a mouthful of food. "Wudfl," he mumbled.

"Come again?"

Aleksandr swallowed hard, still grinning. "Wonderful. Thanks for your help getting in."

Barbara's face peeled back in shock at his manners. Finn resisted a laugh, secretly considering a high-five to his son.

"It pleases me to hear it," Augustus said. He folded his hands in front of him on the table, but he wore the distinct aura of discomfort. Where, months ago, he had presided at the head of this same table, that honor had now passed to Finn… and Finn was fairly certain his father-in-law saw him as a man far less worthy of the role.

"Yes, thank you, Daddy." Ana looked radiant in a light blue dress that brought out the cobalt in her eyes. They sparkled every time her father spoke to her.

"Only a short walk to the campus, too. Your mother lived here while she attended Tulane," Augustus added.

"Actually, to give Aleksei some privacy and a chance to grow on his own, I'm letting him stay in my apartment on Chartres," Ana said.

Barbara crinkled her nose. "That's a party flat."

Ana looked at her. "And when have you ever known me to party, Barbara?"

Finn sensed the chill in the air between the women and jumped in. "Aleksei has a new friend, too. His cousin. Katja's son, Sebastian."

Augustus raised a brow, then lowered it in an apparent attempt to censor his reaction. Sebastian, like Aleksandr, had grown to adulthood in months, and actually looked older than his nineteen-year-old mother. And where Augustus couldn't deny this phenomenon had happened, he didn't have to like it, either. "Friends are an integral part of your formative years," he said, pleasantly enough.

"Sebastian's pretty cool," Aleksandr agreed. "He has a Ferrari."

"Don't get any ideas," Finn said, leveling *the look*.

"A Ferrari? At his age?" Barbara raised a hand to her chest.

"We bought Ana a Porsche when she started college," Augustus pointed out, though he seemed less determined to defend Sebastian's situation than to provide a counterweight to his wife's fusses.

"Yes, but..." Barbara lowered her voice. "Ana was eighteen, as in *actually* eighteen, not that... isn't Sebastian, only..." She dabbed her napkin at her mouth and set her posture straight. "Never mind."

"You're right. He's not even a year old, technically. Just like Aleksei," Finn said as he poured another glass of wine for Ana. Delicacy only led to more awkwardness. May as well address what she didn't care to say. "But what can we do? They grew up. They're adults in every other sense. Aleksei devours knowledge for breakfast and was obviously sharp enough to get into college." He looked at his son. "Is Sebastian in school, too?"

Aleksandr shook his head. "He kicked out his tutor before he could pass the high school equivalency."

"Such a shame," Barbara said.

"And what precisely is he doing with his time, if not school?" Augustus asked, perplexed. "Please don't tell me he's backpacking across Europe or some other liberal arts nonsense."

Aleksandr shrugged. "He says there are more important things in life than sitting in a classroom. He'd rather experience them, I guess."

"Let us see if this wise Sebastian still agrees with his life philosophy when he's thirty and unemployed," Augustus muttered. "And have you picked a major, Aleksandr?"

"He's getting his required credits out of the way first, Daddy," Ana jumped in. She hadn't touched her wine. She added, with a pointed look, "We're trying to take things slowly here. Ease back into things."

Augustus nodded. "He has time. And if he finds himself undecided, a career at Deschanel Media is always on the table."

Aleksandr brightened. "Thank you, Papa."

Augustus nodded with the faintest of smiles.

Finn watched the exchange between his father-in-law and his son with rising interest. While there was discomfiture wherever Augustus was concerned, especially whenever he was out of his element of control, he also sensed something new in the venerable older man: a gentleness that surfaced when a man became a grandfather.

"Not everyone wants to be in media, dear," Barbara chastised. She polished off her third glass of wine. Finn exchanged a look with Ana, wondering if it would be worse to refill her glass or ignore it. "Look at Ana. She practically ran from the trade. You've yet to name a successor."

"That's not true," Ana said and reached her hand over to give her dad's a squeeze. "I just didn't inherit Daddy's head for business."

"Always a dreamer, like your mother," he replied with a wistful look. "But business or not, I *am* proud of you. And my finding a successor should not influence your choices, one way or another. There are many capable Deschanels to choose from."

"Why, what about Finnegan?" Barbara lit up at her own suggestion, as if she'd made the most brilliant contribution of the evening. "Surely he could be trained."

As if I'm a damned circus monkey.

"As you already said, darling, not everyone shares my passion for media," Augustus rejoined. He set his jaw. Finn wondered what their marriage was like behind closed doors.

"Well, what *are* you going to do with yourself, Finnegan?" Barbara pressed. She gazed at her empty wine glass with inflated confusion, followed by disdain at the oversight. Finn obediently filled it, knowing all the while it was a terrible idea. He couldn't wait to ask Ana about her stepmother later, though he was beginning to understand her silence on the subject.

"I haven't really decided," Finn said. "We only just came home, and our focus has been on settling in and making sure Aleksei has what he needs. For now, I have plenty of money socked away from my business back in Maine." He added the last with a sense of hollow bravado, courtesy of the secret part of him that would always feel inadequate in the presence of Ana's family.

"You may find yourself in the need of a new trade," Augustus said. "Even had you remained in Maine, being a lobsterman surely wasn't your long-term goal."

The flush started at Finn's toes. Ana responded before he could. "Actually, Daddy, Finn was at the top of his industry. People from all over the world consulted with him on his techniques, which were legend in New England. If he'd wanted to focus on money, he could have been a millionaire. He had so many businessmen breathing down his neck. Instead, he chose not to sell out and focus on doing what he loved."

Augustus made a sound that came out like *hmm*. His response came by way of a long look at Finn, which the latter could not even slightly read. Then he cleared his throat. "My daughter and grandson are in able hands. If not for you, Finnegan, none of us would be sitting here, enjoying a fine meal and respectable conversation. I asked you to bring my Ana home, and you did just that. I can't ask for anything greater than that."

Finn didn't know what to say. Ana beamed with pride from his peripheral.

"Thank you, sir," he managed.

"And should you require or seek out a change in career—"

"Daddy!" Ana exclaimed. "Your sales pitch about the glorious honor in working for Deschanel Media is going to be wasted on Finn. That's not what he wants."

Augustus watched them both in stoic silence, and then a small laugh escaped. Ana looked as surprised as Finn to see it. "You can't fault a father for trying to keep the business in his own line."

"You can, however, fault him for being a blowhard," Barbara remarked, between sips of her wine.

"Yeesh," Aleksandr whispered into his milk.

"He's proud of what he's created. He did it all on his own, and he created an empire. Isn't that right, Daddy?" Ana said, with a hand on his arm.

Augustus's expression remained solid but a bit of color popped into his cheeks.

Finn had never heard her talk about her father like this. The one time he'd seen them together, they'd been at ends. Now, she was fawning over him with an Uptown drawl that had flared to full force when she was back in her element.

Seeing Ana in such strong defense of her father, both his work and his surprisingly delicate ego, Finn could almost picture them years ago together, as she was growing up. Ana looking after him as he worked his way through life. Barbara doing her best, as far as that went, to be a surrogate mother and replacement wife, and only halfway succeeding, a virtual third wheel.

It had really always only been Ana and her father. Finn had known that, but only now could he see the inner workings of their unusual symbiosis. How they loved and needed each other, even though they could not be more dissimilar individuals.

"I would be nothing without the love of my only daughter," he said to her, as if they were the only two in the room. Finn understood then how hard it had been, on both of them, to be separated for so long, despite their differences.

When Barbara emptied her wine glass and set it against the table with a tad too much force, he added, "And, of course, my doting wife."

Barbara affected a slow blink at her husband, and then turned her gaze on Ana. Her movements had grown jerky and off-balance as the alcohol settled over her. "What have you done with your hair, darling? It's lovely."

"Nothing at all," Ana said, shooting Finn a confused look.

"Maybe you've lost weight, then."

"Of course she's lost weight. She's been to hell and back. You would, too," Aleksandr said. He dropped his eyes when all four adults looked his way.

"We all have our own hell. For me, it's when they forget to stock the avocados at Whole Foods, and I'm forced to drive to the one in Mandeville," Barbara said wisely, and even Augustus gave her an incredulous stare.

Augustus patted his napkin and slid his chair from the table. "That really was a lovely meal. Ana, forgive me, but I didn't realize you could cook quite so well."

"Lord knows I tried to teach her," Barbara quipped.

"My father actually made the jambalaya," Aleksandr said. He smiled at Finn. "He's an excellent cook."

"Well, then," Augustus said. "I look forward to trying more of your culinary delights."

Ana and Finn stood as well. She looped her hand through this. "We're hoping to make this more of a regular thing, now that we've decided to settle down here in New Orleans."

"You know I'd love nothing more."

"Indeed, it's all he talks about," Barbara said.

Ana and Finn escorted her parents to the door amid further efforts at small talk and pleasantries. They exchanged hugs and kisses, and doted on Aleksandr once more before shrugging on their coats and heading toward the awaiting town car.

Ana leaned into her husband as they watched and waved. “I really enjoyed that.”

“Me too,” Finn said, and he meant it. One of the many tests of joining this new world had been passed. He also saw hope in a real relationship with Augustus, where the possibility once seemed too far from his reach.

“Even the part where Nana got drunk and said a bunch of inappropriate stuff?” Aleksandr joked as he wedged in between them, arms sliding around both their waists.

“Oh, *especially* that part.” Finn laughed, and they all waved as Augustus and Barbara drove off down Prytania.

AFTER DINNER, ANA ANNOUNCED SHE WAS TAKING ALEKSANDR TO THE Chartres apartment to help him unpack some boxes. “I’ll be back in an hour,” she said, dropping a kiss against the corner of Finn’s mouth on her rush toward the door. “Without the kid.” She winked.

Finn hugged them both and then stood alone in the central hall of the biggest house he had ever lived in.

Hell, it was so big they *named* the damn thing.

The house echoed with the absence of his family. Without them, he was still an outsider in this lavish mansion, and the world of old money and exotic lifestyles beyond.

Maybe that would pass. For now, he needed to get away.

He called up Jacob, who answered on the first ring. “What are you up to?”

“Sitting alone in the dark, petting Miss Kitty,” Jacob said. He laughed. “That’s my cat. Not a euphemism.”

“Uh, yeah, I know.”

“Amelia went to her mother’s for a bit.”

"Ana is gone, too."

"You're staring at all those frightening portraits of your wife's ancestors, aren't you?"

Finn diverted his gaze. "So... drinks?"

"Head on over."

THEY WALKED UP TO MAGAZINE STREET, WHICH BUZZED WITH activity, even so early in the week. Everyone from college kids to the middle class gathered in the eclectic stretch of urban wine bars and antique shops, amidst more of the Greek Revival and Creole cottages the Garden District was famous for.

Finn thought this was what Summer Island's main drag could look like if the town could ever get the funding to clean it up.

Jacob led them with the expert ease of one who spent a good deal of their youth crawling from one establishment to another. He took them past the busy, hipper joints and settled them into a building Finn nearly walked right past. It was an old cottage, the front almost entirely ensconced by overgrown plantain leaves. He could find no signage that might reveal it was a business. It occurred to him Jacob had taken him to some kind of modern-day speakeasy. It was New Orleans, after all.

Jacob held the wrought iron gate for him and then led them inside. A server's stand bore the first evidence the place had a name: The Delachaise Saloon.

To the left and right of the shotgun house were dining rooms, each decorated in vivid Caribbean color palates. One had a sign boasting *Private Event,* and the other was half-empty. Straight ahead, behind the server, was a large oval bar with a pipe organ stretching to the ceiling in the dead center. Along the ceiling, opposite the bar top were extravagant paintings of some sort of medieval carnival, or at least before there was any modern decency in the business. The images were borderline horrific—bearded ladies ringed by nude, dancing midgets. Jars of shrunken heads, and costumed debutantes riding weary, elephants with foam at the corner of their mouths.

"Charming, right?" Jacob said, and Finn couldn't quite read if he was joking or serious.

"Your standard and mine might detour on this one."

"Those are contemporary." He had followed Finn's appalled gaze. "This place was operated for years by Madame Rosalie Delachaise, whose father ran the carnival circuit in this region at one time. When she grew up, she left that life behind... but not entirely."

Finn broke his gaze away from the strange paintings. "You can take the girl out of the carnival..."

"Exactly."

They pulled up two stools at the bar, only half full in contrast to many of the trendier bars and pubs they'd walked past.

"I'm surprised all the tourists aren't hanging out here," Finn said. "It's unique."

"They don't have signs out front for a reason," Jacob said. "Place is a local secret."

Finn ordered a Jack and Coke. Jacob a gin and tonic.

"So... you discovered your father-in-law might have learned his interpersonal skills from the KGB?" Jacob quipped after a quick clink of their glasses.

Finn laughed. "It wasn't that bad, surprisingly. That was the first time I've met Ana's stepmother, though. She's not what I expected."

"How so?"

Finn swirled his drink. "Ana never said much about her, really, which is strange I suppose, given Barbara came into their life when Ana was very little. I always had the impression she tried hard to give Ana a normal life, but Ana didn't have much of a relationship with her. Now I can see why."

"And your verdict?"

"She seems like she might be a bit of a drunk."

Jacob choked on his gin and tonic. "I'm not much help," he said. "I don't know anything about her. I've met her over the years, at Deschanel gatherings or holidays, and I think once or twice when I hung out with Ana in middle school, but I can't say I've ever said more than a handful of words to her. She seemed nice enough. I don't remember her falling all over Christmas trees, though."

"You and Ana were friends?"

Jacob shrugged. "Not exactly. I was an orphan, and she was kind." He pushed his napkin over the bar to soak up the condensation. "I'm guessing you aren't here to talk about your wife's stepmother?"

"I don't know if I'm here to talk, or just get out of the house," Finn confessed. He signaled for another drink. Three would be his limit, and just long enough to fill the silence of Ana's absence.

"You'll get used to it," Jacob said. "Or, enough anyway that you won't turn into an alcoholic every time Ana leaves the house."

"It's more than the house. I'm anxious. I keep thinking, we're here, starting a family, which is what I wanted. There's nothing in the world I want more than to start a family with Ana. But every time we talk about everyday things, like getting the pool set up for scheduled cleanings, or the grocery list, I can't help but think, did we imagine the last six months of our lives? All of it. The Prophecy, the months we spent overseas, time traveling... fucking *Farjhem.* A place that, by all logical reasoning should not even exist. I feel like the Pevensie kids coming back through the damn wardrobe after too much time in Narnia."

"Well, that's basically what we did," Jacob said. "More or less. Minus the heavy-handed lion Jesus allegory."

"Am I the only one struggling with this?"

Jacob finished his own drink and ordered another. "What? No." He laughed. "Noooo. It's definitely not just you. Amelia was saying yesterday that we should hire her mother's gardener, and I was like, hey, lady, do you remember we just went back in time over a hundred years?"

"You said that?"

"Of course not. But I think it a lot. And I know she does. I think we're both afraid to talk about it, but I can't put my finger on why."

"Maybe because we might decide settling down was a bad idea?"

Jacob shook his head. "Maybe we're all going through our own form of PTSD, figuring out how to make sense of things. And what else is there for us to do, Finn? Where would we go, if not here? Join Tristan and Harriett and the Brotherhood? Colleen would have our heads if we tried to do anything that dangerous. We have one job, according to what we've been told."

Finn winked. "Well, I did mine."

"I believe Ana did the heavy lifting on that one."

"And then some," Finn agreed. "I don't suppose you and Amelia have been able to talk about..."

"I can't bring it up," Jacob said. "And she won't. With some distance between what happened, it's been harder on her, thinking about the baby we lost in that cabin. Sometimes she cries at night, when she thinks I'm asleep, and it bloody *guts* me. She's all I've ever wanted. I don't need a child, only her. I told her that from the very start. My childhood was pretty high on the scale of *worst ever* and I never wanted to potentially screw up another human being. Who knows how much of my pa's madness runs in my blood? I only know I never wanted to find out."

"Ana didn't want kids either," Finn said. He focused his gaze on the bottles of liquor lined up between the pipes on the organ. The deep burgundy of the velvet couches reflected off their glass, creating hazy pink hues all over the room. Like a dream. "I always did, but I know what you mean. I would have given that up for her. I was ready to."

"Thankfully, you didn't have to." Jacob hadn't touched his second drink. Finn wondered more about what he'd said about his father, the madness. Maybe there was a drinking problem there, too.

"There's another thing about the quiet," Finn ventured. "I used to love it. I spent too many years disappearing into the silence, happy there. Now, all it does is remind me of all that's happened. All we've lost."

"I hear you."

"I think about Aidrik every day. I wanted to hate that creature. You have no idea how badly I tried, when he ran off with Ana." Finn ran a hand over his face and through his hair. "But he became like a brother to me. More than a brother. But I can't mourn him in front of Ana and Aleksandr."

"Why the hell not?"

"They lost more. He was Ana's evigbond. And one of Aleksei's fathers."

"And you were bonded to him too, my friend. You lost just as much."

"I have his sword in my closet. I keep thinking one day he'll come back and claim it."

"It was a gift," Jacob said. "He wanted you to have it."

“He gave it to me when he knew he was going to his death.”

“Still.”

They sat in silence. Jacob’s drink remained in the distance, untouched. Finn ordered his third.

Jacob broke the quiet. “I wonder if Ana and Amelia talk like this when they’re together.”

“Ana always comes back less... burdened after she’s spent some time with Amelia. Not unlike how we’re both going to hopefully feel when we go home tonight.”

Jacob pushed his drink away, toward the other side of the bar. “We all have to find our ways of getting through this. Whatever happens, we can’t let it build up. I’ve seen what happens when people don’t deal with their problems.”

Finn knew Jacob was again thinking of his father. How he’d killed his wife and children, except Jacob, who’d barely survived. “You can talk about it. If you want. It’s okay if you don’t, too.”

Jacob looked down at his hands. “Funny what time and circumstances can do. I used boxing for years to cope with my anger. When I met Amelia, I needed it less and less, until I didn’t anymore. But now, after all that happened... in that cabin... now I see my father again, the sharp whiskey smell he wore every single evening... I see his failure to do what he felt was his only real job in life, take care of my ma and us. And I know, in his own very messed up way, his actions came from love. But that’s the problem, isn’t it? Love and madness have always ridden a fine line. It’s hard to tell them apart sometimes.”

“You’re not your father,” Finn said, more sternly than he intended. “What happened in that cabin had nothing at all to do with him. Sometimes bad things just happen.”

“Aye,” Jacob said. His glassy eyes reached into the distance, and he seemed somewhere else. “I’m not.” He shook his head and breathed out. “Anyway, sorry. That got a little deeper than I intended.”

Finn held up a hand. “I’m the one who asked you for a drink, to get out of my own head.” He checked his watch. “And we should probably be getting back.”

Jacob nodded at the carnage of drinks before his friend. “I’ll get us a taxi. Wander around drunk on the streets of New Orleans, never know where you might end up.”

5
ALEKSANDR

"You're spoiled rotten," Sebastian charged. He slouched inside the doorway, inspecting the French Quarter flat on Chartres that Aleksandr's mother had let him use to stretch his wings. "All the way to your smelly core."

Aleksandr hung the jacket Sebastian had thrown to the floor. "Says the guy with the brand-new Ferrari."

"I would kill for my own place." Sebastian made his way around the living room, turning up couch cushions and opening drawers.

"What are you looking for?"

"Money. Do you know how much I've made off my mom and Aunt Olivia, without even having to steal a dime?"

Aleksandr frowned. His mother and father had provided for him as much as Sebastian's had, and he couldn't fathom a need or a desire to steal anything at all. The idea of wronging them in such a way made him sick, and he hoped Sebastian was joking, or exaggerating, as he tended to do. "You don't really steal from your family, do you?"

Sebastian's smile spread nearly ear to ear. His teeth sparkled. "Don't give me that wide-eyed Boy Scout face, Aleks. You're going to straight-faced tell me *you* haven't?"

Aleksandr answered what he felt was a completely asinine question with his own. "Why the hell would I?"

Sebastian kept his penetrating, frat boy smirk—his standard look, Aleksandr came to understand, but it felt a heck of a lot less standard when he leveled it on you—on Aleksandr. He couldn't read whether his friend was ashamed or legitimately surprised that Aleksandr's innocence was not merely for show. "I guess you don't need to when your folks give you a damn *apartment.*"

Aleksandr opened his mouth, but paused in mid-rebuttal. His counter, a refrain now growing old, that Sebastian had way more than most, would be lost on his new friend. It always was. Sebastian was loud, demanding in everything, and always craved more, more, more.

Uncle Jacob, who had come to be his secret confidant, remarked lightly one day that Aleksandr and Sebastian didn't seem to have much in common. Aleksandr knew what he meant. Where Aleksandr's actions reflected his kindness and thoughtfulness, Sebastian's illustrated his boastful, self-centered nature. Where Aleksandr looked for ways to make the lives of those around him richer, Sebastian took whatever he could get his hands on.

This, in many ways, was part of his charm. The only other friend Aleksandr ever had, Fiona, had been more like him, and in the end, his heart ended up broken. Sebastian might be crude and unpolished, but you got exactly what you expected with him. There were no surprises.

And all in all, he wasn't such a bad friend.

Sebastian dropped Aleksandr off at college every day, and was there, promptly, when his classes were over.

He shared his favorite candy, even when he only had a few, even if it meant giving Aleksandr the last piece.

He sometimes let Aleksandr pick the movie.

He listened, with only occasional interruptions to insert his outrageous opinions, when Aleksandr confided how his one and only brush with love had not ended well.

And, while Aleksandr wouldn't admit this was a part of the allure, Sebastian was literally the *only* other being on this earth he knew personally who had been through what he had, growing to his full adult form within months of birth. While others around Aleksandr, even his own parents, approached the changes in him with a careful discomfiture, Sebastian understood what it was actually *like.* To go from knowing nothing one day, to understanding everything. To listen to others talk with wistful yearning about fond childhood memories from years past, and know that he would never relate to that. His careful formation was like nothing anything around him had experienced. He may as well have been grown in a lab.

But Sebastian got it. He didn't struggle with it as Aleksandr did. He was always in a hurry for whatever came next, rarely stopping to contemplate what came before. But he understood, and that was more than enough.

Sebastian threw himself on the couch with theatrical aplomb. He drew his hands behind his head and stretched his arms over the back of the cushions he'd overturned moments before. They sat crooked and unsettled. Aleksandr would have to adjust them when he left. "I wonder how many guys your mom laid on this couch."

"Sebastian!"

"Come on. You know what she was like. Before she met your dad and, uh, your other dad?"

Aleksandr's face darkened a deep pink. "That's my mom you're talking about. I've told you, that's not cool."

"Yeah, well," Sebastian said, leaning his head back, "all hoes are someone's mother." He paused. "Wait, that's not right. Not all hoes have kids. Dammit. I need to work on that."

"Or you could stop talking like that about my mom and things you know nothing about." Aleksandr pressed his feet into the carpet. The rush of blood began at his toes and rose high to his neck and face. Even accepting Sebastian's brashness as part of his charm, this was too much.

Sebastian bolted forward in his seat. "Oh, Aleksei, you sweet unspoiled child, you don't know, do you?" His laugh wasn't unkind, but it wasn't nice, either.

Aleksandr's whole body was on fire. "And what the hell would you know about it?"

Sebastian looked ready to push this issue all the way, but after a quick study of Aleksandr, his smile faded. He, somehow, always knew the precise moment when Aleksandr had had enough of him. "You're right. Not cool. Hey, wanna go fishing?"

Aleksandr brightened in spite of his foul mood. Fishing reminded him of simpler times, when it was his mother, father, and Aidrik, and all they had was each other and nature, and the world was less scary. "Yeah, okay. Sure."

SEBASTIAN'S SUGGESTION OF FISHING WAS ALWAYS FOR ALEKSANDR'S benefit. Sebastian was most in his element redlining his Ferrari, drinking until he couldn't read the names on the street signs, and finally heading to bed at eight in the morning. The enveloping, welcoming solitude of hours on the lake would inevitably be lost on such an adrenaline junkie.

This was another important way Aleksandr saw Sebastian had within him a kindness that he likely wished no one would come to notice. Aleksandr saw Sebastian for the man within. He reminded Aleksandr of his uncle Nicolas in this way. His mother once said that to be loved by someone with the erratic passions of Nicolas Deschanel was a gift unlike any other.

Aleksandr felt this way about his friendship with Sebastian.

Their cousin, Luther Fontenot, had a sprawling lakeside property in Mandeville where he and his family spent half their time. When they were not living there, Luther generously offered it to the family for events or a casual day at the lake.

Sebastian had come to know about it through his aunt Olivia and uncle Greg, who liked to take their young son, Rory, because Greg could rarely get away long enough to leave New Orleans altogether. Olivia sunbathed on the long dock that stretched into the endless Pontchartrain, while Greg took his son out in the little tin boat. The one Olivia said was "unfortunate," but Greg had kept because it reminded him of his childhood and early mornings with his beloved late grandfather.

Aleksandr prepared both his line and Sebastian's, while his friend kicked back on the cherry red Adirondack chair. The sun sat directly above them—*high noon*, his father liked to say, in his best gunslinger voice, reaching for his invisible twin six shooters—and the surface of the lake sparkled like a thousand diamonds. Sebastian had already cracked open his tallboy and let out an almost guttural sigh as he drew his first sip.

Aleksandr grinned to himself as he continued sorting through his tackle box for the appropriate weights. When Sebastian suggested going fishing, what he really meant was for Aleksandr to do the work while Sebastian got completely wasted. Aleksandr didn't mind. He was good at this; had absorbed everything his father taught him like a willing disciple. Where Sebastian could hit the best time on the quarter mile at the racetrack, or pop the clutch and launch into a perfect drift just as they hit the Causeway—something that would never not stop Aleksandr's heart—Aleksandr's skills with nature were untouchable.

He liked to imagine Sebastian watching, with secret admiration and approval, at how skillfully Aleksandr tied his lines —invisible were best in the Pontchartrain—and maybe arching an impressed brow over how Aleksandr knew precisely the right bait for every type of fish. At how carefully he tended the lines, which could be deceptive in this broad span of water.

"Oh, just throw it in," Sebastian barked, crushing the can against his forehead. He started to heave it in the lake when Aleksandr leveled a hard, *don't you even dare* look. He instead tossed it back in the brown paper bag.

"Cast the lines, you mean," Aleksandr said with a burst of pride. Sebastian always acted the alpha in their friendship. The one to lead, to guide. Out here, those roles were reversed. Maybe only out here.

"I mean, get the fuck over here and start drinking."

Aleksandr cast both lines and then carefully set them within the holders. Once satisfied they were far enough from the dock, he settled into the chair next to Sebastian.

Sebastian's hand held out a beer, like an automatic response. Not a question, but a demand. Aleksandr rolled his eyes and took it.

"My uncle Greg moved out," Sebastian said. His tone was flat. He may as well have been talking about a shortage of butter at the grocery store. But his friend wouldn't bring this up for nothing.

"What? Why?"

Sebastian shrugged. His gaze was fixed on the lake. "Fighting with Aunt O. I think it's about me." A wet metallic crunch sounded as he opened another beer. "Not that it's my fault. Everyone needs an escape goat."

"Scapegoat."

"Huh?"

"Nothing. Why would it be your fault?"

"You know. How Olivia took my mom in after my dad blew his brains out." Aleksandr winced at Sebastian's callous words and the subsequent belch. "Greg doesn't like me much. Feeling's mutual. Dude's a fucking square. All he ever talks about are his architectural designs, like he's Debussy or something, creating shit that will change the world."

"I think you mean Da Vinci."

Sebastian squinted into the sun and lifted his glasses. "What the fuck I mean is what the fuck I mean, Aleks. And anyway, it's quieter with him gone. He and Aunt O were always yelling. Rory started pissing his bed because of it."

"Man." Aleksandr didn't know what else to say.

"Yeah. My mom offered for us to leave, since, you know, we all get a property as part of the Deschanel Trust and Mom hasn't claimed hers yet, but Aunt O wasn't having it. She has this weird fixation on saving us or some shit. I don't know. So Greg left instead."

"She must love you a lot."

"Yeah? Maybe. Who cares."

Aleksandr knew Sebastian cared, a lot. He liked to act tough, but he'd said, several times while drunk, how he was "the lucky son-of-a-bitch with two moms, and all those single mom assholes could suck it. Quote me."

"What about your sister?"

Sebastian's mouth wrinkled into a frown, but the corner of his lips twitched. "Stella? What about her?"

"I don't know, have they found her?"

"You and the whole rest of the dysfunctional clan would know if they had."

What did Aleksandr really want to ask? Did Sebastian miss her? Did he care? Aleksandr tried to imagine having a missing twin and all he could come up with was a sense of tremendous loss, like how he felt when he thought about Aidrik's gaping absence in his life. "Hopefully they will."

Sebastian grunted. His glasses fell back on his face, settling with ease on his nose. "Maybe my mom will stop being so fucking clingy if they do."

"She's probably afraid of losing you, too."

"Aleks, don't sit over here and act like you're the expert on relationships, like Dr. Who."

"Dr. Spock? Freud? Jung? Help me out here, Sebastian. I can't fix this one."

"Fuck you."

Aleksandr grinned into his beer.

"When's your girl coming out?" Sebastian asked.

"Fiona?" Aleksandr asked, though there was only one. Only one girl. He tried not to blush. He hated how easily he wore his emotions on his face. "In a couple days."

Sebastian made a crude gesture with his arms, thrusting his hips in the air. "Aleks is gonna get so much ass!"

Aleksandr *did* blush this time. Fiona wasn't the end of someone's joke. She was his heart. And anyway, he wasn't so sure about the sex part. They hadn't parted on the greatest terms, after Aleksandr tried to protect her and only ended up looking like a blustering machismo idiot.

But she'd agreed to come. That had to mean she was at least open to talking to him. And he was ready to fall on his sword and open his heart to her. This was his fault. All of it. She was right, after all. They could figure this out, together. The Prophecy. Everything.

"So I guess that means I won't see you for a few days," Sebastian pressed on, nudging him with his elbow.

Aleksandr flinched and pulled himself further to the left in his chair.

"I don't know. I'd like you to meet her."

Sebastian brushed a golden red bang of hair off his face. He ran his tongue over his lip, suggestively. "Probably not the wisest idea, Aleks. One look from me, and panties melt." He aimed his bedroom eyes on Aleksandr.

Aleksandr smirked. "You're not her type. And she wouldn't do that." He almost added, *and neither would you,* but he wasn't so sure.

Sebastian reclined back in his chair and curled his arms behind his head. "I'm *everyone's* type, Aleks."

Aleksandr had something witty on his tongue when he saw a light twitch in one of the lines. He eased forward, cautious. The key to a successful catch was patience and vigilance.

Sebastian perked. "If you catch another damned anchovy..."

"Hush," Aleksandr admonished. He drew the line back in with a controlled deliberateness. The tug on the line gave more resistance than he'd expected or hoped. A speckled trout, if luck was moderately on his side. He didn't dare hope for...

He alternated tension and slack, his pulse racing at what might be at the other end of his line. Even Sebastian had leaned forward to watch, quiet for once.

At last the fish breached the surface, and Aleksandr angled him toward the dock.

A bass. He'd finally caught a bass.

The thing was at least ten pounds. Perhaps fifteen.

"Jesus Tittyfucking Christ," Sebastian whispered. He whistled as Aleksandr lowered the fish onto the dock for a closer look.

"What was that you were saying about anchovies?" Aleksandr remarked.

Sebastian only gawked at the fish flopping under Aleksandr's hand.

"Have you ever skinned and cleaned a fish?" he asked his friend, enjoying, for once, having some of the control and upper hand. Seeing Sebastian's discomfort make an appearance, however brief.

Sebastian closed his mouth and recovered himself. "I'm just here to look pretty and eat all the food."

6

NICOLAS

Blinding light streamed through the velvet curtains of Nicolas Deschanel's bedroom. Beside him, a soft feminine moan sounded as movement stirred the bed. The source of this intrusion wrapped the bed sheet tighter as she turned to block out the light.

Nicolas blinked. Blinked again.

Who was she?

He didn't have the answer, but that wasn't really the question, was it?

Who wasn't she?

She wasn't Mercy. And if she wasn't Mercy, then it didn't matter.

He ran himself through this tight sequence of questions each night. Every time, the first question had a different answer. The second was always the same.

In his most debaucherous days, which began in high school and culminated in his late twenties, Nicolas Deschanel had easily moved from one amusement to another. Their names, he never bothered to learn, even when they offered them. He thought of these women in more descriptive terms, which worked better for his transient memory. *Redhead with the boob job scar, who only drinks gin and uses a lot of five-dollar words so you don't miss that she paid a lot for her education. Pakistani who loves the Saints and has a nervous habit of running her tongue along her teeth, as if expecting to find them covered in lipstick or perhaps remnants of expensive coke. Exchange student from Taiwan with the Hello Kitty fixation and never stops chewing gum, even in bed and the shower.*

The contents of Nicolas' little black book existed solely in his head, even as the numbers moved from dozens to hundreds. He didn't remember every single conquest, but he didn't need to.

Because it was never about remembering.

It was about forgetting.

NICOLAS HAD A STANDING ROOM AT THE BOURBON ORLEANS. HIS father, years ago, donated to the restoration efforts of many buildings in the Mississippi Valley, the hotel included, and part of his thank you was a suite with his name on the door. A suite that passed to Charles' only son when he died.

Nicolas hadn't always taken his amusements there. It depended on where they'd spent the less interesting part of their evening. If they had taken in some blues or jazz on Frenchmen Street, they crashed in his mother's Victorian townhome on Esplanade and Decatur, or his own Frenchmen flat. If Magazine Street was on the menu, he owned a cottage a mile past the hubbub of bars and shops—he also had a great deal of relatives within walking distance, scattered throughout the Garden District, but Nicolas did not mix his pleasures with his personal life. Years ago, he occasionally also used Ana's apartment on Chartres, but that felt like another Nicolas, in another life. One he tried not to think about too much, because it felt like looking in a very candid funhouse mirror.

On rare occasion, he simply brought his conquests back to Vacherie, to *Ophélie,* and then had his driver take them home when they were done.

This last he hadn't done since opening his home to others in the past year. The sense of privacy, of a space that was wholly his own, had disappeared long ago.

So why had he done it last night?

Why was she here?

HE HAD TO GO BACK. BEYOND LAST NIGHT. TO WHEN HE'D WATCHED Mercy disappear into the moss-covered cabin deep in the gloaming Highlands, following the young woman who promised precisely the healing Mercy was after.

A child. She'd wanted her dead womb brought to life so she could become a mother.

More, she wanted Nicolas to be the father.

Nicolas had stood here, feeling an almost magnetic pull toward the direction she headed, but rooted in place by... what? His better sense? His past self? The knowledge of who he really was?

He might never know. He understood only that he couldn't follow where she was going. Nicolas may have deceived himself, and even altered the fabric of who he was, to be the man she needed, a man worthy of her, but a father?

No.

If there was anyone in the world he would have broken that rule for, it was Mercy. He even tried following her all the way to the doorstep, climbing over roots and fallen trunks of trees. But in that final moment, as she threw him a glance over her shoulder, led by the magical woman who lived within,

Nicolas remained true to himself in what felt now like the soberest moment of his adult life.

That was the cost of Mercy. He could give her everything except what she wanted most. He'd given up his old life and ways, and had domesticated himself, in a manner of speaking. He would pick out sheets and china if she wanted. He would keep his hands to himself where other women were concerned. He would give up the drink.

But he would not further his bloodline.

He had too much of his father in him.

Nicolas had stood outside that cabin for hours. Day turned to dusk. Rain broke through the twilight canopy overhead, littering him with a spreading dampness he hardly noticed. He'd only stared at the heavy wooden door behind which Mercy had disappeared. Willing himself to go after her. To change this one final thing about himself, in exchange for their happiness.

It was the old man who finally came out and helped him to his senses. A wrinkled hand fell over his shoulder. A kind smile appeared. "Nicolas, it's time to go home."

Those words had the power to break the spell. And Nicolas did exactly that.

He turned around and walked back through the woods the way they'd come.

Nicolas Deschanel went home.

He went home and he became, once again, the man he had both embraced and abhorred. His father, those same qualities in his father.

The Hennessy glittered against the silver tray in his study, calling to him. This time, he answered.

Night after night, he revisited his favorite haunts. A new

woman each evening. Sometimes more than one. Why limit himself? He craved this return to his true self as if fulfilling his own personal prophecy, bringing the saga of his life full circle. Whoever he was when he'd taken Mercy to Scotland to save her—to love her—he wasn't that man anymore. He had no time for him. That man had been a fraud, and the time spent wearing the false suit had been only a dishonest interlude meant to confuse him and taunt him with whispers of a different life. One where he did not live like a ghost within the shadows of his dead family.

At least he knew better now. He'd been happy before Mercy, and he would be happy again. Aunt Colleen could threaten to disinherit him from their magic club all she wanted. No one had expected him to succeed on the Council anyway. He'd seen it in their eyes when they all, under Colleen's sway, agreed to swear him in with strong reservations.

Nicolas has grown up. He's ready now. And he's the heir. We always must make a place for our heir.

Yes, but... he's Nicolas.

Nicolas hated to let her down, but that was what he did, whenever anyone set the bar higher for him. He was giving them exactly what they expected. Exactly what they bargained for. He was done playing house, done watching cousins and aunts and uncles exchange knowing glances about how Nicolas had *finally grown up, bless him.* No. None of that. The status quo would be restored. All would be as it once was. The sun would continue to rise and set over the Mississippi beyond his home. The world would go on. And no one would ever expect more than they rightfully should from Nicolas Deschanel ever again.

. . .

BUT *WHY* HAD HE BROUGHT HER HERE?

To *Ophélie*?

Why, when the house wasn't solely his, and hadn't been for many months?

The subject of his questions woke. She stretched her arms and legs, yawning through the exertion.

With painful clarity, Nicolas had his answer.

He couldn't bring someone home who had already been here to begin with.

"FUCK," HE WHISPERED. THE COGNAC SAT ON THE PORES OF HIS SKIN, blanketing the hangover attacking him from limb to limb. Going sober for months had messed with his tolerance. His penance for trying to be a better man.

"Again?" She laughed, but unlike the night before, there was a distance to her laughter, like she was looking upon her actions with a measure of regret.

Nicolas pressed his face into the pillow. How had they gotten here?

Oz had gone to bed early, claiming a headache. The kids and Livia were already sound asleep. Lucia wandered the halls looking lost, as if searching for something undefined.

Nicolas thought she'd always looked half-lost at *Ophélie*. She craved the excitement of perpetual motion. How she'd gone from traveling the world with her partner, Anders, training Empyreans to reach their full potential, to playing house with Oz and his kids was inestimably bizarre to Nicolas, but it wasn't his business any more than what he did every night was the business of others.

He'd been drunk, of course. The throbbing in his temples and his complete rage at the light outside was a sure enough sign if his memory wasn't playing fair. And Lucia had been... what? Lonely? Horny?

Nicolas remembered only two words from her. *I shouldn't.* But *shouldn't* and *won't* were apparently not the same because she followed him into his room, into his bed, and rode him like she was the champion of the Steeplechase.

Those should have been his words. *I shouldn't. I shouldn't because Oz is my best friend. Because even if he won't admit it to himself, he's got some kind of feelings for you. Because if he finds out, it will hurt him. He's already lost too much.*

"I need a shower," Nicolas mumbled. This was usually a cue to his date to get dressed and be on her way.

Lucia, clearly not up to speed with human dating cues, mumbled, *okay,* and turned back over on her side.

"Okay, you need to go to your own room," he said, as nicely as he could muster through the pain radiating through his skull.

She turned her head only and looked back at him, over her shoulder. "I got the hint the first time. Just not a fan of anyone treating me like a dick."

"Sorry?"

Lucia pulled herself forward, sitting up. The sheet fell off her and she made no move to pull it back. Her nipples stood erect in the cold room. She possessed not a hint of self-consciousness.

"I wasn't looking for a repeat, Nicolas," she declared as she stood, searching for her clothes from the night before. "Just another hour or two of sleep. Who the hell is awake at this hour?"

Me, because my fucking head feels like I got the shit kicked out of it.

"Anyway." She slid her panties on, followed by her shirt. She draped the rest of her clothes over her arm. "Thanks? Is that what Children of Men say after a one-night stand? Or am I supposed to pretend like it meant more? These are your rules."

When Nicolas didn't answer, she flashed him a sidelong smirk and sauntered out.

Nicolas never made it to the shower. The amber Hennessy, sparkling against the morning sun, called to him before he could convince himself being clean would be preferable to being drunk.

Around two, he stumbled downstairs in search of food. Condoleezza would have leftovers from whatever she made the kids for lunch. If not, she would make him something. She was always glad to see him return.

Oz stood at the sink, staring into an empty water glass.

"Abracadabra," Nicolas slurred and waved his imaginary wand over the glass. "Water!"

Oz kept his gaze lowered. His jaw tightened. So did his grip on the glass.

"Not water? Coke, then?" He laughed and stumbled into the counter. "Oof. Not Henny. You're too much of a nice guy to drink like a gangster."

Oz looked up with bloodshot eyes. His mouth hung open as he assessed Nicolas. He shook his head. "Nice guy? What do you know about that, Nic?"

"Maybe you do need a drink." Nicolas searched the kitchen for a bottle. He'd never kept them here, though. Not by his own choice, but because Condoleezza insisted some places were sacred, even from him.

"I know what you did," Oz accused. He stepped out from behind the counter, and Nicolas took in a closer appraisal of his friend. Dark bags made home under his eyes. He looked as if he hadn't slept at all. "My *kids* are under this roof, Nic. My children, who, I will remind you, are here because I'm doing *you* a favor. I pulled them out of their schools so I could come out here and run your damn household while you were off doing God knows what with Mercy, who, by the way, you apparently lost along the way. And *this* is how you thank me?"

Nicolas understood at once. Lucia. He understood more, as well. "Your kids?" Nicolas laughed. "This isn't about your kids, Ozzy, and we both damn know it. You wanted her for yourself, but you wouldn't make a move. What, you were hoping she would save herself for the martyr? That she would wait until you passed the appropriate martyr mourning period and realized that, hello, you're still a goddamn man?"

"Save your drunken sanctimonious bullshit for someone who doesn't know you the way I do," Oz spat. He dropped the glass in the metal sink. The clang reverberated across the kitchen. "I'm done, Nic. Done. How many years have I catered to your ego? How many years have I let you walk all over me, claiming to be my friend?"

"Oh, you're done. Sure." Nicolas ran his tongue over his cracked lips. "Just like you were done with Adrienne all those times she played with your emotions and left you in the dust. Just like you were done with Ana when you emo-fucked her a year ago. You're the fucking King of Done, Oz Sullivan. I bow to you and your uncompromising doneness."

"You're absolutely unbelievable."

"And you're a pussy, Ozzy. People walk all over you because you *let* them. Because you fucking love playing the martyr. You don't know any other role for yourself. You can't possibly survive in this world if you haven't been victimized and lived to tell about how you persisted."

Oz gripped the marble counter with both hands, knuckles white. "You're blaming *me* for what you did? So it's my fault, because I'm loyal, that you've spent our entire friendship using me or somehow screwing me over to get what you want?"

The room spun. Nicolas reached a hand out to steady himself and caught the fridge. "You invite it in! You want it, you *love* it, you eat it right up like the self-sacrificing bastard you are. You've been fucked over by the Deschanels so many times you walk with a permanent limp now, but you keep coming back for more."

Oz shook his head, slowly, over and over. The look he wore was several steps beyond incredulous. "Even drunk, I can't believe you would say these things to me. After everything I've done."

Nicolas snorted. "I did you a favor, fucking Lucia. I brought you out of your heroic delusions, friend. You like her, and now you know."

"Oh, *fuck* you, Nicolas! Fuck you!" Oz screamed.

Nicolas stumbled back into the cupboard. Oz rarely swore. He rarely yelled. He rarely fought back.

"You don't get to take your selfish delusions and make them noble. Not with me. Not anymore. I'm done. I'm leaving tomorrow."

Nicolas laughed. "Yeah, right."

"Believe me, or don't," Oz said. His breaths came rapid now. His face flushed from forehead to neck. "I can't do this with you any longer. We're not kids, and I have my own family to think about. I'm too old for games. So are you, but I can't stop you." His eyes closed. He whistled a long, controlled breath through his lips. "I can't be your conscience anymore. Sleep with who you want, Nic. Drink until you black out. I can't care any longer. I can't care about someone who has no regard for me. You're right. I did spend a lot of years letting others walk all over me. Too many." He opened his eyes. "Thank you for helping me finally see it."

Nicolas wished Oz would go back to yelling his anger. This quiet, controlled Oz scared him more. This was not an argument like any they'd had over the years.

A sense of finality settled into the space between them, and Nicolas's head cleared enough to understand he had caused it, with words and actions he could never take back.

The weight of his mistakes, of who he was and always would be, choked him. A yolk around his neck, secured there by no one but himself.

"Ozzy," he said. He had nothing to follow it with. There was nothing potent enough to erase what had happened.

Oz dropped his eyes. "The kids and I will be out tomorrow," he said quietly and brushed past him.

7
LAUREN

"Yeah, I don't know. Just feels like a failure."

The words had become almost a chant for Leander as they returned home for the first time after being on the road for months. Lauren didn't disagree, but his particular form of nihilism had a wearying effect. She'd drawn from every ounce of her own positivity to keep herself pointed forward, eye on the goal.

She couldn't deny Leander's claim that they were proverbially beating their heads into the wall trying to find Quillan, Estella, and Stella. All their leads had run dry. None of the Deschanel family telepaths—not Leander, not any of those back home, awaiting their updates—could locate them, either. Clearly the refugees were blocking to protect themselves. The one telepath in the family who could breach a block, Tristan, was conveniently away from home, fighting another element of the same battle.

"I know this is frustrating," Colleen Deschanel said reasonably, whenever Lauren called for help, or to share their lack of progress. "Especially for us Deschanels, who have grown quite accustomed to our abilities pulling us out of difficult circumstances."

Except Lauren had no idea what that was like. Until she met Quillan, and everything went to hell, she didn't even know magic *existed,* let alone in families she'd known her whole life. Sullivans. Deschanels. Where did it start and end? They had more important things to deal with than her wide-eyed questions, but she tallied them in their mind for a more appropriate time.

"It's not failure," Lauren said, feeling a tremendous responsibility to keep them focused on a successful outcome, versus the alternative. It would be too easy, not to mention disastrous, to spiral into Leander's negativistic way of thinking. "Colleen said she has more information for us."

Leander snorted from the passenger seat. His arms crossed over the ripped Ramones T-shirt he'd worn for more days straight than Lauren was comfortable with. The hair he'd shaved completely off right before Quillan went missing now had a fuzzy, unruly quality about it that made her want to take the shears to him while he slept. "Yeah. That's why she's having us come home to get them, instead of call."

"She knows we need the break."

"Colleen? The woman doesn't know the meaning of the word. She's never taken a break in her life. It's over, Elle. It might have been over before we started."

"Maybe you're right," she conceded, but carefully. "But I believe in the power of positive thinking. We *will* find them."

"And how long are we going to drive around this country trying?" He reached between his legs and took a swig from the can of Mountain Dew that had been wedged between his dirty jeans for the past hour. "At some point, they'll be letting us out of the nursing home for day trips to chase down new leads."

Lauren rolled her eyes, which never left the road. Their conversations had a tendency to grow animated, just the two of them on such an important mission, but she would always first think of their safety. “Are you done? Is that it?”

“No. Hell no,” Leander grunted. “Did I say that?”

“Sure sounds like you’re implying it.”

He finished off his soda and dropped the can in the plastic grocery sack in the backseat that held the remnants of his addiction to all things sweet. At least she’d been able to get him to stop throwing the cans on the floor. A small victory. “I’m frustrated, is all. I’m tired of this car and not sleeping in my own bed. I’m sick of all the disappointment when nothing pans out. I just want to find Quillan and bring him home.”

Lauren nodded. They each had their reasons for leaving everything behind to find Quillan, Estella—Leander’s insufferable older sister—and the young Stella, who had been kidnapped by Estella for reasons unknown. They were together, everyone was certain of it. Lauren’s leave of absence at the firm was indefinite, but her boss, Patrick, Quillan’s father, promised to hold her spot for her out of gratitude. And Leander had dropped out of school to pick up and join her.

Leander’s reason was the simplest. He and Quillan had been best friends for almost two decades. An unlikely pair, oil and water, but Leander’s loyalty to Quillan was unshakeable. Though Quillan had an undoubtedly selfish streak about him, whatever he’d offered to Leander over the years in friendship more than made up for it and earned the loyalty Leander now showed in putting his life on hold.

Lauren’s motivation was more complicated.

When Patrick enlisted her to help his son learn to care about his job, she’d at first taken the charge because she had no choice. But as she grew to know Quillan—apathy and all—she viewed converting him to a functioning member of polite legal society as an interesting challenge, just as she'd once seen law school. He'd proceeded to betray her, nearly destroying her reputation, and then—though she hated to admit this last part—break her heart. And still, she desired to help him.

Lauren saw how everyone in his life, including his own father, had failed him. They'd given up on him. She could relate, in some ways. She'd lived in the shadow of her older sister, Cassidy, for years, a placement her father hadn't discouraged. Cassidy was everything their father had ever wanted in a daughter. She was the face of his empire, Weatherly Department Stores, and the pride of his heart. Lauren was simply a suitable second place. She often wondered in how many other families would a successful career in law only be *second place.*

Whether it be stubbornness or a genuine desire to break this trend in Quillan's life where she could not break it in hers, she was here, and determined to see this through. Whatever fleeting, deeper feelings she'd had for him at one time were long gone. She was relieved to realize this, in part because it restored her self-confidence to know it wasn't some secret hope of winning his heart that kept her pushing forward, but mostly because she didn't want to love him. Quillan had a good heart deep down, but Lauren deserved more than someone who would love her back when it was convenient.

She would not be the heroine who found herself running after the bad boy, only to have her heart broken in the end.

Their time on the road had been more frustrating than anything else. Both of them, in their own ways, had convinced themselves finding Quillan and Estella would take a few days and then they'd be home, back to their own lives. It wasn't unlike when small traumas hit childhood circles. No one ever imagined it would be permanent.

The longer they traveled without progress, the more the situation began to feel real. It grew legs and arms. The expression on the face of the problem changed from one of adventure to the spreading dread of an unsolvable problem. Where Leander often commented that Quillan had a habit of getting worked up and cooling off just as quick, it became clear this was not a situation that fit this predictable side of his personality. Quillan left, and this time he did not want to be found.

Colleen and the rest of the involved Deschanel gang in New Orleans all hitched their wagons to the belief that if they found Quillan, they would find Estella and Stella. No amount of explaining how Quillan had left *because* of Estella, and the horrible things she had done to him, would sway them. Estella was a fish out of water, they said, with no clue how to care for little Stella. She would reach out for the familiar. Someone she trusted.

Leander and Lauren had sat in Colleen's broad office with similar expressions. Trust? Estella? Quillan? How could the venerable Colleen Deschanel be so off with these assessments? *We hurt the ones who will allow the abuse, all the while developing a special respect for the same person we have wronged. Estella may have come too late in her realization, for it arrives in tandem with Quillan's own that he does not need her as he once believed. But Estella is the one we must watch. For it is Estella who fled her home in search of sanctuary. Estella who chose to protect the child instead of turning her over to her beloved great-grandmother, Blanche.*

Leander's sarcastic smirk did most of the talking for him. But he did throw in *You give my sister too much damn credit* and other disparagements. He was here for Quillan, not Estella. He didn't need to be sold on his sister's non-existent merits, nor did he have any desire to.

Lauren, though, heard Colleen's words. She, too, had puzzled over Estella's actions. Everything she knew about Estella pointed to award-winning self-centeredness. What was she thinking when she came upon Stella? When she aimed her car away from New Orleans with the scared little girl in her backseat? She had no verdict on Estella's motive, but her actions were curious indeed. Enough that she wouldn't completely rule out the possibility Colleen was right.

If Estella had sought out Quillan, though, what then? Would he have taken her in? Turned her away? Leander insisted Quillan would advise her to go fuck herself. Colleen had a theory that the girl would be what kept Quillan from shutting the door in her face.

"We should pull over for the night." Leander's sleepy voice pulled Lauren from her reverie. She'd never driven so much in her life as she had these past months. Leander *didn't drive*—"why would I?"—so the burden had fallen on her.

Lauren didn't know if his suggestion came from a fear of ending up in a ditch, or concern for her. She suspected a bit of both, and it was the latter that worried her. Sometimes she would catch Leander watching her when he thought she was focused on the road. His sheepish grin when he ordered her food for her in a roadside diner, so she could refresh in the restroom. Or the look of plain relief on his face when she declared, one night after a particularly grueling day, that Quillan could rot for all she cared.

Her observations of these little nuances in Leander Broussard were touching, but she wouldn't encourage them. Leander was a better person than he wanted others to believe, but it wasn't about him. Lauren just didn't need the complications romance would bring. Not now.

"Yeah," she agreed with a yawn. Her headlights caught the

sign on the freeway. Plenty of options at the next exit. "I'll be so glad for a couple nights in my own bed."

Leander flushed in the passenger seat.

Best if she didn't know what he was thinking.

8
JACOB

Amelia loved to tell the story of the first time she rediscovered Jacob Donnelly.

To hear her tell it: she'd stumbled into the Tulane campus pub to meet some friends. As she craned her neck, searching for a familiar face, her gaze stopped on Jacob, lost to his very enthusiastic drum solo of the Foo Fighters' "Everlong." When the song was over, he'd bowed to the applause of dozens of college kids, and his and Amelia's eyes met on his way back up. She hadn't seen him since high school. Who had the underclassman funny guy become? Her friends were nowhere to be found. Should she go talk to him in the meantime?

This was the defining moment that stuck with her, the one she carried into the future and recalled when she spoke about the moment that changed her whole life. The story she told at dinner parties when inevitably someone asked how they had met.

Jacob remembered that day a bit differently. He recalled

nailing that solo. Her gaping at him like she'd just seen water after a month in the desert.

Amelia rolled her eyes whenever he told his version to friends or acquaintances. Jacob didn't mind. Both versions had led them down the same path, toward a future together.

For Jacob, it wasn't this moment but another.

After their chance encounter in the pub, he'd taken her on a quick streetcar ride into Carrolton, where he bought her a burger at Camellia Grill. Then he'd followed her all the way back to her stop at Jackson Avenue and walked her home to The Gardens. She'd insisted it wasn't necessary; she was, after all, the daughter of feminist icon, Dr. Colleen Deschanel. But it was necessary for Jacob, who knew he had to see her again.

Yet it wasn't this moment either, but the next.

The following day was St. Patrick's. As an exiled Irishman, this holiday was bittersweet. Jacob's only memories of living in Ireland had not been happy ones. He tried to recall how he felt sitting on his dad's shoulders, watching the parades and fairs in Killianshire. His siblings giggling and cheering and pointing out their favorite costumes. But the scar on his chest was the only thing that stuck with him.

Jacob considered asking Amelia out, but it felt too soon, and he didn't know what the rules were. She told him upfront she wasn't looking for a relationship, and really, neither was he, but he nevertheless felt the overwhelming need to be *near* her. To share space, even for brief moments. If friendship was the terms, he could live with that, and that was safer for him, too. But if he called her the next day, she might think he hadn't heard her at all.

So he'd wandered over to Bourbon Street with a plastic glittery leprechaun hat and drank his share of green beers as he made his way down the line of exotic dance clubs and bars waiving covers to get more eye candy in their doors.

Then he saw her. She stood at the corner of Orleans and Bourbon in a sparkling emerald party dress cut several inches above her pale knees. She swung from the street sign, her gold-white hair speckled with green extensions, face dotted with glittery hand-painted clovers. In her other hand was some sort of green-tinted concoction in a clear go-cup with the logo from Lafitte's Blacksmith Shop printed on the side.

Amelia was surrounded by several of her girlfriends. Jacob recognized one of them from high school. The other two had distinct sorority looks, with exceptionally strong hygiene—gleaming white teeth, perfect blond hair, a mouth that never quit smiling—and form-fitting costumes. Amelia smiled along with them, but Jacob saw through the gesture to the heart of her disposition. He saw the truth through her eyes, which held in them a dreamy look, as if she knew she *should* be there, but wished she were anywhere else.

Jacob realized in that moment that the reason he'd never paid much mind to Amelia Deschanel was that he'd automatically placed her in the same bucket as the other popular girls, who had no time for anyone who didn't somehow further their own social advancement in high school. Jacob had been marked his whole life by his difference from other children. By his Irish brogue, which he spent years forcing from his tongue. By the distance he placed between himself and others, after years of solitude and no solid support system. By the scar on his chest from his father's gun that meant hiding in corners to change for gym class, or be assailed with questions he wasn't prepared to answer. By how he was known by his classmates for one of two things: fighting or joking.

As he watched Amelia swing from the street sign, playing the part of Garden District debutante that her friends expected and desired from her, Jacob understood her for the first time. He understood her in the same way he understood himself, and the way he had been interacting with the world since he'd found himself on a plane to New Orleans without a family.

In all his life, Jacob had only found true boldness and courage behind his fists and his laughter. Both afforded him special protection from the world and from the potential of being exposed, and hurt. He had neither on his side when he approached Amelia that night on Bourbon Street and, for once, he didn't need them.

And as he maneuvered through drunken crowds, dodging the dredges of waste littering the street, wincing as he was sloshed with rancid beer, Amelia glanced his way. Her smile broadened. Her eyes lit up.

That, right there, was it. His moment. The one where he knew she would become a fundamental part of his life for whatever remained of it.

"Jacob Donnelly," she'd said, stretching his name with her light Uptown drawl. "What's a guy like you doing in a place like this?"

One of the girls rolled her eyes at another, who cackled and shook her head. *Loser,* he heard. Jacob ignored it. They and the rest of the world faded away.

"Rescuing you," he said, not missing a beat. He was playing a part, too, even if he didn't yet understand the role. "If that's all right."

"It's more than all right," she said and hopped off the curb. She dumped the rest of her drink in the storm drain, to the horror of her friends.

Jacob shuddered as he realized he couldn't tell the difference between her drink and some nearby vomit.

"Ladies, please forgive me. I owe my old friend a dinner and tonight seems like a great night to return that favor."

"Seriously?" one of the girls asked. Her arms went up and

out. Her designer handbag dangled precariously on several fingers. "It's St. Paddy's, Amy!"

"A Deschanel always lives up to their word," she said, adding an edge of regret to her tone, which he later learned was to spare them any slight. That was Amelia, always considering first how her actions made others feel, even if they didn't reciprocate the kindness.

"Are you coming *back*?"

"Go out and enjoy the rest of the night, which has not yet revealed the last of her mysteries." She winked.

She then flashed them the sweetest smile and looped her arm through Jacob's.

She is so weird, Jacob heard one of them say when they'd crossed the street. *Why do we even bother with her?*

She's a Deschanel, Darcy. Hello!

Jacob steered her down Orleans, away from the hubbub of dirty Bourbon Street and the cutting words of the young, insipid women Amelia had called her friends. When the music dimmed enough for them to talk comfortably, he said, "When I bought you lunch, there weren't strings attached."

"Oh," she said, dodging the cracks in the upturned sidewalk in her towering stilettos. Her knees wobbled every few steps. "I know that. But *they* didn't. And anyway, it's still my turn."

"Your turn?" Jacob's heart skipped in hopefulness.

"Well, yeah. I pay my own way. If you subscribe to some antediluvian notion of chivalry, that's your problem, not mine."

Jacob looked down, smiling. She still held tight to his arm.

"I won't complain about anyone buying me dinner." Jacob laughed. "I'm a cheapskate before I'm a gentleman."

"My kind of guy!"

My kind of girl.

"So, since you picked lunch, it's only fair that I pick dinner," she said. They sauntered past an older man plucking B.B. King on his cracked electric guitar as he leaned against a boarded-up building. Amelia reached into her purse and pulled out a twenty-dollar bill, dropping it into his case with a smile. "You aren't allergic to anything, are you?"

Jacob shook his head.

"Thank God. Where we're going is a bit pricy, but you don't get to complain about the cost unless you're buying. Fair?"

Jacob nodded. He didn't know what to think. He only knew he wasn't unhappy.

"Are you sure you don't want to hang out with your friends, Amy?"

"Please, call me Amelia. Or Mia if four syllables is a struggle." Amelia stopped in the center of the sidewalk. Her direct look and sky blue eyes shined startlingly bright against the sea of green she'd decorated herself with. "Can I tell you something, Jacob?"

"You can tell me anything." He internally kicked himself for what he immediately knew was far too tacky a response for the question.

She watched him for a moment, then smiled. "The thing is, I don't really have any friends."

Jacob gestured toward the gaggle of girls still congregating where they'd left them on Bourbon, but the earnestness in her expression stopped him from adding words.

"Girls my age, is all they are," she explained. "In a sorority I joined because it was expected. My mother knows I've never had many friends, and it worries her, even though it shouldn't. I'm fine. Have you ever done something to make others happy, even if it didn't make you happy?"

Jacob started to say no, but then thought of Sister Agnes. How she had nurtured him like a mother and only asked in return that he stop fighting his emotional turmoil with his fists. "Yeah. I guess I have."

"Normal is overrated in my book," she went on. "Normalcy isn't anything more than someone else's standards for how you should live your life. So sometimes it's more important for others to think you've achieved normalcy than it is for you to really do it."

"Pretending, you mean."

"Small deceptions created to put the hearts and minds of those you love at ease."

Jacob had no experience with that kind of selflessness. Not the orphan whose father had tried to end everything for his own weakness.

Yet, listening to her, watching her, he knew not only that she did, but that he could as well.

He wasn't entirely in love with her. If he was honest with himself, he'd been *partly* in love with her, from that moment in the pub onward. But he might have loved her sooner, really loved her, had he known he was capable of not only giving but receiving that gift. It took years of growing comfortable together and exploring their individual boundaries before he would understand this and take action. Before he would let her all the way in, to see through all the dark holes of his past; the pinpricks of light straining to come through.

But that night, Jacob Donnelly experienced a phenomenon he had not felt in all his life: hope.

THEY HADN'T WALKED THE QUARTER TOGETHER AGAIN SINCE THEY'D been married. In their decade together, the night walks down Royal and Chartres, and occasionally, even, the sins of Bourbon, were a routine still steeped in the magic of that long ago

St. Patrick's. They both loved their city, but they loved it even more together.

Amelia suggested the walk. From the time they'd returned home, she'd been both closer to him, but also, somehow, somewhere else. Jacob understood she was prone to internalize her grief, but he was also grateful she'd chosen to grieve *with* him now, as well. Their experiences traveling to the past had helped them both accept how important this was.

She was at the stage of her grief that craved a return to normality. In the last couple of weeks, they'd been out to eat almost every night, visiting all their old favorites. She started running again and invited Jacob along with her. He paced her by the river as the steamboats passed them by.

Yet, at night, she disappeared for hour-long showers, or escaped to the porch, by herself, until he felt compelled to break her out of her thoughts. He wanted to understand, and so he made himself understand. He let her have these escapes by herself, because he saw how much effort she was placing into returning to who they were. To him.

The crowds were thin in the French Quarter on the off season. They walked in relative peace, passing mostly locals on their way to or from somewhere. Amelia pulled her sweater tight, but also leaned into Jacob for warmth. He recollected the girl with the green in her hair and twinkle in her eyes.

He wanted to thank her for not shutting him out where Victor was concerned. She could've handled it herself, which was often her way. But instead, she welcomed Jacob in, and they faced this unfortunate challenge hand in hand, together.

But he wouldn't let Victor steal their private moments, too.

"I was thinking I might go back to work," she said. When the sidewalk narrowed, she led the way, her arm extended behind her, hand laced through his. "I haven't even been able to experience being a doctor since I got my PhD."

"I think that's a great idea," Jacob said. He lifted his voice to carry ahead of him, over the competing music wafting from nearby streets. "I might finish my own PhD. I miss the lab, but I think I'm also ready to lead my own studies."

He felt her smile from behind. "Of course you are. And I think Aleksei was right about us all staying put for a while. Why shouldn't we try to return to what's normal for us?"

She turned on Royal, and he knew immediately where she was headed. The Hotel Monteleone's Carousel Bar. With its light rotation and glittering Jazz Age portraits lining the walls, they'd always been drawn here. To the magic and memories alike.

Under usual conditions, they would have to stalk and wait for a seat at the carousel, hovered in tight crowds of other patrons with the same goal, but they found two without waiting. Amelia skipped forward and secured them in a rush, as if someone might spring forth from the shadows to steal them from under her.

Jacob grinned and sidled up on the seat beside her.

She ordered vieux carres for each of them. Her eyes traveled around the magnificent detail of the bar, the way she did the first time they went together.

Jacob caught something from the corner of his eye and sighed. "All right. We've got one. Creeper. Four o'clock."

"Four o'clock permanently or four o'clock at our point in the bar's rotation?"

Jacob shook his head. "That hurt my brain. Dark hair. Seersucker suit. That's about all I need to say, because who seriously wears seersucker suits anymore?"

Amelia raised a brow. "Have you spent time in the Central Business District? Even Ashley wears one from time to time."

"He does not."

"He does. The fabric is really quite breathable, which is a smart choice for our humid climate."

"Stop rationalizing this antiquated fashion choice."

"Only pointing out the facts, Donnelly."

"Your facts are questionable at best."

Amelia swirled her drink and affected a light nod in the direction of the other man. "As questionable as the creeper's bedroom eyes. He needs to work on his game."

Jacob laughed. The man in the seersucker was hilariously bold with his smoldering look and unnerving stare. With luck, they'd soon hear some terrible pick-up lines they could laugh about later.

Amelia's hand came behind Jacob's neck and she shoved her tongue down his throat like inexperienced teenagers in the backseat of a car. Jacob initially gripped the bar in shock and then wound his hands through her long hair, playing along.

Across the bar, the man tensed his lips. He downed the remainder of his drink.

Amelia laughed and winked. Jacob flushed, wondering what had come over her. This had never been an element of their playful game before. It didn't fit at all with her natural modesty.

"Subtle," he charged and took a sip.

"Yeah? That's what I was going for."

The man threw down a twenty and left.

"I miss some of the mischief we used to get into when we were younger," Amelia said suddenly. She cradled her drink in both hands, watching the amber liquid hit the bright lights. "Do you think we're too old for that now?"

Jacob smirked. "Too old? For fun?"

"Like that time," Amelia said, her face breaking into a wide grin, "you pretended to be Jack from *Titanic* on the Steamboat Natchez?"

Jacob winced in an *oops* expression. "Banned for life. But honestly, I couldn't have been the first. And you know I wasn't the last."

Amelia released an exaggerated sigh. "That's right, it was a *lifetime* ban. Nix my next suggestion about a river cruise tomorrow."

Jacob directed a knowing gaze. "What about Miss 'If I want to ride Andrew Jackson, who's gonna stop me?'"

Amelia's mouth gaped in mock protest before her face crumbled into a laugh. "That was me, wasn't it?"

"Oh, I still have the pictures, in case your memory is failing you. Of course, you riding the statue of AJ, whistling Dixie, is probably burned into my mind forever, whether I like it or not."

"At least I was drunk," she defended, sipping her drink through two tiny straws. "Can't say the same for the time when you tried to re-enact the diner robbery scene from *Pulp Fiction* at Café du Monde."

"Would have been a shame to be drunk during such an important moment."

"Or the time you crashed the Quarter ghost tour in order to begin a serious discussion on slavery and piracy, in no particular order."

Jacob shrugged. "History is important. Which I would expect you know, seeing as you tried to steal Napoleon's death mask from The Cabildo."

Amelia shook her head. "They had that locked down pretty good, didn't they?"

"Obviously, they knew you were coming."

She affected an innocent look. "This sweet face from the nice side of Magazine Street?"

He laughed. "Next time you tell me your name doesn't

matter, I'll remind you that being a Deschanel is the *only* reason we don't have a police record."

"On the flip side, that means our street cred is nonexistent."

Jacob clinked his glass against hers. "Too cool, or not cool enough. The cross is ours to bear."

JACOB COUNTED TWENTY FULL ROTATIONS ON THE BAR. FOUR MORE drinks apiece. Story after story. Memory after memory. Slowly, over time, their eyes glassed over. Their laughter died to low, slurred giggles. Amelia's head fell against his shoulder and stayed there.

He didn't dare voice his gratitude for the happiness in his heart that evening. He didn't trust the universe. Not just yet.

Instead, he lifted his wife into a piggyback ride, and stumbled down the cobbled Quarter streets, weaving and laughing, remembering, once again, what it was to feel hope.

9
LUCIA

Lucia listened helplessly from the next room as drawers slammed closed and metal hangers flew from the closet rod, landing with an ear-splitting clang on the wood floor. Naomi cried in another bedroom as she packed her own clothes in protest. Christian, who Lucia passed in the hall on her way to her own room, wore a look of quiet strength unique to children who are predisposed to wanting to fix the problems of their parents' worlds.

She should go talk to Oz. She'd told herself that over and over as his heavy footsteps fell against the cypress. As he cursed under his breath.

But what would she say? The argument that they were great teachers to the children would hold such little water. They did all right, but real teachers would undoubtedly do better than their patched together homeschooling. And managing the estate? Oz could do this from New Orleans, as he and his firm always had. Lucia couldn't very well say *she* needed him. Maybe she could throw out Livia's name, but that wouldn't be true. Livia required very little, least of all two meddling adults who smothered her and kept her on a tight leash.

Oz was moodier than a tribe of women menstruating in tandem. Lucia had no personal point of reference with which to relate, but she possessed, at least, an intellectual understanding of how unexpected and inconsistent grief could be. For Oz, he'd carried the grief of not only losing his wife—two wives, actually—but of every action or inaction ascribed to him over the course of their tumultuous courtship. Moments in time, blips on the radar, saw him happy and playful. Mostly, though, he was knee-deep in a self-loathing so dense Lucia could find no skills of her own possession to break through.

But this sudden departure from *Ophélie* wasn't about Adrienne. Oz had been dark and depressed at times, but he'd shown no signs of fleeing the property until Nicolas had come home.

Lucia overheard bits and pieces of their fight from earlier. Not enough to stitch together anything coherent, but plenty to understand that Oz's dissatisfaction with Nicolas' gap in character was a driving reason for his decision.

And what would become of her when he did leave? And Livia? She didn't think Nicolas, even at his worst, would kick them out, but she also saw no reason to stay. Months ago, she couldn't wait to break free of this backwards bayou countryside and return to where the action was. She even missed grumpy, insufferable Anders, and his patriarchal bossiness.

Maybe she'd grown complacent. Complacency was a trait she'd turned her nose at in others, and she loathed the idea it might appear in her own character. But she couldn't deny that *something* was pulling her toward this old property.

Naomi flew into the room, her face a red mess of tears and sniffling. "Luc, you have to do something! Daddy will listen to you!"

Lucia knelt down before the little girl who had once annoyed her and now tugged at her heart. "Your father has his reasons for taking you home. Nothing I say will stop him."

"Bad reasons!" Naomi cried, bursting into a fresh batch of tears. She threw herself against Lucia. "Stupid reasons!"

She looked past the girl now pressed into her chest, arms wrapped tight around her. It was a mystery to her why little Naomi would want to stay in this remote property when she could be home again, with all her friends. "Sweetheart..."

"Please!"

Lucia sighed. She kissed the top of Naomi's head and went to find Oz.

A TOWEL WHIZZED BY LUCIA'S FACE AND LANDED IN THE HALLWAY. OZ gave her a surprised, sheepish look and went back to his packing.

"Naomi is pretty upset," she ventured. She hung back in the doorway. If the conversation didn't go well, she could either escape quickly or block his.

"She's been through worse than moving back to the house she was born in." Oz opened another drawer, found it empty, and went back through the rest, which were the same. How many times had he opened and closed the same drawers? Lucia had a sense he was stalling.

Lucia shifted her weight to one hip. "Maybe you should talk to her, then. Don't you wonder why she came to me, instead of you?"

Oz snorted. "Weren't you ever a kid? When one adult told you no, you didn't go to the other for a better answer?" He stopped for a moment to assess her, then rolled his eyes. "No, I guess you wouldn't know about that, would you? You don't know about a lot of things, it seems."

"I definitely don't know what changed your mind so quickly."

Oz looked ready to take her head off. He seemed to force a calm over himself before responding. "With Nicolas home, my work here is done."

It was Lucia's turn to laugh. She thumbed toward the stairs. "The man child upstairs? Really? Meanwhile, Condoleezza and Richard take turns wiping the drool from his entitled chin."

"Not sure how that's my problem." Oz tried to zip his suitcase, but it bulged too high. He dropped his elbow and forced his weight forward, and still had no luck. With a strained grunt, he added, "I did what I signed up to do. I took care of stuff while he ran around the world doing whatever the hell he was doing. He's home. It's not my house. Why am I the bad guy?"

"No one said you were the bad guy."

"You're standing there trying to guilt me into staying by using my daughter. Cheap tactic, Lucia, even for you."

"And why are you suddenly mad at *me*? I thought we were friends, Oz."

Oz stopped trying to finagle the suitcase and glared at her. "In what world would you and I ever be friends?"

She gawked at him. "You're not yourself."

"What would you know about who I am?"

"What has gotten into you? Yesterday, you were completely fine."

"That was yesterday." Oz gave her a blank look.

She slouched in the doorway. "I'm trying to help."

He returned to the problem of the suitcase. "If you want to help me, help me get this damn thing closed."

Lucia breathed out in annoyance and sauntered across the room. With one shift of her torso, she flattened the top of the suitcase and pulled the zipper around with ease. "There. Happy?"

"Thanks."

"Now tell me why you're leaving."

"I already did."

She stood between Oz and the suitcase. "Then tell me why you won't stay."

He met her eyes. She couldn't read what was in them. "There's nothing keeping me here."

The words hit her in the chest. She didn't understand why they felt so personal, and why they should hurt. "Nothing?" she repeated. Her mouth and throat went dry.

"Nothing," he said and pulled his suitcase off the bed as he brushed past her.

Lucia followed Oz and his children down the stairs, like a forgotten pet. She knew a lost cause when she saw one and wasn't apt to chase one like some would. Oz was a man determined, whatever his reasons, and she didn't have the power to change his mind.

Both children sniffled as Oz yanked the heavy oaken door open. Naomi threw herself in Lucia's arms one last time and whispered, "Thank you for trying."

Christian gave her a tight, sad smile and a brief hug. Lucia saw the man he would grow to become.

"Come on, kids," Oz ordered, without looking back.

Outside, Richard had pulled his car around and the doors were open, awaiting them.

Christian followed his father, carrying both his and his sister's bags. Naomi glanced back on her way down the steps, clutching her stuffed blue bear, her wide, miserable brown eyes burning a hole in Lucia's soul.

Nicolas stepped up beside Lucia and reached around her to close the door. Oz and his children disappeared from view. She jumped back, startled out of the daze that had briefly consumed her.

"You and Livia are welcome to stay," he said. She could smell the cognac on him, but he didn't sway or slur his words. He was just getting started. "Until your Brotherhood, or whatever, needs you again. It's no matter to me."

She spun on him. "What the hell happened?"

Nicolas regarded her with one eye cracked closed. "Come on, Lucia."

"Come on, *what*?"

"I know Empyreans have their own crazy ideas about morals and right and wrong, but you've spent more than enough time around humans to understand the difference. Unless you think ignorance goes well with your pretty new heels?"

Lucia squared her stance. "What the hell are you getting at?"

Nicolas leered at her in cruel amusement. "If you really don't know, you're as fucked up as I am."

"I don't have the patience for whatever it is you're doing right now," Lucia countered. "Either tell me or don't."

"Let me spell it out for you." Nicolas' smile sent chills through her. "Oz, our favorite friendly neighborhood martyr, developed some less than friendly feelings for his babysitting cohort. Because the mourning period for such a chap is at least a hundred years to maintain the unreasonable standards set for himself, he could not, in all good conscience, act on said feelings. Here comes the wrench. Said babysitting cohort fucks his best friend. Oh, no, now we *really* have a conundrum because the martyr can neither be angry, which would require a full admission of his feelings, nor can he stay in the situation, because that would interfere with his heroic good guy complex that forces him to always side with right over wrong. Leaving is the only way he can keep up appearances and also protect his tragic heart. This is what we simple humans might call a lose-lose situation, Lucia."

Lucia's jaw hung. "You're crazy. And wrong."

"I *am* crazy," he agreed. "But I'm not wrong."

Lucia stepped away from him. There was no way Oz had feelings for her. He found her impulsive, reckless, and a loud-mouth—everything he wasn't. It was simply out of the question, and she refused to entertain the delusional notions of a drunkard. But if Nicolas thought this to be true, and seduced her into his bed believing this, then how could he call himself a friend to Oz? She had a sudden urge to run after Oz and apologize, but she didn't know what she was apologizing for.

"If you really believe this, why did you sleep with me?" she asked.

Nicolas shrugged. A bottle of Hennessy appeared from the back of his pants. He unscrewed the cap and squinted with delight at the liquid inside. "We all play our parts, Lucia. Some of them we're good at, others not so much. Me? I'm better at the part everyone expects me to excel at."

"Being a lecherous, disloyal asshole?" she spat.

"Ahh." Nicolas grinned as he backed away, toward the stairs. He tipped his bottle at her. "You have a way with words."

10
NICOLAS

Nicolas stood on the uppermost gallery at the rear of *Ophélie,* of which he was the heir and master, and surveyed the wreckage of a transient dream gone to waste. He swung a half-drunk bottle of Hennessy over the railing, occasionally spilling a long, thin stream of amber into the garden below.

This was Mercy's vision. All of it. He'd shared it with her, eagerly, believing, for once, in something greater than himself. Her idealistic theory that they could, somehow, be important to the outcome of the civil war brewing between the Empyreans. That they would provide a safe haven to the youth of that movement, and that, safe or not, them being here could matter. *We will teach them,* she said. And he had blindly and blithely followed, without asking, *teach them what, exactly?*

Now, the outbuildings they had fixed up for housing remained empty. Nicer, he supposed, and in better shape than they were prior to this utopian vision. By all objective measures the property had never looked better. But the lights had gone out, in a manner of speaking. Where he'd been content to live in sepia tones all his life, Mercy had breathed color into every inch of the house and property, bringing it to life like a painter with a canvas. And now he lived in a world of black and white, where the sum total of his failures whispered and screamed: *You are alone, alone, alone, and this is exactly what you deserved.*

"Master Nicolas." Richard's voice appeared from the double door plantation shutters behind him. Richard, who had a heavier hand in his upbringing than his own father, and who had started calling him *Master Nicolas* when he was just five, and only because it annoyed Nicolas.

Nicolas lifted a hand, but didn't turn. "I'm fine. Go away."

"With respect, you are *not* fine." The old man's steps sounded in uneven strides as he made a slow, hobbled approach. "If anyone knows when you are and are not fine, it's Richard."

"Okay," Nicolas said. "I'm not fine. But I don't need anything."

Richard came to a stop several feet behind him. Nicolas let the garden below swim in and out of focus. He could still make out the careful detail in the parterre design. *Nope, not drunk enough yet.* "Your daddy used to confide in me. And his daddy before him. And you, Nicolas, used to confide in me, too, when you were a boy. Ain't no shame in talkin' about what troubles you. All men need the release from time to time."

Nicolas held the bottle over his head. "Found mine."

"That's no release, and you know it. That's your hell. Just like your daddy's was his wife. And your granddaddy, August, his heart was too damn big for his chest. Was a good man, your granddaddy. He saved this family."

Nicolas snorted. "Saved it? Have you had a good look around recently?"

"You and I look at the same scenery and see different

things." Richard approached, less tentative than Nicolas would have liked. "See that oak over yonder, the one that's been dyin' for the past two years?"

"The one the Trust won't let me just dig out and be done with?" Nicolas grumbled.

"Because you see a nuisance. An ugly eyesore sittin' on your otherwise pristine land that has outworn its usefulness."

"And?"

Richard stepped forward and leaned over the balcony at his side. "And I see a life well-lived that deserves the same respect as you and me."

"You want me to give it a proper burial, is that it? Order a mausoleum and etch Robert Frost poems on the side?"

Richard shook his head. "You ain't listenin'. That's your right, but if you start, you might learn something."

"I'll start listening when you stop talking about trees."

"You don't need my analogies, that's fine. I'll come out with it, then. Your family, they've been through a lot. A whole lotta hurtin', more than what any family should expect to handle. No one knows like I do, lookin' after generations of Deschanels. I watched your granddaddy say goodbye to the love of his life, and then turn around and marry her nursemaid 'cos I expect he knew what he needed to do. The heir's line was close to dyin' out, and he couldn't just lie down next to his love and give up. Seven kids he had by your grandma, and whether he loved her or not is a mystery he took with him straight to his grave. Only four of 'em left, but that's more than enough to make a family. Colleen, she always led the family better than anyone, anyway. Augustus, Evangeline, they do their part. Maureen, well, ain't no one ever accused her of good sense, but you can't win 'em all." He shook his head.

Nicolas laughed in spite of himself.

"Your daddy," Richard went on, "was a weak man in a lot of

ways, and I expect you knew that without me rubbin' it in. He didn't have the stomach for the hard stuff, or the grit of his own daddy. But he loved his children, and yes, even you. He jus' knew you didn't need as much of him. Your sisters suffered greatly under the heavy hand of Cordelia, as you well know, and the more he loved 'em, the more she hurt 'em. Sometimes I think they're better off in heaven, where she can't get to 'em. Other times, I think about the women they might have become, and I get mighty sad."

Nicolas tilted his head toward the old man at his side. "This was supposed to be uplifting?"

"If I didn't tell it like it was, I expect you'd make sure I knew it," Richard said with a half-hearted smile. "Your sisters, that's a real, honest-to-God tragedy, Nicolas. It just don't get any worse than that. But the world didn't stop turning when their hearts quit beating. You ain't as alone as you think you are. Sister, brother, cousin, uncle, aunt, those labels never meant nothing to Deschanels. Amelia, Olivia, Anasofiya, and Katja are your sisters as much as Adrienne and the lot of 'em were. And what about poor Anne? You say you wish you'd had a brother. Well, you have them! Ashley, Tristan, Markus, they're your brothers. Y'all are stronger together, and always have been. Colleen, she knows this, and that's why she's the glue."

"It was never like that," Nicolas scoffed. "Don't act like it was."

"If you had come out of your room from time to time, or stayed home instead of running off and away from all your problems, you might've seen it *was* like that. Always has been since August breathed new life into this clan. No one forced you to be the outsider. You chose it, and wore it like an ugly, expensive suit you were too cheap and proud to return."

Nicolas looked down into the garden, wishing he'd had the good sense to drink more before Richard showed up.

"You ain't alone," Richard repeated. "That's all I'm saying. And this fine gal, Miss Mercy, who came and went before the seasons changed, well, if she ain't here, then that should tell you somethin'. You aren't the only one expected to clean up their act in a relationship. I saw a boy turn into a man these past few months, but I saw a woman who wasn't ready for what that man had to offer. I'm mighty sad for you, but give me a man who ain't had his heart broken and I'll give you a man who's never lived."

Nicolas turned away and said nothing. He had no desire to talk about Mercy, not when standing amidst the wreckage she'd left behind, both what he could see, and what he could not. Richard's words about getting your heart broken had some truth to them, but what Richard didn't understand was how this was less about heartbreak and more how Nicolas had finally come to the realization that he was not now, or ever, meant to *be* that man Richard had charged him with. That man had been vulnerable and allowed a woman in who was not ready for him —Richard had that part right, at least—and that vulnerability wasn't endearing, it was weak. Distracting. Pointless.

"That'll be the door," Richard said with a heavy, weary sigh. "You expecting someone?"

"I'm never expecting anyone. Doesn't stop them from showing up."

"And there's some truth." Richard chuckled. He gripped Nicolas's shoulder with a trembling, bony hand. "What we lose is a part of us as much as what we gain. No point in putting more weight on one than the other, neither. Only thing we can change is ourselves."

Nicolas turned to watch Richard limp back into the house.

His arthritis had flared in the few minutes he stood to offer advice, and Nicolas had a pit of regret in his stomach from how he'd treated one of his few constants in life. A man who had grown terribly old while Nicolas was wrapped up in his own set of troubles.

Richard. Oz. The Council. He was apparently going down the whole list, knocking off every ally he'd had.

Nicolas took a long swig from the bottle and waited for the inevitable call downstairs.

Of all the people Nicolas expected to come check on him, his cousin Ashley was the last he would have put on the list. Clean-cut, always-got-his-act-together Ashley, who had undoubtedly been more than disappointed that Nicolas came back when Ashley had done such a great job covering for him on the Council.

After the last meeting, he thought Ashley would have all but written him off.

Then a light went on. Nicolas gave him a withering look. "Doing your mother's dirty work?"

Ashley stood in his tailored suit, looking like a walking advertisement for Brooks Brothers. "I came because I wanted to."

Nicolas set the bottle down on the parlor table. It nearly teetered off, and he edged it back on with a sharp panic, as if he couldn't afford all the alcohol in the world.

"And why would you want to come out here?"

"To offer my help."

"Help with what?"

Ashley maintained his sharp poise, like a young politician. Of all the Deschanels, Nicolas thought, Ashley was the most classically beautiful. The most sculpted. His cheekbones and jaw line seemed cut from fine clay. His hair, that white-blond Nordic color unique to so many in the Deschanel line, was held in place by God Himself. If beauty was a math equation, he would equal out to an even hundred.

"With anything, Nicolas. So much has happened to the family. We're rallying, around my sister, around Ana, around the rescue groups, but no one has come to see if they can help you."

Nicolas belted out a laugh. "Me? Why would *I* need help?"

Ashley's eyes traveled briefly to the bottle, and then back to Nicolas.

"That? You're here because I'm enjoying something I've been doing since I was twelve?"

Ashley winced. "You were drunk at the meeting. I wasn't ready to present, and you knew that, but you were too smashed to think rationally. That's not recreational. That's a problem."

"So, you're mad?"

"No," Ashley said slowly, "I'm worried."

Nicolas slumped into the grandfather chair at the other end of the room. "What is it with everyone in this family trying to rewrite history? We've never been close! You and I were never the cousins who swung from trees and caught crawfish in the river. We never whispered our secrets to each other, or compared the size of our dicks. Don't give me those sad eyes and act like you're here to rescue your favorite cousin."

"Not for lack of trying," Ashley replied. "Don't you ever wonder why everyone else in the family remembers our closeness as kids, and you're the only one who doesn't? It's because you were always the one in the shadows, Nic. While Nat and Giselle and the others played with us and shared their world, you decided you had your reasons not to."

Nicolas leaned back, legs splayed like a wayward prince on his throne. "Again, I ask, why are you here?"

"Whether or not you have the same regard for the rest of us, we love you. *I* love you. And when tragedy hits the family, we get through it by banding together." Ashley made several careful steps in his direction. "Aren't you tired of doing it all alone?"

Nicolas stared at him as if the question could not get more ridiculous.

Ashley pursed his lips. Nicolas imagined he was praying for strength. Some of the Deschanels, at least, were still good Catholics. "We've all lost. My brother, Ben, and his family, I thought that would kill me. And then I lost my daughter. My Katie." He dropped his head. His mouth wrinkled and his hand clenched and unclenched as he fought for control. "There's no pain, no hell, like losing a child. None. And it's as if I've lost the others, because my wife took them and ran away, from me. I think about this every single day of my life, how we got here, and whether I could have prevented it. I wonder what goes through her head, wherever she is. But then I look objectively at the facts. Christine knew what she was doing. Wherever she is now, she planned it well, because even the Deschanels can't find her. She hates me and this family so much that she would literally disappear to get away from us. I might *never see my sons again.* I have to live with this."

"I'm sorry." A lump formed in Nicolas' throat. He swallowed it down. "But that doesn't answer my question about why you're here."

"Because if I can lose my daughter and keep breathing, then you can find your way out of this, too." Ashley's eyes traveled around the room. He stopped trying to hide his tears. "A lot of the family wrote you off years ago. I guess you know that, and I suspect you don't care. They think you're an asshole because it's fun. Maybe it is. I wouldn't know. They think that because you wanted everyone to believe you were indifferent when you lost both your parents. All your sisters. That's because you tried to be, because it was easier than the pain. I know all about trying to circumvent the pain, brother. It just doesn't work. You either allow it at the surface, or it eats you alive from the inside out."

"I didn't realize you had this level of depth in you, Ashley," Nicolas quipped.

"And your girlfriend?" Ashley continued, ignoring the barb. "Well, I can't find the same sympathy. You fell in love, it didn't work out. Welcome to the world the rest of us live in. At least yours didn't take your children and disappear into the nether."

"Don't compare our grief," Nicolas said. "Did Amelia teach you that technique? Or maybe the hours you've obviously spent in therapy yourself. Want my take? Christine is a selfish bitch. She knew who this family was when she married you, and fuck her for suddenly acting like it's a new problem when it directly affects her."

"She has my children."

"Those children are Deschanels, and we'll get them back," Nicolas insisted. "The bitch can only hide in so many places."

Ashley bowed his head. "I didn't come to talk about me. I came to say, I'm here if you need anything."

Nicolas threw one leg over the arm of his chair. He gestured around. "I've got everything I need right here."

"Right." Ashley looked defeated. "Well, I came all the way out here, so you're going to get some advice anyway."

"You made your lack of sympathy over my wrecked love life perfectly clear."

"I wasn't going to tell you to get over it. I was going to suggest getting away. Make a change. Find a purpose for yourself that doesn't involve self-destructing or chasing tail.

You think you're mourning your relationship, but you're wrong."

Nicolas raised a skeptical brow.

"You're mourning the glimpse of the man you thought you could be, but you now believe is lost again." Ashley chewed his bottom lip. His eyes clouded over. "But that's the problem with becoming a man at the side of a woman. We think it's about them. But it's not. It's about us."

Ashley lifted the bottle of cognac and wrinkled his nose. "All your money and you choose to drink this?"

They both grinned.

"It took having my whole life pulled away from me to figure out the man I was," Ashley said as he set the bottle back in place. "I'm not sure if he's a good man, yet, or the man he *should* be, but at least he's a man who's moving forward and once again has hope. And purpose."

"That's all very existential and all, but what makes you think I'm not already the man I'm meant to be?"

Ashley smiled. "Same way you'll know when you are."

11
VICTOR

Immortality was a long time.

In the earlier years of his gift, Victor de Blanchefort considered himself most fortunate. His never sated lust for life would not ever have to end and he could go on, century after century, enjoying life as he always had, picking up new passions to delight and excite him when others grew mundane. Continuous, endless exploration and enjoyment, without limitation.

When he took the gift that made him into a dhampir, he was at a juncture in his young life where he'd begun to wonder if Morrigan's Prophecy was a farce, in the same way the "enlightened" in his time did not completely buy the story of the Resurrection.

And then, after a drunken evening of considerable and felonious self-reflection, Victor came to his grandfather, Etienne, and announced he was ready to join the others in the family who had already made their choice.

Not weeks later, he'd laid eyes on Ophélie and knew. He

knew. The Prophecy was not simply words. He had found his Cerridwen. It was too late.

Victor was being tested all along and he had failed. His crisis of faith had cost him everything.

But young Ophélie was not destined for his arms anyway, as he soon learned. Hers was a life meant for incredible strife and suffering, with an end that would come mercifully, but all too soon.

Between his own failures as a man, and his innate love for the tortured Ophélie, Victor saw before him a second test. One perhaps more important than the first.

He had not failed the goddess by taking the gift of immortality, because he had done precisely what she had seen in her all-knowing mind. Just as Ophélie's short life was part of her plan all along.

Victor could abide that sometimes terrible things happened to good people, but he could *not* sit aside as a pawn in someone's greater scheme. Of all the Cianans and Cerridwens to walk this earth over the many cycles, why was it that they, Victor and Ophélie, should be the ones to suffer most?

It did not have to be this way. As Amelia had expressed in so many ways on her visit to the past, they still had their free will.

Victor exercised his free will by hiding in a dark alcove of Ophélie's bedroom when Charles came wielding the knife that would take his daughter's life. His free will afforded him the grueling patience to watch her bleed out until it was safe to take her. Using his free will, he took her to his father, Marius, who healed her as best as he could. And then, while she lay unconscious for days, Victor decided to use his free will in one last important way.

Even as they approached their dhampir tribe leader Childeric, Victor understood that to exercise his own free will in this decision was to take away hers. But everyone else around Ophélie had taken from her her whole life. What he would give her was a gift no one else could, a gift that would wash away all the pain, all the suffering, all the grief.

They traveled to Slovakia by way of the master's portal in the cypress swamps of St. Charles Parish, to the remote forest-land bordering the Ukraine where The Master's Tree stood waiting. As Childeric brought forth the dhampir sacrifice, the creature who would give their gift of eternal life so Ophélie could have hers, Victor's heart swelled with the unwavering belief he was doing the right thing. He would save her, when no one else could. Not her father, and not the wayward time traveling Amelia and Jacob. He could see her gratitude so clearly.

And then she awoke, and there was nothing but her great rage. She had thrown first the lamps and anything not hinged to the tables in their small hotel room. Then she'd lifted the furniture and sent it all hurling across the room, back and forth, all the while screaming some of the worst words Victor had ever heard from anyone.

She hated him. Loathed him. All because he had given her the greatest gift he had to give.

I had accepted my fate, and you stole from me that power of acceptance. I loathe you, Victor de Blanchefort, more than I have ever loathed my mother, Jean, or both of them combined. You are a plague upon me, and I wish never to see you again!

He didn't know what to do. He was helpless against her violence and anger. At first, he tried to restrain her to the bed, but she broke free and tried to murder him with a candlestick. Realizing his error struck wrong on many levels, he pleaded and apologized, begged her to see why he had made the choice on her behalf.

It matters not, for you cannot undo the crime, and I, whoever I am now, am no longer capable of forgiving you.

The last time he saw her, she huddled in the corner of the room like a feral animal, speaking nonsensical words and phrases to her belly. Victor recalled she had been with child before her father's attempt to take her life. Was she still? Her small bump had not disappeared with her humanity, but what had the change wrought upon the unborn life?

Victor never had the chance to ask her. Following days of no sleep, he'd succumbed to a brief rest, and when he awoke, she was gone.

He never saw her again.

He had spent the past century and some searching for Ophélie Deschanel, and had never found more than a cold trail. While time was fluid and less constraining for an immortal being, eventually Victor grew weary of his failures.

Meeting Amelia in the flesh had provided him with a solution he was shocked to never have considered before.

The Deschanels, Ophélie's own blood, could find her.

And if Amelia would not offer this help, there were others who would.

WHAT VICTOR NEEDED WAS A TELEPATH. SOMEONE WHO COULD search across the family for one of their own. Failing that, a seer who might not be able to locate her in the present, but could find her in the future.

Colleen Deschanel and her fellow Magi Collective Council members had within their vaults a manifest list of all blood relatives mapped to their abilities. Victor could think of no easy way to get to this—he was immortal, not a superhero—and so the only way to this information was to massage it from someone.

Seeing as he himself was a telepath, all he needed was to find someone with the information.

The challenge with telepathy was that you could not pull from someone's mind what they were not already thinking at that very moment. You could not glean the passwords to their accounts if they were thinking about Sunday dinner. So if Victor was determined to find out who among the Deschanels had strong telepathy, he would need to be present among a Deschanel who was thinking about exactly this.

Colleen and her Council had done a top notch job of teaching their family members to block out interlopers. They weren't the only ones who possessed these skills, after all, and they had to protect the family from outside trouble. Knowing this, Victor decided the path to what he needed lay in following one of the Deschanels as they left their Collective meeting. Being somewhere they felt safe, their guards would be down. Someone was bound to have what he needed.

So he hunkered down two blocks over, on First Street, listening to hundreds of minds and their competing thoughts as they filtered out of The Gardens at dawn. He strained to focus, to pull out something of use. Most were scared over the behavior of one of their ancestors, though he couldn't catch a name. Others were worried for Amelia and Anasofiya, for reasons he didn't pick up—though he could guess. He heard some consider leaving town.

And then he *did* hear it.

Maybe we could find Stella if our most powerful damn telepaths hadn't left New Orleans when we most needed them!

Tristan is doing important work. And considering Estella, who took the poor little girl, is the other said powerful telepath...

Why aren't we using the others?

I was wondering myself.

I mean, they aren't the only ones, right?

Well, let's see, we have Llewellyn's girl, Charlotte.

Right. And isn't Kitty's son, Charles, also a telepath?

Yes! Was he here tonight? Why didn't he say something?

I think so. And oh, there's Rex's kid. Julian, I think.

Julius. Our family is endless. There's got to be more.

Oh, for sure.

The exchange went on from there, debating who might or might not be a telepath—most were in the category of "not"—and whether or not their leadership really knew what the hell they were doing. He let them bicker. Victor had what he needed, and it had come to him far easier than he ever imagined.

VICTOR STARTED FIRST WITH CHARLOTTE FONTENOT. HE PICKED UP bits of information about her from Internet searches—technology never ceased to knock him over with a feather. She finished her undergraduate studies at Yale and had started a law program there. She was a year or so into it when her younger sister, Annette, tragically passed away. She returned home to be close to her family.

Charlotte raced crew, volunteered at her local chapter of the ACLU, and was active in the Daughters of the Confederacy. Those last two were a strange pairing, Victor thought, but by all accounts Charlotte seemed to be a kind, thoughtful young woman. None of these facts mattered to Victor outside of providing him a way to engage her.

As it turned out, it all proved to be for naught. His picture, it seemed, had been displayed at the Collective meeting for all who attended to see.

Charlotte, in her pale canary dress and golden hair pulled back in a pearl barrette, had regarded him with so open a hostility he wondered if she might also possess the power to summon a hurricane to dispatch him.

She didn't back away or scream. Charlotte radiated a sharp sense of empowerment, and his guess moments earlier that she meant to harm him returned. Her hands traveled to her handbag, where she opened the top to a small gap, revealing to him an ivory-handled dueling pistol.

"I mean you no harm," he'd said, pointless words, for she had already decided he most certainly did.

"I know precisely what you mean," she said in a soft, but commanding voice. Her fingers gripped the ivory with a comfort suggesting she knew exactly how to use the weapon she carried. "And it won't work with me."

There was no way she knew precisely anything, but he would get no further with Charlotte Fontenot.

Charles Marsolet, son of Kitty Guidry, and a few years older than Charlotte, was next on his list. Charles was in medical school with aspirations to be a cardiothoracic surgeon. No wife or children, and not much of a social life. He had the local notoriety of being the Louisiana State Chess Champion several years running, and spent whatever free time he had fishing in Bayou St. John. He showed up for mass at St. Mary's Assumption Church every Monday, Wednesday, and Sunday without fail. In an article in the Times-Picayune, after his last state chess victory, a friend described him as "the most upright, loyal man you'll ever meet. That's no poker face you see from Charles. It's just that nothing ruffles him. His only breaking point is his family."

As it turned out, this friend was correct.

Charles very politely kicked him off his front porch and let him know, in a most cordial way, that he would be calling his cousin Colleen Deschanel to be sure she was aware.

And so Charles Marsolet was strike two.

The last name on his list turned out to be a peculiar choice. Julius Guidry was only in the seventh grade. A shy, sensitive kid—upon first glance, Victor guessed he might also be an empath—with bottle-thick horn-rimmed glasses and a perpetually brow-beaten look. He shuffled between classes without speaking to anyone and didn't engage when kids knocked him about as they rushed past him, laughing and carrying on in a world he didn't seem to belong to.

Victor thought to himself that this kid would either go on to cure cancer, or start a domestic terrorist ring.

Without a parent around to stop him, this young kid, hungry for social interaction, would hopefully cling to the opportunity to be heard.

Victor waited until the last bell rang. He watched hundreds of teenagers stream from the school in an excited rush, piling onto school buses and pulling bikes from racks. Some congregated in small groups across the street or nearby. He was struck with how different the educational experience was today versus when he was a young man huddled into a barn-sized schoolhouse with the other boys his age.

When he'd almost decided he must have missed Julius, the crowd dissipated to only a handful of kids awaiting rides, the young man stumbled out into the open courtyard, head to his feet.

He turned left, toward home, and Victor followed him for a couple of blocks, until he was certain the schoolmasters wouldn't see him and think he was a predator.

Well, he *was* a predator, in a manner of speaking.

But Julius took one look at him and his eyes flew into wide, terrified orbs. He dropped his book bag and ran, his wide gait making him resemble a very fat penguin.

Victor ground his teeth together in flourishing anger. He could continue to press on, but he would be met with the same results.

There was one person to blame: Amelia's mother, Colleen. She had warned the family, and even the children were not immune. He had avoided her because he was quite sure she was the last person in the family who would give him the time of day, even if she did have the potential to prove the most useful.

Victor accepted now that he had been going about this all the wrong way. He could not circumvent the problem. He must face it directly.

SHE SURPRISED HIM BY INVITING HIM IN FOR TEA.

He followed her across the marble floors, through a home that rivaled the ones they'd built along the river to run their empires, past the parlor and onto a vast screened porch.

Colleen gestured for him to have a seat across from her.

"I wondered when you might make your presence known to me," she said, drawing a sip from her tea. She crossed her long legs and regarded him with a cool, direct look. "I suspect this is because you've found no success with others, and now you believe you can convince me instead?"

Victor smiled. He saw so much of Amelia in this polished woman. "I only hoped we could speak and come together toward a common cause."

Colleen pulled off her reading glasses and folded them, placing them in the breast pocket of her suit jacket. "I'm already well-versed on the purported facts. Amelia filled me in."

Victor's pulse quickened. "And your thoughts?"

She returned the smile. "They shouldn't surprise you. I share my daughter's sentiment. You may have our blood in your veins, but you are not one of us. You and others in your family ceased to be so when you chose immortality. You became something else... something I cannot yet claim to understand, but you are no longer a part of us in any meaningful way. Do you follow?"

"I may not agree, but I follow. Go on."

"If what you have told Amelia and Jacob is true, that indeed Ophélie lives—whatever such a life it is, now that she is no longer human—then that life is hers to decide how she wants to live it. It was not your choice, but yet you made it anyway. She has to live with that, as you have to live with her not wanting anything to do with you."

"It isn't that simple."

"Nothing is ever so simple, Monsieur de Blanchefort," Colleen agreed pleasantly, "but it is, nevertheless, clear. She has run from you for over a century. The mystery, to me, is not why she hides, but why you continue to pursue her as if it is your right."

"Ophélie and I have unfinished business," he explained. He tried his best to sound reasonable, and not a man desperate. "And I would think, given the organization you lead, that you, as well, would want to speak to her and bring her into the fold. I believe she may have given birth to a child, as well. What of that line? What of her descendants?"

"Much as I would love to connect with any descendants of Ophélie Deschanel, I will not do so if it means exploiting the privacy she has sought."

"Your vision is so narrow," Victor accused, shooting to his

feet. "You and your daughter throw around words like consent, and exploit, as if I did not do what I did from love, but from maliciousness!"

Colleen pursed her lips, but showed no other outward signs of being unruffled. "No one believes your actions were malicious, Victor. But intent does not erase outcome. I would discourage you from this errant cause of yours, but I know my words aren't going to dissuade you from a centuries-long quest. A man mad on his own purpose cannot see the forest for the trees." She stood, running her hands over her cream suit to smooth the lines. "But I will *not* allow you to bring anyone in my family into this. You will continue to be met with opposition if you don't cease your behavior. We are many, but we are also one, Monsieur de Blanchefort, and where you seek help you'll only find an impenetrable barrier."

Victor blinked away his sudden rage. Spittle flew from his mouth when he went to speak, but she would be the one to get the last word.

"And if you go near my daughter and son-in-law again, you will find yourself faced with much more than a cold shoulder."

VICTOR LEFT THE GARDENS NOT FEELING DISCOURAGED, BUT renewed. Colleen Deschanel might believe she had her tendrils spread across every last dark corner of her family, but she could not possibly have filled them all in.

He would find one, and when he did, he would find Ophélie.

12

LAUREN

Lauren wouldn't have guessed how deeply she'd missed New Orleans.

It didn't hit her when they crossed the Louisiana state line. The moment came when she saw the signs for Kenner, Slidell, and Metairie, one after another, inching closer to home. The skyline came into view, and the gold-topped Superdome gleamed bright against the sun as they came around the bend of I-10. She switched on her blinker at the Carondelet exit and turned down St. Charles, holding her breath until the Mid-City commerce—including a billboard for Weatherly Department Stores, featuring the gleaming smile of her older sister, Cassidy—turned into a world of Greek Revival mansions and stately cottages.

Lauren's relationship with her father and sister was tenuous, but her relationship with her city had always been untouchable.

Leander had stopped talking altogether about an hour from home. She suspected he was thinking of his own fractured family awaiting him. His drunken mother, ineffective father. Both his sisters gone, Harriett for noble reasons, Estella for reasons unknown.

She took a left on Jackson after the St. Charles streetcar ambled past. She had never actually *been* to The Gardens, but how many times had she skipped past as a girl, gaping at the wide columns and deep berth of a house that seemed to take up its own square block? Wondering what life was like for those who lived beyond the bay windows? Sometimes she would catch a glimpse of Colleen in her garden. Or her beautiful daughter, Amelia, reading under a tree. Once upon a time, Lauren had even had a crush on Ashley—or was it Benjamin? —but that seemed another lifetime now, when she still believed magic existed only in books.

Colleen knew they were coming, but had said she might not be around when they got there. *One of the Council will be there if not, I promise. You'll get what you need so you can enjoy your downtime for a couple days before you're back on the road.*

Lauren eased her car into an open spot against the curb. On cue, a young valet approached and asked if he could help her.

"We're here to see Colleen Deschanel on official business," she recited, as Colleen instructed, through Leander's open window. "In her absence, we're here to meet with one of the Council members."

"I'll pull the car around for you, ma'am," the valet replied.

Lauren opened the door and moved to exit when she noticed Leander staring blankly through the windshield.

"You coming?"

Leander sighed and reached for the door. "Do I have a choice?"

"We always have choices," she said and yanked the bottom of her light pullover down. She wished she'd had some time to clean up first. Her only preparation was a quick glance in the side-view mirror when they were stopped at a red light, and what she saw only made her feel worse.

It occurred to Lauren that Leander's father was on the Council, and this might be the cause of his hesitation. In Colleen's absence, it was a matter of chance who they would get.

They made their way down the cobblestone path flanked with exotically arranged, exceptionally groomed foliage, and then up the stairs to the porch that could have housed an entire party on its own.

A woman who Leander whispered was named Aria answered the door and led them through the cavernous central hall, then down a longer one with paneled walls. Lauren felt like Dorothy in the palace at the Emerald City.

Near the end, Aria stopped to knock.

"Colleen's guests are here," she said, then stepped back with a friendly smile and left them.

The door opened. A man with an impish, almost criminal grin greeted them. Leander made a sound that she thought might be a surprised laugh.

Lauren knew him. It had been years, but...

"Leander, it's been a while. Glad to see your hair is finally growing back. White supremacist chic didn't suit you." Nicolas Deschanel turned his attention on Lauren and tapped his finger against his cheek with a thoughtful expression. "I know you. You're... hmmm... yeah, okay, you're Assidy Cassidy's sister."

Lauren turned a dark shade of plum in an instant. What she wouldn't give for this to be removed entirely from the list of things said when people met her. "Lauren. And Cassidy is married now, so maybe it's time people stop calling her that."

Nicolas wagged his finger in the air. "Yeah, yeah, Assidy! Legs and ass for days. It's coming back. Man. Oz dated her. I might have hit that once or twice myself, but the details are fuzzy."

"Charm city," Leander said, rolling his eyes toward the plaster molding on the office ceiling.

"Yes, Cassidy is my sister," Lauren replied evenly. "And I don't know why people seem to think I need to hear about the things she did in high school. Then or now."

Nicolas ran his eyes over her, scrutinizing. "I see Cassidy in the Weatherly ads, but not you. Dad keep you in the back office? Are you the one who's better at math? A face made for the broom closet?"

"She's a lawyer," Leander chimed in, and Lauren was startled at the sharp defensiveness in his tone. "She works for Sullivan and Associates, which I'd say is a step up from having her picture on a Canal Street billboard."

Nicolas pulled back in mock defense. "Hey, to each their own. I shop at Maison Blanche anyway."

Leander laughed. "Right you do. They went out of business in the '90s."

"If you'll excuse us, we have business with Colleen, or her proxy, if she's not in," Lauren said and moved to continue on. She didn't wait for any returned pleasantries. Her patience for the antics of Nicolas Deschanel, or men like him, was nonexistent.

"I'm a member of the Collective Council you're here to see," Nicolas countered, following her. "You think I don't know what your business here is?"

"Am I supposed to know what that is?" Lauren asked over her shoulder.

"You're relying on them for support, so I should hope so."

"I'll explain later," Leander mumbled. "Let's get in, get what we need, and get some sleepy sleeps."

"Aunt C isn't here," Nicolas said, when they stopped at the

door at the end of the hall that housed the Deschanel Magi Collective meeting chambers. "She briefed me on what you need, and I have the information you came here for."

Lauren's hand dropped from the doorknob. "You? You're her proxy?"

"Is my sexiness that off-putting?"

Leander snickered in bland amusement and picked at his fingernails.

"Offensive was the word I was looking for," Lauren countered. Her face was hot. She knew he could see it, and that bothered her more. After the way Quillan had treated her, she had no time for self-proclaimed bad boys and their ridiculous need to be the sun at the center of everyone's universe.

"Amelia needed her and she had to run." Nicolas shrugged. "It isn't like I'm coordinating an operating room, here. It's a few sheets of paper with some addresses."

"Then please hand them over."

Nicolas smiled a toothy grin. "You didn't say please."

"Just do it," Leander barked, resuming interest. His head rolled on his neck in a long, bored stretch. "We only have two days to chill, and I don't want to spend one of them with you."

"Cut me, Leander. Cut me deep." Nicolas feigned a knife to the chest. "I'll bring them with me when we leave to go back on the road."

Lauren nearly dropped her purse. "You'll what?"

"You can pick me up at *Ophélie* on your way out of the city," Nicolas said as he pulled the Council chambers door shut behind them. "Don't look put out. Your first lead is in Breaux Bridge, so Vacherie is on the way."

Was he joking? He had to be. "If I look put out, it's because I'm exhausted and I didn't come here to have a sparring match with some—"

"Dude, you are not coming," Leander interjected. His hand

tickled Lauren's as they walked side by side. She veered to the left, worried again at the message he might have picked up from their time alone on the road. "We have enough shit to deal with."

"Much as I love to debate, this isn't up for one," Nicolas said. He steered them back down the dark hall, toward the entrance. "I was told to get more active in family affairs. By Colleen, Ashley. Hell, everyone. This is me getting more active."

"Fuck me," Leander muttered, and that was when Lauren knew there was not a thing they could do to prevent this.

"We've had enough incest in this family, don't you think?" Nicolas joked.

Lauren's ballet flats clicked on the marble floors. The sound resonated across her head like the start of a migraine. This was not what she'd signed up for. Leander was often more than enough responsibility, with his long stretches of moodiness and his constant reach for the most negative outcomes. Now she would have to put up with that *and* a spoiled man-child who thought everything was a game?

Nicolas opened the door and brought his hand to his head in the sign of a telephone. "I'll call you!"

LAUREN DROPPED LEANDER OFF FIRST—TO HIS VISIBLE disappointment, leading her to wonder if he thought she was intending to bring him home—then stumbled into her own townhouse with a defeated sigh.

Her purse landed on the counter, then slipped off with a messy thud. She moved toward the wreckage and then shrugged it away, instead heading straight for the bedroom and her own bed. Her own bed, after all this time! It wasn't even a special bed, or an expensive one, but it was hers, and oh, how welcoming it looked...

She face-planted, fully-dressed, and fell asleep almost immediately.

Her ringing cell phone woke her hours later. With one arm, she flailed around, searching for the source of the sound, until she realized it was in her jacket pocket.

She reached inside and squinted to focus on the screen. The number wasn't one she recognized, but it was local, and given their business with the Deschanels, she thought she better answer it.

"Assidy Junior," a cheerful voice chirped in her ear. "You busy?"

"Nicolas," she deduced. She groaned; groggy, annoyed. "Where did you get my number?"

"Council. Colleen. Endless access. Remember?"

"Unfortunately."

He ignored the sarcasm and continued on, with a lightness in his voice that made him sound almost like a kid. "I'm over here packing and wondered if you had any advice on what I should bring?"

"Are you serious right now?"

"Sorry?"

"You don't really need my packing advice."

Nicolas breathed out. "Actually, I wanted to say sorry."

Lauren turned over, wincing at her sore limbs from not having moved for hours. "For?"

"I shouldn't have said that about your sister."

"No, you shouldn't have. I hear it all the time and I'm tired of it."

"Well," Nicolas ventured, "when you have a sister who has banged half of Uptown, people might sometimes use that as a point of reference during introductions."

Lauren gritted her teeth. "So much for apologizing."

"Hey! I meant it. I *am* sorry. The Uptown comment was a

point of fact. You know it and I know it. But we got off on the wrong foot, and since we're going to be hanging out for a while, I wanted to tell you I promise not to use any form of Assidy while we're traveling."

"You answered the phone with it!"

"That was *before* I apologized, in my defense."

"You're hopeless."

"I used to get that a lot from my father."

And probably still do from all the responsible adults in your family, of which you clearly cannot be counted. "Are we done?"

Nicolas lowered his voice. "But first... what are you wearing?"

"Dammit, Nicolas!"

His laughter filled her dark room. "Just playing, Lauren. See you this weekend."

The line went dead before she could curse him once more.

13
AMELIA

Amelia smiled at the group gathered in her dining room, seated in a perfect circle around the mahogany table that once belonged to her grandfather, August. He'd built it with his own hands, in a shed at *Ophélie*, and while his sons thought it too crude for their own homes, his eldest daughter, Colleen, saw within it something greater: a connection to her father that would last long after his death. She gave it to her own daughter as a marriage gift. And should Amelia never have her own children, she would find someone equally suitable to appreciate the heirloom.

How long had it been since Amelia felt the warmth of good company and conversation? Her husband. Ana, Finn, and Aleksandr. Anne and Jonathan. The first four were her tribe, some existing, some new, but all welcome into her inner circle. The last two had the potential of becoming so.

Ana, who had been to Amelia's home a handful of times in the past, was now a constant staple. They jogged together in the mornings, and often sat on one or the other's porch after for coffee and light conversation. They talked about nothing, and everything. Serious topics, like Aidrik, and Amelia's assault. Inconsequential ones like the books they were reading, or gardening techniques.

Finn and Jacob spent an equal amount of time in each other's company. Finn taught Jacob to fish, and in turn, Jacob became something of a personal trainer, teaching Finn on proper boxing techniques. They sometimes spent hours on end together, and Amelia didn't know what else they did, or talked about, only that Jacob seemed better for it.

Anne and Jonathan were both self-possessed of a visible, tentative hope as they sat across from one another at the far end of the table from Ana and Finn. Everyone, even Aleksei, knew the crime Jon had committed against Ana. Only Amelia knew of how it still affected her, almost a year later; how it kept her up at nights. She'd chosen to forgive him not for Finn's sake, as Finn believed, but her own. Holding onto her anger was a dangerous business. Ana wanted only to move forward, with her family at her side, and she'd accepted Jon was a part of that family.

Jon's own contrition was written in his eyes, a permanent passenger. Amelia's empath senses picked up the deep regret he never let go of, even when he was smiling. As Ana's friend and cousin, Amelia would always take her side, but she saw within Jon a keen desire to be a better man and a constant search for the path to get there. Anne seemed to see that, and clung to it, as she worked to overcome her own past transgressions.

Amelia sincerely hoped the two of them could find their way to peace, together or on their own.

For her part, she was slowly finding her way back to her own.

• • •

A WEEK EARLIER, ANA HAD CONFIDED IN AMELIA HER TRUE PURPOSE for this dinner.

"It's Finn's birthday," she had said. She chewed the corner of her mouth, a bundle of nerves. "I know he's completely forgotten. But I haven't. Jon hasn't either."

"Oh? What were you thinking?"

"Well... I have an idea he will either love or possibly take offense to."

"Offense? Why?"

Ana had leaned forward, dropping her elbows to her knees. "I want to send for Forbia."

Amelia frowned. "His wolf? I'm confused."

Ana shook her head. "His ship in Maine. He named the wolf for her. She was his baby, for so many years, and he had to leave her behind when he followed me." She cast her eyes away. "He says it doesn't bother him, but it bothers me."

Amelia beamed at her. "Ana, that's such a wonderful, thoughtful idea for a gift! And he would certainly find use for it here. The Pontchartrain, the Gulf. I don't know how big she is, but there are so many smaller waterways, too. It will be like a whole new world for him to explore."

"She's ocean bearing," Ana said in a low, tense voice. "But small enough."

Amelia leaned in. "Why are you so worried?"

"Because," Ana said after a pause, wringing her hands, "he doesn't like when I talk about his life in Maine, and what he left behind."

"Only because he doesn't want you to feel terrible for his decision. *He* doesn't," Amelia said gently. "He loves you, Ana. Even with everything that's happened, he's happy, and he's right where he wants to be. I can sense it in him, and you know I'd tell you if I thought otherwise."

Ana released a slow breath into her folded hands.

"And I think he'll see this gift for exactly what it is... a way of bringing even more of himself into his household, and this town, where he feels out of place."

"I hope you're right."

Amelia squeezed her hand. "I know I am."

ANNE SAID GRACE. THE MEN FOLDED THEIR HANDS AND BOWED THEIR heads in automatic compliance, a reaction stemming from years of the behavior. Amelia smiled at Ana before they lowered their own in tandem.

After the food was passed around and plates were full, Jacob asked Aleksei about Fiona's visit.

Aleksandr brightened. His hands traveled to his lap, where it was clear he was hiding his fidgeting. "She'll be here tomorrow."

Finn looked at Ana, then back at his son. "Fiona's a wonderful girl. I'm glad you're both open to talking this out."

Aleksandr nodded, looking embarrassed.

Jacob bailed him out. "And school? How's college?"

The young man answered through a mouthful of mashed potatoes. "Fine."

Jacob smiled. "Just fine? What classes are you taking next term?"

"That's the best you're gonna get, I'm afraid," Finn said with a laugh. "I've tried."

"Why does that sound familiar?" Jonathan said with a shake of his head.

Finn rolled his eyes. "I don't remember you coming home from school and being overly talkative, either."

"And what about you two?" Amelia asked Anne and Jonathan. "How are things going? All settled in?"

They exchanged a look. "Well," Anne began, "Colleen

bequeathed my home to me, you know, as part of the Trust, so it's taking up most of my time getting settled and the house decorated."

Amelia nodded. She drew a sip from her wine.

"We'd love to have everyone over soon," Anne added.

"That would be nice," Amelia said. "Which house did Mom give you? The one on Napoleon?"

"I actually asked her for one closer to The Gardens." Anne flushed darker, as if embarrassed at the admission she wanted to stay close to Colleen.

Amelia understood, though, that Colleen was the only maternal figure in Anne's life who had ever made a difference.

"We are in the cottage on Second and Chestnut."

"We?" Ana focused on cutting her steak. "Are you two living together, then?"

"I'm staying in a guest room, until I figure out what I want to do," Jon hedged. He didn't look at Anne.

"We're taking things one day at a time," she asserted.

"So you're staying?" Finn asked.

Jon shrugged. Then his expression lightened and he put a hand on Anne's knee. "Seems like I probably will. They need vets everywhere, and after what happened back in Maine, I don't know if that's the place for me anymore. We need to figure out what to do with the house. Keep it, sell it."

Ana watched Finn carefully. "I don't know why we would sell it," he said. "Dad built that house himself, and I know he would want it to stay in the family."

"I have no problem if you want to give it to Aleksandr," Jon said. "Or we could hire a caretaker, or rent it out. There are other options to selling."

Finn gave a tight, dismissive shake of his head. "We're getting ahead of ourselves. There's no reason we have to decide this now. The house isn't going anywhere."

"No, but we can't have it fall into disrepair, either."

"The house is older than we are."

Amelia flashed Ana a look. *I think your distraction is just what this table needs.*

Ana returned a nervous nod. She blotted her mouth with her napkin, then set it on the table beside her plate, rising. "Before we all end up in a food coma from Jacob's awesome dinner, I had something I wanted to say."

All eyes moved to where she stood. Ana raised her glass. "First, a toast. To all of you here, and new beginnings." She offered a small smile to Anne and Jon. "And second, I want to wish a very happy birthday to the other half of my heart."

Finn's eyes went wide, and then a slow smile stretched over his face. "Oh my God, I completely forgot."

"I thought you might have," Ana said.

"Happy Birthday, Finn!" the room cried, clinking their glasses together.

"Happy Birthday, Far!" Aleksandr added.

Finn looked up at her, a little drunk, a lot in love. "Thank you for remembering."

"Well, that's not all." Ana let out a nervous laugh. She reached behind her to the servant table and grabbed an envelope. She handed it to him.

"What's this?"

Ana gestured with her head. "Open it."

Finn watched her with a curious expression as he turned it over twice before sliding his finger under the seal. He removed the paper inside and unfolded it. Ana's anxiousness became ever more apparent on her face.

"A delivery notification..." He pulled his glasses from his top pocket. "For... one..."

"Forbia, Far," Aleksandr blurted out. "Mora had Forbia delivered to New Orleans!"

Finn's jaw dropped. The paper fluttered in the gap between his hands, which had started a slow, light tremble. He removed his glasses and wiped his eyes with the back of his arm. "Ana... I don't know what to say..."

"Say you're happy," she whispered. "Say you can't wait to see her."

"I can't wait..." Finn choked up. He set the paper aside and pulled in a sharp, calming breath. "Silly girl... you have no idea..."

Finn tugged her, and she fell atop his lap with a cry of surprise. His arms wrapped around her and his face disappeared into her chest. Amelia could only see his knuckles white as he clutched his wife in unfiltered joy.

Jon smiled at them and blinked away a few rogue tears of his own.

"God, I love you. I love you, I love you," he whispered, his words flattened against the fabric of her dress.

Ana sniffled and pulled back. "She's here for you, for whenever you're ready."

"I can't wait to finally take you aboard," Finn said through his tears. His arms were still around her as she leaned back against him. His knees bounced in excitement. "It was so late in the season when you came, and we never got the chance."

"We'll have all the chances now," Ana replied, smiling.

"It's going to be so much fun!" Aleksandr exclaimed.

"Really, Ana, you did good," Jon said quietly.

"You mean we get to do real man fishing now?" Jacob threw in.

Finn frowned. "Hey, now. We've been real man fishing this whole time."

Aleksandr flexed. "All you need now is a real man."

"Time to learn if I have sea legs," Jacob said, furrowing his brows.

Finn reached over and clapped him on the back. "If not, real men also puke off the bow from time to time."

They both laughed.

"Real men also do dishes from time to time," Amelia said with a lowered look at the men at the table. "So the women can go pick a movie for movie night."

Jacob groaned. "This is way too important a decision to just be left to the three of you."

"Says the man responsible for the romantic comedy we suffered through last week."

Jacob hung his head. "It got good reviews."

"I'm thinking hobbits and elves tonight," Ana said with a mischievous grin. "It's been way too long since I've heard Finn passionately pick apart a Tolkien adaptation."

"Hey," he said lightly.

"Hobbits and elves?" Anne repeated with a blank look.

"Time to indoctrinate you, Miss Bayou," Finn teased.

Amelia nodded at the kitchen. "Now, get to it."

AFTER MIDNIGHT, AMELIA AND JACOB WERE AGAIN ALONE. JACOB found her on the bench swing on their back porch. He curled in next to her.

"What are you reading?" he asked, with a glance over her shoulder.

Amelia refolded the paper and slid it into the envelope. "You can read it, if you want. It's from Nora."

"Oh?" He looked interested. "What did she have to say?"

"They're working with the Empyreans now. Birger and Astrid have been there, and they're talking things out. Papers have been drawn up to make their alliance more official. They'll burn them on the altar to seal the words for eternity, she says."

"That's a good thing, right?"

Amelia looped her legs over his lap and breathed him in. His scent, the very *realness* of him, always stabilized her and brought her back to the moment. "I think so. Seems like a step in the direction we need to go."

"But?"

"But... it means things are moving now. She also mentioned the Empyreans aren't sitting back now that their homeland is in jeopardy from Oriana. They're going to do something about it."

Jacob kissed her hair. "What does she want us to do?"

"Nothing." Amelia exhaled. "Except what we're already doing. Staying safe and out of danger. Looking after Aleksei, Ana, and Finn."

He seemed to read her mind. "I know what you're not saying. Don't let her pressure you about the baby, even if she means well." His soft brogue slipped into his words. "The choice is ours."

"I know that." She used the force of her body to increase the momentum of the swing. "I know."

14
ASHLEY

Ashley fumbled in the dark for the candle drawer housing the only sources of light allowed in the Council chambers. He grabbed three, this time, thinking ahead instead of letting the candles burn all the way out and finding himself again alone in the dark.

He struck a match. The dull flame provided enough light to navigate to the wick of the candle. When it came to life, he blew out the match and wedged the wax into the bronze candleholder. He went back to work.

How many nights had he spent here, alone, poring over the archives, over letters, eyewitness accounts, journals, notations from members past and present? The absence of natural light in the mahogany chambers created the eerie sense of time standing still. He might come in after work with the intention of spending a couple hours, but stumble out as the sun was rising. He chose not to wear a watch inside, because he had, most of his life, been a man defined by his attention to detail, of which punctuality was a key characteristic. It was ingrained in Ashley to find subtle ways of checking his wrist or a clock on the wall, of gauging how much more of his time to spend on a given person or activity. In here, this gauge would be nothing more than a distraction from his purpose.

His purpose was largely undefined, another step outside of his comfort zone. Colleen had only said, *See what else you can learn about Margarethe.* And when he probed to understand what she expected him to find, Ashley was deflated to find she actually didn't know. *Anything,* she had said. *Anything at all.*

Before the recent issues, they hadn't known anything about Margarethe Deschanel, except as a penciled in name on an old family bible. Then Quillan Sullivan had stumbled on what they now called "The Sullivan Letters" and "The Blanche Ophelia Exchange." The former, correspondence between Ophelia Deschanel and Seamus Sullivan that revealed the Sullivan blood connection to the Deschanel family, were now a matter of common knowledge. Everyone, Deschanel and Sullivan, now knew of their existence, and while opinions varied, very few doubted the evidence presented—including recent DNA testing—that spoke to their veracity.

The exact contents of the Blanche and Ophelia letters had been contained to the Council only, for Blanche's beloved clan would not be ready to hear the marks against their late ancestress until they had a full story to present. In the letters, Blanche and Ophelia spoke of something "forbidden," something Ophelia strongly discouraged her niece to abandon. Through studying them closer, it was determined that Blanche had gotten herself into something dark and sinister. Over the course of several letters, Ophelia made clear she knew Blanche was preparing to do something terrible, and she meant to persuade her to stop. Her words were indirect, but clear. *I, of anyone, understand and empathize greatly with the immensity of what lies before you as you begin the journey, once again, recently married for a third time and with designs to start a family. But I say to you thus: what you propose is preposterous. More, even if it did produce the results you are expecting—and I truly, do not, in my heart of hearts believe that it will—the cost of said results would be far more burden than I would ever want laden on your kind and goodly heart. I plead with you, Blanche, do not do it. Your great-grandfather's greed and arrogance is what brought this upon us, not some vengeful single-minded spirit. Do not overcomplicate this with flowery explanations... accept it for what it is and pray for the safety of those you love.*

Remember the warnings, with the fervor of faith: seduction to sinners. A legacy in splinters. Beware, the myths of midwinter.

The myths of midwinter. Another prophecy—how many more would they uncover before all was said and done? Ashley wondered—foretelling the end of the family, through the manipulation of the starlight awakener—the necromancer powerful enough to be the vessel that would allow Margarethe to come back permanently. Margarethe appealed to those weak in spirit with promises of immortality. Immense and immeasurable power.

Ashley's better sense was always tempted to laugh at this. Wasn't it always true, that if it sounded too good to be true, it most certainly was? Margarethe's gain would undoubtedly be her pawn's loss. In mathematical theory, they called this a zero-sum game.

But he also didn't doubt how easily others could be persuaded with the right words.

Like Blanche.

Like Estella.

Now it was clear Blanche had been aiding Margarethe even beyond her death. And she had used her impressionable great-granddaughter Estella to do what she no longer could: find the necromancers who were strong enough for Margarethe to come through. This should have been easy, for Stella and

Sebastian were defenseless children. Then, for reasons no one yet understood, Estella broke away from Blanche's sway at the last minute and ran off with Stella, hiding so well not even the Deschanels had found her.

These were what Ashley called the "known quantities." The facts, which were preposterous by non-Deschanel standards. These were the collective articles and knowledge given to him when Colleen asked for his assistance. They hardly knew their adversary, and the less they knew, the more at risk the family remained.

He'd accepted the charge because he was tired of feeling helpless. Christine and the kids were gone. His daughter, deceased, his sons, somewhere unreachable. Ashley had already decided that if Christine came back, he would give her the divorce she wanted. He wasn't the same man who had married her. He wasn't someone he recognized at all, really. He had always been the odd man out in his immediate family; the pragmatist who refused to get caught up in anything unexplained or unexpected. Now, here he was. Ready to move forward. Ready to help. To mobilize, if the need called for it.

Yet he'd made no progress. When he stood in front of the Collective to give an update, he'd been expecting someone to call him out and ask why he was repeating what they already knew. It would have been a fair thing to do. There was literally *nothing* in the archives he hadn't scoured through, and he had hit a dead end.

Then it occurred to Ashley that their knowledge on Margarethe thus far had not come from the Collective records, but elsewhere: lost letters found in a box at *Ophélie*.

He'd first asked Oz—since Nicolas' desire to cooperate was largely driven by his blood alcohol level—to see if they could search *Ophélie* for more boxes. Oz had said he would send someone from the firm again, but that what they'd already pored through was the last of the un-accounted for inventory. Not helpful. But Oz's next suggestion had been.

"Have you checked *Femme Forte*?"

Ashley didn't know what he was talking about and said as much.

"Blanche Deschanel's old property on Bayou St. John. She built it before her children were born and lived there her whole life, I believe. Her daughter, Eugenia Fontenot, inherited it. She wasn't the oldest, but she basically wrote off any of the children from her Guidry marriage, as you probably know. Eugenia gave it to her son Luther when he married Jo, I believe, and they use it more as a weekend and holiday house. They lend it out to some of the cousins from time to time, too. But I seem to remember stories about Blanche turning into a Miss Havisham type in her old age, roaming around in old dresses with her sawed-off shotgun. The house was a mess when she died, and her children didn't know what to do with it, so they just shoved it all in her attic and agreed to sort it out later."

"And did they? Sort it out?"

Oz had laughed. "Apparently later never came. As far as I know, that attic is still filled with endless crap."

"Any suggestions?"

"If you can get Luther Fontenot to sign off on giving us temporary power of attorney over anything we remove, the firm would be happy to put some junior resources on sorting and tagging."

Ashley was grateful about the Guidry oversight in Blanche's will, because it meant dealing with someone much more reasonable. Luther had first sighed, then collected himself and said that the attic would take years to go through. *We don't have years,* Ashley had said, and Luther had nodded and agreed to let Sullivan & Associates manage the laborious task.

Earlier that afternoon, Oz had sent a box to The Gardens with a note for Ashley. *I didn't read the letters. That's not our job. But this box is full of them. Might be what you're looking for.- O.S.*

Five candles later and a yawn that wouldn't quit, Ashley Jameson deduced that this was, in fact, what he was looking for.

Blanche Broussard had kept a diary since she was twelve years old.

Even before Ashley cracked open the first in the stack of tattered notebooks, his logical mind grasped he would need to treat anything he read with a grain of salt. These being personal journals, he was dealing with a highly unreliable narrator, and her thoughts and feelings would be largely open to interpretation, as well as the back of mind belief of the author that one day someone would come to read it and pass judgment. How she described events might or might not be as they actually were. But that didn't make them without value.

With that in mind, he proceeded at the beginning.

Blanche, as far as he could see and as far as his knowledge about adolescent girls stretched, seemed fairly normal at twelve. She talked about the books she read and the games she played with her friends. She liked to sew with her aunt, Ophelia, with whom she shared a special relationship since her mother, Amelia, had died when she was only four. Blanche and her aunt enjoyed long talks as they picked pecans behind *Ophélie*.

Ashley found nothing of interest in these early years, though he read every page.

When she was eighteen, she met and married Ellis Kenner, who died under strange circumstances less than a year into their marriage. Blanche's thoughts on this, unlike her flowery retellings of day-to-day activities, were very clinical in nature. *Ellis did not return home from the office yesterday. Authorities have uncovered his body in the swamp of Bayou St. John. Mass is set for two days hence. Today's pecan load exceeded expectations.*

She never spoke of it again. The next interesting thing to happen to Blanche was meeting Johnson Guidry within months of Kenner's death, and the math around the birth of their first child together, Pierce, seemed to indicate she had known and socialized with Guidry before her husband died. As with Kenner's death, Blanche curated this piece of her life story with a careful precision. It was as if she knew someone, someday, would read this and she had a very specific conclusion she wanted them to draw.

Guidry eventually also met an untimely and unusual death, and she moved on to Claudius Broussard. In the years between the birth of her first two children by Broussard, and that of their last two, something notable happened to Blanche. Ashley's last candle had burned halfway to the quick when he realized it, through a very careful read between the lines.

Her general disposition when speaking of her children had always been lively, animated, as one would expect from any mother. Even the Guidry children, whom she favored less than her Broussard offspring, were dear to her, and she mentioned, on several entries, how she would die before she let harm come to them.

Then she began to refer to her youngest sons, Wyatt and Noble, as if settling a distance between them and her heart. She first spoke of them less, and then stopped referring to them by name. *Those children* or *those things* she would say, as if they were animals... or abominations.

When Wyatt and Noble both died, Blanche's entries grew more sterile than ever before. *W. Broussard and N. Broussard deceased. Gardener scheduled at home upon the morrow, expected around noon. A casserole seems suitable for supper.*

Ashley re-read that week of entries seven times, assuming he had clearly missed the passage where she mourned the loss of her two sons. He had almost given up when he stumbled across an obscure sentence.

M assures me our prosperity is on the rise.

M. Ashley flipped through past entries for any search of this "M." He found similar, oblique lines. *M's directives are clear. M is on the rise. M is fond of me. M will always see to my needs.* They were so brief that he saw now how he'd missed them. Before and after each mention of M were her usual missives about her day. These one-line mentions seemed dropped in, like Easter eggs for the most observant.

Ashley blinked the dryness from his eyes. He sank back in his chair, mouth open. All these weeks of fruitless reading, and here it was, finally, *something.*

After a detailed backtrack, Ashley came to several conclusions:

M appeared in Blanche's life, or at least entries, not long after she had her second child with Claudius Broussard.

M's presence in her life was received as generally fortuitous and full of promise.

M seems to have offered something of value to Blanche.

M expected something in return. A *quid pro quo.*

M was almost certainly Margarethe.

Between the Ophelia and Blanche letters, and this journal, Ashley's deduction came down to this:

Blanche sacrificed her youngest children on a promise from Margarethe that her others would be protected, and so would their descendants. In addition, came a promise of power for Blanche. Not simply to survive, but to thrive. Eternally. *Once M comes through, it is only a matter of time for me.*

Ashley combed through the remaining journal entries long into the morning, or so he guessed, given how his eyes sagged heavy with fatigue and his mind blurred the words together into Rorschach blots. He read every last one and noted every single mention of M, or anything relating to M.

When he reached the final page of her very last journal entry, dated February 21, 1990, the day she died, his heart surged. Then skipped.

Estella. Estella is the one. She will continue my work. She becomes the path to M. To eternity.

And if she will not... Ah, if she has a crisis of conscience... then there is another.

Ashley pushed the journal across the table and stared into the empty room.

Estella took Stella because Blanche asked her to, of that they'd already guessed. Just as Blanche had offered her sons to Margarethe, half a century earlier.

But Estella's refusal to play had been anticipated by her great-grandmother. She had a way around this, and for all they knew, she had already employed that tool.

Stella was *not* safe.

"Jesus," he whispered. "Damn it all to hell."

Ashley dug in his pocket for his cell phone.

15
SEBASTIAN

His mother was crying. Again.

Sebastian had learned to tune her out, but it didn't make her shrill, pointless keening any less annoying. If Katja wasn't carrying on about her failure to protect Stella, she would caterwaul about Sebastian, and how he was so *closed off* to her, whatever the hell that meant.

"Mother," he huffed, intimating his irritation with an eye roll so severe his irises disappeared under his upper lids with a flutter.

Katja sucked in a chain of jagged breaths. "How c-can I expect anyone to f-find my own daughter if I'm h-here?"

Sebastian glared at her with undisguised annoyance. "I've told you before, *go*. I don't need..." He almost said *you* but stopped himself. He wanted her to quit the incessant self-loathing, not move into round two. "I'm *fine*. How many times do I have to say it? Olivia is here."

Katja's eyes bored holes in him, two tragic orbs of self-loathing. "You h-hate me. I don't blame you. You should hate me, and your father, too. We're m-monsters."

His eyes rolled again, harder. “Your words, Mother, not mine.”

“Do you deny it?”

Sebastian crossed his arms and groaned. “I’m not having this conversation with you every single day. You’re supposed to be the adult and I’m the one over here trying to be rational with you. See a problem?”

“It’s a little hard to be *rational* when your son looks older than you are!”

“Do you ever listen to yourself? Aunt Olivia goes on and on how you were going to be a scientist, how reasonable you were. Where did that woman go?”

Katja’s lips quivered. She rolled her wheelchair in reverse, backing away. She didn’t need it anymore, but she used it anyway, a bizarre form of self-punishment. “She died with your sister, Nora, and your father.”

Sebastian shook his head in exasperation as she rolled away in her wheelchair, likely in retirement to her bedroom where she spent half her days pining over her poor decisions and the depressing results. Or something. He didn’t especially care.

He had something sitting on his mind far more pressing. More urgent. More *important*. Margarethe had chosen him as her disciple, and there could be no greater honor than this. Stella was afraid, and, he supposed, she should be, considering she wouldn’t survive the starlight awakening.

If Sebastian was anyone else, this would make him incredibly sad. She was his sister... his twin sister. He had read about twin connections and how bonded they should be. He didn’t remember much about his childhood, for whatever it actually was in the few weeks it lasted, but he guessed for at least a short time he must have loved Stella. In a way, he always would, even if his particular form of love wasn’t what others would look for him to exhibit in a traditional sense. Margarethe had showed him love revealed itself in many ways. He could love Stella and still take her life and make it his own when the time was upon him. In that way, he and Stella would be together forever.

But, despite his innate telepathic link to Stella, he had not been able to find her. And the closer he came, the better she learned to block him out.

He *would* find her, though. The bitch could only hide so many places, and she was growing weary of always fighting him.

Katja thought Sebastian to be a cold and almost surgical child, lacking in complex emotions and anything more than a distant regard for family. She wasn't far off, but he didn't worry too much about what she thought. His birth mother was no better than a blubbering idiot, displaying only flashes of usefulness and clarity. He hadn't known the budding scientist and struggled to see that she ever could have been so practiced and disciplined.

He worried more about his aunt Olivia, who was as observant as a buzzard circling fresh carnage, especially after Uncle Greg had left. She had always kept a careful eye on him, stepping up when his mother stepped away from reality, but Uncle Greg's decision he'd had enough of the Deschanels had only amplified Olivia's paranoia where her children were concerned. She didn't have the good sense to be afraid of Sebastian, as Katja did. She trusted him with her young son, Rory, although he had never given her a reason to think this was remotely a good idea. He couldn't decide if this was hopeful ignorance on her part, or utter cluelessness.

He didn't honestly care, either. Olivia's decision to trust him was irrelevant. Sebastian wouldn't hurt Rory, because there wasn't anything the least bit special or useful about him.

Not in the way Margarethe would want, and there was nothing Sebastian did or didn't do these days that did not somehow serve her greater purpose.

Such as Aleksandr. Sickening sweet and pure as the driven snow. Sebastian didn't know another person could be so malleable. He could say anything, do anything, and Aleksandr was so hungry for a friend who could relate to their crazy growth anomaly that he was willing to overlook how Sebastian continuously bullied him into submission, breaking him down, word by word.

You must do more than win him over, Margarethe whispered to him. She came to him mostly at night, when the only other sounds were the settling house and the garden wildlife. *You must isolate him. Control him. Destroy him, and then lift him high in your love. His destructor and savior in one.*

Margarethe refused to tell him why Aleksandr was important—only a small reassurance that *no, darling, he is not replacing you as the starlight awakener*—but her secrecy was a small price to pay for his eventual reward. All she would tell him was that plans had changed, and Aleksandr was as important, if not more, than finding Stella.

Sebastian at first had no inkling how he would *destroy him and lift him high in his love,* but it was Aleksandr himself who presented the idea, without ever realizing it.

Fiona.

Sebastian had paid careful attention to Aleksandr's correspondence with his on-again-off-again Irish lassie, monitoring closely the plans they'd made. Her flight from Dublin had landed ten minutes ago, and she would be at the Hotel Monteleone, awaiting Aleksandr, within the half hour.

Or so she thought.

The night before, Aleksandr had left his phone alone for a single moment—a moment was all Sebastian needed—and

Sebastian sent Fiona a small change in plans. *Let's meet at the Monteleone instead. Your cab driver will know where it is. My apartment is a mess. I would hate for you to see it!*

Sure, Aleksei. You know I'll be happy to see you anywhere.

Sebastian had quickly deleted both messages. Aleksandr returned from the bathroom with a smile on his face, and for a moment, Sebastian felt a twinge of guilt tickle his stomach.

While Sebastian prepared to leave for the Monteleone, Aleksandr awaited Fiona at his apartment, almost certainly wringing his hands while overthinking every last word he planned to say, stressing over what she might say in return. When she was late, his anxiousness would fester. When she never showed at all, that anxiety would turn to paranoia and then despair.

Eventually, he would learn the truth, but until then...

Destroy him, and then lift him high in your love. His destructor and savior in one.

Sebastian snatched the keys to his Ferrari off the kitchen counter and grinned on his way out the door.

FIONA WAS NOT HARD ON THE EYES, HE DECIDED. SHE DIDN'T QUITE deserve the pedestal Aleksandr placed her on, but she had a softness about her features that made him think, *feminine, lovely, wholesome.*

Not for long.

Her suitcase was upright in the corner of the room, a wool jacket draped over the top. She stood in front of both looking travel-weary and more than a little unsure.

Sebastian—Sebastian the illusionist, Sebastian who had projected to her that he was Aleksandr and so that was who she saw before her—sat on the edge of the bed, masking his Cheshire cat grin with a burst of unusual self-control.

He patted the blanket to his left. "Come sit down."

Her focus followed his hand. She wanted to do as he asked, he could see it in her eyes, but something gave her pause. "We should talk before... before, I don't know, anything else. I don't want to confuse things."

The last thing in the world Sebastian-posing-as-Aleksandr wanted to do was talk. The longer they stayed in the room together, the greater the risk to his discovery. He could mask his physical appearance all day, but eventually she would begin to note the oddities of his mannerisms, or cadence of his speech. She was no stranger to magic herself, and her senses wouldn't fail her for long.

"I agree, Ona. We need to talk. Wanna start?"

Fiona sucked in a sharp breath. She leaned into the wall, hands folded in front of her. Like Aleksandr, she must have practiced this moment a hundred times. "I was wrong to guilt you about wanting to protect me. I was just so tired of feeling like everyone knew what was better for me than I did myself, from my mother to Flynn to Declan, and I thought what we had was different." She looked down. "I know that was unfair of me. What we had *was* different, and you were scared, and I should have seen that and tried to understand it instead of ascribing motivations to you that you didn't deserve. I lashed out at you when I should have pulled you closer."

Sebastian listened to her with what he hoped was a gentle, understanding look. He drew his response from the dozens of times he'd heard Aleksandr yap on about his lost love. "We all make mistakes. I shouldn't have said what I said either. You're right. You're my equal, not some damsel in distress."

The worry in her face melted. She sagged in relief with a choked laugh. "I honestly didn't know what I'd be walking into."

You still don't.

Sebastian rose and held out his arms. "Can you forgive me, then?"

Fiona pressed her lips together to suppress her incoming tears. "Aleksei..." She flew into his arms with such force it almost touched his heart.

Almost.

With a move he rehearsed for Margarethe's approval, Sebastian lifted her chin and kissed her in one fluid gesture. She moaned against his mouth, and he knew the rest would be so, so easy.

"How I've missed you," she whispered. Her breath smelled like rosewater. The scent of her hopes and dreams preparing to die smelled even sweeter.

"Mmm," he replied and hoisted her into his arms. Her legs came around his waist as she cried out, in as much pleasure as surprise. He eased her away from the bed and onto the desk. A notepad and pen went sailing. The lamp knocked back against the wall.

Sebastian read the question in her eyes—what's the rush?—but he wanted, no needed, to get this over with. He had not studied Aleksandr nearly enough to be sure he could stay in character for long.

He silenced her question by slipping his hand under her dress, beneath the thin sheath of fabric between her legs. Her head fell back and her legs spread wider when he inserted two fingers and worked them in and out, his thumb making small circles against the small bundle of nerves.

"Goddess," she hissed. She bit her tongue so hard she drew blood. Her dark eyes were wild. "Have you been practicing?"

When her hand came for the bulge in his pants, he didn't waste time. Sebastian unzipped his trousers and let her do the honors of extracting his hard cock.

Not hard for you, sweetheart. Hard for a future you can't even begin to understand.

Fiona's pretty eyes traveled down, then up, and again. Sebastian didn't wait for an invitation. He pitched forward in a powerful thrust, filling her, delighting her as she fell forward against him. Her hands traced scratches across his back. Begging. For him. For more.

No, not for me. For Aleksei.

Sebastian pumped harder, increasing his rhythm. His heart raced at the culmination of the moment he had waited for, which was almost there, finally, but even more so at the realization that he *had done it.* He had done it! He had never before employed his illusionist skill with such need for precision, and not a single thing had worked against him.

When at last he felt his own climax approach, he yanked back her hair, hard, so her face stretched before him, trapped in place.

Sebastian revealed his true self.

Fiona's face erupted in pure terror as he released inside her. They screamed together as his orgasm rocked through them both: him in the unmarried pleasure of true power. Fiona, in unabated, animalistic fear.

She struggled to pull away, crying out with unintelligible words and guttural sounds. He pinned her in place until he had spilled every last drop.

Sebastian backed away, tucking his cock back in his pants. He snarled at her as she curled up on the table, trying to flee from him, and from whatever horrors had happened that her mind had yet to grasp.

"What's going on? Who are you? Where's Aleksei? What just happened? Oh, goddess, what has happened?" Her shrill fear was deliciously evident. Success.

"He was never here, if that isn't already clear. If you tell him, you'll destroy him. And I'll lie and say you wanted it." Sebastian wiped the back of his hand over his mouth, to wipe away the residue of her kisses. "That you've been texting me all along with a plan to hook up behind his back and leave him in the dust."

"That's crazy. He would never believe you." Fiona's voice was low, ringing of defeat. "He knows me."

"He'll only know you fucked me," Sebastian countered. "And loved it."

Fiona's head shook furiously, as if she could expel the past twenty minutes. "Who *are* you?"

"You don't know?"

She gaped at him.

"You do know."

Tears streamed down her cheeks.

"Go home, Fiona. Don't call him. Don't attempt to explain yourself and how you *accidentally* fucked his best friend. He won't understand, and why should he? Things were rocky between you at best." Sebastian leaned over her. A thrill passed through him at the raw exertion of power. She tried with commendable desperation to show her bravery, but she wore her fear like a sharp scent. His name sat on her lips like a threat, barely audible. He enjoyed watching her simple mind piece her new reality together. "He doesn't forgive you. And now? He never, ever will."

"Does he know you're a monster, Sebastian?" Her voice cracked. "Does he know what you are?"

Sebastian reached in his wallet and withdrew a stack of bills. He counted a thousand dollars and threw it on the bed in a messy heap. "For services rendered. And a flight home." He glanced at his wrist. "Next one leaves in two hours."

16
VICTOR

Victor's efforts to find a willing assistant fell victim to prior patterns. Recognition, indignation, outright refusal. Usually in that order. Without the list of attendees at the last Collective Council meeting, he had no way of knowing who had heard Colleen's warning. It was probable those not in attendance had been given the same warning, passed down through the family like an intricate web.

If he had to sift through every last Deschanel on the planet, he would.

He first saw Olivia Claiborne, daughter of Maureen Blanchard—Colleen's sister—as she locked the front door of her flower boutique on Magazine Street. Her tear-stained face was half-hidden behind the high lapels on her tan jacket as she hurried to her car. Once behind the wheel, she collapsed into fresh tears. Her head leaned forward on the wheel in fleeting surrender. When she sat back up, she shook her head, dabbed at her eyes, and started the car.

What did he know of Olivia from his limited research? Very little. She was married to a local architect, and they had a small child. An Internet search of her name brought up several write-ups, from the Times-Picayune, the Advocate, The Tribune and others, about her inspired floral boutique, The Secret Garden, which was lauded for the shop's unique design. The interior largely resembled an outdoor garden, complete with a bonsai maze and live trees growing straight from earth to sky. Parents even took their children in to let them play, while Mrs. Claiborne freshly clipped their bouquets.

Interesting, perhaps, but not terribly useful for Victor.

Her mother, though... Maureen. Maureen had nagged at the back of his mind. She'd perked his interest not from his online searches, but from bits and bobs floating across conversations the night of the meeting at The Gardens. One thing in particular was abundantly clear: Maureen was a staunch enemy of the magic in their veins. More, since the death of her son, Alain, she had become a callous hermit, denouncing the family altogether, especially her sister, Colleen.

Like mother, like daughter? Victor wondered as Olivia put her car in drive and took off down Magazine.

When she was out of sight, Victor jogged up to her shop and checked the hours. Open again at ten in the morning.

He would be there.

WHEN VICTOR INFORMED HIS FATHER, MARIUS, OF HIS PLAN TO appeal to a member of the Deschanel family to help him find his beloved Ophélie, the response he received was not a favorable one. His father believed, as Colleen did, that Ophélie was empowered to make her own choices, including the one she already made to be free of Victor.

"However," he'd said, "should you decide to pursue this, to not heed my advisement, you must understand the Deschanels are not our enemy. We have always enjoyed civil relations with our distant cousins, and I will not have you tearing this apart with your whims. Your careless confession to Amelia has already exposed our darkest secret to the clan. I have no reason to suspect they will use that to harm us, but your untoward meddling may give them a reason, Victor. We cannot have that. Do you understand what I am telling you?"

Others were less diplomatic. His aunt Flosine had whispered a threat in his ear while he slept. "I will drain the blood from your body if I even smell a *hint* that your behavior has wrought an enemy upon us."

As news of his behavior continued to spread across the de Blancheforts, both those living immortal as dhampir and those still human, he found himself on the receiving end of many other warnings and admonitions. What was Victor thinking, telling this Amelia Deschanel their greatest secret? The whole family must know by now! And now, tempting fate further by angering the family matriarch? His behavior should not be borne!

Victor acknowledged their concerns. He assured them this was why he had chosen not to employ any great force in his solicitations. He might have had his information by now had he taken a different tack.

"I only need to find one not under Colleen's sway," Victor told his mother, who listened to his distress, night after night, with sad eyes. "Just one. There has to be one."

"Please exercise caution, *mon ange.* Madame Deschanel is a great woman, but she is a woman to equally be feared. What you feel for us, and for your Ophélie, imagine that magnified on an immeasurable scale. She bears the weight of a thousand of her ilk, and she would defend them to her last breath."

"Maman, *you* are a great woman."

Francoise closed her eyes. She squeezed his hand. "Would

that I had been born in another time, your words might ring true."

"And what would you have me do? Forsake my one, singular desire in life? Forsake my heart?"

She kissed his forehead. "I would see you happy, *mon ange*. But not at the cost of your own self."

VICTOR DECIDED HE SHOULD MAKE HIS APPEARANCE AT THE START OF Olivia's workday, counting on the bulk of her business to show up around noon or after given the laid back clientele of the city. He required time to speak to her, uninterrupted, and this seemed to be the only way to get her attention without scaring her off. It was unlikely a married woman would agree to meet a strange man for drinks.

When he entered the store, she sat upon a high stool in the center of the garden, reading a book.

Olivia glanced up. She took quick measure of him and smiled. Her eyes, bloodshot and heavy, told of a deeper story beyond the courteous gesture. "How can I help you?"

Victor returned her smile. "I'm looking for a bouquet. Something bright and colorful. Eye-catching."

"Are these for a special someone?" Her eyes traveled to his left hand. He guessed she searched all her clients for certain "tells," to better anticipate their needs and assess them. "A girlfriend?"

"If only," he said and chuckled. "Would it be strange to admit I wanted them for myself?"

Olivia continued her routine scan, looking for other give-away signs of his personality. "No, I would say you have great taste, if you're looking for flowers to brighten up your own world. Do you have any favorites? Lilies, roses? Any colors that particularly strike you?"

Victor took a look around her floral paradise as he approached her. "What if I wanted you to pick? To surprise me?"

Olivia looked taken aback. "I can, if you like. But it would help me to know a little bit about you, if that's all right."

"Oh? Why's that?"

"I know some might say they're only flowers," she replied, wistful. "But, as with anything in life, we're influenced by our environment. From the people we surround ourselves with, yes, but also a step deeper, the colors, the shapes. Have you ever heard of the Chinese philosophy of *feng shui*?"

"Vaguely." He had not.

"It speaks to the theory that the arrangement and orientation of your surroundings is correlative to the flow of energy in that space. That these arrangements and orientations can have both positive and negative effects on this living or existing in that space."

"Fascinating," he said, though it sounded a bit too abstract for his liking. Like something one of the Renaissance-era dhampir might go on about. "And you believe you can capture, as it were, my appropriate *feng shui* by knowing me better?"

"I believe I can try."

Victor swept his arms in a shallow bow. "Ask away. I'm an open book."

Olivia stepped off her stool. "Favorite color?"

"Anything dark. Burgundy. Gray. Black."

She squinted. He mused at what might be going through her head. Her thoughts were blocked, a trick she'd likely not learned from her headstrong mother. "What style of music do you listen to when you want to relax?"

This one was easy. He had no grasp on the modern genres. "Classical. Baroque."

Olivia didn't write his answers down, but she appeared to

be committing them to memory with a quick glance up each time he delivered an answer. "Any scents you find especially relaxing?"

"The river. Freshwater carried off an evening breeze. I could almost drink it."

This brought a new smile to her face. "A lovely smell, but I certainly wouldn't drink anything from our river."

"Heavens, no!"

They both laughed.

"Sunset or sunrise?" she went on.

"Sunset."

"Silence or noise?"

"Silence."

"Indoor or outdoor?"

"In Louisiana, indoor, except precisely two weeks in January."

Olivia chuckled. "And the last question, and you must only pick one option, so consider carefully. Idealist, optimist, nihilist, realist, or pessimist?"

Victor crumpled his mouth into a frown. The answer was not difficult for him, but he sensed this question would set the background for whatever their relationship evolved into. What would she most like to hear?

"Idealist," he decided. "The realist within likes to remind me that I am a flawed creature living in a flawed world. But to have hope is a beautiful thing. To see the world through the eyes of an idealist is to believe, truly, that no matter our pain, no matter our scars, we still have hope for a better world. A better life."

Olivia's eyes filled with tears. She snapped her head away and mumbled an unintelligible apology.

Victor stepped closer and handed her his silken monogrammed handkerchief. "I'm the one who's sorry, if my words upset you."

She dabbed at her eyes with a thanks, still looking away. He sensed as much shame in her as sadness. "I shouldn't bring my bad days to work. I'm so sorry, Mr...."

"De Blanchefort," he said softly. A gamble to give his name, but playing his hand later would mean wasting more of his time if she was forewarned. "Victor." He ran his hand over her hair for a brief, fleeting moment, and then stopped. She looked up. She wasn't running yet. "Never apologize for your pain, Mrs. Claiborne. We are complex creatures with a great many nuances. Our pain is a part of us, and it is simply inhuman to expect anyone to turn it off for the sake of others."

Olivia's face went blank, but her eyes swam with question upon question. Who was he? Where did he come from? Why was he being so kind?

He was now almost certain she had not recognized his name, his face, or his intentions. His gamble had paid off.

She was the one.

"I don't know what to say to that," she said after a comfortable silence. "Things have not been easy lately, but I shouldn't be making that the problem of others around me. Especially not my patrons."

"You know way too much about me now for me to simply be a patron. I mean, how can I leave here, knowing how aware you are of my love for rivers and sunsets?"

Olivia tensed until she realized he was playing with her. She laughed into his handkerchief. "Never know what I might do with that information."

"Friends, then," Victor declared. He leaned into the counter across from her. "And now it's my turn. What has you so upset?"

Olivia's mouth parted. "I couldn't possibly..."

"You could. And I insist. Your secrets are safe with me, and I'm a good listener. You may add that to your *feng shui* questionnaire as well."

She shook her head in surprise. "What about your flowers?"

"I believe they aren't going anywhere, unless there's something you'd like to tell me about floral militarization techniques."

Olivia chewed her lip. "I'm not that good. Not yet, anyway."

"So, tell me. I'm as neutral as you'll find in a listener. I do not know you, or any of the others involved in your sorrow."

"It's a lot to tell," she said, easing back up on the stool. "My family is complicated."

"Nothing unique there, I'm happy to tell you."

"Yes, well... it's unique in ways I can't really discuss, but it may be enough to say that this uniqueness of ours causes a lot of problems."

"Something I can relate to, for certain."

"This um... uniqueness causes more than problems, though. It creates division. Most of the family falls on one side, but there are others who fall on the other. My mother is in the minority group, and she raised my brother and me to be as well." She handed him back his handkerchief, but he waved at her to keep it. She balled the cloth in her hands and settled them into her lap. "My brother committed suicide last year."

Victor's face fell. "I'm so sorry to hear that."

"He was my world, next to my son. I adored Alain. I would have done anything for him, except when he really needed me, I failed him."

Victor's hand fell on hers. "We're human, Olivia." *Well, one of us is, anyway.*

Olivia nodded. "That's what everyone says, but words

won't bring him back. But things got even harder. My mother became worse about her beliefs. Even more closed off and prejudiced against her own family. She hates them all. Her sisters, her brother, her nieces, nephews, because they all represent that uniqueness that divides us. When I chose to help Alain's children and their mother, mine shut me out completely. She says I chose the wrong side, and she wants nothing to do with me now."

"That's a terrible thing to go through," Victor said. "Though I hope you know that decision was about her, not you."

"Maybe," Olivia agreed. "But it doesn't make it any easier for me to live with. I lost my mother and my brother in an instant. I don't have a great relationship with most of my extended family because for years I listened to my mother, and even let myself agree with her. And now I've lost my husband."

"Your husband?"

Olivia tapped her foot on the metal rung. "He... well, he left me."

"Oh, Olivia..."

In her fidgeting, she dropped the fabric. He knelt to pick it up, and one of her tears landed on his hand.

"Things were tense for a while, but they got worse after Alain and the twins and then the miscarriage and... God, okay, maybe I wasn't always the best wife. I can be *difficult* at times, like my mother. But I've always put my son first. And when Alain and Katja's son became mine to protect, I put him first, too. But it was too much for Greg, and even though things got better for a time, I guess that was only the calm before the storm. He walked out a few days ago. Said he couldn't handle me or my family anymore."

"You poor dear." Victor reached for the handkerchief and this time he used it on her, pressing it gently to the corners of her eyes. "You have the whole world on your shoulders right now."

Olivia hung her head as the sobs rolled forth. "I'm sorry. I can't believe I told you this! A complete stranger... how unprofessional..."

Victor bent his knees and bowed his head so he could see her face. "I told you, we can't possibly be strangers, knowing what we do about one another now. And as for professional, I say with complete authenticity that you run the most unique flower shop in all of New Orleans. I would buy from you even if you were screaming obscenities at the customers as they walked in."

Olivia sniffled and laughed. "I haven't done that yet."

"We've only just met, and I can see your heart and your kindness."

Olivia blinked the tears from her eyes and looked up. "You're an unusual man, Victor. I don't think I know anyone like you."

"I'll take that as a compliment."

She squeezed his hand. "You should." She pulled in a gulp of air. "Well, then. You wanted a colorful bouquet, and you're going to get one."

"There's something else I would like." He considered his next words carefully. This exchange had been easier than he expected—he hadn't known about her husband, but this unfortunate timing for Olivia ended up fortuitous for Victor—but he could clearly see she was a smart woman, even if she was guided by her emotions. He would need to tread with caution.

"Yes?"

"I'd like to see you again." Pause, let the words settle. Let her think exactly what she should, that he was coming on to her. "I apologize if that was too forward."

"No," she said quickly. "I mean, no, it wasn't too forward, it's just..."

"Your husband. Of course! This is my fault, for not being more clear with my invitation. I'm not looking for a date from you, Olivia. Only your friendship." *Now, reel your interest back, so she sees how ridiculous she was for assuming I was coming on to her. Peel her guard away.* "It's only that this conversation was so refreshing, and I'd like to continue it, or perhaps begin another. Maybe at a time where you're not working."

"Oh! Hmm, I suppose that would be all right."

"Only all right?"

"What did you have in mind?"

"Dinner, tonight, Galatoire's? Say, seven?"

"I would need to see about my son."

"Your brother's girlfriend. You mentioned she lives with you?"

"Yes, but I can't just dump my son on her at the last minute."

"You've done so much for her," Victor said gently. "I'm sure she would do this for you."

The corner of her mouth twitched in the hint of a grin. "I can't believe I'm going to have dinner with a man I just met, who only knows I'm miserable and cry a lot."

"Isn't that the point of getting to continue this later? So I can learn more about you?"

"You're sure about this? You really want to take me to dinner?"

I may want so much more. "Very much so."

The bell on the store door rang. She looked past him and waved at the customer. "Okay. Seven, then. I'll meet you there, though. It's probably best Rory, my son, that is, doesn't see you and get confused. He's too young to understand. He still thinks Daddy is coming back."

"Oh, of course. I'll meet you there at seven, and I'll make sure we get an upstairs reservation."

"Yes, please! I don't know why they would ever seat anyone in their downstairs area. May as well go to a diner."

Victor grinned at her bourgeois breeding shining through. "Indeed. I look forward to our evening."

17
FINNEGAN

Finn held the beer by the neck. He squinted one eye and positioned the other over the small hole, examining the remaining contents. He gave the bottle a quick swirl and swallowed the last of the swill.

Captaining Forbia once again offered him a sense of purpose he didn't even realize had been missing.

Neither he nor Jacob had said a single word in hours. It was nice to have someone to share the silence with, and Finn was almost sad to break the peace. "Hey. You awake?"

"Just thinking about whether a lobster would beat a crab in a cage match, and also if their pincers were capable of wielding small thrown weapons."

"Wanna hear something weird?"

Jacob tilted his head. "That wasn't weird?"

"No, dude, that was plenty weird."

"All right. Hit me, then."

"Maybe weird was the wrong word, knowing how your brain works. And the answer is the lobster would always win." Finn grinned. "While you spent the past few hours making a hierarchy of badassery in the arthropod crustacean circuit, I was thinking of Ana."

Jacob made an *awww* sound. "Who says chivalry is dead?"

"*Over*-thinking, I should have said. Usually, when I'm on the water, my mind goes blank. Complete blank slate. *Tabula rasa*. But I've had a lot on my mind. No surprise there, I guess." He wedged the bottle between his thighs and lifted his sweater over his head. Now past noon, the day had finally started to warm up. He straightened out his white undershirt and settled back in. "I'm pretty sure I know my wife, especially after all we've been through. In the ways that matter, anyway. But we spent most of our relationship on the run overseas, or apart, or in some kind of danger. And now we're playing house and starting a life, in her world. I'm seeing her now, how she was before she met me, raised in a world of privilege, and it occurs to me how little I actually know her."

"What do you mean? Like you think she's someone else here?" Jacob lifted the dirty white lid of the cooler and withdrew another beer. He tossed one to Finn, who caught it effortlessly at his side, with the easy dexterity of a receiver. With his other hand, he chucked the empty one in a white bucket.

"No, it's not even her, not really. I know nothing, or almost nothing, about how she was raised. Her world feels more like I stepped into another country, not another state."

"You're living in the house she grew up in. Bentleys and cotillions. Our wives are as Uptown princesses."

"Yeah, but that's not Ana," Finn replied. "Or Amelia. At the same time, it is, and I'm not sure how to reconcile the two sides in my head. Am I making any sense?"

"Maybe how she was raised isn't important to who she is now, though. I'm not the scared Irish kid who watched my family die. Not anymore. Amelia has grown into someone... amazing. She's a warrior. She's my hero. And even though

Amelia and I were raised in entirely different worlds, I rarely ever feel that gap."

Finn nodded slowly, listening. "Maybe what's really bothering me is that I don't know her family at all."

"They're a hard family to know," Jacob conceded. "I didn't know them right away, either."

"But you do now?"

Jacob shrugged. "Her parents and Ashley, anyway. They're the only family I've ever really had, other than Sister Agnes, and they've always treated me like I was one of them. And I was in school with some of her cousins, like Ana and Olivia. I hung out with Nic once or twice, but I doubt he remembers it the way I do. But there's always been this void where everyone else was concerned, because of the secrecy of the Magi Collective. The others all treated me fine, but I couldn't really be a part of any of it until we were married. And for a hell of a long time, she refused to marry me."

Finn raised a brow.

"When we still lived and died by the Curse. She didn't want a piano to fall on me, or something." Jacob laughed. "It seems stupid now, knowing what we know, but it made sense at the time. Love turns us backward sometimes."

"Doesn't it, though."

Jacob went on, "They have their secrets, and for good reason. It's nothing you don't already know after the last year. We have ours, too."

"Her dad is an interesting guy," Finn said. He studied the sun to gauge the position, the degree of movement since they set their traps. "We need to check the nets soon."

"We've talked about this. You lost the father-in-law lottery, comrade. The man is Stonewall Jackson."

Finn laughed and cast his eyes toward the sparkling water. The sun hit it directly, heating the water's surface, a phenomenon he was completely unfamiliar with in the frigid northern Atlantic. Cold days and cold nights. That was his life for twenty-seven years. This was his life now. "He doesn't scare me. But I know how much it means to Ana for us to get along."

"You said dinner went well when you had them over, minus Barbara pulling a drunk Joan Collins."

"It was. Better than I expected. But he wasn't happy when she stayed with me in Maine instead of coming home, and he doesn't seem like a man who forgets things. I know he wanted an investment banker or congressman for her. I'll never be either."

"Doesn't matter what he wants," Jacob replied. He stood and raised his arms above his head, stretching away the long day. "She picked you. And you're not just her husband, but also her baby daddy. That's gotta count for something with him."

"Who knows? The man rations his words like he gets them from a Communist bread line. You'd need a degree to read him. He's good with Aleksei, though. That makes the rest seem not as important."

"Bingo. And if you really want to get to know her family... all the cousins, the aunts, the whole clan... join the Magi Collective. Membership is open to spouses, and a majority of the Deschanels are members. Now that we're married, and back in New Orleans, I'm probably going to pursue it myself."

"You don't think that would be weird?"

"Weird? How?"

"I don't know. A proletarian at a table of Deschanels. A Yankee who wrangles lobster for a living. Just seems weird, like I don't belong."

"Weirder than telling people that Aleksei, who looks *maybe* a year or two younger than you, is your son? Weirder than you having deep and meaningful conversations with your arctic wolf?"

Finn laughed. "You have a point."

"You might have a harder time convincing Ana. She's never been an official member of the Collective."

Finn hadn't known this. "Why not?"

"Remember who her father is? Amelia once told me you could divide the Deschanels by those who are cool with their abilities on one side, and those who act like they don't exist on the other."

"If I don't get to live in denial, neither does she," Finn said and stood. He was eager to check the traps. A day earlier, someone had stolen them right from under him, an oversight he wouldn't allow to happen twice. "Hey, I was thinking I might invite Jon to come with us next time. That cool with you?"

"Yeah, man," Jacob said. "But if things go sideways, and you decide to Natalie Wood this thing and throw him overboard, the official story will be, what?"

Finn restarted the boat's motor. His body shook with laughter. "With your whack-ass imagination, I'm sure we'll come up with something."

18

AMELIA

The sound of the front door opening and closing interrupted Amelia's light rest. She blinked away the sleep, then squinted to gather her bearings. She let the afghan fall away, only to realize she'd fallen asleep on the couch again.

She hadn't meant to, but she'd been so tired in recent weeks. She thought of it as her body demanding some catch-up from the difficult months past. The physical effects of stress often manifested latently, and the unusual calm they now enjoyed seemed as good a time as any for stress to show up.

Jacob leaned over the couch and pressed his lips to hers. He laughed into her yawn. "Have a nice nap, Sleeping Beauty?"

"Mm. How was your first experience as a true mariner?"

Jacob hung his jacket on the hook by the door. He pulled his arms behind his back and groaned into the stretch. "I'm basically an expert now."

"Did you engage in a lifelong power struggle with a giant white whale?"

"I thought I'd save that for the next time."

"Then you're still an amateur," she charged. "How many times did you hurl?"

He made a *pfft* noise. She cocked her head at him. "Fine. Once. I think of it as christening the lake."

"Or a variety in diet for the fish," Amelia teased. She unfolded herself into her own stretch, but everything about her, from muscle to bone, felt stiff, like she'd spent the day mountain climbing, not engaging in random household chores.

Jacob pulled up behind her. His hands went to work on her shoulders, kneading. "Mail came for you from Tulane Medical Center. Their employment department. Did you send them an interest letter?"

Amelia sagged with an aggravated sigh. "Jesus. No. Mother. You know, she sure gets on a high horse when Uncle Augustus pulls strings for people in the family, but when she does it, it's perfectly okay. She just *assumed* that's where I would want to work. She never even asked me! If she had, she might have known I was interested in Oschner. Or, crazy thought, joining a private practice! But, no, she's off on her own, doing whatever she thinks is best."

"Hey, what's wrong?" Jacob hopped over the back of the couch and landed beside her. Usually, Amelia hated when he did this, insisting it would ruin the elasticity of the cushions, but at that moment the inanity of it made her want to hug him. She might have, if her mood hadn't turned so foul in an instant. "This isn't about your meddling mama."

Amelia fell into him. "I talked to Aunt Evie today. She called me. And yes, in a way I guess this *is* about my meddling mother, because she doesn't get to pick and choose what I should know. I told her everything. Now, she's parceling out information like I'm a child who needs to be monitored closely. I'm almost thirty years old and have a PhD, for the love of God!

I think I can handle knowing what the hell is going on in my own family."

He ran his finger in circles around her knee, and it calmed her. "Let's back up. Aunt Evie called you and said what?"

Amelia yanked the blanket over them. Her anger grew more acute as she continued her retelling. "You know the meeting we missed? Where Mom warned everyone about Victor?"

Jacob nodded.

"Thank goodness she did, because that jerk has been harassing the family."

"What? Serious?"

Amelia looped her fingers through the gaps in the crocheted blanket, tugging and stretching. "And I would have never known that because Mom told Aunt Evie I was *in a delicate state* right now and couldn't handle more stress." Amelia bounced on the cushion, pivoting in a rage to face her husband. "Do I look like I'm in a delicate fucking state?"

Jacob tried to respond, but a laugh escaped instead. "If I saw you in a dark alley, I'd back away slowly."

Amelia flopped back into place. "Six people, that we know of, including my mother. That creature went to see my *mother,* Jacob, and she decided I didn't need to know this. And I can't even yell at her, because Aunt Evangeline made me promise I wouldn't break her trust. The last thing I need on my conscience is a rift between my mother and the only sister left she actually likes."

"I can see why you're angry," he said carefully.

"Oh, not you too!" she cried. "There are no eggshells on this floor, Donnelly."

Jacob tucked a stray hair away from her face. "I would be mad, too. It's not up to Colleen what you can and can't handle right now. Or anytime, really."

"*Thank* you."

"But please don't let it eat at you, *Blanca.* We knew Victor wasn't going to give up, right? The dude just showed up at our house this week, but, for him, he's been trying to get this show on the road for over a hundred years. I don't know why it only recently occurred to him he might be able to leverage the Deschanels to find her, but now that he has, he's probably going to keep at it until he either finds someone to help or someone takes the bastard out."

Amelia gave him a look. "Are you volunteering?"

"All I'm saying is, if someone finds that dude in a dumpster, I was with you all night."

"That's a thought. That someone might try to stop him in a more permanent way. Imagine the war with the de Blancheforts, though."

Jacob leaned back until their heads were touching. "I wouldn't lose sleep over it, but I think we have to assume he's not done and accept it has nothing to do with us."

Sigh. "Yes."

"If it would make you feel better, I can hang some garlic in the doorways."

Amelia frowned. "He's immune, sadly."

"We can amp up the cross level in this house to gratuitous, then."

"He probably goes to church more than we do. He walks freely in the damn sun, too. Prefers gold, but isn't especially bothered by silver."

Jacob's hand flew to his chest in indignation. "What the what? What kind of vampire is he, then?"

"The kind that doesn't give a damn about what others think or want. The kind that would drive Ophélie into hiding because he can't conceive that everyone else doesn't think like he does."

"I know you want to find her. But if she wanted us to know where she was, she would have made herself known."

"Or maybe she knows he's prowling around the Garden District and she's afraid."

"He wasn't five years ago. Or ten. Or fifty. She had plenty of time to come out to the family."

"It wouldn't have meant anything before we went back in time and got to know her. She couldn't have come to us before we returned, and now that we have, Victor won't leave us alone."

Jacob's eyes crossed. "I've never liked chicken-egg arguments."

Amelia socked him. "Stop playing dumb. You know what I'm saying."

"I do," he agreed. "But us aside, she could have come out to your mother, or others in positions of power in the family, and she chose not to. If Ophélie wanted to be found, she would. I believe that."

"And what about the fact that we might have a whole line of Deschanels out there somewhere descended from her?"

"If you want to make that point, let's think of all the Deschanel bastards running around with their own lines, too. Your uncle Charles probably sired half the current generation of Louisiana before he kicked it. There are things we can change and things we can't." Jacob laced his fingers through hers and looked down. "I spent my life wondering about my father's choice. If I had paid attention when he disappeared into the shed while Ma was still cooking breakfast. He never did that. I remember thinking it, too, *Pa never does that.* Our instincts are supposed to protect us, but sometimes they don't. If I had asked my ma what he was up to, she might have stopped and found him in those split seconds when he was still conflicted about what he was about to do. I picture my pa in tears, hugging and kissing her, unable to believe he almost did something so horrible. But I didn't. I said nothing. And there is no way, no matter how much I might wish otherwise, to know if speaking up would have changed anything. I couldn't control my pa, Amelia. We couldn't control what happened in that cabin. And we can't control Victor or Ophélie, or anyone. Some things, we just have to let go. Just let... it... go."

"Stop saying smart stuff," Amelia pouted, tightening her grip on his hand.

"Let it go," he whispered in her ear. His tongue grazed her neck. She shivered. "All of it. Victor. Your mom. The Saints not making it into the playoffs. Let it go."

A giggle sat on her lips, but as she turned to him, she saw no evidence of his playfulness. Desire pooled in his eyes instead. His mouth parted. His pulse quickened through his warm skin.

Amelia fell back against the length of the couch as Jacob parted her legs with his knee. He buried his face in her neck, moaning through his increasingly desperate kisses.

She slid her legs over the side of him, running her bare skin over his clothes, then his own skin as his shirt came up. He brought his hands around to her thighs and squeezed. She pressed them tighter until her ankles locked behind his back.

Jacob paused in time, for a solitary moment. He regarded her with a look so powerful it sent the blood rushing through her limbs.

Amelia snaked her hands behind his head and pulled him toward her, sliding her tongue into his mouth, wrapping it around his own, the gesture sloppy in the way her first kiss was, but equally as demanding. His skin burned so hot against hers she gasped.

Her hands fumbled at his shorts, searching. Jacob bit his lip and groaned when her hand circled his cock. She tugged and his mouth fell open.

"Let it go, you say," she demurred. "But what if it's mine?"

"Yours," Jacob panted.

Amelia squeezed the hardness in her hand. She bit her lip at the enthusiastic response it produced. "Mine?"

Jacob's head fell forward against his chest as he moaned again. "Yours."

She reached her hand around to his ass, sneaking under his belt and beneath the waistband of his trousers, and spread her fingers across his soft flesh. She drew him closer and slowly released her hand as she guided him inside her.

Jacob slid his hand behind her back and lifted her toward him. His other hand tangled itself within her hair, making a knot at the base of her skull as he kissed her.

Amelia flexed her thighs, tightening her hold on him with every powerful thrust. She gritted her teeth in ecstasy as he drove harder and faster, losing himself, becoming someone else, as he always did when she held him in the throes of his deep-running passion.

She surrendered as well, to the pleasure of making love to her husband, but also, to something more powerful, the release of her fears.

Jacob pulled down her shirt and took one of her nipples in his teeth. She cried out and squeezed his ass tighter, digging her thumbs in, deepening his hold on her.

Amelia moved her arms to around his neck and maneuvered them both so she was atop him. Pressing her hands to his chest for control, she commanded as she rode him, "Come for me."

Jacob's eyes fluttered closed in tandem with a languid, drawn sigh.

He shuddered as he filled her, his release sending his body

into short spasms of pleasure. She held him close as he came, as he gave her what was hers and always would be, the one thing she would never, ever let go of.

She stretched back out on the couch, and he collapsed on her chest. His labored breathing delivered in uneven spurts.

"I need to say smart stuff more often," he gasped. The saliva at the corner of his mouth seeped through her thin shirt.

Amelia kissed the crown of his sweaty head. "I'll give you an encore round for free."

Jacob's limbs came to life again in an instant. His head lifted up off her chest. His black hair had a life of its own; his damp face grinned at her. "I accept your offer." His hand traveled down her belly and landed between her legs. "But we have other unfinished business first."

19
VICTOR

Now that he'd waken up next to Olivia, Victor realized he had never quite gauged exactly how far he was willing to take his plan. He liked to consider himself a good man, for the most part. Good men occasionally twisted the fabric of their lives for their gain or advantage, but they were careful in their delivery, and in their considerations of others. Victor had already filled his quotient of making decisions for others with Ophélie. Despite how he protested to Amelia, Jacob, and Colleen and defended his decision—and he did defend it to himself, as well, insofar as he would make the same decision again if he had it all to do over—his guilt over the same kept him up at nights. This, perhaps, more than anything else, was why his determination to find Ophélie hadn't waned. It had grown. He needed to apologize. To make amends, if that were even possible.

He also wished to care for her descendants, if she had given birth to the child growing within her at the time of her disappearance. Victor didn't expect her to accept. But if he could even get a hint as to where they might be found, he could establish trusts in their name. He could ensure every single one of them had the money for college and never struggled to pay a bill. The de Blancheforts' wealth was as vast as the ocean beyond the Gulf. Immortality had opened up immeasurable opportunities, and they had spread their investments across many industries, many names. The seers in his clan had known precisely the best places to invest. He *could* do this, provide for Ophélie's children, grandchildren, great-grandchildren, and on and on. It would be nothing, and it would be everything.

He intended to elicit Olivia through their friendship, but their talks turned to an intimacy, in words and in gestures, that led them through her house, down her hall, and inevitably, to her bed.

Olivia's dark hair pressed against the pillow. The soft down on her pale arm caught the light peaking through the blinds. He wanted to reach out and touch it. To run his hands down the length and kiss the back of her bare shoulder. He pictured her turning with a sleepy smile, which he would kiss until he felt her body arch in response, in desire for his body against hers, again.

Where did the path between planning and desire sever? He could have convinced her to help him without taking her to bed, so why did he?

"I wanted to," he whispered against her burgundy silk pillow. "That's why."

One dinner turned to three. Victor surprised her every morning when she opened with a coffee from a nearby shop, which after the second time was no longer such a surprise. He appeared when she locked up, only to say "see you soon." From there, she would go check on her son, then later meet him for dinner.

Olivia unfolded like a flower, in each conversation growing bolder and less restrained in how she talked about her life. Victor sensed she had been desperate for a confidante, but had no one to fill that role. Olivia had lost her brother, mother, husband. Her cousins thought her to be insufferable—a trait Victor only saw within her in flashes. Her son, Rory, wasn't even in kindergarten yet. Katja was a mess of self-loathing delusion. This was a woman alone in all the ways that mattered.

Victor had never known the intimacy of an equal partnership. His wife, Elisabeth, had been chosen for him, for the advantage the Romans brought to their family. He had taken his share of lovers, but practiced careful discretion to avoid bringing shame to himself or his family.

Olivia Blanchard was the first woman he had taken to his bed for what lay within her mind, rather than behind her smile.

Throughout their long conversations, which stretched far enough into the night to produce a mother's guilt in Olivia, Victor found himself so pulled into their shared words that he'd forgotten why he sought her out to begin with.

He learned more about the degree of her strife. Alain's suicide had ripped the Deschanels apart, with her own small family at the nucleus. For Olivia, this had been her Great Epiphany, as she called it. Her mother's philosophies about the evils in the family being caused by embracing their distinctiveness had been ingrained deep in Olivia, from her childhood on. She had shared Maureen's self-righteous platform of denial with a child's blind trust, only allowing this tight grip to unwind itself when Alain had taken his life as an indirect response to this belief system.

Olivia decided then and there she would embrace Katja, whom she had previously turned her back on, and do everything in her power to help Alain's surviving twins, who were not abominations at all, just innocent babies who needed someone to love them.

Maureen, alternately, turned into a grief-stricken lunatic. No one even knew where she'd buried Alain, so they couldn't visit his tomb. When she learned Olivia was helping Katja and the babies, she forced her to choose. *Me or them.* Olivia told her family should never be about choosing, and she would choose not people but doing the right thing. Maureen closed her out of her life.

"I'm your *daughter,* Mom," Olivia had pleaded.

"I have no children," were the last words Maureen said to her.

Olivia had turned to Greg for support. Greg, who had always gone through the motions of the marriage with all the right moves on the outside, but none of the emotional punch behind them. Olivia admitted she hadn't done much better, but she wasn't the same woman now, and never would be. She required more... was ready to give more in return.

Greg, at first, stepped up, thrilled at the increase in affection and intimacy. For a while, they both remembered why they had married in the first place.

But this honeymoon period lasted less time than the first. Greg knew when he married Olivia that her family was special, but he took comfort in Olivia's refusal to participate. When she found herself at the center of it, these were not circumstances he would live with.

Special. Olivia had used this word, and *unique,* in very obtuse ways, fearful of sharing her family's great secret with a strange man. Eventually, Victor had played his own hand, moving a salt shaker across the table, to gain her trust. From there, she held nothing back.

Olivia was a great seer. Unpracticed, after years and years

of her mother's heavy hand, but her visions of the future were precise and long-reaching. With practice and discipline, she could be incredible.

Three glasses of wine, and her eyes had turned glassy. He read the invitation there before it made it to her lips.

"I've never been more alone in my life," she'd said, voice husky with Syrah and the heaviness of her confessions. "I don't want to be alone tonight."

And in the end, it was not Victor, Seeker of Ophélie, Fearsome Dhampir of St. Charles Parish, who landed in Olivia Claiborne's bed.

It was Victor the Man.

VICTOR LET HER SLEEP. IN THE END, HE *HAD* STOLEN THAT KISS ON THE back of her freckled shoulder. She stirred with light, sleepy sounds, and he smiled. He pulled the blanket up to her neck before he left her.

The clock in the kitchen said it was only six. Rory would still be asleep. Olivia said he slept until nine unless someone made him get up sooner. And though she'd never said it, he suspected Olivia wasn't ready for her son to meet her lover, if that was even what he was. She might even be seized with regret when she awoke and realized what she'd done.

Of Katja's waking habits, he wasn't as sure. Olivia said very little about her cousin, only that she was fiercely protective of the younger girl, and her son, Sebastian, whom he took to be of a very young age, given Katja was hardly out of high school herself.

Should he leave a note, or wake Olivia on his way out? He was so out of his element.

A voice down the hall caught his attention. Two voices, actually, both male.

Victor stepped in the direction of the discussion. His first panicked thought was Greg had returned. The last thing he wanted was to cause trouble for Olivia's marriage, which might or might not be salvageable—inching closer to *might not* if Greg discovered his wife's lover in the house, drinking from his *Architect Monthly* coffee mug.

When the words gained clarity, he paused to listen.

"Sebastian, I said I *don't* want to talk about it."

"I don't get it. After all this, and your girl doesn't even show up? Come on, Aleksei, that's bullshit and you know it."

"Can we go back to sleep? Please?"

Victor frowned. The voice belonging to the one called Sebastian was clearly developed. An adult. Were there two Sebastians here? Perhaps the younger was named for the elder?

That made no sense, either. Sebastian's father, Alain, was dead and gone.

"We can when you tell me you aren't going to be some damn chump who lets a girl walk all over him," Sebastian barked in a bossy, know-it-all tone.

"I don't even want to think about it."

"You have no choice, my friend."

A chill passed through Victor the more he listened to Sebastian. His words at the surface had the ring of a concerned friend. What he sensed just below was far from friendly.

"No? Fine, I'll go home. I thought staying here would help me clear my head, but if you're just going to keep bringing it up, then I'm better off going home and just being alone."

"You can't ignore the snub," Sebastian insisted. He sounded like a commanding father. "She's obviously a flaky bitch. She needs to pay."

Aleksei's voice cracked. "Pay? Listen to yourself. If she didn't want to see me, then there's nothing else to be said. It's clearly over for her. The end."

"For her, maybe. But look what she did to you, Aleksei. Look at yourself, man. Are you really going to let her get away with the pain she's caused you?"

Sebastian's steps sounded loud across the bedroom floor. "We could kill her, you know."

Aleksei erupted into sobs.

Victor backed quietly down the hall.

Going to bed the night before, he thought he'd known nearly all there was to know about Olivia and the life she led.

Now, he wasn't so sure.

20
ALEKSANDR

Sebastian continued to harangue him about Fiona's defection all through the morning until Aleksandr couldn't handle anymore. *She's been playing you. She's bad news. She toyed with the wrong motherfucker.*

Aleksandr was sure he was trying to help, but his words only put a finer point on Fiona's bizarre actions. How could she have done this to him, not showing, not even a note or a call to say she wasn't coming? They'd hardly exchanged any words since extending the invite, but everything she'd said in her return messages to him gave him the impression she was as eager to see him as he was to see her. He was so stunned by events he hadn't yet had the presence of heart to tell his parents. They'd been so happy when she said yes.

"You still thinking about that crazy ass Irish bitch?" Sebastian barked from the bed.

Aleksandr finally escaped by saying he was going to the bathroom and slipping out the front door instead.

Sebastian immediately began blowing up his phone with one text after another, then when that didn't work, calls. Aleksandr finally decided to turn it off. As he went to press the power button, another message came in, but this one wasn't from Sebastian.

Aleksandr sat in his parked car in the private lot outside his mother's apartment, staring at the screen. He didn't recognize the phone number, but the first few words of the message were enough. More than enough.

Aleksei, I feel sick about what happened.

Aleksandr glanced around the lot and determined he was alone. He shook his head at how silly this was. Then he flicked open his phone and scrolled down the rest of the message.

Aleksei, I feel sick about what happened. He wiped his hand across his brow, where sweat began to form. *I borrowed this phone from my mother after I got rid of mine. It's our community phone, for emergencies, so don't reply. I want to explain to you what happened, but I don't have the words, and I don't believe the timing would benefit either of us. I never meant to hurt you. Please believe this. Never. No matter what you might hear later, or think, remember that, if nothing else.*

The silver phone bobbed in Aleksandr's shaking hands. He flipped it closed and clutched the plastic to his chest. He scrambled to open it again, to type a response about how she wasn't making any sense, but realized she had asked him not to.

He choked out a short, desperate cry and dropped the phone at his feet. After accidentally kicking it under the brake pedal in an effort to retrieve it, Aleksandr dropped his face against the steering wheel and gasped for breath, trying his best not to cry. He couldn't lose it, not here. Not like this.

Aleksandr didn't want to be home, but if not home, then where? He couldn't face his parents. Sebastian only made the wound fester, with all the delicacy of stampeding elephants.

There was one person. Really, the only one, because, aside

from this kind individual, he'd only confided in Sebastian about his experiences with Fiona, and he was learning now that maybe he shouldn't have. No one else but this person knew how he'd agonized for days over the right words to say to her when she arrived. Or how he had been ready to give up everything for her.

Aleksandr hopped out of the car and knelt by the driver's side door, fishing under the pedals with one hand. His fingers found purchase on the phone and he drew it out, sniffling.

He punched in a quick text to his uncle Jacob.

ALEKSANDR HAD SEBASTIAN TO THANK FOR HOW HE DISCOVERED Armstrong Park. Sebastian had a love for several uncomfortable topics, with Anasofiya's colorful past unfortunately being one of them. One night he rambled on and on about her trail of lovers in the Faubourg Tremé neighborhood. Before Aleksandr could shut him up, his own interest had been piqued. It occurred to him, not much later, that his real anger at Sebastian's fixation with Ana was less about his thoughtless words and more that his friend knew more about his own mother than he did.

When Aleksandr was little, she would speak in her low mom voice, as he thought of it, and whisper about her childhood as a Deschanel, running and playing with her cousins at *Ophélie,* growing up at Magnolia Grace. She told him about how she met his father in Maine, and what their courtship was like. But there was a glaring gap of about ten years in her stories, one he noticed but never asked about. He was afraid to. Of learning something about his mora that might be upsetting to him, something he couldn't un-learn.

But Sebastian had stirred this curiosity anew, and not in the ways his friend probably expected. Aleksandr was no longer afraid of what he might find. He only wanted to know. He wanted to live in her world and see what she saw.

Tremé was only a ten or fifteen-minute walk from his apartment on Chartres, just a skip and a jump across Rampart. The beaming, almost blinding lights of the Armstrong Park arch boasted a glaring invitation. *Step right up!*

On his first time in the park, he wandered the grounds, inspecting every sculpture, pausing in reverie at the monument of Congo Square. He fed the ducks and swayed to the jazz that was always, inevitably, there as a soundtrack to his venturing. He adored the jazz funerals and stepped in time to the second-line parades. The spirit of the past and present of the African American community of New Orleans was alive at all times in this fascinating district of his city, and especially within the park. His enjoyment stretched so far that he never did venture further out to any of the bars and clubs Sebastian had named in his attempts to bring Ana's past to shame.

Aleksandr's love of Tremé and Armstrong Park was another secret he kept from his parents. At first, he was ashamed, seeing as his reason for even exploring that area was to learn more about his mother's dark past, but over time that shame faded and was replaced by a childlike desire to have something his parents *didn't* know about.

But Aleksandr was not great at keeping secrets, and so he eventually told his uncle Jacob.

He couldn't pinpoint what, specifically, about Jacob made him so willing to open himself up to the man, but he couldn't deny he was drawn to others with atypical childhoods. Adults who could only smile awkwardly when other adults recalled a fond story from their youth. Sebastian. Jacob. They both understood this sensation of being ostracized from society, in their own ways. Because of this gap, where most adults had a very "adultiness" about them that made it hard to talk about difficult things, Jacob still possessed a great deal of youthful innocence in him. A desire to make others laugh, or smile, to make up for that gap in his own development.

Jacob knew about Armstrong Park, and also the precise motivation that brought Aleksandr there to begin with. While Jacob said, with some trepidation, that it wasn't his place to fill the holes in Aleksandr's story of Ana's life, he could say with great confidence that Ana had left a powerful impression on him in his formative years. And he, Jacob, didn't take kindness for granted the way others might. When it appeared for him, he remembered it and held on to it, and never let it go, not entirely.

This was why, of his broken friends, he had chosen Jacob, and not Sebastian, in his time of need.

JACOB PLOPPED BESIDE ALEKSANDR ON THE BENCH AND THRUST A BAG at him. "Oats. For the duckies."

"Oh, you remembered." Aleksandr half-smiled at the lunch baggie, which had been so haphazardly packed that the grains were spilling from the top.

Jacob poked his temple with his forefinger. "Irish memory."

"Is that a real thing?"

Jacob lifted his shoulders with a light laugh. "I don't know, but you're the first person who bothered to question me saying it."

Aleksandr didn't bother to quibble with small talk. His chest hurt so bad that if he didn't know better he'd say he was on the verge of cardiac arrest. He thrust the phone at Jacob. "Here. Read."

Jacob looked at him, then down at the phone. With his thumb, he pressed the down key until he had finished. "Yeesh. Sort of vague, huh?"

Aleksandr nodded. He squeezed the bag so tight that oats spattered to the ground. Several ducks surged forth from the water in delight. He moved his legs in a robotic fashion, not keen on getting mobbed by water fowl but lacking any energy to get completely out of the way.

Jacob knocked on his knee with a loose fist. “Sucks. I’m sorry, Aleksei. Really. Life can really be a fuck-all sometimes.”

“But see...” Aleksei screwed his mouth into a tight pinch when he felt the tears come. “I don’t even know what I’m supposed to take from this. I have no clue what she’s talking about. I was hoping...”

Jacob turned his brogue up to eleven. “Tha’ I might put on ma Irish hat and decipher the lass’s meanin’?”

“That’s a thing, too?”

“Not in this case, I’m afraid.” Jacob read the message again, then slipped the case in Aleksandr’s pocket. “There’s a secret to this, though. To taking someone’s elusive words and making them clear. Wanna know what it is?”

Aleksandr lit up. “Yes! Please!”

Jacob sighed and leaned in. “Ye need to ask ’er.”

“Seriously?” Aleksandr grunted and swung back against the wooden bench. “She said not to reply.”

“She said not to reply to the text,” Jacob clarified for him. “Which, come on, would you want your mom reading your texts?”

Aleksandr reddened. “I suppose not.”

“So call her,” Jacob went on. “Ring her up. And if you’re worried that’s awkward, then write her a letter. I can tell you how that works. You find a piece of paper, any will do, and then—”

“I *know* how to write a letter, Uncle Jacob.”

Jacob threw his hands up. “All right, then. Your generation is so tied to their electronics, I wasn’t sure.”

"I mean, I've never actually sent one, but I'm sure—"

"Aha!" Jacob cried, pointing his finger at him like a sword. "As I suspected."

Aleksandr rolled his eyes.

"Call her, mate. Or attempt the archaic form of communication known as letter writing, but *communicate.* You asked me here for my sage advice—"

Another eye roll.

"—So here it is. The one and only thing that has ever honestly hurt my relationship with Amelia is when we weren't communicating right."

"But... what about..."

"What happened in the cabin?" Jacob finished. He leaned forward, folding his hands out over his knees. "That wounded us, both of us, in different ways, but what hurt us as a couple was that we forgot how to talk to each other."

"Fiona said what she wanted to say, though, and if I push her, she might get angry."

"Stop."

"What?"

"Making excuses," Jacob said. "There are a million reasons your girl might not want to be direct with you, but there's only a single way to find out. Only one. The worst thing that will happen is she won't tell you and then you know she doesn't value you enough to be forthright. That leaves you exactly where you are now, except with the advantage of a wee bit more closure."

"I don't know."

"Or she tells you. And there are so many outcomes for what she might say, but whatever the words, you can figure them out together, instead of stressing alone."

Aleksandr reached into the haphazard oat bag and drew out a large handful. He chucked it as far as his arm would throw. The ducks fluttered to the scattered food. "What should I say?"

"Maybe start with your questions."

Aleksandr puffed out a gust of air. "I have so many."

Jacob pulled the bag from him and dipped his hand in. "Then start at the beginning, Aleksei. And don't stop asking until you have your answers."

21
ANASOFIYA

Anasofiya refilled Amelia's mug, then her own, from the ceramic decanter on the veranda table. The steam from the pressed coffee swirled like a fine mist on the surface.

"I can't believe I'm about to do this." Ana's voice was shaky. It echoed full of cracks, full of doubt.

Please, Aidrik, Wraith, both of you... respect my need to get calm before I do this. Be silent for me, if you love me.

Yes, Anasofiya. Wraith.

My will is yours, Kjære. Aidrik.

Thank you.

Amelia gripped her mug from across the table with an encouraging smile masking heavy eyes. Ana wondered once again if her cousin was getting any sleep. "This is exciting, Ana. Truly. If it works, if I can see him... then think of the gift you'll be giving to Finn and Aleksei."

Ana breathed in the steam from her cup. "I know, but what about all the unknowns?"

"We've talked about them. Would it help to go through

them again, one by one?" Amelia had slipped into her therapist voice. Ana suppressed a grin.

"Yes. Okay," Ana said, with a quick nod.

"You start."

"What if this is all in my imagination?"

Amelia took a sip. "We'll either confirm or put the thought to bed today, when you show me. If I, someone with only obscure connections to Aidrik, can see him, then anyone can."

"What if I'm not strong enough to keep him visible?"

"You were strong enough to create him," Amelia said evenly. "And your Wraith, whom others saw in Farjhem, right?"

Ana said yes.

"Then you're asking the wrong question, and the right question is already answered."

"Which is?"

Amelia leaned forward. "The correct question is, can you make him visible at all, and that answer is yes. We'll find out today if others can see him. Don't put more pressure on yourself than is needed, Ana. Even if you can only bring him back for short visits, that's significantly more than what Finn and Aleksei have today. Five minutes with Aidrik would be a tremendous gift for the two men in his life who never got to say goodbye. That's the right question, Ana. Would they rather have five minutes with him, or none at all? I think all the time about what I would give, for five minutes with my brother, Ben. And I think I would give everything I have."

Ana considered her own losses. She would have said the same about Aidrik, before he appeared within her. Her focus had been so rooted in being able to deliver in a big way, when perhaps a small way would be more than enough.

"You're right. As always." Ana forced a smile. "What if… what if it's not really him?"

"You don't really believe that's a possibility."

"When I see him, and hear him, I know, in my bones, deep in my marrow, that it's him. It's my evigbond, back. Within me. *Here.*" Ana rapped on her heart with a fist. "But I also know how badly I wanted him to be back. How many times has someone created their own reality to deal with grief? And how *real* has that reality felt, when matched against the strong desire to combat loss?"

"Do you want my professional opinion?"

"If you're comfortable giving it."

"Yes, people do sometimes retreat into their own head and create a reality that takes them back to a time before their life changed for the worse." Amelia drew her knees up onto the chair and wrapped her arms around them, locking her hands. "But there's often a great underlying disorder to accompany that. Dissociative personality disorder, schizophrenia, bipolar disorder, something. It's very unlikely that a perfectly healthy woman grieving her mate would create something as vivid and real as what you've described to me. Stress can produce a lot of unusual symptoms in a person, but the more likely way it would manifest for you is through sickness, fatigue, anger, and so on. Oftentimes, the effects of stress come latently, even months or years after the painful event. And what about Wraith? Wraith was certainly not something you asked for." Amelia paused for a moment. A spot of color appeared in her cheeks, while a visible pallor spread over the rest of her face.

"Are you okay?"

Amelia pursed her lips as if fighting back a wave of nausea and waved her hand. "Fine. Sorry. That happens sometimes. Speaking of the effects of stress." She breathed in and hugged her knees tighter. "Ana, I don't think you've created this in your head, at least not in any psychological way. We should talk to my mom and see what she knows about etheric summoning, because she might be able to put some of your fears at ease. As far as I know, we don't have any in the family. I don't ever recall even seeing it mentioned in the records."

"I've been told it's the most uncommon ability there is." Ana sighed. "Of course, I would be the family weirdo. If I can't heal someone back from the dead, I can manifest them apparently."

"I won't tell you how badly I wish I had either of those gifts," Amelia said softly. "Because I know your anguish is real. But I do think the vast majority of the stress you have over this is because you carry the burden of the success or failure. Ana, I know you're scared about the unknowns, but *life* is all about unknowns. We could be here one minute, laughing, enjoying life, and the next dead of a heart attack. I could leave to go home and get in a fatal car accident. This could happen to any of us, at any time. I don't envy the seers in this family, because that's no way to live. All we have to decide is what to do with the time that is given to us."

Ana cocked her head with a sideways grin. "I'm married to a Tolkien nerd. Did you think I wouldn't notice you slipped in a *Fellowship* quote?"

Amelia looked down with a short laugh. "I hoped you might. You're smiling again, anyway."

"I had really wanted to deliver this for Finn's birthday," Ana mused.

"Girl, you sent for his damn *boat.* On the scale of gift giving, you're basically the messiah. We should all bow down to you."

Ana laughed.

"But if it works today," Amelia went on, "then you can consider it round two for his birthday. An encore."

"Hell of an encore."

"Exactly. Messiah." Amelia gestured toward her cousin. "I

think we've worked through your biggest questions. Wanna give it a shot?"

She did. She didn't. While this step would lead her one closer to unveiling Aidrik to Finn and Aleksei, it also meant there was no turning back. That the voices in her head, and the faces that materialized, so far, only for her, were real.

If they were real—and she believed they must be, or she wouldn't be sitting in front of her cousin ready to prove this—then their lives were forever changed. Amelia had said she would give anything for five minutes with her brother, but not everyone felt this way about their dearly departed. For some, grieving led to a closure of a door that wasn't easily re-opened. So much of grief was a private business that Ana wasn't completely certain where her loved ones were in the process.

"Ana?"

"Yeah, okay. I'm ready."

Amelia gripped her mug tighter. Her face colored with nervous anticipation, but she didn't flinch or look away as Ana stood and drew in a breath for strength.

All right, Aidrik. I'm ready for you. Are you ready?

Aye, Kjære. I have been ready for this.

What about me, Anasofiya? Wraith asked.

All of Farjhem saw you, you voyeur.

Right. I'll be here in the darkness, awaiting your moment of need.

Don't be flip.

Tell me when, Kjære.

"When," she whispered, eyes closed tight.

Ana heard Amelia's chair skip across the stones and an audible, throaty gasp. Ana's eyes flew open.

"Jesus, Mary, and Joseph." Amelia clutched the lattice on a nearby trellis, a vine of bougainvillea balled in her fist.

"Hello, Amelia. We are well met." Aidrik's voice sounded

clear and crisp, as well-formed as either of the two women standing in shock on either side of him. His red hair flowed over the top of his head like a fresh flame. His pale, youthful face offered a disarming, kind smile. His scar, nonexistent, replaced by smooth, unmarred flesh.

"Nice to meet you finally," Amelia managed. She loosened her grip on the plant. "You're... uh... younger than I pictured."

"Empyreans cease to physically age beyond approximately twenty-five years of age, in human equivalency. So while I have walked for over four millennia, this is the face I have borne through all but my very earliest years of existence."

"Fascinating," Amelia said, slowly inching out of the protection of the trellis. "Can I... touch you?"

Aidrik's smile stretched wider. "You may."

Ana watched in stunned silence as Amelia stepped sideways toward Aidrik, hand outstretched.

Her eyes registered her shock as she made contact. She first poked his arm and then moved closer so she could run her hands across his flesh. "Ana, he's as real as you or me."

Ana's knees went weak. She couldn't stop the tears, which lurched forward in a flood. "Yeah?"

"Yeah," Amelia answered. "Oh, yeah."

Panic appeared in Aidrik's face. "Anasofiya, the chair. Quickly!"

Ana had only a second to register his words before Amelia crumpled like a rag doll. Aidrik scooped her into his arms before she hit the flagstones.

"Disregard the chair. I will carry her to the couch. Fetch a glass of water and a damp cloth."

She's in shock, Ana thought as she rushed to comply with Aidrik's request, but even as she thought these things, a voice in her head, Wraith, whispered, *not shock.*

Amelia's head lolled to the side. Her glassy eyes fluttered as they fought to stay open. Ana knelt beside Aidrik and handed him first the dish cloth, and then the glass of water.

"You must call Colleen," he said, without taking his eyes off Amelia. He spread the damp cloth over her face and then folded it and rested it upon her forehead.

"What's wrong with her, Aidrik?"

"You must listen to me, Anasofiya. You cannot leave Amelia's side. Not now, or later, if you can help it." Aidrik took Amelia's hands in his and used his thumb to massage small circles in her palm. She moaned and stirred in response.

"You're scaring me. What's happening to her?"

"Call Colleen," he reiterated.

Ana answered the door to see her aunt looking precisely as she always did, groomed and dressed for all of life's most important matters. Her face, by contrast, was deep with worry.

"Tell me," she commanded.

"I..." Ana turned to look for Aidrik, but he was gone. She felt the fullness of him within her once again.

Colleen brushed past and hurried to her daughter's side. In the ten minutes it had taken her to get to Ana's house, Amelia had slipped from consciousness. A sheen of sweat coated her face, her silvery hair plastered around her temples, soaked. "I'm here, darling. I'm here, baby girl."

Ana stepped forward and lifted the glass of water, handing it to her aunt in a helpless thrust.

"Where's Jacob?" Colleen asked over her shoulder.

"He might be at home. I'm not—"

"Call him. Now."

"Aunt Colleen, what the hell is happening? Do you know?"

Colleen's hand fell on Amelia's bare belly. She rubbed slow circles over her flesh, whispering words Ana couldn't hear.

"Amelia is pregnant," she said, rocking back on her heels. "Not pregnant as most are pregnant, but pregnant in the way you were with Aleksei. Short in duration. Violent. Dangerous. Do you understand?"

The blood rushed from Ana's head and out through her limbs. She sagged against the grandfather clock behind her. "Oh God. But she's not carrying an Empyrean. I don't understand..."

"No, but she is carrying an heir to The Prophecy," Colleen said evenly, hands still connected to her daughter. "I don't understand it either, but I can see for myself this is not typical. Now, call Jacob, darling. And then prepare a bed. If you have plans, cancel them."

"All right. Okay." Ana fumbled with her phone.

Colleen stretched one hand back and gripped Ana's. "Be calm, Anasofiya. I know you're afraid, but we must be strong for her, as Aidrik and Finn were for you. Only you know what this experience will be like. She will need you, more, perhaps, than her own husband."

Colleen is correct. Your calm will benefit not only you, but Amelia. She needs you now.

Aidrik, I almost died. I almost died, and what if...

You mustn't even think it, Anasofiya. Not even for a moment of weakness.

"Call Jacob."

THE STORM

“The snow doesn’t give a soft white damn whom it touches.”

e.e. cummings

22
TRISTAN

Tristan navigated the crowds of the Djemaa El Fna, using both his eyes and his less traditional senses to locate the booth Anders had sent him to find. Sandy green umbrellas balanced in the open courtyard, blocking his view of the clay-colored market beyond.

Half of those congregated came to a slow stop as a warbled voice sounded across a series of loudspeakers. Tristan didn't speak Arabic, but he recognized the Muslim call to prayer, Adhan, and turned in the direction others now faced, which he assumed was the direction of Mecca.

There was something altogether beautiful, almost enchanting about the unseen muezzin voice speaking to the masses from the nearby mosque. Anders explained to him that the prayer was a continuous recognition of Allah as their one and only God. He broke into Arabic and recited a single line, which he then translated to Tristan as, "There is no strength or power except from God."

"Why do you know this?" Tristan had asked, for what need did an Empyrean have of Islamic doctrine?

"Why do we study anything, Tristan?"

To learn, Tristan replied in his head as Anders walked away. Everything was a lesson with his mentor, and Tristan continuously felt as if he was ten steps behind where he needed to be.

This trip to the medina was no different. Anders wouldn't tell him the name of the man he was to see. *Use who you are,* he had said, a strange set of instructions for a young man who still had no *idea* who he was.

Tristan wrapped himself in the loose-fitting serwal and thobe and ventured from their mountain enclave on Djebel Toubkal, and out into the vibrant city of Marrakesh without a clue of his goal. When he paid the rickshaw carriage driver in what little dirham Anders had given him for his journey, he jumped into the dusty medina and kept his eyes low and his senses open.

The rich scents of saffron and clover burned his nose as he passed a vendor calling to him for a sample. Tristan tripped and almost overturned a large cart of nuts and legumes towering six feet high, where the shop owner stood in a giant podium, like a god.

Tristan pivoted, pressing through the crowd. A hiss sounded in his ear as a snake charmer lowered his dazed, drugged python to Tristan's shoulder, nudging him to go ahead, touch, hold him. He started to refuse when a monkey wearing pajamas rode by on a unicycle, confusing his senses further.

He broke into an open area. More green umbrellas surrounded him, overwhelming him, but he also spotted, finally, an entrance to the market.

Tristan positioned himself sideways and squeezed through a break in the bustling activity. He stood before the entrance to the narrow market. The stalls crowded tightly together, filled to every inch with vibrantly hued textiles, from elaborate handbags to woolen blankets, to silver and gold jewelry.

He lifted his gaze and let his eyes scan the proprietors. Men and women, leaning forth to the passersby, using their persuasion to get anyone to stop, even for a moment. None looked at Tristan with anything more than the same passing interest—"Pretty hijab for your pretty wife." "Wallets of real leather, see how soft, how smooth."—and he wondered again how far he would have to wander before he found the strange man who was the key to the African sector of the Brotherhood's resistance.

Dagr, our Moroccan leader, was captured by Oriana's men. We must seek out his second-in-command. We need Africa, Tristan. We need them all, if we can.

Second-in-command to all of the African-based Empyreans. Seemed fairly prestigious, so what would such a powerful creature be doing in a dirty, crowded market?

Use who you are.

In the beginning, Tristan fought bitterly against Anders' strange authority, where he withheld just enough information to drive Tristan to frustration, but taught him enough that he couldn't completely complain, either. Anders seemed to enjoy the discomfort of others if it came as the result of an important lesson.

"Use who I am," Tristan muttered, knowing he would, because he must, but wishing he didn't need Anders and his vague wisdom.

Tristan opened his mind and allowed the flood of the market in. The assault nearly sent him careening into a cart of glass animals. Too much, too soon.

He imagined himself hitting the "X" button on all the minds in the crowded hall, one by one. He was positive none were the right ones, because the one he was looking for would have a wall where there should be an open vault.

His world cleared again as he eliminated the noisiness of everyone else's thoughts. As he progressed down the line of stalls, he pressed the invisible "X" above each person he passed, the other part of his mind already steps ahead, searching for the wall.

The bright glare of the sun peeked around the next corner, as he reached the end of the line. Tristan reached up to shield his eyes when darkness passed before him.

He looked up and found the wall.

"Come," said a deep voice behind a carefully swaddled turban.

Tristan was yanked forth into the sun.

THEY DOUBLED BACK THROUGH THE OPEN MEDINA AND THROUGH A building on the other side. Up several sets of crumbling stairs they climbed until they emerged onto an empty rooftop.

Tristan looked across the sea of other roofs on the outskirts of the medina. Many housed cafes, or other gathering places.

The man unwrapped his face, setting the cloth in a neat pile on the table. His translucent pale flesh explained immediately why he had needed to cover himself as a shopkeeper.

He gestured for Tristan to sit in the metal chair on the other side.

"Tarek, you may call me," the Empyrean said. "And you are Tristan."

"How did you know?"

"Same as you. I, too, can breach a telepathic block."

Tristan balked. Anders had said his gift was rare, and here he was, having a conversation with someone just like him. "I never got the chance with you. It was like you ambushed me or something."

Tarek smiled. Dirt creased the corners at the sides of his mouth. "You might say I was waiting for you. I know of Dagr's fate."

"That he was captured? Yeah, everyone is pretty upset about it."

Tarek set his mouth. He folded his hands over his lap. "Is that what they told you? Captured in the beginning, yes. Tortured, without doubt. I very much doubt Dagr still lives, though. Our adversary is not known for patience, or mercy."

Tristan sighed. He'd never met Dagr, but he'd heard stories. Of his bloodlust, of course, but also his wisdom. He was very, very old. "Wow. That's awful."

"You look surprised. Your mentor is not so," Tarek said evenly.

The rising intonations of the ancient Berbers singing their songs carried upward. Tristan looked away, toward the sound. "I don't know what Anders' motivations are. All I know is, he wants you to come back with me."

Tarek followed Tristan's attention. "Do you know the meaning of the Djemaa El Fna, Tristan?"

Tristan looked at him. "I wouldn't have even known how to pronounce it."

Tarek's smile was placating. "No one can agree, to tell you truthfully. There are several interpretations, because each word has different meanings depending on the context. Most speculate it translates to 'the assembly of death', in homage to the public executions here in the eleventh century.'"

"Sweet," Tristan said, perking up at what would surely be the start of a juicy tale.

"Fna means death, but it also means courtyard. You see,

very different implications. As Djemaa also means mosque, many call it 'the mosque at the end of the world.'"

"Um, okay." This was less interesting, by far.

"There are others yet, Tristan, who equate the life of the dead with the life of a nobody," Tarek went on. "Those who do come here to blend in, to become part of the medina itself. By this definition, we sit atop the 'assembly of the nobodies.'"

Tristan thought now he understood why Anders wanted Tarek. They were both a fan of obscure, random lessons in history that most others could do without.

"You wonder why I tell you this," Tarek finished.

"I'm double blocked now, so I don't know how you could know this," Tristan said in defense.

"A deduction only," Tarek said with a grin as he tapped his temple. "I would want to know why the old man rambles on about seemingly pointless facts."

Old man. He doesn't look any older than me. "Yeah, okay, so why?" Tristan didn't wear a watch, but he checked the position of the sun. If they didn't leave soon, they would be stuck in the city after dark, which Anders strongly cautioned against. Pick-pockets would be the least of his problems. Oriana's scouts prowled at night.

"Because a nobody is a threat to no one," Tarek said. He reached into an old, faded cooler beneath the table and produced two Cokes. Tristan couldn't read the words, but the logo was universal. Tarek handed him one. "One who is not a threat escapes harm. They get to live their life in peace."

Tristan sipped from the sugary drink, which was so much sweeter than the ones back home. "What does that mean? Is that a way of telling me you'd rather be safe and comfortable here than join us and actually fix the problem that made you go into hiding in the first place?"

Tarek's brows lifted. "Not such a child, after all. I will

follow you, Tristan, to Anders. To the others with you. I tell you this because the African contingent of the Brotherhood has never had the cohesion of, say, the European sects. Many have blended in, within the Djemaa El Fna, within the medinas of Fez, the markets of Egypt. They travel with Bedouins. They become healers in villages in the Sierra Leone, or businessmen in Johannesburg. We are less affected so far from Farjhem that we have turned to a life that is vastly different. Very few have ever even *seen* Farjhem, save for in the minds of their brethren. To them, this is a life that does not exist, and does not need to. What is a revolution to those who don't feel the burn in their hearts and the passion in their fingertips? These are not Birgers and Astrids, young Tristan. They are not disenfranchised, only displaced, but without the experience to comprehend what is missing."

Tristan slumped back in his chair. He drained half the Coke in one swill. "You're saying we came here for nothing."

"You came to learn what you needed to learn," Tarek amended.

THEY REACHED THE CAVE SHORTLY AFTER SUNDOWN. ANDERS AND Tarek disappeared for a walk, but Tristan could hear the escalating voices; the disappointment in Anders.

Tristan had read enough books, watched enough movies to know that not everyone had the desire to fight for what was theirs. But Anders was searching for more than allies in Africa. He sought some sort of self-validation. To show up to the conclave with Birger, Astrid, and the others and have something of value to produce.

Tristan found Harriett in a corner, wrapped in a long chador, scribbling on paper by candlelight. The smile on her face when she rose her head to welcome him lighted up the small space, and Tristan's troubles of the day—of, specifically, the fear he had disappointed Anders somehow, as if he could be blamed for the complacency of their African contingent—slipped down and into the ground, where they belonged.

"Who are you writing to?" he asked, though he knew.

"Dad," Harriett said, her voice soft. Though she hadn't spoken for over a decade until recently, she seemingly had no desire to exercise her vocal chords. She always spoke in a tone just above a whisper. "Anders said we could post it on our way back through Marrakesh."

"I know it must be hard, sending him letters when there's no way for him to write back." He should write to his dad, too. He even thought of the words he might use. But he couldn't bring himself to pick up the pen, and Harriett never shamed him for this failure, though he felt it nonetheless.

Harriett closed her eyes and shrugged with a dreamy smile. "The letters are for him anyway. Not for me. I sleep better knowing he sleeps better."

Tristan kissed her on the forehead. "Yeah? That's because you're a sweetheart. You always think of others first."

"How was the medina?" she asked, folding her letter. She slid it into the envelope and turned it over, scribbling an address on the front.

"Crazy." Tristan laughed. "Overwhelming. Anders isn't happy."

"Not everyone wants to fight," Harriett said, and Tristan had a small warmth spread across his chest as he realized she'd said exactly what he'd been thinking moments ago.

"Yeah, well, I just want to be useful," Tristan countered. He scooted across the dusty ground, settling in next to her. "I feel like an errand boy."

Harriett grinned and tapped his head. "An errand boy with a very important weapon."

"Didn't even get to use it today. Tarek already knew we were coming."

"I bet you could learn something from him, if he's like you. No one else knows what you can do the way he does."

Tristan shrugged. "Yeah. Maybe. If Anders can talk him into coming with us. We leave soon for Spain. Thorvald's territory." He shuddered. The creature intimidated him.

"No one to convince there, at least," Harriett said and squeezed his hand. "Don't trouble yourself with what happened today, Tris. Because of you, we have all of Southeast Asia now. Yiva is only in because of your quick thinking and persuasive words." She leaned her head on his shoulder. "And anyway, I think Anders is overreacting. It's not like this is going to be a gunfight, right? These are all supernatural creatures. Whatever we do, we don't need numbers so much as we need an advantage."

"Aren't numbers an advantage?"

"Only if you have the right ones."

Tristan didn't respond. After the chaos of the medina—after the chaos of the past weeks traveling in subterfuge, always steps away from very serious danger—he wanted instead to bask in the quiet comfort of Harriett's warm body and the heady glow from the half-burned candle. Here, away from the world, they were no more or less than the sum of their parts.

He closed his eyes and dreamed of his mother.

23
ANASOFIYA

Ana and Finn's home had turned into a virtual pup tent, family healers coming and going at all hours.

Amelia had been well enough still to go home, but Colleen requested she stay put at Magnolia Grace. She cited the size being nearly double Amelia's cottage, which would allow for precisely the scenario that now played out in Ana's home.

Ana didn't mind. She remembered those early days, when the fatigue settled over her not in a gradual way but all at once, throwing her body into a tailspin. From there, nothing was the same again, not until long after she'd recovered from childbirth.

She talked Amelia through this as she sat at her bedside while one family healer after another stopped in for their shifts. Soothed her when she cried from the pain and discomfort. Joked with her when she had moments of clarity, and ultimately, joy.

Amelia, like Ana, had never wanted children. And now

Amelia, like Ana, discovered she was having one and had never wanted anything more in the world.

But Amelia, unlike Ana, struggled more with the changes taking her body hostage. She spent more time asleep than awake, something Ana hadn't started until she was several weeks further along than Amelia was now. When she was conscious, she often drifted somewhere neither Ana nor Jacob could reach her.

Jacob left the room only to use the bathroom. He had his meals brought in, and he slept at his wife's side, running his hands in gentle circles over her belly, whispering about the moment their little girl would emerge into the world. What they might name her, the things they would do with her.

Ana tried to reel in her warnings about what Amelia would go through in the coming weeks, because it was important Amelia stayed mentally cogent—imperilment was a serious risk, Aunt Colleen had said—but she did make a point to prepare Jacob. He needed to understand what Amelia's body would experience, but also to understand how it would affect him. Finn talked to him as well and shared his own reflections from that time. Namely, his fears, as he worried daily if Ana would die before she saw her own son born.

"Things are so much different this time around," Finn told him. "We were in the wilderness, with only ourselves. Amelia is surrounded by an entire family of healers, as well as legitimate medical doctors."

"I don't think they teach supernatural childbirth techniques in medical school," Jacob murmured as he massaged Amelia's hands lightly enough not to wake her.

"Your baby might be unique, but she's still a baby. Not a single one of us will let anything happen to her," Ana comforted.

Jacob looked up. "She?"

Ana and Finn exchanged a look. "Didn't Colleen tell you?"

Jacob's head slowly shook.

Ana's face erupted in a smile. Good news, that was what Jacob needed right now. "You're having a little girl, Jacob."

ANNE CAME TO RELIEVE THEM. "YOU'VE BEEN BY HER SIDE ALMOST A full day. Aunt C is working on a rotation so y'all can go back to some normalcy."

"We don't mind," Ana insisted.

"She *also* said we have weeks ahead and she needs you to stay fresh."

"I see." Finn pulled on his sweater. "Shall we pop in on Aleksei, then?"

"While he's with Fiona? What if he wants his privacy?"

"They've had a whole day of privacy."

"What if they're..."

Anne snorted. "Aleksandr is a good boy. He would never."

Ana and Finn both gave her a look. "You must have missed what happened in the Quinlan base camp," he said with a brow raise.

Anne's mouth formed a wide O, and she quietly slipped into the bedroom where Amelia slept.

Ana laughed when Anne was gone. "You scandalized the poor girl."

Finn lifted his shoulders. "Have to get my entertainment somehow, right?"

WHEN ALEKSANDR DIDN'T ANSWER HIS DOOR RIGHT AWAY, ANA TRIED not to imagine her son and Fiona twisted in his bed sheets.

"Should we use your key?" Finn asked.

The door swung open before she could decide. Aleksandr's

face stared out at them, red-faced and tear-stained. He sniffled, lips quivering. With a glance back and forth between the two of them, he buried his face in his hands.

Ana dropped her handbag on the floor and pulled Aleksandr into her arms. Finn let out a sigh and closed the door, leading them to the couch.

Ana ran her hands over her son's face in haphazard appraisal, wiping away his tears with her thumbs. She kissed his cheeks. "What happened? How long have you been here like this?"

"All day." He got the words out before more tears assaulted him. He bit his lip so hard a bloom of red appeared in the center. "Mora, she never came."

"Never came?" Finn repeated. He sat at the other side of Aleksei with a hand on his shoulder. "She never came to your apartment?"

"To New Orleans."

Ana eyed Finn from behind Aleksandr's head. The confusion in his expression matched hers. They had the call from Nora, saying Fiona made it off from Dublin. She'd been worried, because it was Fiona's first time on a plane, but Ana assured her there was nothing to be worried about, that she would be in good hands.

So where was she?

"Aleksei..." Ana began, but he reached for her hands pressed to his face and lowered them. The man looking back startled her. "Honey, we're trying to understand."

"I really just need to be alone right now."

"That's too bad, because we're not going anywhere until we get to the bottom of this," Finn asserted.

Ana shook her head at him. "What did she say, sweetheart? Fiona? What did she say about her visit?"

Aleksandr looked at his hands, which rested on his thighs. "Nothing. She said... see you soon. And then I didn't see her."

"Why didn't you call us?" Finn pressed. He fitted one of his hands to his son's. "That's what we're here for, Aleksei."

Aleksandr shrugged. His eyes stayed down. He sniffled and blinked away fresh tears.

"I just don't understand..." Finn sat back. He seemed to be puzzling through all they knew, and now, all they didn't. "Nora just call—"

Ana's eyes widened to silence him. Until they knew what had happened with Fiona, adding more details to Aleksandr's turmoil would be torture, not relief. "We'll contact the Quinlans. They'll know what's happened, and then we can sort this out."

"No." Aleksandr's head swung back and forth. "Please, don't get involved. This is my problem to solve."

Finn moved his hand up Aleksei's arm, to his shoulder. "Son—"

"Far, I mean it!" Aleksandr cried. His head shot up; his cheeks flushed so dark, Ana couldn't tell if this was caused by his distress or his parents doing what parents did best: interfering. "Stay out of this!"

Finn's own face took on a spot of color at the shaming from his son. "Okay, Aleksei. If that's what you want."

"It is."

Finn nodded. He wore his distress plainly. "Can we get you anything? Dinner?"

The fire went out of Aleksandr. "Some privacy." He offered them both a pitiful smile that only made Ana's heart sink further into the couch. "Please."

There was nothing to be done. Aleksandr was an adult, in the ways that mattered, and he was only asking them to leave, rather than telling them, for their benefit. Ana looked helplessly at Finn, who dithered somewhere between tears and rage.

"Okay, sweetie." Ana stood first. She pulled her hair in a tight fist at the nape of her neck, looking around the room for something she could spot that might need her help later; an excuse to return.

Finn took another few seconds to gather himself. He squeezed Aleksandr's knee, several short grabs, then stood. "Call us, if you need anything. Hell, even if you want me to walk down to Central Grocery and get you a mufaletta—"

"Far. Dad."

"Sure. Yeah. Okay." Finn did a similar vulnerable pass around the room as she had, then sighed, a sound full of defeat and so much more.

They kissed their son and left.

"SOMETHING ISN'T RIGHT," ANA SAID AS SHE SLID INTO THE DRIVER'S seat. "Nora watched her enter the airport. She watched the plane take off."

"Where did she connect?"

"Chicago, I think."

"Maybe she missed her connection."

"Maybe." Ana sensed Finn was searching for a way to deal with his son no longer needing him, so she didn't point out all the obvious reasons this made no sense. If she was delayed, she would have called Aleksandr. And certainly, by now, she would have found a new flight to New Orleans.

There is no gain in dwelling, Anasofiya.

Dammit, Aidrik. Not right now. You have no idea how hard that was, to just walk out.

He is my son, as well.

Ana turned the key and the engine of her BMW roared to

life. Beside her, Finn fidgeted, chewing his nails, tapping his foot. When she looked at him, he didn't seem to notice. Within her, Aidrik exhibited his own form of anxiety, a restless stirring that made her anxiousness flare.

"Let's not go home just yet," Finn said abruptly beside her.

"Where would we go, then?"

Finn's sad eyes sparkled. "Somewhere you haven't been."

FINN REACHED HIS HAND DOWN TO ANA. SHE TOOK IT, AND HE GAVE A quick, comfortable tug as she came up and over the bow of Forbia.

Forbia was a forty-foot glass trawler, built for long hauls. Finn fixed her up when he was a teenager and turned her into his constant companion. To hear others on Summer Island speak of Finn was to see him through eyes Ana never would: running his nine and ten trap trawls with buoys the colors of the Irish and Scottish flags, spitting in the face of the season's change as he boldly pushed Forbia well into winter, daring Mother Nature to stop him.

The deck revealed even more about her husband. Where he was fastidious around the house, this was a piece of his life where not everything needed to be in place. The flooring was half-painted and peeling up, stained by saltwater and the sea life that had been dumped on the surface for years on end. Nearly everything, from the rails to the bolted-in chairs, had a layer of film, a residue of nature's mark.

For weeks, Finn had wandered around her world, lost and looking for purpose. Now, Ana would experience his.

"Hang on," he called from the captain's area. "She's a bit jerky on the start, but once we get her offshore, she's smooth as silk."

Ana gripped the back of one of the once-white passenger

chairs. She pitched forward as the engine surged to life, planting her feet to maintain balance, but more, to show she could belong here with him, too.

Finn's muscles tensed under his sweater as he navigated his ship from port. Long ripples appeared on the surface of the lake behind the ship, leading back to land, to their life beyond. But what lay ahead was far more interesting to Ana.

Once she gained her sea legs, she stumbled carefully toward him, joining him in the bridge. He smiled from his peripheral and looped an arm over her shoulder as they steered through the dark Pontchartrain under the sky and stars.

FINN SET FORBIA TO DRIFT FAR ENOUGH OUT THAT ANA COULD SEE NO sign of the life on land except dots of lights. It never stopped amazing her how vast the lake was, never more apparent than when you were floated in the center of her.

"You did this for me," Finn said, turning to her. A breeze whipped his blond hair, which he'd let grow to his ears since they'd come home. He kept saying he was going to sheer it off, but Ana loved to wrap her hands in its softness, bringing it to her lips as she made love to him. "I want you to stop and remind yourself of that, every now and then, when you get silly ideas in your head."

Ana sipped her beer, smiling as she swallowed. "I don't know what you're talking about. I've never had a silly idea in my life."

"You married me."

"You're right." She pulled the sweater he'd given her tighter. It was one of his, a dark gray wool piece he'd brought from Maine. The fabric smelled of him. "That was pretty silly."

Finn's eyes had a sheen to them as he observed her, wordless for several long moments. His mouth parted. He reached his hand out to push her hair from her face. "I've never taken another woman on my ship, Ana. Not one."

The admission caught her in the stomach, leaving her breathless. Their quick courtship, which was only now coming up on a full year, despite all they'd been through, meant every moment with her husband led to the possibility of further discovery. "I guess I must have left quite the impression," she said, when she caught her bearings enough to find words.

"Tonight, when we were at Aleksei's, watching him deal with a very adult thing, and choosing to do it without our help, it made me realize something so important."

"What's that?"

"We have to let him," Finn answered. He twirled the end of one of her red waves over his index finger. "But our life doesn't stop because his begins."

Ana breathed in the cool breeze that passed over, giving Forbia a slight nudge. "And what does that mean, do you think?"

Finn's hands slid over her shoulders and down her back. He settled them under her bottom, startling her as he lifted her, up and onto the ledge just beneath all the gauges Ana couldn't read. He pressed his face into the curve of her neck. "The very first time I saw you," he said, breathy, "I only wanted to know you."

Ana leaned her head back, lacing her hands behind his waist. "As opposed to?"

"Getting you straight into bed." Finn's kisses trailed up her neck and across the line of her jaw, settling into the curve just under her bottom lip.

"And now?"

Finn took her lower lip in his teeth as he moved his calloused palms down her back, unsnapping her bra in a swift move. “Getting you straight to bed is the *only* thing I can think about.”

Ana knotted his sandy sailor’s hair in her hands and let his crystal blue eyes take her somewhere far away from the world beyond. “And what does Forbia say about this?”

Finn plucked the button on her jeans and tugged. They landed in a pile on the deck. “She says it’s about damn time, Finnegan.”

24
COLLEEN

Colleen hated to leave her daughter for even the hour or two she needed for this meeting. Although Amelia was surrounded by some of the strongest healers in the family, not to mention her husband, her father, her brother, Ana, and Finn, Colleen couldn't suppress the irrational belief that her presence was the one most needed.

Evangeline and Luther were at her side in the Collective chambers. Initially, she'd asked Luther to stay behind, with Amelia, as his healing prowess was as strong as hers, but he assured her she had thrown more than enough resources at Amelia. *There is such thing as diminishing returns, you know.*

Colleen had already lost one child. Ben's death haunted her through every moment of her life. And she had come so close to losing Amelia months ago. One close call was one too many. Ashley's findings in the Blanche journals—*Estella is the one. She will continue my work. And if she will not... ah, if she has a crisis of conscience... then there is another*—had not left her mind for a moment, yet another threat plaguing her family that she could not solve until she understood. She hadn't puzzled out who "another" was. It could be anyone.

Despite her reservations, Luther was not wrong. Colleen herself had reminded others of the boundless capability within their family, and that they should not always look to her for there were many others equally able. She must follow her own advice, she decided. Her absence was a few hours at most.

Evangeline checked the clock. She tapped her pen on the long table, notably empty with only the three of them present.

"You're making *me* anxious," Luther growled, though he, too, looked unsettled.

"They will be here. Rory gave me his word, and he's a man of his honor," Colleen said.

Evangeline had let her hair free and wild this night, and seemed now to regret it as she alternated one hand for another, over and over, to smooth it back. "I find Rory a bit droll for my tastes."

"That's a character trait, not a flaw," Colleen admonished.

"Isn't that why you broke up with him? All those years ago?"

Colleen flushed. "It was more complicated than that. You know that."

"Don't you think..." Evangeline chased away the thought with her hand.

"No, go on. Say it. Before they arrive," Colleen urged.

Evangeline dropped the pen, chewed to a pulp at one end, next to her notebook. "I only wonder if offering them spots on the Council was premature. They don't know our ways, Leena. And if they're put in a position to make decisions for not only their family, but for all of us, this has the potential to backfire."

"That could equally be said of them now, when they have no seat at the table but all of our decisions nevertheless impact them," Luther said.

"You're saying they're the colonists and we're the British overloads taxing them without giving them a substantive voice," Evangeline said. "I get it. I'm only wondering if it might have been more prudent for them to attend meetings as Collective members before offering them Council seats."

"Those who choose to join the Council will be allowed in without questions. They only need to be willing to sign our non-disclosure agreement and speak the vows. This is true for all our blood."

Evangeline groaned. "It feels very cart before the horse to me, but I defer to you."

"We are equal, sister. And we agreed, all seven of us. This was not my draconian measure."

"The vote was unanimous," Luther added. He cleared his throat and straightened his tie.

Evangeline rolled her eyes toward him with a dramatic look. "Yes, Luther, I know. I'm only voicing some concerns so that we might talk through them before there's no going back."

"I didn't hear these concerns from you when we all voted," Luther said.

"There was no going back once we learned they shared our blood and our abilities," Colleen said pointedly. "They get two seats, Evie. Two of nine. And in the future, they will need to be voted in like the rest of us, on equal footing. The two now is only to bring them fully into the fold and provide them with a vested interest. I don't want the Sullivans joining with one foot straddling the doorway. They are in, or they are out."

Evangeline resumed chewing on her pen in silence. Colleen wasn't concerned with her sister's eleventh hour questioning. She had expected it.

The chime from the door at the other end of the house startled all three of them.

Colleen smiled at the others. "And that will be the

Sullivans."

Rory Sullivan had not given any advance indication of who he was bringing. He promised a small group, to keep the meeting intimate and on task. Beyond that, Colleen could only guess.

One face certainly would have surprised her: Oz's father, Colin, seeing as he was part of the reason Oz's abilities had been suppressed until very recently. This river of denial was not unique to Colin, either, as most Sullivans had kept the secret of what they could do very close to their well-tailored vests.

The real question was, how many were ready to come out?

Luther returned with four individuals, three men and one woman. Colleen recognized two of them immediately. Rory Sullivan had not only been her good friend, but also her boyfriend, once upon a time, and was now an integral member of the team at Sullivan & Associates responsible for overseeing the Deschanel Trust. Their friendship had continued on into recent years, and Rory's wife. Carolina, who had once been Colleen's best friend, was now someone she enjoyed afternoon tea with.

And staid, strong Jamie Sullivan... now an old man, but how many years had she known the father-in-law of her beloved, departed sister, Elizabeth? A good, honest family man, lacking entirely in imagination. He had further ties to the family through his grandson, Tristan. Colleen assumed he was here as one of the most respected elders at his law firm.

The other two were familiar faces, but Colleen was ashamed to not recall their names. Rory graciously offered introductions all around, saving her from the question.

The youngest in the room, a serious young man roughly Amelia's age, was Cameron, Rory's son. *Of course,* she thought.

I recall now. Cameron married into the Weatherly family. Cassidy, the oldest. Noah and I attended the wedding. The last, the lone woman in the bunch, became familiar as soon as Colleen watched her embrace Evangeline.

"Chelsea," Colleen said, offering a light hug herself. "I haven't seen you since you and Maureen were sneaking out at night to meet wayward boys."

Chelsea grinned, a gesture both polite and mischievous. "Careful. I married one of those wayward boys."

"Mason Landry, if you can believe it," Rory said with a teasing look at his younger sister.

"Mason was quite a looker, as I recall," Colleen offered, thinking to herself that one of her sisters had once dated him, maybe.

"Still is. My three rambunctious boys favor him," Chelsea said. "And you, with Noah Jameson. I wouldn't have seen that coming."

Colleen laughed, in spite of her wrecked nerves. "No one did."

"Maureen and I kept in touch over the years, so I heard things here and there. Then Elizabeth married our cousin Connor. What a wedding that was!" She turned to Evangeline. "I always regretted not being able to make it to your wedding to Johannes. Mason had just opened the bar, and we were always at the doctor for the in vitro treatments. Who knew a year later we would have triplets?"

"Think nothing of it. We didn't expect many, having it in Sweden and all," Evangeline replied, still smiling at her childhood friend. "How are the boys?"

Chelsea gave her the look Colleen once knew herself as the Wide-Eyed Mom Stare. "In college now, but still as crazy as ever."

Colleen turned to Rory. "And how is Carolina?"

"She's well. She asked me to extend an invitation for lunch, when your schedule opens up."

"I would love that. And Clancy? Robyn?"

"Clancy is finally getting married next spring. You might remember the tough spell he and Angela had, but it seems to have passed," Rory said. "Robyn is buried in her work at the firm, as always. Did you know her daughter, Ruby, helps Jasper in his shop? Only odd jobs, of course. She's not even fourteen."

The seven of them continued their catch-up, each sharing the most noteworthy of their life's moments. Evangeline giggled with Chelsea over old jokes, harkening back to a time where neither of them took anything very seriously. Colleen discovered herself, for the briefest, fleeting moments, remembering how she had once upon a time loved dark-haired Rory, who was now only a glimpse of the fun-loving boy he'd once been.

Each of their lives had diverged and taken unique paths, but yet, here they all were, intersecting again, possibly for the long-term. *Hopefully* for the long-term.

"So here we all are," Colleen said. She spread her arms and gestured for the guests and her fellow Council to take a seat.

"I must admit, most of us are still in shock," Rory ventured. Colleen noted how the other three deferred to him as their de-facto leader of this mission. "There are broader implications, of course. Marriages between families. Jamie's son Connor and your sister, Elizabeth. Colin's son, Oz, and your niece, Adrienne. And though it never resulted in more than a fling, my son, Clancy, and Augustus' girl, Anasofiya, had an inappropriate relationship in their high school days. With Oz as well, I believe."

"We've missed the point of the meeting, I see," Luther groused.

"Not that this should have an impact on how we move

forward, but Elizabeth and Adrienne have both since passed on," Colleen replied. "And as you said, Clancy and Ana were a childhood romance, nothing more. Same with Ana and Oz. Now that we know of the connection, we can prevent further such relationships."

"There are children to consider," Jamie said. "My grandson, Tristan. Oz had a child by his Deschanel wife. A son."

"Christian," Evangeline replied pointedly. "And her name was Adrienne."

"What do you suggest we do about it?"

Evangeline lowered her pen. "What are you asking, exactly? You want us to put them in concentration camps, Jamie?"

"There's nothing *to* do," Luther added in a clear attempt to diffuse. "What's done is done."

"And while I wouldn't have encouraged the unions had we known what we know now, the blood connection between all those you mentioned was not only legally irrelevant, given the distance in the family tree, but posed no genetic dilemmas, either," Colleen said. "I myself have examined Tristan on many occasions and have also had the opportunity to spend time with Christian. They are perfectly healthy young men." She pressed at her thoughts to prevent annoyance. They weren't here to discuss marriages between the families.

Evangeline massaged her temple, a less subtle sign of her own budding vexation.

"So we agree then," Rory said, as if they had all voted. "No more Sullivan-Deschanel marriages."

Evangeline bristled. "We aren't here to debate family breeding habits, Rory."

Luther sat forward, again clearing his throat. He had always used this as an advance pronouncement he was preparing to speak, and others should take heed. "We're here to discuss how we bring the families together toward future prosperity. Specifically, offering you and other Sullivans access to what we know."

Chelsea looked vaguely amused, the corner of her mouth curling. She wore the face of a woman who had already heard every excuse and story in the book from her own boys. "What you *know*?"

"The Deschanel Magi Collective," Colleen answered. "Rory is aware, at least, of the existence. I believe this is an element of the redacted version of your file on us?"

Rory blushed. "I believe that's correct, yes."

Colleen smiled. "We have trusted you all these years. I see no reason to stop now." She turned to look at the other three. Cameron in particular had said nothing beyond introductions, but watched with wide-eyed fascination. "Our Deschanel Magi Collective exists as a governing body for the family, from many angles. We catalogue our history, our present. We research others like us and make a point to seek out any leads on others from our bloodline that have not been on our record."

"Others like you?" Chelsea repeated. "Forgive me, but you'll need to be more clear."

Evangeline slapped a hand on the table. "Oh for heaven's sake, Chels, you know *exactly* what Colleen means. How many times did I heal you when we were kids?" She turned to Rory. "And I *know* Colleen healed *your* ass a few times."

Chelsea looked stricken. "I just wanted to be sure we were all singing from the same hymnal. I have three teenage boys. Vague doesn't work with them if I want their attention, and I'd rather we spell things out so there are no misunderstandings."

Colleen recovered her icy smile before it could fall over the group. "When I say those like us, I mean those who share our supernatural gifts. Healers, telepaths, illusionists. I could continue to list them, but I believe that's enough specificity to get the point across. We also know of others out there, not of our family, who are like us, but we only observe them. In some cases, if we deem it safe, we make contact, and occasionally even form alliances. We, of course, knew all about the Sullivans for years."

Cameron shifted nervously in his seat.

"The discovery of the Sullivan letters only added clarity to *why* you had these abilities," Luther added.

Jamie sat straighter. "You presume our blood connection means we are... whatever you call yourselves."

"Witches." Evangeline grinned, tapping her pen against her teeth.

Jamie's mouth hung. Colleen couldn't decipher if he was horrified or smitten.

Cameron let out a long, exasperated sigh. "Can we stop pretending? Here, of all places? Please?"

"Cam," Rory cautioned.

Cameron turned in his seat. "No, Dad, I'm not going to keep quiet. We agreed to come here, but under false pretenses? I'm sorry, but if they're willing to trust us, we need to be willing to trust them." He turned back to face Colleen. "You're right. Most of us can do things we have no business doing. All of us have kept it to ourselves, for fear of hurting the firm and bringing unwanted attention to the family."

Rory shook his head, but offered no denial. Chelsea studied her folded hands.

"Before we go further," Colleen said, eyes on the young Cameron who might prove to be the most useful of the bunch, "we need to get some necessary paperwork out of the way."

"NDAs," Rory said pleasantly, as if they were discussing any ordinary business arrangement. "Mind if I look them over?"

"Please," Luther said. He slid the manila folder across the

table. “The wording will look familiar. You wrote it.”

“Ahh, yes,” Rory said with a light, uncomfortable chuckle as he scanned the small print. “I do recall putting this together at your request. Pen?”

Evangeline extended hers at him, then snickered at Rory’s panicked expression. She tucked it behind her ear and let Luther offer several from his own, un-chewed stack.

All four of their Sullivan guests signed their non-disclosures. Luther stacked them neatly in the folder and set it aside.

“Right. With that behind us, we have an offer to make,” Colleen said.

“What sort of offer?” Jamie asked, eyes still glued to the wild witch Evangeline.

“If we are to work together, there is information you must know. Histories and current events alike that have as much impact on you as they do us,” Colleen began. “Now that you’ve signed the disclosure, we can, of course, discuss some of that with you. However, we want to take this discussion a step further.”

“Must be juicy if you can’t tell us without an NDA,” Chelsea quipped.

“Our history goes back thousands of years,” Evangeline snapped, then settled back in her chair, getting ahold of herself. “As Leena said, there are things you should know.”

“No one knows their history back that far,” Rory charged.

“We do,” Luther and Colleen said in tandem. “And there are elements of our bloodline that are highly irregular, in many ways,” Colleen added.

“What we have to offer,” Luther pressed. “Is a spot at the table. All Sullivans are welcome to join the Collective once they have signed their non-disclosures and taken the sacred vows. But we wish to offer two of you a role in the Council, where we make decisions that affect every single one of us. Two seats, two voices. And an opportunity to be considered in the votes for any future vacancies, across all nine seats."

Rory was taken aback. "That's quite generous, all things considered. But what does this give us that we don't have now? I won't claim Cameron's words didn't have a ring of truth, but the Sullivans have done more than fine throughout the years *without* embracing this aspect of who we are. In fact, I would say we have thrived in our normalcy."

"Drowned," Evangeline corrected.

Rory narrowed his eyes at her. "We may share ancestry, but that doesn't mean our paths have to be the same. Addressing this other... thing is not a requirement to our success."

"No," Colleen agreed. "But before now, you could at least claim ignorance. I would imagine many Sullivans were confused, and even ashamed of their telepathy and telekinesis. Scared. Now, however, you know who you are, and we are offering you not only brotherhood but also answers as to *why* you are this way and access to information that could impact all of your family, for better or worse."

"Two seats," Cameron mused. "Full voting power?"

Luther nodded. "Two of nine. We were seven but have agreed opening two additional was the right decision in light of this new branch of our family."

"And the opportunity to be considered for roles in the other seven positions in the future?"

"In the event of openings, yes," Luther affirmed.

"And, as members, we will have access to... all you know?"

All three Council members nodded.

"Without exception?"

"Cameron—" Jamie gruffed.

Cameron ignored his uncle and looked at his father. "We should consider this. The offer is more than fair."

Rory rubbed his neck, eyes elsewhere. "We need to discuss

this as a family. We're not deciding here."

"Of course. We would expect nothing less," Colleen said. "On top of everything, I imagine this has been as much of a shock for all of you as it has us. We've always treasured the Sullivans as great friends and allies, of course, but never imagined we shared so much more."

Rory looked at his fellow Sullivans. "Any other questions for the Council?"

"None they'd answer directly, I'm afraid," Jamie said, massaging the age spots on his sagging cheek.

"If we did take your offer," Chelsea said as she stood, folding her cardigan over her arm, "how would the decision be made as to who gets the seats?"

"We would defer to you," Colleen replied. "And allow your family to vote on who you feel would best represent your interests."

"Fair enough," Chelsea replied and nodded at Rory. "Ready, brother?"

Rory reached a hand across to Colleen. "Thank you for taking the time with us."

"No, thank you," she replied, both relieved to be done quickly but also that the meeting had stayed relatively on track. "We truly do want to welcome the Sullivans as part of us. This is the best and most meaningful way we know to accomplish this."

Rory nodded. "We are honored. I promise we will give the matter the serious consideration it deserves, Colleen."

"That's all we ask."

"Expect a response within two weeks' time," Rory said and flashed her one last short smile before they disappeared from the Council chambers, leaving the three standing alone in the big room, each lost to their own interpretations of the last half hour.

25
MAXIMA

Maxima asked herself no less than three times per day if her duplicity was worth the tension.

Four hundred years she had served the Brotherhood, under the guise of the Eldre Senetat. She had been on the Senetat far longer, over a millennium. Like so many others, she had taken her sacred oath with stars in her eyes. To be closer to Emyr! To live in opulence! To serve Farjhem in the most sacred of roles!

Then she learned what Emyr's Mark really was. Then she witnessed not one, but three defections from those most loyal to Farjhem, and to the Senetat. Three Empyreans she greatly respected, wiped from the map. But their Marks had not been "activated," so where did they go?

Her peers in the Senetat were unconcerned with this question. They blithely assumed these creatures had found themselves in trouble and perished untimely. But Maxima did not think this was a coincidence, and she couldn't let it go.

The more she learned of the Senetat's true purpose—the control, the unchecked power, the poison within the chambers that could not be contained and seeped through their beloved motherland—the further died the light in her eyes.

Maxima was no weak thing, though, and where one part of her expired, dissolving and draining into the cracks of the snow white marble of her bedroom, another sprung to life.

Typically, the Senetat were not permitted to leave Farjhem. Business required outside their land was dispatched to lesser, more expendable of their ilk. Finding one of those errand boys she could trust took over twenty years. She couldn't even deign to risk so much as a single errant word to the wrong individual, or it would be her own neck. Maxima had watched this in action herself, in the early days of her tenure, as one of the Senetat was discovered doing exactly this. His execution had not been painless. Hers, in the center of the rise of a new insurgency—not Runa's band of misfits, not this time—would be far worse.

Then something entirely unexpected happened. Her errand boy found *her.*

He had been recruited by a creature named Thorvald, a name unfamiliar to Maxima. When she searched the grid of Marks, she found no such Empyrean.

The page had been sent to test her, but in the end, as she told him, she could not leave Farjhem to meet with Thorvald or his fellow conspirators.

"There is a way," said the page, and so she followed him down through the armory, and into a tunnel she didn't even know existed—closed since the days of The Blacksmith, said the page.

She closed her eyes in Farjhem and awoke on the sandy shores of a land foreign to her.

"Spain," said the page, beaming at a group of glorious creatures standing in a circle around her.

Glorious was the only word she could muster. They were

exquisite! They had no silver in their bright red manes, not even a strand. They didn't sag with the weight of the Mark, which was meant to resemble the weight of Emyr's faith. Yet these were not newborns... not young at all. The bearing suggested an age she couldn't even calculate.

"I am Thorvald," said one of the oldest. He extended his arms in welcome. "And we have not much time until the Senetat discovers you are no longer in Farjhem."

THUS BEGAN HER SUBTERFUGE, SERVING THE SENETAT WITH THE outward piety required to keep up appearances, while ferrying messages to the rebels. The Dragon Brotherhood, they called themselves. They consisted not only of those who had removed their Marks—including the three she had seen fall off the map, thank Emyr—but many, many born outside the knowledge of the Senetat. Those most ancient were believed dead by the leaders of Farjhem. How shocked they would be if they ever knew Brynja, Einar, and Trygve still walked this earth at large. And others, like Dagr—ahh, not Dagr, not any longer. Maxima had mourned him, even as Oriana threw a massive fete—Birger and Astrid.

And then these things grew less and less secret. Agripin brought his halfling toys to Farjhem—and Aidrik the Wise! What a shock to so many of Farjhem who had heard of his ascension and mourned his loss years before. Emperor Aeron's death had sent their relative calm into a fury. As Agripin rose to power, his pets in tow, the Senetat began to suspect the timing was perhaps less than coincidental.

Few knew the Senetat had orchestrated Aeron's death. That they had done so because they viewed Agripin with high mistrust and wanted him close, where they could manage him. Where they could watch him hang himself and then quash whatever mischief he had in him, and at the same time, discover his accomplices. So they could return to the status quo. The Brotherhood equally seized the opportunity of his accession as a tool for the resistance.

The Brotherhood played a dangerous hand with Agripin. Maxima warned Birger that the duke-cum-emperor was too unpredictable a creature to rely on. They didn't disagree, but they had no better hand to play. If seating him in Farjhem went as they hoped, they could begin the slow process of dismantling the Senetat and restoring a benevolent, faith-based rule.

Then the world fell away. Agripin was exposed, and he constructed a case against Aidrik instead, putting him out front as the turncoat. A move that, had it ended there, would have been horrifying enough. The Brotherhood, including Maxima, never agreed to Aidrik taking the fall. He was beloved to so many.

But that was exactly how things played out in Farsengel, the prison, and then the most unexpected thing happened.

Anasofiya of the Darkness.

An etheric summoner. Even now, Maxima mused on this. Had Aidrik known? Had Agripin? Maybe this was Agripin's plan all along, to force Anasofiya to face who she was and bring Farjhem to its knees.

Whether planned or not, Anasofiya's destruction launched the Third Runean War. But Maxima didn't blame the unhinged halfling. She blamed Agripin.

He had taken a plan that could have worked and brought the world down around them.

Maxima had followed the Brotherhood as far as Trondheim. She ached to be where the planning and action was, but more, to be among like-minded Empyreans. But her value to the cause was in the Senetat. Without her, the Brotherhood was blind to anything in Farjhem.

So she returned to Farjhem, affecting a degree of shame she did not feel, and pledged fealty to the terrible, horrible Oriana, for a purpose greater than herself.

How she loathed Oriana. The narcissist. The despot. Oriana had no designs on governing at all. She wanted the war over, so she could return to the limited world of rule-breaking and hedonism. Then she would seat a puppet in her place, someone who would follow her whims as she ruled from The Menagerie.

Grand Empress Oriana's reign of terror made Maxima long for the days of Grand Emperor Aeron's passive apathy.

In this new world, treason was even more challenging. In the first weeks of the transition, where Oriana rebuilt the Senetat from her own minions—creatures with no experience of designs on politics; creatures that, Maxima was dismayed to say, made her miss her old peers—Maxima was under a watchful eye at all times. Oriana seemed to realize she needed *someone* in her administration who understood how to govern, but she had yet to understand how and why Maxima had even survived the carnage that had taken every last Senetat member except her.

But Oriana was out of her element in the emperor's seat. She was a cunning goddess in her world, The Menagerie, but here, she was a fish out of water, searching desperately for the nearest relief, even if temporary. She had no middle ground within her. She either walked around in complete bliss, or threw herself into wild fits of rage. She'd been entrenched in the latter when she ordered Dagr's execution. A savvier leader might have seen him for the potential asset he could be. But not volatile Oriana.

This volatility made her both predictable and unpredictable. Good news elated her, and bad news incited her. But either direction on the pendulum could lead to things unexpected.

So Maxima watched. She practiced her public obedience and prayed in private to Emyr, for strength in this lawless land she hardly recognized. For the opportunity to use her devotion to Emyr; for something to present itself that made her useful once again.

THEN, HER PRAYERS WERE ANSWERED.

As Oriana pranced around in a cloud of euphoria, Maxima listened. Her adrenaline surged with every word from her wayward empress, both with fear of what the creature had planned but also with hope.

For Maxima finally had information she could share with the Brotherhood.

HER PAGE OF THE OLD DAYS HAD PERISHED IN THE WRECKAGE OF Farjhem, so Maxima had no one but herself as a conduit to the outside world. In those days, all telepathic communications were strictly monitored, but that was a time of supreme organization. Oriana had not the experience or the sense to design such a structure.

Maxima again found herself wandering through the cobwebbed and collapsed world of The Blacksmith, which was as far from the palace as she could venture without leaving Farjhem. She imagined a great veil around her thoughts, one that blocked them from behind but opened them up for those beyond.

Birger, we have a significant problem facing us. Oriana has found herself a weapon, and it's one we never could have predicted!

No one will have seen it coming, and so, unless we stop it, there will be no prevention. We must warn the—

Maxima was ripped from her telepathic reverie as the magical bindings swirled around her limbs, wrenching her forward.

"Eldre Maxima," barked a guard she did not recognize. More of Oriana's new regime. He lacked the authority of the old guards and reminded her of a child playing a game he'd seen the older kids play. "You are ordered to Farsengel for the unauthorized use of outside telepathy, and for conspiring with the enemy against the crown."

Maxima spat at the guards. There was no escape from her punishment, and her bindings would prevent her from finishing her message. She should have known that Oriana's lessening of the reigns was a trap. That she had walked right into it, and had not even been able to deliver the most important words of all, and now, never would.

Maxima escaped into her mind as she was dragged up the crumbling stairs. *Please, Emyr, deliver the wisdom to Birger another way. We must not let Oriana's plan see the light of day! For if we do, all is lost. All is lost... all is lost.*

26
QUILLAN

Their cramped motel room in the small getaway town of Rockaway Beach on the Oregon coast had come to feel like a prison cell.

Stella, whom Quillan had weeks ago called *Little Stella* but was now not the least bit little, used her limited strength to shield them from the broader world. She was undoubtedly a powerful child, but Quillan saw within her the world of restraints that kept her from her potential. Her fear of herself. Of her brother Sebastian. Of the bitch, Margarethe.

So they stayed in Rockaway Beach, which, while almost three thousand miles from New Orleans, was still too close to home for Quillan's comfort, probably a significant part of why what he'd been running from, Estella, found him anyway.

The Estella who did all their grocery shopping, who had upgraded their room to include a kitchen so she could cook for them; the one who read to Stella at nights and hummed old Cajun songs as she watched the waves crash against the piles of logs accumulated during pre-winter storms... *she* may as well have been a stranger.

This abrupt shift in character from the woman who had curb-stomped his life with heartless abandon didn't lead to any great revelation for Quillan. He experienced no change in heart, or inevitable warmth at finally seeing the woman he always, naively, believed she could be.

The truth was, he didn't know Estella at all. He never had. And now, he never wanted to.

Somewhere in their shared, determined quest to protect Stella, a child neither of them had any great reason to help but found themselves drawn to anyway, a mutual respect had formed in place of a friendship, which would never be a factor between them. When Estella kept herself at a distance, looking after their needs without searching for the benefit to her, Quillan could almost tolerate their situation.

It wouldn't take much to snap the tender thread holding it all together. A single, extended look. An unasked question behind her eyes.

When she first arrived, it had taken two weeks of Estella's silence before he accepted she hadn't used the poor little girl as a bargaining chip in exchange for Quillan's necromancy. But the question never came. Not then, and not later, and eventually, Quillan stopped worrying about its arrival.

His loathing for her hadn't waned, however. He would eventually heal from the hurt she had caused his own heart, but he would never, not ever, forgive her for being the cause of driving Riley from his life, forever.

Riley had been his one and only constant. His twin brother who never aged, but never left him, either. True, at times he had shooed Riley away, or made fun of him, but isn't that what big brothers did? Riley's death at seven hadn't changed anything between them.

But Estella had. Estella, the unimaginable monster who

had occupied his thoughts and life long enough to do damage he could not undo.

Quillan spent his days ignoring her and his nights hating her.

Stella was an interesting child, even if "child" no longer described her at all. When she'd shown up, a girl of no more than six or seven with tight blond ringlets and wide, scared eyes, Quillan's heart seized with purpose. Later, he would see it as atonement, for how his defection of Riley had come with permanent consequences, but at the time he only knew this child needed him.

She was a quiet, introspective little human, who preferred books to spoken words. She played with sand, shaping it into human-like forms, carrying on silent plays in her mind until Estella ventured out Highway 101 and found a knick-knack store that sold various amusements. She'd returned with a sand-pail and shovel, some giant conch shells likely made in China, and a bag of key chains.

Stella's sweet gratitude at these odd gifts showed her sensitivity to others. She used the pail to shape her sand castles and stationed the conch shells along the inside of her moats. The key chains dangled precariously from the turrets as decoration, inevitably crashing back to the untouched sand from the uneven weight.

She ate whatever Estella cooked her, which made her something nearing a saint in Quillan's eyes. He grudgingly appreciated that Estella had stepped up to try and provide Stella with food other than takeout, but it was evident she'd never had to cook a meal in her life. And the lone grocery store in town, a tiny Thriftway where half the items were expired and others sold out, didn't help. Stella's protection only stretched so far. Even the other end of town was too far to venture safely.

When the unthinkable happened and she began to stretch and grow out of her clothes, Quillan didn't know what he was seeing. Estella explained that both Stella and her brother were special, and they better get used to it. It wasn't going to stop there.

So Stella graduated from her adorable Sunday dress to tourist T-shirts, hoodies, and sweatpants Estella procured from the same store she'd found the gifts. And when eventually her height stretched as tall as Estella, and her hips and chest blossomed from awkward teenager to a fully-fleshed young adult, Quillan realized they had more than they bargained for.

"We should take her to Colleen Deschanel," he said to Estella one day. She stood in the small kitchen, heating a box of macaroni and cheese on the stove in her goofy apron with the words *Keep Oregon Weird* embossed in chipped green paint.

Estella paused, half-melted spatula in hand. "If Colleen could help her, I wouldn't be here."

"Did anyone give her a chance?"

"Not even Colleen is all-knowing, Quillan. People put that woman on a pedestal, but she's flesh and blood, like you and me. If I hadn't found Stella that night, she would be dead. This isn't a game."

"Only you would use the word game when talking about a child's life."

Estella dropped the spatula in the boiling water and pivoted. "Lay it on me, Quillan. All the things you want to say. I can take it."

"Whether or not you can take it is irrelevant," he'd said. "You're not worth it."

The impact of his words reflected in her drawn face, but she didn't stop. "I was, once."

"And I was a man, once. But you took that, too."

QUILLAN WONDERED IF HIS FATHER MISSED HIM, OR IF HE MOURNED only how his absence would lead to questions from the rest of the family.

He thought of his mother, who loved her theatrics, but she had also loved her sons, and now she had lost both.

He wondered how Leander was faring without his friendship. Better, maybe.

He pictured how beautiful Lauren had looked that last night over dinner. And how different his life would have turned out had he not answered Estella's call and stayed.

But mostly, he thought of Riley.

THANKSGIVING WASN'T FAR OFF. QUILLAN HAD A BORDERLINE nihilistic view of the family unit, having been raised by a blustering social climber of a father and a histrionic mother, but holidays had a way of erasing reality long enough to feel grateful for what you had, instead of wishing for something you didn't.

Thanksgiving, for Quillan, meant the smells of his mother's homemade dressing and fresh baked rolls. It meant cousins running in the backyard of Rory Sullivan's place, playing tag or red rover. The men watched the football games, connecting, finally on something other than law.

Estella shyly suggested they try to make a turkey, but he only barked at her. He later regretted it, though his regret only angered him. He owed her nothing. She had no right to look at him with those pitiful eyes and make him feel even worse about himself.

He thought more and more of the third person in their motel room, the striking woman-child who, in another world, Quillan might have even tried to date. This was so far beyond what either he or Estella was capable of. And she might not think reaching out to Colleen was the best course, but her judgment wasn't exactly something to be regarded, either.

Quillan sat on the back porch, toes in the sand, reflecting on their situation when a shadow fell over him.

He glanced up. Pretty, shy Stella bowed her head down, blocking the sun.

"Riley still loves you," she said in her husky voice. She smiled from one corner of her mouth, and there was something very sad about the gesture. "He isn't angry with you."

"Riley..." Quillan's chest burned. His toes went stiff in the wet sand. "Do you talk to Riley?"

"Sort of." She kicked at the loose ground with her dime store crocs. "He visits me in my dreams."

"What?" Quillan ran his hands down his face, sighing through his fingers. "What do you mean? How?"

Stella shrugged. She always picked gestures over words when possible.

Quillan shot to his feet. The blood rush rendered him dizzy. "Stella, tell me! Please."

She shook her head and pursed her delicate mouth. Tears ran from the corners of her eyes, and Quillan worried he might have caused them. He took her soft hands in his. "I'm not angry, Stella. But, see... I thought Riley was gone forever, and what you're saying means maybe he isn't. He's so special to me, and I miss him so much."

Her head shook harder. "He's gone," she said in a near-whisper. "He can't come back. Not even for you."

"But you?"

Stella's tears quickened. "When I sleep, I go to places not even a necromancer can go."

"Where? Where do you go?" Quillan pressed.

"Where the dead are."

Quillan didn't have the slightest idea where the dead went, but from the haunted looks Stella wore every morning when she woke, he guessed it wasn't a place he wanted to go.

"Do you want to go there? Or are you, I don't know, sent there?"

Stella dropped her hands back to her sides. "I go because he can't get me there."

"Who?"

"Sebastian."

Quillan should have been asking more questions all along. He'd taken her silence for granted. When Stella said they were protected, he assumed exactly that, and never pressed for anything more.

He saw now that she had been enduring her own private horror the whole time.

"Tell me what to do," he said. He glanced back to see if they were alone. The room behind the dark orange curtain was empty. Estella was still out shopping. "Do you want us to leave here? If you know how I can help protect you from Sebastian, tell me, Stella."

"He's going to kill me."

Quillan caught her before she collapsed in tears. He eased her into his chair. "Like hell," he answered as he knelt in the sand in front of her. "You hear me? He'll have to kill me first."

"Oh. Yes. He will kill you," Stella said blandly.

Quillan blanched. "Do you want to go back? To New Orleans?"

Stella's tears fell on his hands. She lifted her head, and he wondered again at how beautiful she was. How delicate and soft, like an angel. Like something not even remotely real.

"You'll know. The time will come, and you'll know, Quillan."

27
JACOB

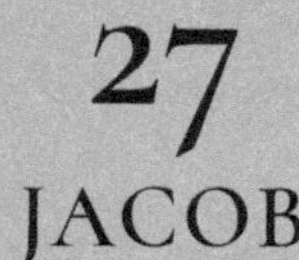

The last time Jacob learned he was going to be a father, he'd had only a moment to digest the information before the child was taken, in the blink of an eye. He had never been given the chance to decide how he felt about the news.

This time around, he'd had a full week, and he still didn't know what to think.

He couldn't grasp how it happened to begin with. Amelia started taking her contraception again when they returned home, or so he thought. Now, he wasn't so sure, and he was afraid to ask. He feared the question might read as an accusation. He didn't want any of his words to lead her to believe he wasn't as over-the-moon as she was.

Because he *was* excited. But he was also scared to death.

Maybe it had something to do with the extreme cavalry Colleen had ordered to look after Amelia. Every single one of the family's registered healers was on shift, sometimes two or three at a time. She couldn't even venture to the bathroom unattended.

Or maybe it was the white-faced terror Ana often wore whenever Amelia moaned or winced.

"What aren't you telling me?" Jacob pulled her aside. "Every time you walk out of her room, you look like you've just come back from her wake."

"I *have* told you my concerns," Ana said. "What she's going through now is nothing compared to what she will go through. There were many nights I didn't think I was going to make it, and when I look at her, it brings back a lot of memories." She eased Amelia's door closed. "She has a lot more goodness on her side than I did. But no one else but me knows what this is like, and watching her is like reliving it again, because I know what comes next, and it's a bit like watching a horror movie."

"That's comforting," Jacob muttered. "Really, you should charge for your speeches."

Ana shoved her hands under her crossed arms. "Amelia has the entire force of the Deschanels behind her, Jacob. And I'm here to spot things they might not know to look for. But it won't be easy, and if you're not prepared for that, how will she be?"

Jacob navel-gazed, wondering what had happened to the man who'd come home so ready to fight.

Ana bent low and stuck her head upside down under where he hung his face. "Hey, look, maybe it doesn't help that Aunt Colleen has sort of taken over this whole thing, you know? If it were me, I'd ask her to clear out for a bit, give you two some time alone."

Jacob snickered. "Right. You try that."

She smiled. "I will."

• • •

WHATEVER ANA SAID TO COLLEEN HAD BOUGHT HIM AN HOUR ALONE with Amelia, which was less than he wanted but a lot more than he'd had.

With the house again quiet and settled, Jacob heard every last small creak and breath as he walked up the stairs of a home not his own, and pushed open the creaking door to the bedroom where Amelia slept.

Amelia had been tucked into the covers like a child, a washcloth neatly folded across her forehead. Her colorless face had the sheen of persistent sweat. She groaned in her agitated sleep.

Jacob slid in beside her, careful not to disturb her. Her hand rested on her belly, which had begun to protrude in the slightest way, enough for him to look upon it with a wash of horror and wonder.

A child grew within her. A daughter, if Colleen was to be believed. As they spoke, the child's cells were coalescing faster than they should, bringing together a development that would astound the scientist in him if he wasn't also the father.

"Donnelly." Her hoarse voice startled him. He ripped his eyes from her belly.

"*Blanca*. How are you feeling?"

"Sore. Spoiled." Her dry lips spread into a tired grin. "Maybe overwhelmed."

"Your mom really knows how to throw a party." It wasn't his best joke, or even funny, but he'd lost his desire for humor. The acrid scent of her sickness hit him like a punch to the gut.

"You're afraid," she said. Her hand slid from under the blanket. Her movements were slow, sluggish. How had she become so invalid in such a short span of time? She wrapped her clammy hand over his. "I was, too. I didn't think I wanted this. Actually, I was sure of it."

Her eyes traveled south where her other hand still cupped

the small protuberance. "But Moira needs us both to be strong now."

"Moira?" Jacob repeated. His laugh was short, clipped. "You already named her, eh?"

Amelia's head shook against the pillow. She nudged the washcloth with a jerk and it fell to the side. "She told me her name."

"She did?"

"I know what you're thinking."

"Not this time, you don't."

"You think I've lost my mind, that I'm delirious with what this pregnancy has done to me," Amelia said.

Jacob rolled his head to the ceiling, settling deeper into his pillow. "Fine, you're warm."

"I don't expect you to understand. Not even another woman could. Not my mother. Ana does, though, and I'm so grateful for her right now. Before my mother confirmed I was carrying Moira, I thought something might be awfully wrong with me, Jacob. That the stress had caught up, and now I was going to fall apart at the seams, literally."

This is where Jacob knew he should jump to reassure her that he didn't need to understand to love her and be her strength through this. This was where he should kiss her, run his own hand over where his child grew within her, and whisper his love for them both.

"I'm not going to die, Donnelly."

These were the words that did it. His eyes closed and the tears leaked, rolling down his cheeks, cutting across his cheekbones on their way to the pillow.

How could he tell her he would rather lose their child than her? He couldn't live without her, and this brought upon him such an immense selfishness that he could hardly face her in his shame.

"You won't have to choose." Amelia brought his hand to her belly. When he stiffened, she unwrapped his fingers and spread them across her flesh. "And trust me, you won't want to, once you get to know her."

Jacob's voice cracked. "Stop reading my mind."

"I didn't have to. I know you."

"Then you should know this is three times in a year I've almost lost you, and I'm losing my grip, Amelia. I'm completely losing it, and I can't believe these words are coming out of my mouth even as I'm saying them, because I'm supposed to be the strong one for you right now."

Amelia moved his hand from her belly to the side of her face. She grunted as she rolled to her side, toward him. "I'll let it slide this time, Donnelly."

Jacob pressed his forehead to hers. He squeezed his eyes shut tight, forcing the tears out. The hand resting on her face twitched, an old fighting reflex. A feeling that surfaced in his most helpless moments.

Amelia's breath smelled of bile, but also, somehow still of her. "This is where you tell me you've loved me forever."

A sob choked deep in his throat and he clapped his free hand to his mouth. *Get it together, Donnelly. Pull it together. Rein it in. This is the moment, now, it's here.*

He licked his lips, clearing them of the salt from his tears. His eyes remained closed tight. "I've loved you forever, Amelia."

Her cracked lips pressed to his, lingering, before she collapsed back against the pillow. Her eyes struggled to stay open. "Then love me forever."

28
VICTOR

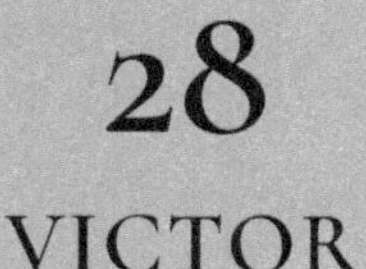

Victor had spent more time at Olivia's house than his own in the past week. His father's suspicions mounted as Victor's moods improved. *What are you up to? What have you done?*

He hadn't made any progress toward finding Ophélie, but each moment he spent with Olivia felt like building an important equity toward that aim. And she wasn't difficult to be around, despite what she might say about herself. He enjoyed her candor and brevity. Her strange mix of curiosity and guardedness.

And yet, he could not help but be drawn to the house across town that housed the closest to Ophélie he might ever be again.

He reminded himself Amelia didn't want to see him. That Jacob had threatened him should he show his face anywhere near their home again.

Still, it didn't stop him from wandering down Coliseum, stopping just before Seventh, checking for her car. For lights on in the house, or a silhouette passing behind the curtains.

But the house had been dark for days. A clueless neighbor mentioned he thought she might have gone to her cousin's house following an illness, but didn't know which cousin. She could be anywhere.

His own gentle stalking of Amelia produced the answer quickly. She was on great terms with most of her cousins, but one in particular had occupied her time more than others since she'd returned to New Orleans.

Victor made the ten-minute walk to Magnolia Grace with a new lightness in his step. There he found himself, morning after morning, night after night. Lurking in shadows, far enough from the action to be detected but close enough to observe.

In recent days, there had been a great many cars, and a great many lights outside the mansion. Bodies streamed in and out of the house with drawn, somber faces, and for one singular, horrifying instant, Victor thought Amelia had died, and these were family coming for her wake. He remembered the neighbor's words about her coming here *following an illness.*

He chided himself for even thinking it. If Amelia were dead, he would know. He might not have the spirit of Cianán moored within him any longer, but he was no less connected to Amelia, same as he was Ophélie, and even Jacob.

On the second day, when he had taken little Rory on his afternoon stroll under the guise of spending time with him, Victor noticed the influx of relatives swarming like security guards and stopped to listen with his mind.

He picked up less than he would have liked, but more than he'd started with.

Amelia was ill. Those coming and going were family healers, sent to be with her. He gathered their presence would only increase in the coming weeks, when whatever was wrong with her worsened.

Beyond that, he could gather nothing more.

He had to see her. To see with his own eyes what had befallen her and determine for himself if her malady was fixable.

And if it wasn't? Would he take her, too, to the Master's Tree?

Victor did not answer himself.

While Olivia busied herself with shop business, Victor made his daily sojourn. This time, when he came to the intersection at Eighth and Prytania, the street in front of Magnolia Gardens was empty.

Entirely, completely empty.

His heart surged with a bevy of irrational thoughts. Had they moved her? Had she, after all, died from whatever plagued her?

But no, nothing had happened to her. It was not possible. He would have felt it, deep within, like the death of an organ.

Emboldened by the lack of Deschanels prowling around, Victor turned down Prytania and approached the house. He paused in front, looking up into the window of the only room streaming light. He deduced she must be there, but there was only one way to know for sure with the curtains drawn.

He glanced around. No one, still. With an easy control, careful not to let the metal clang, Victor shut the front gate behind him and made his way around the side of the house. He listened for the thoughts of others, but found none this time, except Amelia's. She could be in there alone, but it was also probable he had failed to pick up on someone on the other side of the mansion.

To his great surprise, the front door was unlocked. Maybe she wasn't home alone, after all, and her companion or companions were blocking exceptionally well. He would deal with that, and any other obstacles, as they presented themselves.

He settled the door closed behind him with the lightest of clicks. A glance around the foyer and living room revealed no one, so he made for the stairs.

At the top of the stairs, he kept his steps light on his way to the bedroom where he believed her to be. He could not be certain his senses were working in his favor here, and he couldn't risk being caught. His father's words about the Deschanels not being their enemies had stayed with him, even as he pretended they were ridiculous. As of now, he was merely an annoyance. Being caught at her bedside would escalate his meddling to a perceived threat.

He eased the door open. The creak made him wince, but there was no one in the room. No one except Amelia, asleep in her bed with the blankets drawn high to her neck. A layer of sweat and sickness covered her visible skin. The room was heavy with it.

"Amelia," he ventured, kneeling at her bedside. "Forgive me. I couldn't stay away."

Amelia's eyes cracked open with great effort. Her mouth formed a tight circle as her whole face melted from confusion to fear.

"I would never hurt you. You must know this. You must," Victor insisted. He wanted to reach for her, to feel her flesh. Not to claim her for his own, only to know she was still real, and still a connection to who she once was.

Amelia ran her tongue over her dry lips and coughed. "How did you get in here?"

"The door was unlocked."

"But Jacob..." Her hand appeared from under the blanket, and she floundered toward the nightstand. He recognized she was looking for her water and slid the glass into her hand. She drew it to her mouth with a shaky advance, draining half the glass in a sip. It nearly slipped from her hand and he righted it, resettling it on the table.

"He must not be here," Victor said. "I see no sign of him."

"What do you want?"

"Only to see you."

Amelia coughed again. She winced. "No."

"What ails you?" He leaned across her bed, running his eyes over her blanched face. "I may be able to help you."

"Not your business. And I don't want your help."

"You will always be my business, no matter what words you use to drive me from your life."

"Stop." Amelia closed her eyes, steadying herself. "I don't have it in me to fight with you. So if you mean what you said... if you mean it when you say you care about me... you'll leave and let me be."

The bedroom door sailed open. Victor caught a very angry Jacob over his shoulder and turned just as Jacob launched himself.

Victor recoiled against the nightstand as a closed fist connected with his face. Amelia's glass teetered back and forth before falling over, spilling the remaining water down the side of the oak stand.

Jacob clenched and unclenched his hand. He regarded Victor, gauging him, calculating his next move. He looked at Amelia.

"What did he do? Did he touch you?"

Amelia shook her head. "I don't know why he's here."

Jacob pressed his right fist into his left hand. Then he lowered both to his sides. "I told you I'd kill you if I saw you here again."

Victor looked up into Jacob's wild, but focused eyes, and he believed him. He had no doubt Jacob would do exactly that.

Footsteps sounded in the hall behind them. An elegant, middle-aged man appeared. Victor knew him. Real-estate mogul Luther Fontenot.

"Luther," Amelia croaked.

"What's going on here?" he asked as another man, a sandy blond Victor didn't recognize, appeared. "Amelia, are you okay?"

Jacob turned toward the newcomers. "If this *thing* doesn't leave, I'm going to kill it."

Another appeared, and then another. *Noah Jameson. Ashley Jameson.*

"That won't be necessary, Jacob," Luther said. "Unless you have your heart set on it. Don't let me steal your joy."

"I'll help you bury the body," Ashley hissed. At his side, Noah held himself in a stance not unlike Jacob's, his silence speaking louder than any words.

Victor's laugh cut through the tension. "I'd like to see *any* of you try."

Colleen stepped through the forming crowd. Christian Louboutin heels clicked on the wood floor. Her outfit, dark from head to toe, made her seem a black widow coming to devour him.

"Remove him," she ordered, forming the words through her blood-red lips.

All the men stepped forward and reached their hands toward Victor, who scrambled to find grip and pull himself to a stand, on even footing with his assailants. "Off me!" he cried. Did they know... no they couldn't... that he could drain them of every last drop of their blood... that he could do it before they could process the fate that had befallen them.

He pressed through the group of men wearing smug, self-satisfying grins, as if they had no doubt of their own power, and how it could be used against him.

Victor's anger roiled to the surface as he side-stepped down the stairs, looking up only once to see Colleen and her male harem regarding him with a whirlwind of potent hostility.

"You will regret this," he hissed before rolling around the edge of the banister and landing on the bottom floor. By the time he reached the front door, his entire body was a torch.

"You haven't yet known real regret, Monsieur de Blanchefort," Colleen answered and pivoted, walking away, leaving him to his own growing rage.

VICTOR'S BLOODLUST HAD NOT BEEN THIS HEAVY IN YEARS. HE DIDN'T need blood to survive, as other vampire races did, but he craved it in the way a drug addict desired a fix after a dry spell. The desire grew keener when he felt a loss of control. Taking from another was the only balm.

He couldn't drink in New Orleans, or at least, not in areas where the victim would be missed. He was expressly forbidden by his father, his grandfather, but also Childeric, who had extracted this promise in blood before each of them took the gift. The blood must be stolen in dark bayous, or under the cover of cypress. It must never, ever draw suspicion to the taker.

Victor roared at the sky as he ran down the upturned side-walks of the Garden District, his speed escalating as he pulled farther and farther away from Amelia's.

Everything, all his life, was for nothing. Nothing! He could not find Ophélie. He could not have Amelia. Neither was his, and only because of this fact did he truly crave them to begin with. He was going mad. Mad!

Olivia opened the door to him doubled over on the porch, exhausted from his exertion, from his grief, from his misery.

She offered him a somber smile. It was not pity in her eyes, but kinship.

But Victor did not need or want her kindness just then.

He lifted her into his arms and carried her to the bedroom.

29
LAUREN

They were headed west. Their last adventure had taken them around the southeastern portion of the country, peaking up the Eastern seaboard around Southern Virginia. They'd operated on the premise people never really ran that far from home.

Whoever made that rule hadn't met Quillan. Lauren was beginning to question the veracity of these so-called tips they'd been chasing down.

When they crossed the Texas state line, Nicolas finally offered an explanation on the source of their information.

"You know those things that come up on your phone when a kid goes missing?"

"AMBER Alerts," Leander said over his shoulder from the front seat. "An acronym for America's Missing: Broadcast Emergency Response, put in place after the disappearance of nine-year-old Amber Hagerman, who was abducted and killed ten years ago in Texas."

"I didn't ask for the backstory, Rainman." Nicolas threw his hands up as if to say, *hopeless.* They landed on the backs of the two front headrests. He peaked through, looking at Lauren. “The Deschanel Magic Club has our own version of that.”

“Deschanel Magi Collective,” Leander groused. “And to think, you’re one of our leaders. God help us.”

“What do you mean?” Lauren asked, keeping her eyes on the road. They had nothing ahead but long stretches of endless highway and a speed limit that terrified her. “Like y’all have family all over the country that keeps an eye on things?”

“Not exactly.” He popped his head in Leander’s direction. “Has she signed an NDA, bro?”

Leander rolled his eyes to the ceiling. “You can trust her. Or you can shut up. Either is fine by me.”

“It’s like this,” Nicolas said, winking at Leander, taking evident pleasure in his annoyance. “We aren’t the only family in this world who can move shit across the room with our minds, if you know what I mean.”

“I think I’ve got it,” Lauren said, gripping the wheel tighter. She didn’t get it. She didn’t even *remotely* get it, but this was not the man to whom she would show her vulnerability. She’d left the patriarchy of the law firm and traded it for the same treatment in the cramped quarters of her own car.

“So, Colleen, who’s basically the captain of this ship, she makes a point to know these families. Mutual benefit. We help them, they help us. And part of that is a system of notification, like this AMBER Alert business. Someone goes missing—boop! —we throw it out on the network.” The word “boop” was accompanied by a light bop to Lauren’s head. “Someone wrongs us, boop! We get wind of something amiss, boop! Imagine it like lighting the beacons, except there’s no fire. Or beacons.”

“So...” Lauren slowed her speech, searching for the right question. One that would show she was not just some dense non-magical human without a clue. "Colleen put Quillan, Estella, and Stella out on this network—"

"Boop!"

"She booped them out there, and these tips we're following are from others like you?"

"In a nutshell. Much better than an ordinary tip line that relies on memories of license plates and recollections of people's faces. Besides, we can't really put this one out to the cops, can we?"

Lauren started to respond, then realized she didn't know how to contribute.

"Magical child who was born months ago is suddenly old enough to get a fake ID, being held by two people who are not her parents, who claim to be protecting her from someone who died centuries ago but is one stubborn bitch."

"I see your point."

"You damn well should. If that case landed on your desk, your only chance would be an insanity plea."

Lauren laughed, and Leander shot her a look. She readjusted her hands on the wheel. "So, shouldn't these tips be more reliable, then? Leander and I have stopped at dozens of places and none panned out at all. I wish I could say I was more confident about this new list."

"Look at my face, Lauren."

Lauren frowned. "I'm driving. And I would rather not."

Leander pitched forward, pressing his face so close to Nicolas' that their noses were almost touching. "I'm looking. All I see is a spoiled little darling."

Nicolas knocked him back in his seat. "When I want the opinion of the son of the man who peddles conversations with Marie Laveau to stupid tourists, I'll be sure to ask."

Leander looked ready to punch him, but instead he turned his head to look out the window.

"So, Lauren, when you look at me, what do you see?"

"I said I'm driving. Do you want me to get us all killed?"

"You've looked at me before. What do you see?"

"I don't think you want my answer."

"I'm out of your league, so let's skip the superficial. You see a man, yes? A human?"

"Wherever you're going with this, I'm already annoyed."

Leander snickered and mumbled something she couldn't hear.

"You annoy easily," Nicolas said. "Must have something to do with your incredibly hot older sister."

Lauren shoved him into the backseat. "You promised you'd leave her out of it."

"No, I promised not to use the name that rhymes with flaccidy."

"That's not even a word!"

"It sure is when you've been drinking all night and someone's counting on you."

"Piece of work," Leander said.

"Work of art," Nicolas corrected. "This network is made up of men and women, who are, by nature, fallible. We may have grandiose abilities, but we are human beings, just like you."

Lauren tensed her mouth. "Thanks for clearing that up."

"What he's not saying is that Colleen tossed a million-dollar reward on this one," Leander said, pressing his face against the glass. "You better believe people will see anything for a million dollars. Hell, I might go find a Quillan lookalike and disappear to the Canary Islands."

"That's a lot of money," Lauren whispered. Even as a Weatherly, she struggled to envision having a million dollars at her disposal. Though her inheritance would one day be far more, she lived solely off her own salary from the firm, and nothing else. Her trust fund had paid for college, but when she turned down a career at the stores, her father locked the remainder of the money, hoping to change her mind. She didn't.

"Thus, most of our leads will continue to be false," Nicolas said.

"Remind me why we're following them, then?"

"Because if we *don't* find them, some crazy ancient psychopathic has-been will, and I don't know about you, but I'm not ready for the Rapture yet. Me and Jesus, we ain't exactly homeboys."

Nicolas reached into his bag and pulled something out. Lauren caught the amber bottle in her rearview. "Uh-uh. No you don't. Not in my car."

Nicolas lifted the cognac in the air and broke the seal in clear view of her mirror. He tilted the bottle and let the liquor pour in an unsteady arc a foot from his mouth.

"Lighten up," Nicolas said with a grin. "We're in Texas now, darlin'."

THAT HAD BEEN DAY ONE OF THEIR ADVENTURE. NICOLAS' DRINKING started just outside Houston and never let up. If he wasn't drunk he was hungover and drinking even more, mumbling about the "hair of the dog."

They had visited a few stops in the Midwest. A woman in Paris, Texas—Leander said she was a shaman; he could tell by the way she inspected them for ailments—who had detained a young man, young woman, and a small child in her basement. The three were very clearly *not* Quillan and company, and so Lauren advised her to release them and pray the poor captors didn't press charges.

A rancher couple in Oklahoma—Leander couldn't read their abilities, but said right off he didn't trust them—

admitted they had no actual lead for them, but they wanted to offer their services in exchange for half the reward. Lauren declined.

They traveled all the way into the Rocky Mountains to a family of five who said they'd seen people matching the description pass through... weeks earlier. No, they did not know where they were going, or even in what direction.

Three more leads, one in Nebraska and two in Wyoming, produced similar frustrations.

Now they were headed to the Pacific Coast.

Lauren had never been there. Her mother had been on a quest to visit every state. She had her map with the pink pins all stuck in to every place she'd been, mounted to a cork board in their motor home. Every summer, they would venture out and knock off a few more states for Mary, who always knew how to make the adventure fun for the girls, who would have rather been playing at the beach in Destin. She combined each visit with something unusual, something they couldn't see at home.

Then Mary Weatherly died, and the motor home was sold, the map relegated to the attic where it remained unfinished, the entire west coast empty of pins.

For Lauren, this had been the worst of the changes after her mother's passing. Mary had been most real to her daughters when she was following her goals and taking them along for the ride. When Lauren suggested they finish the map for Mom, Daniel Weatherly gruffed, "Nothing to see out west," and that was the end of it.

Daniel opened more department stores, as sure a sign as any to Lauren on how he would be dealing with his grief, and the girls were sent to boarding school.

The trio stopped for the night outside Reno. Lauren had been content to stay in whatever motel was most convenient for them when they were too tired to push on, but Nicolas was horrified at the suggestion they stay anywhere not fit for a Deschanel.

He lost the battle in the end when Lauren refused to drive into Reno, and he was too drunk to take the wheel. She paid for the rooms from the envelope of cash provided by the Council and then steered Nicolas to his own room, making sure he was safely inside before retrieving her bag from the trunk.

Leander stood against the car with an agitated look. “You’re enabling him.”

“Sorry?”

“Walking him to his room, nursing him like you’re his mommy. You think that helps?”

Lauren pulled her bag over her shoulder and slammed the trunk. “He’s got a problem, Leander. A very real one, and it goes way beyond him being an asshole.”

“And?”

“And, I’m *not* his mother, but I also won’t let him stumble off into a ditch. He’s in his room, and what he does from there is his business, but at least I know I didn’t leave him to fend for himself.”

Leander shook his head. “You’re the one with the problem. First Quillan, now Nicolas. Can’t help it, can you? Everyone else sees them for the assholes they are, but not you. You see their *potential.*”

Lauren brushed past him. “Go to bed, Leander.”

“Oh, I will. Without another thought about that selfish drunk asshole two doors down.”

She dropped her bag on the faded, frayed rug outside her motel room door. “The only selfish one right here is you.”

Leander touched her arm. “Elle, come on. You can’t see what he’s doing?”

Lauren fumbled with the key. She was uncomfortable with

the softness that had crept into Leander's voice and wished she'd just disappeared into her room and said nothing. "I didn't want him here any more than you, but he's here, and he's a mess. He's broken. I don't care what you think of me trying to make sure he doesn't die on our watch."

"Wouldn't be our fault."

Lauren finally got the door open and she rushed inside, positioning herself on the other side. "No? That's not enough for someone with a conscience."

She shut the door in his face before the tears started.

30
OZ

Oz had thought going back to work, after a couple months away, would be hard. What he found instead was that the limbo of waiting for his first day back was harder than the thought of stepping onto the forest green carpet and facing fifty faces with endless questions.

His home on Seventh was quiet. Too quiet. Ashley had gone to stay with his mother at The Gardens, now that his housesitting was no longer necessary. The children were spending two weeks with his parents while he "sorted himself out," as his mother tactfully put it. Her underlying insinuation seemed to be that he was on the verge of a complete nervous breakdown.

His parents. Nicolas. They all looked at him like that, as if he was hanging on by a thread, that Adrienne's death had sent him into a lifelong period of mourning that rendered him incapable of tying his shoes or finishing his vegetables.

The people in his inner circle had always ascribed this level of depth to his emotions, throwing around words like "martyr," or "hero complex," without really understanding the density of his commitment to those same people. Yes, Oz loved hard, and he loved deep, but he wasn't a one-dimensional man defined by that love and nothing else.

Only Lucia didn't condescend to him on the matter. She teased him about it, but her method involved words like "get over it" and "let's go for a run." She fell on the exact opposite end of the spectrum from Oz, a free spirit un-tethered to anyone or anything.

Oz supposed her dalliance with Nicolas shouldn't have surprised him all that much, but it did take him off guard. Nicolas had it wrong, though. Oz's feelings had nothing to do with how he reacted; he couldn't have put it adequately into words, either. He only knew that what had felt untainted in his life now no longer was. Whatever sheltered innocence they'd shared, no matter how unorthodox or temporary, had been shattered.

Lucia's name popped up on his phone several times a day. He sent each call to voicemail. He couldn't explain those feelings to someone like Lucia, whose most complex emotions involved reactions to battle scenes in movies. She wouldn't get it. She'd tell him to get over it. She'd invite him out for a run, like everything was the same.

The grandfather clock chimed noon. When the intonations died down, he was again left in a silence so loud he could very nearly hear his pulse through his skin.

Oz grabbed his blazer from the coat rack.

THOUGH HE HAD CHANGED, THE OFFICE HAD NOT. THE SMELL OF FINE mahogany and lemon furniture polish welcomed him, as did the smiles of so many of his relatives and peers. There were no downcast eyes or unasked questions, as he had feared. They were happy to see him. It was time.

He made his way down the long hall, past more friendly faces, and stopped in front of his office door. The sign was the same, and why wouldn't it be? C. Sullivan III. And next door, his father's office would read C. Sullivan Jr. And while retired, his grandfather's remained unoccupied, C. Sullivan Sr.

Farther down, the offices of Rory, Jamie, Jerome, Robyn, and all the others. His uncles, aunts, cousins. His people. He didn't belong outside of town in a secluded plantation. He belonged *here*.

His uncles, Patrick and Rory, huddled together in some kind of office talk. When they saw him, they brightened, clapped him on the back, and said they were glad he was back.

Oz released the long sigh he'd been holding. His first interaction with his peers wasn't so bad.

He opened his office. He was glad, too.

HE'D BEEN AT HIS DESK NO MORE THAN FIVE MINUTES WHEN HIS cousin Connor knocked.

"I heard you were back," he said, looking around. "I just came back, too."

Oz's own pain pushed to the surface as he remembered. "I was so sorry to hear about Elizabeth."

"Listen, I'm even sorrier I didn't come to Adrienne's service," Connor replied. "I don't think I realized how bad off I was for a while."

Oz shook his head. "We've both had more to deal with than we should."

Connor nodded. "Wanna get lunch?"

"Lunch?" Oz couldn't recall a single time Connor had asked him anywhere.

"Yeah. Marcello's has their meatballs on special, and I could use the company."

Oz looked out his window onto Carondelet. The air was crisp, but the sky clear. A short walk and a hearty meal might be just the thing.

THEY WALKED DOWN CARONDELET TO GIROD, AND THEN CUT OVER TO St. Charles Avenue. The low rumble of the St. Charles Streetcar drowned out whatever Connor was trying to say, but Oz welcomed the familiarity of the old green beast. He decided he might go for a ride into Carrolton later in the evening, after the work rush, when the car only ferried the occasional straggler after the route passed Louisiana Avenue.

"As I was saying, it's really not good for business, but you know your father. He's always carried a different view of philanthropy."

"Yes," Oz agreed, having missed most of the story. He watched the streetcar amble down the tracks, in the direction of the Garden District, while Connor gave their name to the hostess.

"Wanna sit outside?" Connor called.

"Huh? Yeah, sure."

The hostess led them to a small metal table, tilted too far to the left on the uneven sidewalk. She took their drink order. Oz said tea and was surprised when Connor did as well.

"No Scotch today?" Oz asked as she walked away. Connor, even more than others in the office, was known for being the one to go to if you needed your afternoon beverage. He always had Johnnie Walker or Macallan to spare.

"No, and not anymore, either," Connor explained as a somber pall fell over his expression. "I mentioned I was in a bad way when Elizabeth died. Two fingers of Scotch a day turned into twelve. It was bad when my Danielle died, too, but Elizabeth was there to hide the bottles or sometimes outright dump them down the kitchen sink. I used to get so mad. 'Do you know how much those cost?' I would rail on at her, sobering up, nursing the worst headaches imaginable. This time, there was no one to stop me. And then Tristan... he started doing it, too, taking after his dad, and I didn't know what to do. I knew he needed help, but he laughed at my attempts to help him. Who wouldn't? The drunk telling another drunk to sober up. When he crashed into that restaurant, that was my wake-up call, come way too late."

Oz nodded. His own escape had involved helping a good friend, which, in the end, was also unhealthy. "I'm glad you found it, even if it came later than you wanted. Tristan needs you."

"Maybe he does, maybe he doesn't. I haven't heard from him since he took off with Harriett." Connor smiled at the waitress when she delivered their tea. "I don't even know where he is. Maybe this is God's punishment for me."

Oz realized Connor had no real grasp of what Tristan was involved with. His marriage to Elizabeth had given him a glimpse into her world, but he'd never dipped more than a toe. "Tristan needed to figure things out for himself, that's all."

Connor drained half his glass. "He was always closer to his mother. Did everything with her. When she was sad, he was sad. When she was excited about something, he was, too. I don't think he knows which way is up, to be honest, but I hope you're right. I hope he's figuring things out."

When the waitress returned, Connor ordered for them both. When Oz gave him a *what the hell was that* look, Connor laughed. "You haven't had the meatballs in a while, apparently. I'm doing you a favor. You'll thank me later."

"You certainly seem confident about it."

Connor leaned back in his chair. "How are you holding up, Oz? Figuring out your new routine yet?"

"Me? Oh, you know, I'm fine. Kids are good. We're just taking things one day at a time."

Connor lowered his gaze. "You can't bullshit a man who just went through a very similar loss. The Dead Wives Club isn't one I ever wanted to be a member of, but here we are."

"Here we are," Oz repeated in a daze, wondering why he'd agreed to come to lunch.

"You're like your father. He never wants to talk about anything either," Connor said. He adjusted his suspenders and snapped them back into place against his carefully starched white shirt. "A Sullivan thing, really. I was like that, too, until I saw I was feeling things, all right, just at the bottom of a bottle."

"I don't even really like alcohol," Oz said. He swallowed down the lump in his throat.

"Everyone has their booze," Connor said wisely. "Be careful, yours might be less obvious but just as toxic."

"I'm fine, really. Going back to work is the best thing for me, and for the kids."

Connor scrutinized him, and Oz guessed he was looking for signs that Oz was not fine.

Before he could dig into him further, though, two plates of meatballs arrived. Connor rubbed his hands together and licked his lips, shooting Oz an eager look.

"Now, Marcello's meatballs are a *great* replacement for booze," Connor said and went to work.

With a long breath inward, Oz picked up his fork just as his phone screen lit up. Lucia.

He watched her name blink with each ring until it went to voicemail.

Connor pointed with his fork. "Whoever *that* was, you look like you might be happier next time if you answer it."

31
SEBASTIAN

He could almost read Aleksandr's thoughts: *Why did I even come here?*

Sebastian imagined their entire friendship had been a series of Aleksandr inching closer to this question, reaping the benefits of having someone he could relate to while somewhere, deep down, also realizing he had absolutely nothing in common with that same someone.

At some point, Aleksandr would view this dynamic on a scale and see how drastically things tipped in the wrong direction. This was why Margarethe was a visionary; a genius, really. She saw Aleksandr was growing close and devised a way for Sebastian to weaken him enough to expose his greatest vulnerability: the fear of being alone.

"You hear from the bitch?" Sebastian asked. They sat side by side on the dock at *Femme Forte.*

Aleksandr skipped a rock across the surface of the lake. Five jumps. "Stop calling her that."

"What should I call her? Backstabbing slut? Traitorous whore?"

"Dammit, Sebastian! I'm serious."

Sebastian grinned into his beer. "So, have you?"

"Why should I tell you? You're just going to twist around everything I say and make it worse."

Sebastian shrugged. The questions were only for show. The things a friend *should* ask. He already knew Aleksandr hadn't spoken to her in any meaningful way, or the two of them wouldn't be sharing beers together.

"No, okay? I haven't." Aleksandr picked another rock from his pile. He rubbed his thumb over the smooth, black surface. "I've been planning to call her. I just don't know what to say."

"Maybe that's because she's the one who owes you words, not the other way around." Sebastian prided himself on sounding so reasonable.

"It just doesn't make any sense. You don't know her."

Only in the Biblical sense. Sebastian tapped his skull. "Maybe that's your problem, Aleksei. You're in too deep, my friend. She's got you by the cock and the heart, and you can't even see straight. You can't see that she's fucked you over, my man." *Fucked me right over, too.*

Aleksandr belted out a sigh. "I should probably go."

"You just got here!"

"And it's not helping. I need to do something... else. I haven't gone to class in days, and I need to get caught up before they kick me out." He tilted his beer bottle, which he'd barely touched. "This isn't even good, Sebastian."

"What are you, a beer expert now?"

"No, but it's gross. And I feel more depressed sitting here. I need to do something useful. My cousin Anne is serving meals to the homeless today in Algiers, so maybe I'll join her after I get some studying in."

Sebastian sprayed beer out of his mouth. "You'd rather be serving meals to the homeless? Is this a joke?"

Aleksandr hopped to his feet. "If you said it, it might be."

"Ohhhhhh!" Sebastian tapped the wood with his open palm. "You *did* make a joke!"

"I make a lot of jokes. Most of them go over your head." Aleksandr dusted off his pants and reached for the pile of rocks.

"Because they're not funny," Sebastian defended. He squinted against the bit of sun peeking through the clouds. "I have an idea."

"I'm not in the mood for one of your 'ideas.'"

"You said you needed to do something else. I have just the thing."

Aleksandr dug in his pocket for his keys, but Sebastian was up in a flash, hand clamped to his wrist. Aleksandr glared at him.

Sebastian turned them both to face the lake. He pointed to a buoy he could hardly see. It had to be two, maybe three miles out, just a speck of red and white bobbing in the distance. "See that?"

"What? See what?"

Sebastian pointed with one hand and gripped Aleksandr by the shoulder with the other. "The buoy. Way out there."

"Yeah, so. What of it?"

Sebastian pressed his lips to Aleksandr's ear. "Swim to it."

Aleksandr recoiled. "Swim to that? Have you lost your mind?"

"You're the one who lost his mind. Over a girl." Sebastian knelt at the edge of the dock and cupped his hand, dipping it in the water. He threw some at Aleksandr, who winced and put his hands up in defense. "You want to feel something else. How about a surge of adrenaline? The kind that only comes when you do something truly dangerous, like a fucking badass."

"It's not badass, it's stupid. Foolish," Aleksandr retorted. "I'm not even a strong swimmer!"

"How does anyone become a strong swimmer? Necessity."

"What? No, Sebastian. They become a strong swimmer by practicing."

Sebastian nodded his head toward the vast, endless lake. "There's your practice."

"What's wrong with you? I would drown if I tried that. I wouldn't even get halfway."

Sebastian shrugged. "I can see why Fiona wouldn't show up if you'd let fear get in the way of an adventure."

Aleksandr shook with building rage. He didn't erupt. He wouldn't. Sebastian was still all he had, even if he was trying to get him killed.

"Pussy," he goaded. "Because you're a pussy."

"Yeah? Maybe I am. I might just be. I wouldn't ask you to do something dangerous for my own amusement, and I guess that makes me weak. But at least I'm not a bad friend."

The rocks slipped from Aleksandr's hand and dropped in a cascading fall, one after another. He shot Sebastian one last scorching look and marched off.

Foolish, careless boy.

Sebastian perked up. The voice of Margarethe almost never came to him in the daylight. Only at night, or in his dreams.

"Me?"

Yes, you. You were charged with winning Aleksandr's affections, not getting him killed.

"You said build him up with one hand and knock him down with the other. I thought I was doing what you asked of me," Sebastian whined. Margarethe was disappointed in him... could it be true? His palms began to sweat. He had the strange urge to whimper like a dog.

You did such a spectacular job of gaining his trust. Then taking away something dear to him. But you kept taking! What did you think this would do?

Tears pooled in Sebastian's eyes. "I thought you would be proud."

You did not think, is nearer to the truth. We are so close, Sebastian. So very close. If he does not trust you, how can you come through for me when it matters?

"How am I supposed to know if what I'm doing is right or wrong, helping or not, if you won't even tell me why we need him?" Sebastian cried.

I asked you once if you trusted me to be your mother. Your one true mother. You said yes. Is this no longer true?

Sebastian gasped for air. He was near to losing control, and he struggled against the awfulness of this sensation. "Of course it's true, Mother. You're my only purpose in my life. Everything, it's for you."

Not everything. Your lavish lifestyle is not for me. Your indulgences are not for me. Ah, do not defend it. I don't begrudge you your enjoyments at all, little though they may mean when you fulfill your destiny as the starlight awakener.

"I would give it all up."

And you will. But we are too close to the end for errors. I have found an ally—the one we required all along, but did not know it. Aleksandr is the key to this ally, but we cannot reach him if he thinks you are a madman.

"Tell me how to fix it, Mother!"

Listen carefully, my child...

32
CYLER

Cyler perched at the edge of the boulder wedged between the rock formations, one of the few places in Farjhem not easily visible except from the mountaintop. The spray from the waterfall created a misty sheen over the surface of his bare skin. Even for an Empyrean, born of fire, winter in Farjhem was not anything to mess around with, but Cyler preferred himself when his senses were at their peak. If he was going to be cold, he'd rather be freezing.

The icy chill served as a reminder that he was still a living, breathing creature with at least some measure of his own free will remaining to him. Oriana's tether was long, but it was still a tether. Farjhem was his playground, but he never forgot a single step outside would lead to his incarceration. And that while inside, his every move was watched.

Oriana liked to ask him if he knew why she continued to offer him second, third, fourth chances. She dangled the question like a promise of extortion disguised as love. He told himself the answer was nothing more than an indulgence of her ego, but at times, he did wonder. Why had she kept him around? He was nobody. He had no bloodline to speak of. No great war record. His sole and single claim to anything was his relationship to Agripin—once duke, then emperor, now nothing. A crownless prince locked away in a gilded cage.

What did Oriana think of Cyler's obeisance to her now? That his fealty was sincere? That he had given up? Cyler wasn't convinced she cared about his motivations, only the outcome. Her entire world had been constructed on the careful appearance of control; of her environment, of the activity of her patrons. She thrived in the expected and reacted violently to anything vaguely resembling opposition. Having Cyler back under her thumb was as much about restoring order to her meticulous world as it was about punishing him for his defection.

Cyler had spent his life serving others, so falling in line once again was akin to muscle memory. Yet, he was not the same fledgling who had vied so hard for Agripin's attentions, nor was he the trained soldier who had followed him across the world, questioning nothing. He had grown into himself with the desire to find meaning in one notable way: finding the leader worth his service and serving that leader through the end of the world, if it came to that.

Agripin had been that leader, until he wasn't. Oriana never had.

Yet he was trained enough in the art of service that he could look at this charge as a job to be done. If Oriana noticed the absence of sincerity in what he offered, she said nothing.

Cyler's greatest fear when he decided to accompany Agripin back to Farjhem for certain punishment was that Oriana might re-brand him with a new Mark of Emyr. Slicing his off had been more than a freedom from control of the Senetat; it had been a symbol of his own freedom. Permission to serve in a less limited way. To go from wings clipped to soaring as far and as high as he so pleased.

But she hadn't said a word about it. She knew, surely. Nothing escaped her. Whatever else others whispered about Grand Empress Oriana behind her back, she was no fool. Perhaps this was yet another layer to the cage she'd built for him. A prison constructed of illusions, to lead him into a false sense of autonomy.

Cyler knew better. He knew precisely what he had gotten himself into by joining Agripin in Farjhem.

The only thing he did not know was how long this new, improved Cyler was capable of tolerating it.

It took weeks before he was capable of visiting Agripin at all. Oriana, from the beginning, authorized Cyler to come and go to Agripin's secured room as he pleased, accepting, in her own way, that Cyler's return had always been about Agripin. He saw this not as a kindness, but a move of practicality on her part, for no matter his crimes, Agripin still had a right to certain luxuries afforded to someone of his station, and attendants was one of them. Another move to lull Cyler into her web, but she didn't count on Cyler's reticence to be anywhere near Agripin with his heart so conflicted.

"Don't underestimate his power as a now and future ally," Eldre Maxima whispered one evening as she passed him in the palace, her long crimson robes swishing against the marble. Cyler turned to respond, and she was already at the other end of the corridor, turning toward the entrance.

Maxima's words angered him. Between the Brotherhood and now this Senetat defect, they all boldly assumed Cyler should be on their side, even when they had done nothing at all to deserve that loyalty, nor had he given them the impression they'd earned it. He had always been on whatever side Agripin said they were on.

If they took his going along with Agripin's incarceration as a sign of anything other than unfinished business between Cyler and his master, they could choke on their assumptions. He didn't owe them anything, certainly not an explanation as to where his head was at.

And how could he, when even he didn't know?

Day by day, he avoided the corridor leading to Agripin's secured chambers. Agripin had asked for him; he knew that because the other attendants passed him messages quietly, in drive-by whispers, as if there were any such things as secrets in a royal court led by Oriana.

One day, his feet carried him with a mind of their own, and he found himself outside Agripin's door, without a plan. The door opened as if commanded, and a guard stepped aside to make way. When he was ushered inside, his heart fluttered with an emotion he couldn't quite describe.

Agripin was splayed across a velvet chair, half-clothed, crimson hair affright. Bottles upon bottles of whiskey lay piled around him like a slapdash attempt at art. "Well, look who wandered down from his perch. Cyler. The honor is all yours."

"Hello, Agripin."

"So it's Agripin now? Am I no longer your emperor?"

"Are you?" Cyler kept his eyes on his former master.

"How insolent you become when I can no longer punish you," he slurred.

"The question stands. Your sister sits on your throne, while you do... whatever it is you're doing."

Agripin chucked his half-full bottle at the wall. The glass shattered, amber liquid dropping a line of trails down the tapestry. "Something I might have had the agency to do something about had you not led me straight back to her!"

The two guards flanking Agripin tensed, ready to restrain him. Cyler mused at this... how these guards were here to protect *his* safety for a change. When had he ever had this kind of power over Agripin, save their journey back to Farjhem?

"You decided your own fate when you brought Anasofiya with you from Farjhem instead of leaving her to face her punishment. You were returning to Oriana with or without me," Cyler explained with unusual, measured patience. He felt like he was explaining a simple concept to a stubborn child. "I thought you might prefer to do it with someone who cared for you."

"And you thought that would be you?" Agripin snorted, searching his hand beneath the cushions for another bottle. The guards exchanged a look at each other, and then behind the chair, where the unopened stack was piled. One grinned. Neither made a move to help.

"Birger and his buddies wanted you dead. I did what I could."

"Do not take credit for my existence," Agripin returned, spittle flying from his lips. Cyler almost pitied him, but he decided instead what he felt was disappointment. The emperor he had loved and followed would have been scheming his way back into power, not drowning in self-loathing. "I know it was Anasofiya who convinced them to spare my life."

Cyler laughed before he could think to stop himself. "Still on about her, are you? After all she did? I wonder if you know she spared your life in order to continue to use you to further the agenda of the Brotherhood. It wasn't from any great affection."

"An agenda that did not need my continued presence to thrive," Agripin said. "I won't discuss this with you. Your small mind has never possessed the capacity to understand mine."

"You're right, I don't understand you," Cyler said, turning

to go. "Something that used to bother me, once upon a time, when I lived and died by your favor."

"I haven't dismissed you, fledgling."

"Go on, if it makes you feel better."

"She's using you. My sister. And you're allowing her, as you allowed me."

Cyler turned. "Do you have something novel to tell me, or are your only contributions to this conversation going to consist of insults and things I already painfully know?"

Agripin stood. The guards at his side looked ready to tackle him at a moment's notice, and even a little eager at the notion. He shot them both disgusted looks. "She will destroy everything we love, Cyler. Everything you and I have ever stood for. She will do it on a whim, without motivation beyond shaping the world to her own desires. Do you think she cares about Farjhem, outside of serving as a front door to her brothel? She never asked for this honor, and she does not want it, but she has no choice but to accept it. It annoys her. It eats at her that she cannot be back in The Menagerie and she will do *anything* to rectify that. She'll see our whole kingdom crumble around our feet to see it done."

Cyler shrugged. "Even if you're right, what of it? She's the one on the throne, Aggie. It's time you realize this." He swallowed, with a cautious look at the guards. "And what you're saying is grounds for treason."

"Aggie." Agripin licked his lips. "I wonder if you would stand there playing the role of arrogant bastard if I hadn't made you who you are."

"You deserve the credit for creating me," Cyler agreed. "But you're also responsible for my undoing."

"We both know why you've avoided me so long."

Cyler crossed his arms, awaiting Agripin's next words.

"You're a soldier, Cyler. You were born to serve and you will always serve, as you draw breath." Agripin tried to step forward, but was immediately halted by his jailers. He shrugged them off, but stayed put. "You think you serve me no longer? The choice is only easy if you don't bother to face the challenge."

"Get some sleep," Cyler replied, again turning to leave.

"Aye, I intend to. And Cyler?"

Cyler stopped at the door, but didn't turn.

"With Maxima in Farsengel, there is no one else to play the Brotherhood's games. No one to thwart Oriana from her reign of ineptitude and the downfall of Farjhem. If you don't define your loyalties, be assured, they will become defined for you."

Blood froze in Cyler's face. Maxima, arrested? When had this happened? Would he be next?

He left before Agripin could take pleasure in his horror.

33
ANASOFIYA

Amelia's face boasted a spark of color along the cut of her cheekbones, peeking out from the blanket Jacob had triple wrapped her in. She leaned back in her deck chair, feet propped up on another nearby.

"The good days make all the bad days worth it," Ana said. "I promise."

"I'm just happy to have one where I'm not being ordered to bed rest by my mother." Amelia stretched her legs and her toes peeked out from beneath a gap in the afghan. She wiggled them in the cool air. "Takes me back to being a kid. I almost forgot how overbearing she can be when she decides she's in charge."

"You have the best mother in New Orleans, and you know it."

Amelia's tired face broke into a muted grin. "I hope I can be half the mother she is."

"You will be. Bad mothers don't worry about what they'll be like." Ana inspected her cousin closely, looking for signs she recognized. The dry, stretched skin, bagged eyes from malnutrition. They were present already in Amelia, and she still had a couple months to go, from Ana's estimate. "How are you feeling mentally? Emotionally?"

Amelia pulled the blankets tighter, huddled in her chair like a swaddled baby. "Excited and happy. More so every day. Until I knew Moira was here, all I could think about were the risks, and now it's like there's no risk big enough to take away the joy I feel over her arrival. The risks seem almost silly now, like what on earth was I so worried about?"

Ana nodded. Her own reservations about being a mother had slipped away as soon as she felt Aleksandr's presence stir within her. "But?"

Amelia sucked in her bottom lip. "What if I'm not strong enough to carry her?"

"Of course you are. Don't let yourself think that. I was strong enough, even on the worst days."

Her cousin's head shook under the pile of blankets. "It's not that. Mom has the healing brigade dedicated to my physical health. I think I could survive dismemberment at his point." Her laugh faded to a cough. "I'm afraid of becoming imperiled again. I don't think of myself as a delicate person, but it's like anyone with a mental illness. They don't make you weak, or less than anyone else, but they do change your life. You learn to live with it, but it requires adjustments. A lot of times they're little changes. For me, I have to separate myself emotionally from someone's struggles, and being a doctor of psychology has actually helped me a lot, to train that muscle. It's not so easy with family."

"Last time it happened, it was when Aunt Elizabeth died, right?"

"Tristan's grief over his mother is what sent me over the

edge," Amelia said. "I felt it like a knife severing me in half, and there wasn't anything I could do about it. I was frozen... entirely helpless. Much as I love Tristan, he's my cousin. Not my husband. My child. If it was that bad for Tristan's agony..." Amelia reached her hand from the blanket and pulled her mug of tea back to her. It disappeared under the pile. "I can hear her, Ana. All the time. Moira. She isn't talking, exactly. There are no words.... I know she's only a cluster of developing cells right now. It's more like messages. As if I know her heart and all its contents."

"I know exactly what you're describing," Ana answered. "There will never be anything more personal for you than now, where it's only you and her, Amelia. You'll be close when she's born, but she'll belong to the world, too. But don't lose yourself to this closeness, no matter how much it calls to you, or how tempting it seems. I nearly did, and it drove me mad."

"That's my fear. I can feel myself slipping into her emotions, absorbing them as my own. That's so dangerous, I know it, but I can't stop it, and a part of me doesn't want to. Because how bad would it really be if it was just me and her and no one else?"

"Have you told your mother? Or Jacob?"

Amelia looked down.

"Amelia, you have to. You have to prepare the healers for this. Now that I know, I can watch you for signs, but what if I'm not there, and you lose yourself to this?" Ana pitched forward, pulling the blanket down so she could see all of Amelia's tired face. "And don't even *think* things like slipping into imperilment like it's some romantic place for you and Moira to hide from the world. Amelia, you will *die* if you stay in that state too long. I'm sorry to say it so bluntly, but that's a truth you already know but are willfully forgetting because you're losing yourself to this pregnancy, as I did with mine. *Stop* and *think*. Your one and only goal is to get through this confinement with a healthy daughter, and a healthy you. The ideas taunting you along the way will only hurt you and steer you off course."

Amelia rolled her bottom lip into her mouth, chewing harder. Blood beaded at the surface. "You don't know how hard I've tried to be more than the things that have happened to me."

"That's where you're wrong," Ana said softly. "Everything I do is an effort to carry me further away from the nightmares."

"You took down an entire world with your anger, Ana. You're far from helpless. You're my damn hero." She set the mug back on the table. "My last imperilment, I needed to be rescued by Oz. In that cabin, where I was raped—where my child was taken from me—it was Jacob's intervention that saved my life. I'm not a damsel in distress, or a woman who needs to be saved. I don't want to be that person, and I'm not going to go crying to Jacob or my mother so they can save me this time, too. If I can't save myself, what kind of woman am I?"

"It's not a weakness to ask for help. Or to need it."

Fat, heavy drops trickled down the sides of Amelia's cheeks. "I know it's not. So why is it so hard?"

Ana reached into Amelia's blanket and pulled both hands out. They were both bony and swollen at the same time. "Then use me. Let me be that person you unload on. I'll be by your side every second of every day if I have to, if it means keeping you safe. We can keep this our secret for now, but you have to promise me you'll tell me what you're going through every step of the way. And if it gets to the point where you need saving, we'll work on a way to make sure you're saving yourself this time."

Amelia wiped her tears away and sniffled into a handkerchief with the initials LF on them. *Luther,* Ana thought with a grin. *Of course the man carries monogrammed hankies.*

"If I agree, can we stop talking about it? For now?" Amelia asked.

Leaning back, Ana noted what a nice day it was for November and how she wished they could go for a walk. "What do you want to talk about?"

Amelia smirked. "How about Aidrik? When's the big day?"

Yes, Anasofiya. I would also like to know this, Aidrik chimed in.

Ana's groan started all the way from her belly. "I think that's on hold for a bit."

"Why?"

"Well, I can't say, because we promised not to talk about it."

Amelia pulled one of the four pillows propped behind her and threw it at Ana. "That's not a reason. What does one have to do with the other?"

"I've never been very good at juggling more than one major life crisis at once," Ana explained. "Look, I know you think I'm looking for excuses, but I'm not. When I do finally reveal this to Finn and Aleksei, I want them to be able to enjoy it. If it makes you feel any better, it's not just you. After Aleksei's failed reunion with Fiona, he's really not himself right now."

"All the more reason to give him such an amazing gift!"

Ana shook her head. "I... I want it to be just right."

Excuses, Anasofiya. You can't fool your own self.

Shut it, Wraith.

"What about Thanksgiving?" Amelia pressed on. "Isn't that a couple weeks away?"

"I completely forgot." Memories of Deschanel holidays came back in a rush. Of rich, cloying seasonal scents and ringing laughter. No matter what was happening, no matter the tragedies, they always came together on Thanksgiving and Christmas. They never moved forward as well as they did during the holidays. "Do you think we'll even have it this year?"

"Why wouldn't we?"

Ana wondered, briefly, if Amelia was experiencing some degree of denial about her condition. "With everything going on, I mean. Your mom usually coordinates with Nicolas to use *Ophélie,* but he's off in one of his self-loathing phases again."

Amelia ran her fingers over her cracked lips with a thoughtful look. "What about *Vivra sa Via*? Your dad still owns that plantation, right?"

"I really don't think you should be traveling that far in your condition…"

"Then what about Magnolia Grace? This house is huge, Ana. Almost as big as The Gardens. I seem to remember your dad hosting the Krewe of Magus ball here one year."

"A few years, actually." Ana had more rebuttals on her lips, but as the idea settled on her, she realized how much she wanted to see this happen. She was only now, finally, leading her own household, at the age of thirty-one. Thanks to Aidrik, she would never age past this point, and neither would Finn or Aleksei, nor Amelia and Jacob if The Prophecy was to be believed, but most of the Deschanels would. She recalled Aidrik telling her once, *every occasion with one beloved to you is a gift when you are immortal.* She hadn't known this facet of herself long enough to understand from experience, but she grasped his meaning. They would always, always have excuses to cancel a get-together, but time not spent was time they would not get back.

"I can sense your excitement over here," Amelia charged with an impish grin. "If you're worried about cooking, we can get Condoleezza and her catering team out here."

"Last time she invited them was for Uncle Charles' and his family's funeral. I assume you remember how that went?"

"Feels like a lifetime ago. I don't remember the food much."

"Because you blocked it out. What they served was criminal."

Amelia laughed. "Okay, okay. What about three Thanksgivings ago? When we had it at The Elms on St. Charles? That was a great meal."

"There's no way we're getting a caterer a week before Thanksgiving," Ana said. "You know what? I can do this. I can cook Thanksgiving dinner. How hard can it be?"

Amelia leveled a skeptical look. "Talk to my mom. She's cooked Thanksgivings for us all in the past. I'm sure she can help."

"Are you trying to say I'm hopeless?"

"Well... you did burn a box of macaroni the other day..."

Ana recoiled in mock offense. "Come on, who hasn't forgotten they were cooking something before?"

"Or Finn could tackle this. He's great in the kitchen."

Ana smacked her with her pillow. "Don't be shocked if your serving of turkey comes with a side of arsenic."

"I should warn you, it's very detectable in toxicology tests nowadays."

With one hand, Ana flipped her hair behind her head in an exaggerated gesture. "Prison might favor me. Fashion experts are now saying orange actually pairs quite well with red hair."

Amelia laughed into her blanket, masking the coughing that suddenly came over her. One hand reached for Ana's and gripped tight. Ana squeezed and forced a smile to overcome the unexpected wave of sadness that hit her.

I won't lose her, Aidrik. When the time comes, I need you to help me.

I will always aid you, Anasofiya, as I always have.

Whatever it takes. She has to survive this.

Aye, Kjære. Then it is time you accept my presence is more valuable as my own entity, once again.

34
TRISTAN

Nerys held her audience in rapture.

"We stand at the greatest impasse of our existence. At a critical crossroad where we will either find a way to move forward, together, or decide that our lives are to mean no more than a race perpetually in exile."

They were in Thorvald's world, an elaborate system of decorated caves and casas on the Costa del Sol. Altogether, it was a feat of designer architecture that reminded Tristan of those million-dollar homes shows his mother used to watch.

Tristan didn't know Thorvald, or much about him, but the creature had an ancient pall about him, one that made him both deserving of a unique respect but also, terrifyingly intimidating. Tristan was in love with him and also afraid of him as the creature stood tall and erect at Nerys' side.

To her other side, Birger and Astrid bore looks of stoic veneration. Anders told Tristan the Brotherhood by design had no leaders, but if they did, this power couple would be the ones to do it. Already, everyone looked at them as if they were, and deferred to them when decisions needed making.

Their only daughter, Eydis, had made her way back to them days ago. She stood in the audience now, but earlier they'd fawned over her like she was their perfect darling returned home from an expensive boarding school. Tristan wondered if they knew how their innocent girl had seduced and screwed Nicolas during her wayward stint at *Ophélie*.

Tristan knew so few of those gathered. He'd overheard names others appeared to revere. Stian, Leif, Jorun, Trygve. Leaders of great regions. Yiva he knew, from their time in Thailand, though even among decorated riches she seemed as foreign and feral as ever. Tarek hovered in the corner, aloof but listening.

But there were Quinlans, also. Of this group, Tristan and Harriett knew next to nothing, so Anders had given them a brief history and explanation of their relevance. Their coming together with Empyreans now filled Tristan with a jittery excitement. He knew, from his favorite fantasy stories and comics, that there was nothing that could heal a past like a new alliance.

"We have borne, for centuries, the injustices of the Senetat. We have hovered in the shadows, watching with only a vague interest, telling ourselves the lives we had were sufficient," Nerys boomed. The red rope of her braid was slung over one shoulder, her bow over the other. *An Amazonian Queen,* Tristan thought. "Friends, there is none more guilty of this than me. The famous pacifist among us, I was content to live as we were if it meant peace for most of us. I told myself that we were thriving in our own ways, and that this was enough."

No one spoke. No one dared interrupt. Tristan's eyes passed over all the onlookers, who were rooted in deep reverence for their speaker.

"We, now, all of us, have been thrust from our placid complacency. I will not rehash the reasons. We all know them.

We all feel the newfound urgency surge through us as we think of my vagabond sister, Oriana, ruling from Farjhem. Make no mistake, we have entered the Third Runean War."

Nods and murmurs of assent filled the cave. From his peripheral, Tristan saw Harriett's eyes glisten with tears as she listened, roused by the same words.

"Friends, we must decide, here and now, what sort of creatures we believe ourselves to be. Are we true Children of Emyr, as we have always sworn, in the relative safety of our exile? If so, we cannot be still as those of us still bearing Marks are eliminated, one by one. No one here knows Oriana as I do. No one knows what she is capable of as I do. I believe, deep in my soul, she is growing weary of a crown she never asked for, and never wanted. As this weariness ebbs, she lashes out in the only way she knows how. She has no loyalty to our homeland as we do, not beyond how it provides her with a shield protecting her and her beloved Menagerie. Do *not* bury your head in the sand one moment longer. We cannot afford to. Not any longer! More *will* fall. This lull is only temporary. Who among us can abide the deaths of our own people on their conscience, as the cost of our continued freedom?"

Tarek stepped forward from the shadows. He threw back his hood. Several voices remarked in sadness over the appearance of this new leader, for his arrival signaled the loss of Dagr. "It has been said that this is not a game of numbers. That we do not need an army of thousands. Yet, we do not know what awaits us in Farjhem. If not numbers, then what?"

"Tarek, it has been many years. You look well." When Nerys smiled, the effect was as dazzling as it was authentic. She had no visible guile in her, no agenda. Tristan could see why she was so beloved to her people. "I believe, as do the other leaders present, that we must play to the strength amongst us. A dozen of our most powerful is a greater weapon than a hundred of their weakest. You are right; we do not know what we will find in Farjhem. Not entirely. We know we will not find mercy. Your presence, and the absence of our dearest Dagr, speaks to this quite loudly."

"We are amassing our most powerful," Thorvald added. His deep voice boomed across the cavern walls. Even the ornate tapestries could not contain it. "Our most rare. A shaman is as common as the weeds growing on the hills of Malaga, but a resurrection shaman? Now, imagine we have ten at our disposal. Because we do, Tarek. As we have one among us who can breach a telepathic block. Two, with your presence."

The shock of this last announcement reverberated across the room. Harriett squeezed Tristan's hand, and he realized Thorvald was talking about *him*.

"And others," added Birger. "Not only Empyrean, but Quinlan. We have signed a new blood pact, one scorched on the fires of the sacred pyre in Nora Quinlan's tribal land. Amongst them, they have those who can commune with nature and wildlife in ways even we cannot. Their draoi is an army unto itself. Between us, we are ready."

Nerys bowed her head for several long seconds. When her head rose to greet the gatherers once again, she was crying. "And we have a weapon no one, not Oriana, not the Senetat, and not even the Brotherhood could have anticipated. We have our most ancient. Our Brynja and Einar."

Her words garnered the same reaction, Tristan thought, as if his Catholic church back home had resurrected Jesus for Sunday mass.

Anders had told them about Bryja and Einar one night as they sat around a campfire in Myanmar. *Children of Men and their Christian faith have the tales of Adam and Eve being the first of your kind. Their original sin then led to all of mankind, for better or worse. We have no original sin in our past. Emyr had always envisioned to create a race of gods in his image. The first of this legacy were Brynja and Einar. There are no Empyreans, living or dead, as powerful as the first two. From them, we all descend. Including you, Tristan, and Harriett, through your blood heritage of Aidrik. This was long before the Marks, before the Senetat. As the years wore on, and our government in Farjhem saw formation, Brynja and Einar were pressed into legend; long dead, if they even existed. But they did exist, and they exist still. They sequester themselves high in the Ural Mountains, where the land meets the Arctic Ocean. Many have searched for them, but none have found them. Only a few among us know how to reach them.*

Tristan expected to see two creatures as old as Methuselah come hobbling out of the corridor behind Nerys. So did others, as Empyreans and Quinlans alike strained to see past the group assembled to speak.

"They are not here, but I have seen them," Nerys continued. "Spoken to them myself."

He looked to see if anyone would call her out on their absence. Then he understood. They might have, if anyone else had been speaking. The choice to put Nerys at the lectern was a brilliant one. No one was more beloved, more trusted. If she said she spoke to the ancient ones, she did.

"They have been reluctant to aid us in the past. They looked unfavorably on the Brotherhood's choice of my brother as their pawn. They did not believe it would end well. They were not wrong."

Birger and Astrid exchanged a strained look.

"But they are stirred to action by the increasing deaths of our own. Like so many of us, they know complacency will not make this horror go away."

How was centuries of activating Empyreans with Marks

different from activating them now? Slaughter is slaughter, Tristan wondered.

Nerys trained her cobalt eyes directly on him. Her smile dropped his stomach. "I see you, Tristan of the Sullivans. And as your question rests on the hearts of others, I will address it." Her gaze remained on him long enough to send his heartbeat into a frenzy, and then she turned it on the gatherers. "Tristan wants to know how thousands of years of the Senetat choosing the time and place of an Empyrean's death using their Marks is different from the systemic massacre we see now. The answer is, it is not. And if that answer leaves us all feeling hollow, it should. We turned a blind eye and in doing so, we normalized the behavior. We let ourselves think, those being activated lived long, meaningful lives and they are now somewhere better. Now that the Senetat is not discriminating on who they're activating, we are enraged! How dare they pick the fledglings, the youth among us? What gives them that right?"

Nerys flung herself forward on the podium and raised her voice so loud the cave rattled. "I beseech you now, what gives them the right to murder *any single one of us?* What will it take, my friends? What more has to happen before we open our eyes and see the destruction wrought in the name of our beloved Emyr?"

Harriett lifted her head. Her hair fell back over her shoulders, and tears streamed down her face. "First they came for the Socialists, and I did not speak out, because I was not a Socialist. Then they came for the Trade Unionists, and I did not speak out, because I was not a Trade Unionist. Then they came for the Jews, and I did not speak out, because I was not a Jew." She wiped her eyes. "Then they came for me, and there was no one left to speak for me."

"I met Martin Niemöller," Trygve said in a low voice. He walked over to Harriett and pressed his hand to her cheek. "I walked with him in the second world war of the Children of Men. I listened to his words on the tyrant Adolf Hitler. And I mused on the similarities between the German people and our own. The blind eye, as Nerys has said, takes from us that what makes us compassionate. What makes us real. We are not immune as the powerful Children of Emyr. We are not above the conditions of the Children of Men. If we now retreated to our caves and our mountains, our sanctuaries where we can pretend the atrocities are only stories, then we are, as a people, utterly lost."

Anders appeared at Tristan's side. He dropped his head and pressed his lips to Tristan's ear. "That's the most words anyone has heard Trygve speak in one sitting in centuries."

"We have seen it with our own eyes, in Ireland," a woman spoke up. She was not Empyrean, so she must be Quinlan, Tristan deduced. "The enslavement and massacre of the Irish people by their own brethren. By a culture that is now revered as one of the most powerful in the world. *That* is what will happen if we do not put an end to the madness. It will become acceptable and will become who we are."

"Harriett, Trygve, and Nora all speak true," Nerys said, resuming command. "If there are any among us who are not stirred to action against the false leaders in Farjhem, you may leave us now."

Tristan looked around. No one budged an inch.

"If we win..." A small voice piped up from the back of those gathered. Tristan didn't recognize her. He looked at Anders, who shrugged.

"When we win," Nerys gently corrected.

"When we win," the voice said, unsteady. "Who will replace Oriana? Who will lead us if we cannot even pick a leader of our own Brotherhood?"

At this question, Nerys' collected calm faltered slightly.

"We have always decided our emperor by two rules. First, by blood inheritance. And the second, by rule of conquer, like the Saxons. These two methods are in direct conflict with one another and make little sense as we move toward a world of peace. We, now, are rising up, together. And thus, we must decide, together, with each of our voices counting.

"But not today. Today, we have set in motion the revolution that will remove a regime steeped in control and hatred."

"It should be you, Nerys," the young girl answered. "It always should have been you."

As Nerys flushed and protested, the room erupted in chants of her name, escalating in volume until she was ushered away from the crowd, back into the corridor.

"So that's what Nerys has been doing. Building her army," Anders said when they were again alone, in the casa on the hillside overlooking the Mediterranean. "While we've been looking for numbers, she's sought out the best and brightest of all the Quinlans and Empyreans. I can see the brilliance."

"Will her plan work?" Tristan asked as he tore into the large leg of the chicken one of Thorvald's servants brought to their cabin.

"It may." Anders went to work unlacing his heavy black boots, one eyelet at a time. "But we are not giving enough attention to the problem of not knowing our enemy as well as we should. Thorvald told me this morning that Maxima was captured."

Neither Tristan nor Harriett knew who this was.

Anders shook his head. "I forget sometimes I may as well be dealing with fledglings. Maxima was our one and only source on the Senetat. Over the years, we've used her information to guide our movements. Unfortunately, she was caught in the middle of a transmission to Birger. They only got a piece of it."

"What was her message?" Harriett asked. She picked at her meat.

"That Oriana now has a weapon of her own," Anders said. He cursed under his breath as he snagged his finger on a sharp piece of metal on his boot. "And that this weapon is what has her calmed down, for now. It would take something pretty significant to calm her down, wouldn't you say?"

"So, what's the weapon then?" Tristan pushed.

Anders groaned as he pulled his boot off and tossed it in the corner. He went to work on his right foot. "That's the problem. She was cut off before she could tell us. All we have are our guesses."

"Wow," Tristan whispered.

"That, my friend," Anders said. "Is where *you* will come in."

"Me?"

Anders stopped messing with his boot. "How many times have you asked me why you're here, and why you matter?"

"Only daily," Harriett teased, looking at Tristan.

"He never shuts up about it," Anders agreed with the slightest hint of a smile. "What you can do, very few can. We have always known your telepathic breaching would be useful to us, but we needed a plan."

"Why don't we just have me all willy-nilly trying to read anything and everything in Farjhem?"

"Because," Anders explained, "no matter how powerful you are, your skill cannot rupture Farjhem's barriers. Sorry to inform you, but you do have limitations."

"How the hell is that useful then?"

"We have to get you in," Anders said as if this would not be the most challenging thing in the world. "You and Tarek, if he agrees to join us."

"You're kidding."

"No, I'm not very good at that, as you know," Anders replied. His second boot came off and whizzed across the room with a heavy thud. "Ah, now I'll sleep well tonight."

"Anders, focus! You're serious about getting me into Farjhem?"

"Yes. Which brings me to the second point. Once you're in, we won't have long before they sense the intrusion. You'll have to know exactly who you're looking for, and you won't have time to find them."

Tristan dropped his chicken thigh. "This sounds hopeless."

Harriett squeezed his leg.

"Not hopeless and not impossible. Only challenging," Anders said. He rose and stretched. "This is where I say good night. If you value your limbs and life, please, do not knock on the door to my room, or do anything otherwise that might disturb this well-earned slumber I intend to enjoy."

When they heard his door close, Tristan spun on Harriett with an incredulous look. "He's completely crazy!"

"He's a little mad sometimes," Harriett agreed. "But it sort of makes sense, doesn't it?"

"Makes sense? How? I'm just a little halfling punk with a non-average ability, Harriett. I'm just me, the awkward Sullivan kid who didn't even have a girlfriend until he was an adult, and still hasn't finished college."

"What does any of this have to do with what Anders is asking of you?"

"It just does! Because..." Tristan faltered, searching for the answer, or one that made sense and validated his own fears. "Did you see all the folks out there? It might as well have been a gathering of Zeus and his Gods, and we were just the mortals who stumbled in as one of their pets. I'm *nobody,* Harriett."

There. Finally, there it was. The nagging fear he'd carried in the back of his mind since they'd left home, and the one that continuously reminded him that his presence here was a more elaborate version of the games he played with other boys in his youth.

"No," Harriett said, tenderly wiping the grease from his fingers with a nearby cloth. "I won't listen to you say these things about yourself. And I won't let you think them."

He didn't guess how she could possibly stop him, but he nodded. She was the last person on earth he ever wanted to cause distress. "How long do you think we'll be here?"

Harriett leaned forward into her satchel and pulled out her notebook. Tristan recognized it as the one she used to write letters to her father. "Long enough for you to write to your father and make your peace."

He didn't know what to say. She never asked anything of him, and her demand hadn't come in the form of the question. He could say no. "Can't it wait until we're done figuring all this Farjhem battle lord stuff out?"

"I saw the way Anders looked at you when you asked about how hard it would be, to get you into that land," Harriett said. Her voice shook, and she set the notebook down to steady her hands. "I'll be by you every step of the way, Tristan. For better or worse. No matter the outcome, we'll face it with our hands linked, and our faces brave. But do you really expect us to make it out alive?"

Harriett's stark words stole the warmth from the room. She'd voiced the question he hadn't had the courage to ask Anders before he disappeared.

Tristan looked at the pen.

35
VICTOR

Victor found Olivia at the back of her house, in her garden pulling weeds. Her dark hair was pulled back into a ponytail with a single perfect mahogany curl; her matching paisley blouse and capris reminded him of the image of a 1950's housewife in the magazines his mother used to collect.

"Isn't the season over?" Victor asked, amused by the little hop she gave at the sound of his voice.

"Hell's Bells, Victor!"

"I didn't mean to startle you."

Olivia laid aside the hand trowel and wiped her face on the back of her sleeve. "We haven't had a deep enough frost yet, sadly. The weeds are relentless. Not unlike you and the way you like to sneak up on people."

"And steal kisses?" Victor bent in for one before she could protest. Instead of smacking him, as she was wont to do when he was slightly out of line, she looped one dirty hand behind his neatly combed hair and deepened the kiss.

Rory's uneven toddler steps sounded on the flagstones and

they broke apart before he turned the corner. Olivia blushed. She pressed the back of her hand to her mouth.

"Mama! Come see my castle!" Rory declared, tugging on her arm. His blond curls, which Olivia was reluctant to trim, bounced against his ears in unruly rebellion.

"Give Mama one minute," Olivia protested. She took Victor's offered arm with a sideways smile and pulled herself to a stand.

"One... two... three..." Rory ticked off on his tiny fingers with a petulant shift in his stance.

"It will be twenty minutes if you don't drop that sass, little man!"

Rory *harrumphed* and skipped off back into the house, singing to himself some song from a show Victor had come to know as *Thomas and Friends.* A show about a talking train and all his friends, which was one of many oddities about the future that he could not quite reconcile with what he knew of the world.

When he was certain the little one was no longer anywhere nearby, Victor slid his arms around Olivia's tiny waist and drew her in. His voice was husky against her milky neck. "Tonight? Galatoire's? Our favorite table?"

Her giggle, an audible representation of how low her guard was lowered around him, sent chills through him. "We have a favorite table now?"

"Don't we?"

Olivia swayed in his arms with a sigh. "People are going to start talking about us."

"What about us?" He had no suitable answer for her. He couldn't even define what constituted the relationship ending with the two of them joining in an "us," or why he had let things escalate beyond fulfilling his need for her abilities.

Further, why he hadn't yet even approached the topic... why even the thought of it made him sweaty with nerves.

"Come on, Victor, I'm a married woman."

"To a man who left you, not the other way around."

"For reasons I can't entirely blame him for," she said. She ran her hands up and down the arms of his sport coat. "Rory already wonders why you're always here. Katja gives me these thumbs-up gestures whenever she sees us together. Who knows what Sebastian thinks, but he's more astute than the two of them put together. It's only a matter of time before the family busybodies get wind and start whispering. God help us if Aunt Colleen finds out!"

Victor tensed at the name of the woman he now viewed as an adversary. Amelia's mother or no, there was only so long he would allow her smug, satisfied grins and dripping self-importance. And after the run-in at Magnolia Grace, she'd climbed to the top of the list of mortals he might like to enslave in his plantation and drink from at will.

"I can be less present," he offered, already knowing her answer, and his.

Olivia's expression fell. "I didn't say that."

"And I hope you never do." Victor buried himself in another kiss, feeling his whole self surrender to the fleeting intimacy. None of this was required to get what he desired from her. He was already certain she would provide anything he asked for, in her vulnerability; in her need to be *seen* and, even briefly, loved.

So why not ask her and be done with it, you fool?

Ah, were it only so simple! The greatest obstacles to our success are the ones we never see coming.

"Mama!" Rory's shrieks sounded again in the garden, and Olivia backed away slowly. She flashed him one last parting, longing glance and hurried off to play with her son.

Victor moseyed around the garden, absent of purpose, but also without motivation to go anywhere else. He really shouldn't stay. Her points about her child and cousins were entirely valid. Rory thought he was "helping around the house," but Katja and Sebastian, surely, had no doubt to the truth of the matter, even with Katja locked in her room most hours of the day and Sebastian off skulking about the world in his designer car.

He moved around the side of the house, admiring Olivia's careful artistry. He had never been one to stop and smell the literal roses, but he could appreciate her gardening as a representation of her own emotions poured into every last element of her design. This was her artist's canvas, and it told the story of her life. Her heart.

He passed outside an open window. Sebastian's low voice floated out, peppered with an intensity that made Victor pause. He noted this was the second time Sebastian's words had intrigued him.

"He isn't even speaking to me, Mother." And then, as if responding to someone whose voice was too low to hear. "I did what you asked, and he's unhappy. What am I supposed to do about that?"

Again, Sebastian went entirely silent before speaking again. "I'm no good at it. He sees right through me. He knows I'm an asshole, but he was okay with it until I really hurt his feelings." Several seconds went by. "I know, all right. I know the lake was a bad idea." Moments later: "Maybe we should focus on finding Stella, then. I don't know why you made me stop. I almost had her."

This one-sided exchange went on for several more minutes. Victor was perplexed. The young man was suffering from some kind of delusion that caused him to argue with himself.

It dawned on him then that he could be having a phone conversation. Victor himself never learned to rely on this strange form of communication, which had only grown more and more advanced over the years.

Curiosity overtook him, and he entered the house through the screened porch and headed in the direction of Sebastian's room. He found the door closed, but given the advanced age of the house, there was a convenient gap between the door and the frame.

Sebastian stood facing his closet door, hands balled at his side. His face was flushed a deep red, and he had the look of a man embroiled in the start of an argument.

There was no one else in the room with which to argue, though... nor was there a phone anywhere near his hands.

"If you would only tell me, Margarethe... I'm not a child anymore. I can be trusted." Pause. "Of course I have faith in you, *Mother*. I'm trying to prove it. I'm capable of more than you think I am." Pause. "Please don't say that! Stella will never be as powerful as I am, and when the time comes, you know I'll do whatever I need to. Whatever I have to. You know this." A near full minute of silence followed this last set of pleas.

Whenever Victor ventured to ask more about Sebastian... specifically the improbability of this grown man being the child of Katja, who could not hardly even be twenty-one herself, Olivia would dismiss it as a private and complicated matter. But this seemed neither private nor complicated—he was quite sure there was an explanation here that defied any normal conventions. He knew of their magic, of course, but Olivia did not know the full scale of his own. She certainly did not know of his *dhampir* roots, and telling her seemed patently out of the question... though it might have opened up a quid pro quo, where she felt safe in revealing her own secret. For whoever—whatever—Sebastian really was, was undoubtedly a secret of great significance.

Sebastian abruptly hung his head and stopped talking to his concealed friend. He threw his head back and yelled at the top his lungs, a visceral sound couched in a rage greater than the moment.

Victor stepped back into the hall, away from the door.

Whatever he'd witnessed, he knew he should not have. He also knew it was important, though to whom and for what reasons remained as much of a mystery as Sebastian himself.

He had come to Olivia Claiborne with the hopes of solving his life's greatest mystery and had stumbled upon another that piqued his interest in a way nothing else, before Ophélie, before Amelia, ever had.

Wherever this information led, perhaps... just maybe... it would provide him with another means of gaining assistance toward the aim of locating Ophélie. Colleen had turned him away with her haughty self-importance, but he had a strong feeling, by the way Olivia sought to keep her aunt away from the house, that Colleen did *not* know about whatever was happening with Sebastian.

And now, Victor had something she wanted. Something that would compel Colleen to help him.

For Victor had begun to accept that though Olivia would probably help him, he would never be able to bring himself to ask.

36
LAUREN

They had six stops remaining before they ran out of leads. Lauren pressed the negative thoughts from her mind and tried to replace them with positive ones, to believe it was still possible a lingering lead would bring them to Quillan; but her natural optimism was as exhausted as the rest of her, and eventually she stopped silencing Leander and Nicolas when they ranted about the pointlessness of their journey.

They detoured first down into Mexico, south of Tijuana to Ensenada, where they came upon a small commune of mages residing in what looked like a resort, along the *Bahía de Todos Santos*. Upon walking through the walled gardens lined with stone-faced militia, it was Nicolas who first called it for what it was.

"Five dollars says we stumbled into the den of the Tijuana Cartel," he mumbled from the corner of his mouth as they followed several men armed with weapons more extreme than Lauren had ever seen in a Southern man's arsenal.

"I thought you said these guys were in your network," she

hissed in return. Her mind went to all the fear-mongering stories she remembered about American tourists disappearing in Mexico, never to be seen or heard from again.

"We don't exactly demand background checks."

"If I had known *this* was why we had to bring our passports..." Leander gruffed.

It turned out they were not in any real danger. The leader of the commune, *Marqués* de los Santos—Leander promptly made a point to remind everyone that the nobility was abolished in Mexico in the early nineteenth century, earning him the stares of a dozen very serious onlookers—as it turned out, was a big fan of Colleen Deschanel. Perhaps even a little smitten, by Lauren's estimation. De los Santos would consider it a great honor, he said, if Colleen would entertain doing business with him. To keep the money "*en la familia,*" was of great interest to him. He went on to describe his vision of the *brujas* and *brujos* of the world united, *como uno*.

Specifically, he saw an opportunity for a market amongst the New Orleans elite and had an elaborate plan using South Padre Island to get his product into the city. He would take their million-dollar reward and triple it within weeks.

"So... you don't know where our missing people are?" Lauren asked.

The drug lord blinked. He gestured around the elaborate walls. "Why would they be here, *señorita*?"

AFTER THEIR LONG, TIRING AFTERNOON RUBBING ELBOWS WITH DRUG lords, Lauren had no argument left in her this time when Nicolas insisted on nicer accommodations. They stopped in La Jolla at a colonial lodge cresting above the Pacific Ocean that looked to Lauren more like a Spanish alcazar. *This will do,* Nicolas had said, glassy-eyed from the cognac.

Nicolas was stumbling drunk by the time they arrived. He slurred nonsense into Lauren's ear as she struggled with the front desk to find any rooms at all. First they had none, and then they found a single bed on a last-minute cancellation. That wouldn't do for three people, though, and she was so exhausted she didn't think she could drive even another mile without some rest. So Lauren finally played the card she said she never would.

"We're representing the New Orleans Deschanels on business. Nicolas is the head of the family," she said with a long sigh.

The front desk host didn't know what to do with that, so he got his manager. The manager, a middle-aged woman who had a similar air of authority as Colleen, declared she had a honeymoon suite she could offer two of them, at no charge.

"Great, you two can share," Lauren said, glancing at her male companions. "And I'll take the single."

"Forget it." Leander backed away with horror spreading across his face. "I am *not* staying with him so he can mess with me all night. Let him take the single."

"You're not my type, daffodil," Nicolas said.

"You and I aren't sharing a room, Lee," she said plainly. Leander blushed.

"Then let him have his own room. I'll sleep in the car."

Lauren gave him a look she hoped conveyed the annoyance she felt burning in her marrow at his childish stubbornness. Of all Leander's faults, his selective charity was the most grating to her. "You know what? Take the single."

"What, you're going to stay with Nicolas?" Leander's eyes narrowed. His face deepened with color. "You'll share with him without a second thought, but get all worked up at the idea of sharing with me?"

Lauren shifted her weight to the desk, sagging in rapidly

escalating fatigue. “What choice do I have? If you’re going to act like a grade-schooler about it, then feel free. I’m too tired to argue, and we have a long day ahead of us. It’s already almost midnight, Lee. Either take the single or sleep in the car. I don’t care.”

The manager offered a patient, placating smile, and Lauren wished she could read her mind like a Deschanel. On second thought, maybe she didn’t.

She took both the keys offered and held one out to Leander. “Do you want it or not?”

Leander snatched it from her hand, his hard look drilled on Nicolas, who was having a thrilling conversation with a nearby potted palm and didn’t notice the gesture.

“You’re enabling him,” Leander accused as she went to retrieve the heir of the Deschanels from his palaver with the foliage.

“I’m trying to get us through this trip without any major issues. You might not care about your reputation, but mine means a great deal to me. I’m not facing Colleen Deschanel and telling her we left him to his own devices and he crawled off and died in a gutter.” She pulled the handle of Nicolas’ rolling bag and tugged on his arm. “I’m not his mother. Not his sister. Not his wife. I’m not even related to him by blood the way you are. You could help me, but instead you think it’s more prudent to throw accusations.”

“I don’t have any sisters. Or a mother,” Nicolas offered, with a whimsical look. He gripped Lauren’s arm as she pulled him toward the circular staircase she was certain he would tumble down. “Almost had a wife, but she wasn’t human, and you know how those things go.”

“Totally,” Lauren appeased and pushed the handle of his bag back into the case. She lifted both suitcases and looked at Nicolas. “Can you manage the stairs on your own?”

"I can manage a lot of things on my own, if you catch my drift."

"What I'm *not* catching is your ass if you fall down the staircase."

Leander passed a look over the two of them that was so brief Lauren almost missed it. Jealousy.

Oh, Leander. If only you knew the strength it took to put others first, especially when they don't deserve it in the slightest.

NICOLAS AIMED FOR THE PLUSH BED, DECKED IN HONEYMOON RED velvet, but Lauren steered him toward the chair and ottoman. "Nope. You'll pass out just as fine here."

"I'm paying for the room," he grumbled into the seat back as she lifted his feet and situated them on the ottoman.

"The hotel comped the room. And if you weren't such a mess, you'd have your own," Lauren chided. She searched the closet for an extra blanket. Finding one, she spread it over him and also tossed a pillow from the bed. "And, not to split hairs, but your aunt is the one funding this trip."

"I can't even escape her draconian leadership on the road, can I?"

"Does your vocabulary always improve correlative to your alcohol intake?"

"I leave home and I still catch shit. Unbelievable."

"Don't worry! We'll be home before you know it and then you can go back to doing whatever it is you do!" she called from the bathroom as she searched her case for her face wash and toothbrush. She hadn't the energy for much else, but she always, always washed her face and brushed her teeth. One of the teachings from her mother that made a lasting impact.

Lauren got no response from the sulking prince. Not a bad thing. He was probably already passed out, which meant *she* would sleep, and she needed this so badly. The sagging darkness under her eyes was not the only sign. The acute ache between her shoulder blades that no amount of stretching or adjusting in the driver's seat seemed to relieve. In their early days on the road, Leander helped with a shoulder massage each night before they turned in, saying it was the least he could do if he refused to drive, but she stopped that when his eagerness to do it became apparent.

She craved swimming, something she'd done daily until this trip. She missed the resistance of the water against her muscles and passing over her skin as she pushed herself harder and harder, losing herself to the motion.

Cassidy often asked her, usually with a martini in hand and her long, unusually perfect legs dangling from beneath a skirt most women would never be able to wear, "Why would you ever want to swim, of all things? You're a Weatherly, Lauren. You should be out enjoying what the world has to offer. Hell, darling, if you want to swim, then at least go to the French Riviera!"

Lauren often declined to answer her sister's vapid questions, which were not questions at all, really, but assessments. Cassidy was no prettier than Lauren in any objective sense, but she was infinitely more pliable. Lauren had not seen her sister without a face full of makeup and coiffed hair since fifth grade. When their father lost his wife, Cassidy filled the spot of the pretty, spoiled princess in his life, and with great satisfaction. Cassidy lived and died by the attention she received, which was why Lauren so loathed to be asked about her sister's sexual proclivities. To acknowledge them had the double-edged impact of both finding her ashamed on Cassidy's behalf, and further validating that Cassidy wasn't the least bit ashamed herself. Cassidy *wanted* people to know she was universally desired, even if it meant also exposing her for her being a disloyal wife. Nor did she care about what this did to her husband, Cameron's, reputation amongst his esteemed peers.

That Nicolas claimed to have been one of her conquests only made Lauren angry at them both. In her darker, more pessimistic moments, she often saw the world in two buckets: those who had or would sleep with Cassidy Weatherly, and those who would never even entertain the thought. Anyone in the first category was both undesirable to Lauren and also inaccessible in a way that almost made her jealous. The type of men who would pursue someone like her sister—the Nicolas and Quillans of the world—were the antithesis of those whom Lauren was attracted to and, more, were less than what she deserved based on what she was willing and able to give herself. But she had always, her whole life, been drawn to them as well, in a near-scientific manner, as if hoping to discover some secret about them that would reveal them as more than one-dimensional. More than a cliché.

Quillan had been the last straw for Lauren. She hadn't even realized what she was doing, looking for these same things in him, hoping he might be able to see her for who she was and break the mold, until it was too late, and her heart had already been broken. Not by him, but by her own self; her own weakness.

Lauren no longer desired to solve the mystery of men. She had outwardly embraced her differences from her sister her whole life, while secretly looking for validation... but no longer. She was nearing thirty, and to possess such a skewed, conflicted sense of herself was something she could only change now that she was fully aware of it.

She wiped the soft washcloth across her face and ran the brush through her light-blond hair in quick, expedient strokes. It was past her shoulders now, since she'd had no opportunity to get it trimmed. She'd only kept it so short because everything about her appearance had been an antithesis to Cassidy: short bobs to Cassidy's long, buoyant curls; a splash of mascara and lip gloss to Cassidy's fully contoured face; conservative business casual to Cassidy's flamboyant South Beach fashion.

As Lauren observed her tired, clean face in the mirror, she saw, for the first time, her mother looking back. The hollowness at the middle of her cheekbones, and the gray eyes that caught the color of the surroundings and changed with them. She even shared her mother's pale blond hair, where Cassidy had to bleach hers regularly to get the same color. Their father always said Cassidy was the spitting image of Mary Weatherly, and while Lauren had never seen that evidence, when you heard something enough, you began to believe it.

He chose Cassidy to resemble her dead mother, whether it was true or not. Because Cassidy was the malleable one, the one who would continue on as the face of Weatherly Department Stores, and be Father's doting sweet girl.

Though her father would never realize his own self-deception, Lauren decided it was enough that she did.

LAUREN EMERGED FROM THE BATHROOM IN HER PAJAMAS TO FIND Nicolas sprawled on the bed again, curled to one side. He peered across the room at her with gleaming eyes, as if he'd been crying or was about to.

She sighed. "I'll go sleep on the chair, I guess."

"I'll sleep on the chair. Don't worry."

"Then why are you in the bed?"

"Do you ever think about your life, Lauren? I don't mean about ordinary stuff, but about your choices?"

She leaned against the frame of the door. She couldn't read

him, or his intentions. His words now, like always, felt like a trap. "Most people do, Nicolas."

"Mercy was the one thing I did right in all of it. I wasn't a good brother, and I wasn't a good son, but my parents sucked royally at their job, too, so that was a wash. Definitely not a great friend, as Oz would tell you."

Lauren didn't know what to say, or what he was looking for from her, so she said nothing, hoping his drunken ranting would taper off quickly and she could kick him back to the chair.

Then she noticed the bottle of Hennessy on the dresser across the room. She'd been monitoring the levels for her own sanity, and it appeared he hadn't touched it since they left Mexico, which meant his drunk was likely wearing off, if it hadn't already.

"I hated them both. My mother was so fixated on being right that she never saw me as a person. She only wanted me to inherit the keys to the kingdom. Never thought if I wanted them." He wiped at his eyes. "And my father was so busy hating my mother that he wasn't any better. He made the girls heirs just to spite her. He might have loved me if she would've let him see me as more than a bargaining chip."

"Look," Lauren said, stifling a yawn. "Everyone's parents suck. There's not a child alive that doesn't need therapy for something."

"Do you know," Nicolas went on, "that we don't even realize the full impact of our upbringing right away? It can't be seen objectively when you're at the center of it. When you're older you can look back and see the good and the bad, but only where it's obvious. Later, you find your values and beliefs, the way you see certain things, were all shaped in your parents' values and beliefs. Do you ever give an opinion on something then stop and wonder where it came from?"

Lauren shrugged at the strange esoteric waxing of the man-child holding her bed hostage. "That's why we're born with the ability to reason. At some point, our opinions become our own. Can we sleep now?"

"We spend our entire lives unwinding the words and sins of our parents," Nicolas replied. "And questioning whether our decisions are pre-wired, genetic mutations continuing through generation after generation."

Lauren stepped to his side of the bed. "You've had way too much to drink today. This week. This year. Probably in your lifetime, really. You'll feel better after you sleep it off."

"No," he said. "I won't. Do you know, I thought I had beaten it, finally? Mercy was my test. I failed along the way, but in the end, I was ready to pass it. Only to find out, she was also being tested, and her failure to pass becomes my failure as a man."

Lauren shook her head, clearing away his lack of sense. "I don't think you know what's even coming out of your mouth anymore."

Nicolas pulled at her arm, and she sank to the bed, sitting beside him. "Lauren, I'm not drunk. That ship sailed hours ago."

"You were discussing the political ramifications of photosynthesis with plants in the lobby."

Tears pooled in his bottom lids. "I didn't want to be alone."

Lauren felt the sigh start deep in her chest and radiate out through her limbs. No, no, no. She was not going to let *this* one get to her as Quillan did in his own moments of vulnerability. Whether Nicolas was like the others or not, her innate kindness was not to be confused with the measure of his character.

"I don't know what you were expecting..."

"I'm not trying to fuck you, Jesus Christ," Nicolas snapped. His face fell after the words were out. "Sorry. I shouldn't have said it like that. Sex is the last thing on my mind right now, for once. Whatever you must think of me after this past week, I'm really not just trying to get in your pants." His eyes ran up and down her. "Or, your unicorn pajamas."

Lauren flushed. "I wasn't expecting anyone to see them."

"They're not usually what women I share a bed with would wear, but you get points for being different."

"We're *not* sharing a bed."

"You know what I mean."

"So, what is it going to take to get you to sleep?" Lauren asked. The heat from his legs through his blue jeans pressed into her lower back as he shifted on the bed. The effect startled her. His warmth from the blood coursing through his veins helped her to remember he was a real man.

"Tell me why your parents suck."

Lauren smirked. "You don't actually care."

Nicolas propped himself up on an elbow, watching her. "Consider me curious. Reflective. That, at least, you can believe, I'm sure."

Lauren folded her hands over her legs and shrugged. What did it matter if she told him this, or not? His opinion, in the end, meant little, and if this was what it took to get him off her bed... "My mother died when I was eleven. My father compensated for it by choosing a replacement. He chose Cassidy."

His eyes widened. "Man, that's fucked up."

"Not like that, sheesh," she said quickly. "I mean... he needed someone to love and spoil. Someone pretty and amenable and pliable."

"You're not exactly ugly," Nicolas said graciously.

Lauren shot him a look and rolled her eyes. "Thanks. I'm more than just 'not ugly,' but that's beside the point. I wasn't as willing to be his doll as Cassidy was. In fact, I wasn't willing at all, really, and so his choice was easy."

"So you have daddy issues?"

"Oh for the love of... you aren't really curious, are you? You just wanted to taunt me some more?"

Nicolas squeezed her hand, briefly, then withdrew it. "I have daddy issues myself. And mommy issues for days. My old therapist claims this is the reason I keep fucking my way through South Louisiana. Boo hoo."

"Did you really sleep with Cassidy?"

Nicolas grinned. Then he must have seen something in her face, for it faded. "I just said that to get under your skin. It worked."

"Why?"

"Because I'm an asshole, I suppose."

"No, why didn't you sleep with her?"

Nicolas laughed. "First you're mad that I did, now you want to question why I didn't?"

"No, I want to understand why, if you slept with all the other girls at Sacred Heart, that you'd skip Cassidy. It doesn't make any sense. No one skipped Cassidy, if they had any choice. Unless... she turned you down?"

Nicolas cast his eyes away. He didn't respond immediately, and she had the impression he was searching for the right words, instead of just the first that came into his head. "She didn't turn me down. It was the other way around."

"What? Why?" Lauren chuckled. "She was one of the hottest girls in school. Everyone wanted her. Why?"

"Lauren..."

"Tell me why!"

He met her eyes again. "Because she was damaged goods, okay? She'd been with everyone at Brother Martin and then worked her way through the other private schools. My standards weren't exactly high, but I did have some."

Lauren rocked back on her hands. "You're serious?"

"You don't believe I could have standards?"

"I'm..." *I'm what? I'm relieved, for reasons inexplicable to me, that you didn't do it? I'm surprised? I'm skeptical? I'm angry?*

No, I'm tired. That's all.

"She's your sister," he went on. "I know the rules about siblings. Even when they're assholes, you can say it, but no one else can. So I could either tell you I slept with her, which would come as zero shock to you but isn't true, or I could tell you she was a little too loose even for me, which is also not brand-new information to you but might offend you more... even though it's the truth. I chose to offend you less. But the truth is, no, I didn't sleep with her, and my reasons stand."

"Okay, then."

"Why did you really want to know? I have my guess, but I want to hear you say it."

Lauren gaped at him, furrowing her brows. "Not everyone has hidden intentions."

Nicolas pulled himself up so his back was against the headboard. "You're still trying to size me up. You want to know if I'm really as much of a dick as I put myself out there to be. Sleeping with your sister was a piece of the puzzle that fit neatly with your assessment, but now that I've debunked that... you don't know what to do with that, do you? I can almost see your mind trying to re-arrange the pieces of the puzzle to figure out what the end picture will actually look like. Am I a castle or a horse barn?"

"Are you sure you're not drunk?"

"Have you ever been in love?" Nicolas pulled himself to the other side of the bed and pointed to the spot where he'd been moments earlier. "Go ahead. I won't do anything to offend you. When we're done, I'll go back to my chair like a good boy."

Lauren tentatively slid into place, keeping her distance. Her shoulders stiffened. "That's not really your business."

"Tonight has been all about each other's business, so go on. Out with it."

"I suppose so. I was engaged once."

"Why didn't it work out?"

Lauren shook her head. "Why do I feel like all your questions have ulterior motives?"

Nicolas grinned. "Because I want you to feel that way."

"Then you can take your question and place it somewhere inappropriate. Why didn't things work out with Grace?"

"Mercy."

"Okay, why didn't things work out with Mercy?"

"I changed. She refused to."

Lauren cocked her head at him. "How self-aware of you, Nicolas. Next you'll tell me she drove you to drink, too."

"Oh, she did. In the same indirect way my parents drove me to drink. But I gave it up for her. I gave it all up for her—the booze, the women. I gave up the part of myself that even wanted those things because the pull to be a better man, for her, was stronger."

Lauren realized with horror she almost preferred Nicolas drunk. This stark look inside the inner workings of his mind made her uncomfortable. "And now? You're just going to go back to that man because one woman didn't appreciate it enough?"

"You don't understand. I wouldn't expect you to," he said with a lift of his shoulders. "I'd guess you've spent your whole life avoiding men like me, or trying to change them."

"If you don't want me to stereotype you, then don't do it to me," Lauren charged. "Just because I'm not like Cassidy doesn't mean I'm living in her shadow, trying to be different." *Oh, but it's not as far off the truth as I'd like it to be.*

"No one would blame you if you were." He turned his head against the oak headboard. His dark eyes burned holes in her.

"That's the problem with being a guy like me, Lauren. We get the Cassidys. The Mercys. Deep down they're capable of love, but they have to be willing to change to give it. But I'll never deserve better because I'm no different. Like attracts like."

Whatever sympathy he might have earned from her over their discussion disappeared in an instant. "Jesus, are you serious? Then change."

"What if we're incapable of change?"

"Nicolas, you said you changed for her. She didn't like it, or appreciate it, or whatever and you reverted back to... this. You act like she's your only choice. The only chance you have at this."

"You say that like you care."

Did she? The answer was less complicated than the question. She could be kind to someone without wanting to be involved in their troubles. "You decided to talk to me for a reason. Maybe you think I'm safe because I'm not like the girls you sleep with? Not sexy enough? Not easy enough? Whatever motivated you doesn't matter to me. I always speak my mind, even if it's not what people want to hear. Regardless of what I think of you, I'm not enjoying your misery."

He leaned over and kissed the top of her head before she could swat him away. "Good night, Lauren. Thanks for listening."

Lauren watched him slide out of bed and stumble over to his chair, where he curled up and didn't say another word.

The old Lauren would have spent the next hours, no matter how exhausted, deciphering his every word, puzzling over the meaning of each syllable, wondering how his behavior fit into her pre-defined narrative of him.

This Lauren was asleep in under a minute.

. . .

She rose before Nicolas with an hour before their departure time. Deciding to take advantage of the extra time, she slipped into the shower and let the hot water roll over her skin until every inch of her flesh was bright red.

Lauren took her time getting ready, enjoying her fresh gourmet coffee on the veranda and picking at the chocolates left by management.

Nicolas slept through it all. She tapped him on the head. "I'll meet you in the car. You've got ten minutes before we leave you behind."

He grumbled his understanding in response, and she left him.

"Interesting night?" Leander asked. He leaned against the fender, Mountain Dew in hand.

"It was fine," she replied, brushing past to lift her suitcase into the trunk. He watched her closely, but didn't offer to help.

"Don't need to get you checked for STDs or anything, do we?"

Lauren slammed the trunk. "I expect better from you, Leander." She left him standing there, shame-faced, and slid into the driver's seat.

Five minutes later, Nicolas jumped into the back. "All right, Assidy Junior! Let's get this show on the road!"

Lauren glanced at him in her rearview, searching for any signs of the vulnerable man of the night before.

As he popped the plastic seal on his fresh bottle of cognac, she found none.

37
COLLEEN

"I'm so glad you called," Colleen breathed as she settled into the leather grandfather chair in her office. "I was just in a debate with myself as to whether I should call *you.*"

"Then you first," Evangeline said. Something rustled in the background; something involving paper. She sounded distracted, divided between the call she'd made to her sister and whatever was in front of her.

"Are you all right?"

"I probably shouldn't have come to New Orleans for a few days with everything going on here in Washington. Johan has been off in Sweden with his ailing mother for weeks, and I don't know a thing about how he deals with our bills and other obligations. It's nothing I can't figure out."

"I should hope so, with your expensive education," Colleen teased. "But that's not why you called."

"No, but we'll get to that. You go."

Colleen felt a twinge of guilt. Her need to talk was entirely selfish, where she suspected Evangeline had a genuine concern driving her. "Before I get distracted and forget to ask, remind me, when is Markus coming out to help with *Ophélie* for Nicolas? Lucia is fine, of course, but I will feel more comfortable with a Deschanel leading things in his absence."

"Oh, yes... soon. Days at most, I would think. He's working out plans with his professors to take his classes online, and he's all but got it sorted. One is giving him fits, but I think they'll work it out in the end. Once we're sure he can continue his schooling from Louisiana, he'll be on the next plane. I promise. When is Nicolas returning?"

Colleen sipped her tea. "I would love to answer your question, Evie, but to understand when Nicolas was returning to his duties would require me to possess an understanding of why he'd left them in the first place."

"Uh-oh."

"Yes. It's all very strange. I didn't even hear it from him, you know. Lauren called to give me an update and mentioned her concerns about Nicolas and his drinking. Until then, I thought he'd been sleeping off a bender out at the plantation. To think, no one was there at all!"

"Except Lucia and Livia. Except Richard and Condoleezza and the other staff."

"You know what I mean."

"Be careful, Leena. Your smug is showing."

"You dare," Colleen said, with less challenge in her tone than her words suggested. "You know very well what I mean. Part of leading both the Deschanel Magi Collective *and* The Deschanel Trust is ensuring the best interest of the family, including the heir... but more than that, the *office* of the heir."

"He's not the King of England. We're not protecting a throne."

"Don't be reductive," Colleen said with a tsk. "You're only

contrary because you're upset about something, so why not just tell me."

Evangeline sighed. Her chair creaked as she rocked it from across the phone. "It almost seems silly now that we're talking."

"You always say that. It's never silly."

"It's not Katja, as you might suspect," Evangeline said. "It's Olivia."

"Has she done something?"

"No, not at all. In fact, she's been a dear, sending me weekly emails to check in, always telling me stories about Katja and Sebastian. She's sent hundreds of pics! She makes the absence of my daughter and grandson almost bearable." Evangeline covered the phone and coughed. "Did you know Greg left?"

Colleen nodded at the empty room. "It's all so sad for Olivia and poor Rory. I wondered how long Greg would survive this family when they married, but back then Olivia was as disconnected from us as Maureen. Now that she's begun to see the light, I fear this was always inevitable."

"Inevitable or not, I feel terrible for her. Olivia may be more independent than her mother, but Maureen's teachings aren't so easily unwound. Olivia was raised to believe having a man to help run the household was the only way to make a go of it."

"Yes, well, she will soon learn that is simply untrue."

"I suspect she might be seeing someone."

"Oh? Well, no one could fault her for some casual company in her grief. She's had a terrible year, first losing Alain, then her miscarriage. And now, Greg."

"Leena, it's more than that. This man has been coming around the house."

"How do you know?"

"I was talking to Olivia earlier this morning, and she set the phone down to wipe up some juice Rory had spilled, or something, and I heard him talking about his new daddy and asking if his new daddy was coming over today. Olivia, of course, said he only had one daddy, but Rory responded that, if so, who is the man who lives there now?"

Colleen settled her teacup in the saucer and leaned back in her chair. "Now, that *is* interesting. And you don't know who this mystery man is?"

"If I did, I would have led with that."

"And I take it you didn't ask Olivia when you had her on the phone?"

"I wasn't about to risk having her get angry with me, and then stop talking to me altogether," Evangeline defended. "She's my only lifeline to my daughter, Leena."

"I know," Colleen said gently. "In the end, perhaps it doesn't matter. Olivia is a woman capable of making her own choices."

"But aren't you the least bit concerned? This is completely out of character for her."

"So was breaking ties with her mother in favor of us, but she has. It is not at all uncommon for people to go through a metamorphosis of sorts following tragedy. This may be part of Olivia coming into herself and learning to fly."

"Will you check on her? To put my mind at ease? I would also like your assessment of Katja, if it's not too much trouble."

"It's never too much trouble. Of course I'll check in." Colleen released a sigh. "If it would set your mind at ease."

"It would, thank you. I'll try to make it back down as soon as I can. I had hoped Johan would be back by now, but his mother isn't doing well at all. When is our next Council meeting?"

"I haven't scheduled one, but you've reminded me that I need to do this."

"And who is covering for Nicolas, should he still be out harassing Lauren and Leander? Ashley?"

"Yes. And if he doesn't pull himself together, it might become a permanent change."

"Would the other Council members allow your son to serve, though? You know I would approve, but I'm not so sure about the others. Luther maybe."

"He's done a fine job," Colleen said. "And if they believe that's due to bias, then we can pick another. But Nicolas won't get away with being absentee for long."

"There's an edge to your voice today. Your turn to talk."

"I'm worried about Amelia, is all." Colleen closed her eyes as she spoke. It was a catharsis to get the words out, to someone who would understand what they meant to her and not expect the great strength others did. "She's never liked the way I dote on her. I've always struggled to teach her to be an independent woman, which she very much is, but then I turn into an overbearing crow whenever something in her life becomes challenging. When she told me about her rape, I have never exercised more self-control over my emotions, Evie. Not ever. I stayed calm, because I knew it was what she wanted. What she *needed.* Yet now that she's pregnant, with a child that could very well kill her, I find myself unable to draw from that same strength of control."

Evangeline's tone was soft, soothing. "Leena, she's your daughter. Of *course* you're having a hard time. Turn off the magistrate for a moment and remember you're a human being as well."

"Yes, well, she hates it, and I'm struggling to find a balance between keeping her safe and smothering her. I can't tell her how much sickness I sense in her; how this child is taking everything she has. Had Ana ridden out her pregnancy in New Orleans, I could have studied her and had a better idea of what to prepare for and expect, which might give me some comfort. And the knowledge with which to help my daughter."

"You turned off your magistrate and turned on the scientist."

"I'm better at those things. They make me a better mother, because I can, mostly, separate my emotion from the facts."

"Then here are the facts. You're already doing everything you can to keep her safe, and if that isn't enough, then what is? There's nothing else, sister. Ana had only Aidrik's healing and Finn's love to push her through, and she not only survived but seems stronger than she ever was. Amelia has an army of Deschanels, not to mention the medical force of Louisiana, should she need it. How many other women can claim to have such a support system?"

"How many other women have such unorthodox pregnancies?" Colleen countered. She tugged at the pins holding her bun in place and let her hair tumble out. She was exhausted, all the way to the bone. The weight of her family's needs had always fallen on her, but now the weight of her grief—the loss of her sister, her granddaughter, nieces and nephews, her daughter's struggles—seemed heavier than even she could bear. Staying strong meant having a barrier, but the barrier was growing weaker by the day. How long could she withstand it?

"I'll drop in on Olivia now," Colleen decided. "I'm due back at Amelia's in two hours, and in the meantime, perhaps I can set at least one of our minds at ease."

OLIVIA WAS AT HER FLORAL SHOP WHEN COLLEEN STOPPED BY, A FACT that would have occurred to Colleen had she not been distracted with so many things. But Katja was home and invited her in.

Katja wheeled ahead to the living room. Colleen's heart sank. When would Katja accept that she was healed?

"I know what's going on in your keen mind, Auntie," Katja called as she pivoted her chair deftly and situated it across from the couch in a small nook. "And thank you, but no."

"You can't fault me for trying to understand."

"I'm fine." Katja's smile was less constructed than it had been in the past, but it nevertheless belied the truth. "It keeps my mind fresh when I'm not focused on what the rest of my body is doing. I would think you'd understand that, as a scientist yourself."

"I understand the desire to keep your mind sharp," Colleen replied, removing her leather gloves. She tucked them inside the front pocket of her Vivienne Westwood suit. "But there are many ways to accomplish that."

The smile stayed plastered to Katja's face. Her white-blond hair floated in a messy knot atop her head, disheveled as if she'd slept that way for days without readjusting. "I'm guessing my mother sent you to check on me."

"Yes and no." Colleen wouldn't deceive her. Katja was far too clever, in any case. "I was actually hoping to speak to Olivia, but I forgot she would be working during the day."

"Always."

"Yes, well. How is she? With Greg gone, that is."

Katja's expression remained impassive. "She's dealing."

"Is she seeing anyone?"

Katja rolled her eyes. "Getting right to it, huh? What Olivia does is her business, Aunt C. I know you're gonna say whatever happens in the family is your business, too, but sometimes it's really not." She flipped loose the brake on her wheelchair. "You can tell my mother I'm fine. Sebastian is also fine. If you really wanna help, you can watch Rory while I take a bath."

"Yes, of course. Do you need..."

"Help?" Katja laughed. "No. We both know I'm not actually paralyzed anymore." She leaned forward, toward the next room over. "Rory! Aunt C is here. Come say hi!"

Rory came toddling in, and Katja fluffed his hair and gave him a brief kiss. "Be good," she ordered, just as he yelled, "Aunt Lee!"

Katja wheeled past Colleen with a cautious look, then turned her cheek for a kiss. Colleen furrowed her brows for a moment before leaning in to kiss her niece.

Colleen lifted Rory with a quick *oomph.* "My goodness, how you've grown!"

"I'm this many now," Rory said proudly, holding up four tiny fingers. "How many are you?"

"Too many," Colleen replied and set him down. She wondered, briefly, why he wasn't in Montessori and then recalled he only went three times a week. That she hadn't remembered that right away worried her, just as forgetting Olivia's schedule had. She was slipping. "What are you playing in there? Dora the Explorer?"

Rory gave her a scandalized look. "No way! Dora is for girls."

"Uncle Ashley's sons love Dora."

"Because they're girls."

Colleen had no argument for Rory's child logic. "You wanna show me while your aunt Kat takes a bath?"

"Where's Mama?"

"At work, love. She'll be home for dinner."

"Yeah, right."

Colleen pulled her great-nephew into her lap. "And why would you say that?"

"She goes to dinner with that man all the time." He made a sour face. "The one that replaced Daddy."

"No one can replace your daddy, sweetheart. Adults sometimes have friends, too, just like you. Your mommy just has a new friend, that's all."

"Well," Rory pouted, crossing his arms, "why does *she* get to have sleepovers with her friends and I don't?"

"That's a fair question," Colleen agreed. Her mind raced. From Katja's attempts to divert her and Rory's directness, she had all but confirmed what Evangeline believed. She saw no problem with Olivia finding comfort with another man, or woman, or whatever helped her through her challenging time.

Still, something didn't feel right. Her senses were all over the place.

"She makes me call him sir," Rory went on, indignant with injustice. "But that's not his name."

"What is his name, then? Do you know?"

"Mama calls him Victor."

COLLEEN SAT IN HER CAR FOR TEN MINUTES BEFORE GIVING THE DRIVER a destination.

She needed to see Victor. She had to stop this, for Olivia's sake. For all of their sakes.

Yet she'd done all in her power to drive him away, and so she did not know where to find him. She didn't think it wise to drive out to *Coquillage* or any of the other plantations alone. She had no reason to believe the de Blancheforts would harm her, but she also knew so little about what they were: dhampir.

"Take me to Amelia's," she decided. Impulse had never steered her anywhere but wrong.

She could not act on this new information until she was ready.

38
JACOB

It had happened.

His worst fear in all the world had come true... the one he had pushed far from his mind, believing deeply that thoughts had power, from the moment he'd learned of their future.

This pregnancy was killing his wife.

Jacob had been lying next to her, only half-asleep, when Amelia sounded the gasp. A death rattle, he might have called it, but he'd never heard one, and the idea of her emitting a death rattle was horrifying beyond what his mind could accept.

When he tried to rouse her, first with words, and then with gentle shaking, he already knew. If he was being honest with himself, he'd known even before he tried, because that fear—the very same one that had nagged at him despite his best efforts to expel it—had never quite disappeared, not really.

The child within her had overtaken her. Amelia was lost to

the emotions of the person closest to her and most part of her, even if this person was not yet born.

"Moira," Jacob whispered through his tears, pressing his face to Amelia's belly. "Please. You have to help her come back."

"I CAN'T LOCATE OZ." FINN APPEARED AT THE DOORWAY IN A FRENZY. His cheeks were ablaze from a worry harkening from his own experiences. "I called, went over. I used the spare key. He's not home."

"His father said he's not in the office, either," Ana said, coming up behind her husband. She was equally flushed. "I called out to *Ophélie*, and Lucia hasn't seen him in a week, maybe two. Nicolas isn't answering his phone."

"Nicolas is on a road trip," Jacob said in a daze. "Have you tried Catherine Sullivan? If Oz is off doing God knows what, he would've left the kids with her."

"I asked Aunt C to stop by on her way over here, but Colin said Oz came to get the kids two days ago and hasn't been back."

"I can't believe I'm wishing for Oz right now," Jacob groaned. He rose from the bed. His greatest urge was to bury himself against his wife and will her to snap out of it, but the best way to serve her now—and himself—was to find himself a use. "My God, what are we going to do if we don't find him?"

Ana pushed past Finn, to Jacob. "Jacob, I need you to listen."

He diverted his gaze.

"I know Aunt C, and you, and others, see imperilment as a pretty serious sentence for Amelia. And I know why. But I think, what it really is, is her mind's way of protecting her. Like a cocoon. And, as long as we can keep her safe, maybe that's exactly what she needs right now."

Jacob closed his eyes. "You didn't see her last time."

She pressed one hand to the side of his cheek. "Maybe having a couple optimists isn't a bad thing."

"And if the worst does happen..." Finn stepped forward with a tentative grimace. "Ana is a resurrection shaman."

Ana shook her head quickly at him.

"Oh dear God," Jacob whispered as the shock of that possibility rolled over him.

"Finn's just trying to be helpful. It won't get that far," Ana soothed, flashing a look at her husband.

The front door opened and a half dozen anxious voices swarmed from the foyer. Jacob recognized one of them as his mother-in-law.

Where Amelia might have found her mother's presence overbearing, Jacob had always felt relief whenever Colleen Deschanel was on the job. She had a way of instilling confidence in others in their worst moments, through the power of her own.

The patter of many feet coming up the stairs was the only sound in the bedroom. Amelia's breathing was so shallow, Jacob had to lean close to her to hear it.

Colleen appeared, power suit and all, followed by faces Jacob both recognized and didn't.

Luther and his youngest brother, Lowell.

Alton Guidry.

Little Maybelle Guidry, with the serious face and lace Easter dress, who couldn't have been more than seven or eight.

Four healers. Six, with Colleen and Anasofiya. Eight if you counted Finn and Jacob still coming into their abilities as draoi.

The last face was unfamiliar to him, but it was someone he'd seen before, somewhere.

"Cameron Sullivan has also offered his services," Colleen said, gesturing toward the young man in a crisp seersucker suit. "Which we appreciate beyond words."

"Yes, thank you," Jacob managed. It came to him that he'd gone to school with Cameron, though they'd never run in the same circles. Cameron had football and class president written all over him, just as he clearly wore the badge of successful lawyer now.

"It's been a long time, Jacob," Cameron said, hands in his pocket. There was an awkwardness about him that confused Jacob. "You probably don't remember me. You were one of the cool upperclassmen."

Jacob knit his brows. Was this guy messing with him? "I remember you. Thanks for coming to help."

"It's still weird for us. Sullivans I mean," Cameron said, shifting his gleaming Allen Edmunds shoes on the wood floor. "But I want to do what I can. Maybe it will help others in my family do the same."

More returned to Jacob. Cameron had married sexy, haughty Cassidy Weatherly, wet dream of every young man in Uptown. Every young man but Jacob, anyway.

Upon closer inspection of Colleen's drawn face, Jacob's confidence faded. He'd never seen her so haggard and less her poised and controlled self. "Luther and I will each lead shifts," she announced, finding her voice. "I will take Ana, Maybelle, Jacob, and Cameron. Luther will take Llewellyn, Alton, and Finn. This should balance the healing strength nicely and give everyone enough time to sleep and recharge. Those not at Amelia's bedside will sleep in the spare rooms, and there is also the couch in the living room and one in the office, if our ranks expand. We have no shortage of room. Those not healing will also be in charge of ensuring the house is stocked with everything we might need, from groceries to other basic requirements. There is no need to leave, as we have staff we can send after whatever list you give them." She placed a hand on Maybelle's head. "You will be on night shift, little darling, and your father has arranged for a tutor for two hours each day before you rest, so you don't fall behind on your studies."

"Yes, ma'am," the bright-eyed child said.

Colleen straightened her jacket. "Keep chatter to a minimum. Take bathroom breaks as you need them. If you find yourself dozing, excuse yourself for ten or twenty minutes and get some fresh air. If you need food, or a shower, do so, but in shifts. Any of us who are not our best selves cannot give our best selves to Amelia, and she needs nothing less of us right now. Amelia and her daughter, Moira, both. In fact, they need all of us."

"Will it be enough?" Jacob asked. He didn't want the answer, but the question would remain on his mind until he asked.

"The power of one of us should be enough. We are offering Amelia the power of nine," Colleen answered. "And if Oz re-emerges, we must find him and bring him in immediately." She moved her eyes across all those watching her. They landed on Jacob last. "No matter how that ended last time, we will deal with the consequences. The alternative is far worse."

Jacob knew precisely what consequences she meant. He'd watched Amelia, confused and in love with Oz, against her own judgment and experience. He'd even left her when she asked him to.

But Jacob would not ever leave his wife again... or, now, his daughter.

Whatever armor he needed to wear for this battle upcoming, he would wear it.

39
TRISTAN

They weren't invited this time.

Their last meet-up at Thorvald's coastal hideout in Spain, had been for all. A rallying cry that riled up Empyrean and Quinlan alike, in a way that made Tristan finally understand pep rallies in high school. The louder the words, the greater the applause. The more excitedly said, the more real they felt.

Now they had numbers, but they required a plan. And for that, they trusted only their highest levels of leadership.

Harriett rested her head on her folded arms, gazing out the window at the stormy Mediterranean. In the last couple of days, she'd reverted back to only speaking to him through her thoughts. She didn't offer an explanation on why she'd returned to her more reflective self, but he had his guesses. She hadn't minced words about what she saw their future to be, if Tristan was put into service in Farjhem.

"You haven't touched your empanadas," Tristan scolded lightly. "They were pretty damn good. I think this is the best food I've eaten in years."

And you haven't written to your father yet. We are both derelict in our duties.

"Hey, I never said I would," Tristan retorted. The shame burned anyway. He didn't know what to say to Connor. It was easier to say nothing at all.

You never said you wouldn't. You're angry at him, but as far as fathers go, you don't have it so bad, you know.

"What are you looking at out there, anyway?"

Harriett flashed a sidelong smirk to show she saw through his attempt to change the subject. *I can see the cave entrance. Lights. I can't hear them, of course. You could, if you tried, though that would be a violation of trust.*

"Uh, yeah. I'll pass on that," he said. "What do you think they're saying?"

I think they're arguing. Some leaders want strength, others won't feel comfortable without numbers.

"How do you know that?"

Deduced it from the meeting a couple days ago. When Thorvald said that thing about only needing ten of the strongest, half the room got nervous.

Tristan looked again at the pen and paper she continued to leave for him, a wordless reminder. "Why can't we have both?"

Why can't anyone ever agree on anything? Human nature. Or, Empyrean nature, which doesn't seem so very different to me. The only thing I do know is that Anders is growing agitated and I see it in others, too. Restlessness, maybe, is what it is, I don't know. But we aren't far from action now.

"I sure hope they can agree, then." He eyed her cold empanadas. "Or, we can stay here and eat this amazing food, forever, too. I'd be good with that."

Write to your father, Tris.

"Harriett, why do you care so much about my dad's feelings? Honestly?"

It's not your dad's feelings that keep me up at night. It's yours when we cross the point of no return and you're stuck with regrets you can't fix.

ANDERS KICKED THE DOOR CLOSED, STARTLING THEM BOTH FROM THE light sleep they'd each fallen into. Tristan held his breath, waiting for Anders' wicked temper. Instead, his mentor grinned from ear to ear.

Harriett's tired eyes widened, hopeful.

"The leaders agree, we're done being idle!" Anders cried. He started to unlace his boots, then grumbled and marched into the dining area. He yanked one of Harriett's cold, hard empanadas from the plate and devoured it in two bites. "I need to send for Lucia at once."

"What does that mean? Are we leaving tonight?" Tristan asked. He followed Anders, but kept a safe distance in case he'd misread the creature's mood.

Anders laughed at him. For once, Tristan didn't care. "Tonight? No. We're spread all over the world, Tristan."

"Everyone's coming here?"

"Not exactly." Anders snatched the second empanada and made quick work of it. The activity behind his eyes was a frenzy of information as he worked it around, evidently deciding what to share. "We have a rendezvous point in Norway. Some, those in the west and the far east, have already left, but if we leave tonight, we would only be waiting. Not all of them have a Stian who can open a portail. No, we get a couple more days... a week, at most... and then we are off to take back our damned homeland. At last!"

Tristan tried to suppress his relief. While he'd wanted so badly to feel useful, now that the moment was close, he wanted even more to enjoy what time he had left. If Harriett had already written them off as dog meat, then he might only have a few days left on this planet.

Don't be so dramatic, darling. I can't see the future. I can only predict the probabilities like anyone.

"Stop reading my mind," Tristan accused lightly. He never blocked around Harriett, and now he wondered how often she milled around his thoughts.

"I wouldn't waste the energy," Anders replied. "Do we have any more of these... whatever they are?" He gestured at the empty plate.

"Not you," Tristan said, looking across the room at Harriett, whose hair had fallen down over her face as she watched the two of them. "And no, but I'm sure Thor's dudes could whip you up some more."

"I wouldn't ever call him that if I were you," Anders said.

"Thor? It's a reasonable nickname."

"And he will reasonably take your head off for using it." Anders pressed the button behind the desk, the one that called Thorvald's staff from the estate. "Aye, send up some more of that food, would you?"

A voice returned an affirmative and Anders stopped his anxious pacing. "Right. Well, now that we have a plan, don't go crazy. No venturing far from the compound. A walk on the beach would be fine, but no going into Malaga. There's a protection over the property that spans as far as the sea, and down to the other side of this hill, but that's it."

"Who is it going to be?" Tristan asked.

"What?"

"The new emperor, when they take down Oriana? Will it be Nerys?"

"You're a part of this 'they' you speak of, so time to start thinking that way. And the answer is, I don't know. Nerys doesn't want it, but everyone wants her to want it. That's a choice that's beyond and above me, and it's no matter to me who they choose. Politics aren't my thing. Anyone within the Brotherhood who will uphold our values is suitable in my estimation. I care more about getting Oriana and her thugs out and stabilizing our homeland."

"But isn't that important?" Tristan pressed. "What happens if we get the bad guys out and no one wants to lead?"

Anders sighed. "You're overthinking this."

"No, actually," Tristan went on. "I'm not. Our history is filled with toppled regimes where the replacement wasn't any better, or they couldn't find one suitable to lead. The worst thing that could happen to Farjhem is that we take out the trash and then no one can agree on what happens next."

"I don't take my history lessons from Children of Men."

"Tristan isn't wrong." Harriett found her voice. It scratched and broke as it returned to life. She cleared her throat. "And I won't let him walk into a war zone if your plan isn't solid. That includes a peaceful transition and a new government."

Anders grinned at Tristan. "She speaks for you?"

"I'm a lucky guy, what can I say?"

Their mentor shook his head in disgust. "You know why Children of Men have wars? Why they never make progress? They overthink everything. They're incapable of simplifying. You can read a textbook full of the winner's words, but how many wars have *you* fought, Tristan Sullivan? Harriett Broussard? How many regime changes have you physically been present for? How many centuries of progress have you witnessed? Oh, yes: none."

Harriett's face flushed red with anger.

"You think I'm a callous bastard. I have my moments," Anders said, passing his gaze between them. "Mostly I'm a realist. I admire the idealism and passion in you both. I mean that more sincerely than you're going to receive it. But I've seen the tides of history turn, and I know what it takes to turn them. It matters not who takes over Farjhem, because if the replacement proves unsuitable, thereby the wheels continue to turn. The cycle of history repeats. We will find another. We will fall, and we will rise, and this is a pattern that is unshakeable in its inevitable truth."

"And if you're wrong?" Harriett whispered through her furious tears. Tristan knew they were for him, and they'd arisen not from Anders' speech but her own fears and uncertainties mounting from the moment they'd learned what his role would be. "You can live with all the sacrifices having been for nothing?"

"Nothing? Dear Harriett, you have it all wrong. Without the sacrifices, the wheel would no longer turn. The tides of history would run flat. We are who we are—Child of Man, Empyrean, and all other races on earth—because we fight and because we sacrifice. I don't know if your Tristan will survive this. You won't get meaningless platitudes from me. I simply can't see that future. But I do know, and I know this with great certainty:

"Should Tristan not make it past the days of the Third Runean War, his sacrifice will become the watermark on the annals of our history."

40
LAUREN

They made their way north along the Pacific Coast Highway. Unlike the endless stretches of flat earth and road along the southern states, Lauren's entire view was filled by an ocean she had never seen until now. A behemoth of power and sound and white crests of waves. It was different from the Atlantic, though she couldn't say why. But she could feel it.

Leander's agitation had evolved since their night in La Jolla. Instead of being angry with himself for his unwillingness to help, he seemed angry at *her* for trying to be responsible. He'd all but ignored her, and when she tried to strike up a conversation, he pretended not to hear her. Only when they stopped for gas or food would he offer a few words. Even then, they stopped short of friendly.

Lauren had already decided this was her last trip for this rescue mission. She was exhausted, but that alone wasn't enough to turn her around. Between Leander's silent grudge, which felt an awful lot like punishment, however unearned, and Nicolas growing increasingly more intolerable since the night he revealed his vulnerability, she had very little fight left.

Back home, her career awaited her. It would be tough to face Patrick Sullivan and tell him that she had no luck in finding his son, but the look in his eyes when she left the first time told her he never really expected her to.

When they stopped for lunch in Carmel-by-the-Sea, Nicolas snuck away to the bathroom after they ordered. Lauren and Leander sat in uncomfortable silence, her swirling the water in her glass, him picking at his napkin. When the food arrived and Nicolas still hadn't returned, Lauren's annoyance turned to worry.

"Can you go check on him?" she asked.

"What? No!"

"Lee, please."

"He's a grown man. And food just got here!"

"I can't go in the men's room," Lauren said with a pointed look. "You can."

Leander's stare could have melted the ice in her water. She couldn't interpret what was behind it, but it was more than anger at being asked to do something, or at Nicolas.

He threw down his fork and napkin and stormed past a waitress carrying a large tray. She teetered, and then, through great skill, corrected herself with a light curse in the direction Leander flew.

Lauren glanced down at her food. She wasn't hungry anymore. Her appetite had waned since Nicolas joined them. She didn't blame him entirely; it was only one of the many ways she wore her exhaustion. But constantly worrying about his well-being, when they had enough to worry about, wasn't helping.

Leander returned wearing a smirk so self-satisfied that Lauren had the unexpected urge to punch him in the face.

"What?" she demanded. "Is he okay?"

"Oh, he's more than okay."

"I don't speak 'Leander.' What are you getting at?"

He grinned into his folded hand, then at her. "You didn't happen to notice our waitress disappeared right about the same time as Saint Nicolas?"

Lauren shook her head. "What has that got to do with anything?"

Leander flopped back in his chair and slow-blinked at her. "They're fucking in the bathroom."

Her breath hitched. She didn't know if it was the news or Leander's flippant delivery. "Fine. Eat your lunch."

"I told you. You wouldn't listen to me, but I told—"

"Eat your fucking lunch and don't say another word!" Lauren's shriek reverberated across the quaint diner, drawing dozens of eyes in their direction. She wanted to cry. To scream again. She didn't ask to be the responsibility of two grown men who couldn't care for their own actions or emotions. In one corner, she had the mess of Nicolas Deschanel, Prince of Louisiana. In the other, Leander sulked and pouted, refusing to add any value other than his occasional broody observations.

Most of all, she wanted to be home, where she would never have to deal with the Deschanels or their sprawling set of cousins again.

For the first time in her life, she actually missed her father and Cassidy.

THEY MADE TWO STOPS ON THE TRIP UP NORTH. NICOLAS AND Leander both rotated attempts at making conversation with her, but she kept her determined eyes on the road.

Leander eventually busied himself in daydreaming out the

window. Nicolas opened yet another bottle of cognac, though with less enthusiasm than in prior days.

They were all tired, Lauren realized. She wasn't the only one ready to be done with this mission. Leander had come to pay a debt of friendship to Quillan, but seemed to be arriving at the slow realization Quillan did not wish to be found. And Nicolas had joined them out of a need to find himself useful, but had shown no inclination to living up to that promise.

During the long silences as they veered inland from the Pacific Ocean, up through the forests of redwoods, Lauren practiced her speeches to Patrick and Colleen. She would be sorry to let them down, but she'd done more than what anyone could expect of her. She;d committed weeks of her life, and, on this last trip, had gone well above the duty ascribed to her when she signed on.

Three more stops were all they had. Then the long drive back to Louisiana, but she could manage that, knowing at the end was the return to her old life. Cassidy liked to call it "dolorous" and her father took every chance to remind her that her life could be more fulfilling if she came to Weatherly Department Stores, but it was *her* life. She had built it, by herself, without aid. Unlike Nicolas, who had fallen into his by virtue of his birth, or Leander who had everything but was willfully blasé, Lauren appreciated every last bit of what awaited her at home. Every fork and knife, every speck of dust accumulating along the edges of her Quarter townhome. Her furniture might be IKEA instead of antique French Rococo, but it was hers.

Her father could have his clothing empire. Her sister could have her dozens of lovers and perfect showcase children.

Lauren found herself most happy in the simplicity.

• • •

THEY MADE IT JUST OVER THE OREGON BORDER BEFORE LAUREN waved the white flag. Ashland, which Leander rattled off some facts about—home of one of the biggest Shakespeare Festivals in the world and a notable bohemian community, she caught, despite his mumbling—was blanketed in snow and set to a majestic range of mountains called the Siskiyous. Lauren tried to imagine living with a backdrop like this. Louisiana was one of the flattest states in the country.

She found an inn with over half the rooms vacant. It would have been so easy to book three rooms and give them each their peace and quiet. But her conscience wouldn't allow this slip so close to the end.

"Two is fine," she said, wondering how long it would take her to regret this decision.

Nicolas settled into one of the rooms while Leander helped Lauren retrieve dinner from a nearby fast food restaurant. They did so with minimal dialogue, though she could see Leander burning to say something.

When they got back, Lauren paused outside Nicolas' room. "One of us has to stay with him. I've been more than fair about it so far. It's your turn, Lee."

Leander snorted, casting a nod toward the door. "All yours."

"We're not even going to talk about this?"

"What's there to talk about? You think he needs a chaperon. I think he needs to grow up. Do what you need to do, but don't drag me into it."

She sighed. So much for her hypothesis he was regretting being a jerk. "I don't know why God put Nicolas in our path, but He did, and he's our responsibility, at least until we can wrap up this trip in a few days. He's in bad shape. It's not our fault, and you're right, he needs to grow up. But he's not going to do it in the next few days, so the problem is ours. For now, yes, he's our responsibility."

"Responsibility?" Leander's brows knitted to a single line. "You know the man is thirty-one years old, right?"

She frowned and shot him a piercing look. "Quillan isn't much younger, and he's needed your babysitting most of his life."

"Quillan never needed my babysitting, just my friendship, for whatever that amounted to. Nicolas needs a kick in the nuts and a wake-up call. He's been nothing but a burden to us since he got in the car in New Orleans."

Lauren shifted, defensive. The mingled symphony of insect life and humming from the Pepsi machine grated on her almost as much as Leander's apathy. "He's your cousin. Family."

"And he's also a spoiled brat who has had the world handed to him his whole life. He's supposed to be the heir of this clan, but he treats it about like I'm treating the situation now, with strong indifference. And now he falls off the wagon because of a bad breakup? Here, let me call in all the violins to play him a swan song."

"That's a cold assessment, even for you," she judged. "I'm not going to justify his behavior, but he's family and he's in trouble. You think Quillan is the only one who needs help?"

"The whole world needs help, Elle, but Quillan is the only one I'm prepared to stick my neck out for." He shoved his hands deep in both pockets, lengthening his arms. Lauren thought he might have reconsidered the gesture had he realized how vulnerable it made him seem. "Why do you care so much?"

"Sometimes the journey is more important than the destination," she said carefully. "The choices we make along the way matter. And maybe I have no personal attachment to Nicolas Deschanel—frankly, I can't wait to be rid of him—but if I turn my back on him now, on the logic Quillan is more important, that the only thing that matters is Quillan when someone with an immediate need stands before me, what does that say about me? I don't know that I can live with the answer." She swallowed. "Besides, do you want to face Colleen and tell her we couldn't even handle keeping Nicolas in one piece?"

Leander yawned and looked toward his own room with a look of bland disinterest. His sagging posture told another story. "That's where you and I are different. The only thing I see ahead of me is a good night's sleep." He gave her arm a light squeeze. "Night, Elle. Be careful around him."

"He's not the one I need to be careful around," she snapped. Her eyes burned holes in his back as she watched him walk away.

"You're a fool," Nicolas said as she linked the chain across the door.

"Can't help yourself, can you?" Lauren replied, tired of him, tired of Leander, tired of every man who had made her feel as if her efforts were not enough.

"I've done nothing but make you feel worthless. But you keep coming back," Nicolas replied. He lay sprawled on his bed. Thankfully, in this room, there were two. "You keep looking after me, like I'm going to see the light and realize what a sweet, bland girl you are, and that I should give up the sexy sirens and go for a sweet bland girl, that my life will be so much better with a sweet—"

"I'm done listening to your incoherent rants," Lauren hissed. "I'm not sweet or bland, though if that's what you see, all the better for me, because then there's no chance of you worming your way into my life when this trip is done!"

"But you *do* want me."

Lauren threw her coat across the back of the paisley chair. "You're delusional when you drink. Or are you always like this?" She glared at him. "I wouldn't know."

"No one would do what you're doing if you didn't. No one is that selfless," he accused. His head rolled to the side, limp. His limbs were dead weight. She wondered how much he'd had to drink. She'd stopped tracking hours ago when she decided she was ready to go home.

"No one? You need new friends." Lauren dragged her suitcase to her bed, flipping it open with a snap that nearly ripped off the hinges.

"People don't do things that bring them no benefit. That's human nature. We're inherently selfish creatures."

"The benefit," Lauren said through clenched teeth, messing up her neat packing as she rifled through her clothes for pajamas, "is that I deliver you back to your beloved aunt in one piece and not in a body bag."

"Ahh, see, you do have a reason. Your reputation."

"Fine, you're right. There's no further need for us to talk tonight, because you've got me all figured out. Discussion closed."

He rolled to his side with great effort, regarding her. "My aunt wouldn't have blamed you for something happening to me. She's been expecting it since I was a teenager and my family turned into swamp food. What's more, I think you know she wouldn't blame you, and you're doing this anyway."

"We all make choices," Lauren said. She looked up from her valise, fighting back tears. All her life, Lauren had been a stoic child with no need of tears. Only in periods of great anger had they emerged, and now was no different. "I'm choosing to do the right thing, same as you're choosing the wrong one."

"I could have you if I wanted," he declared. Spittle ran out the side of his mouth.

Lauren watched him in disgust. She could see, beyond the desperation and decay, the beautiful man others had desired and been charmed by over the years. His eyes had a deep and haunting quality, a way of using them to see through you. He had dimples that made you tempted to rest your hands against them as you kissed him.

But Nicolas on the outside was beginning to match Nicolas on the inside, as if the rot could not be contained.

"I would stab myself a thousand times," Lauren said, controlling herself, every word, every gesture, "before I ever let you touch me."

For this, for once, Nicolas had no response. The smile died on his lips and he settled slowly back into his pillow.

They watched each other in silent standoff, Lauren challenging him to dare say another word; Nicolas evidently decided there were no other words worth speaking.

He kept his gaze in her general direction as she sorted out her pajamas and toiletries. When Lauren returned from the bathroom, he hadn't moved.

She sighed and thought of something else to say, but immediately saw the futility in any further discussion. Better to enjoy the gift of silence.

Only a few more days. That's it. I can do this.

Lauren closed her eyes and fell asleep in minutes.

41
LUCIA

Markus traced haphazard designs across the damp skin of Lucia's lower back, his eyes and other hand glued to his phone as he scrolled.

"Yeah?" he repeated, a perfunctory response to her upset, even if it was the wrong one.

"You're not listening," Lucia charged. But she was past any anger at Markus. The whole of her ire was to the words on the page that should have warmed her but instead left her as cold as Markus' return. "I don't care, either. I don't need more from you."

To her surprise, Markus set his phone on the nightstand and sat up to rest his head on her shoulder as she read the crinkled parchment in her hands. "Sorry. Got a lot going on myself. So, Thorvald called you back. That's supposed to be a good thing, right?"

"Yes... no... it's more than I could explain to a Child of Man." She rolled forward, shaking his chin loose.

Markus was unfazed. "Drawing conclusions before

attempting a reasonable experiment sounds pretty human to me."

"Scientist," she hissed under her breath, meaning it as an insult, even knowing he would take it otherwise.

"Start by telling me what it says." He nodded at the letter, written in the ancient script of Farjhem. Empyreans never fretted much about their letters falling into human hands. No linguist could crack the script, because it bore no relation to anything existing within the languages of Children of Men, past or present. Where their spoken language had, over the years, become a derivative of Old Norse, as they learned to live with the world around them, their written language was entirely unique. One linguist studied it for twenty years before finally declaring it must be extraterrestrial, from Mars or even somewhere beyond the galaxy. He was laughed out of the scholarly world.

"It's not what it says," Lucia replied, her voice low and husky.

"Let me guess. He's cold. No emotion. Nothing to betray his feelings."

Lucia nearly rolled her eyes, then stopped short of the betrayal of her own feelings. "He's always been like that. It's nothing new."

"But you love him."

"Also nothing new."

Markus wrinkled his forehead. "If we've established that how he said it was in character, and so not the cause of your distress, then we're back to *what* he said." When she glared at him, he softened. "I thought you'd be happy to go. You couldn't wait to get out of here."

That was before. "I am happy."

"I may lack the full register of emotions most people possess, but I can see clearly that you're *not* happy."

Lucia twisted to look directly at him. "Are you happy to be back here?"

"We're not talking about me. I'm not the one upset over a letter."

"Well, are you? You left to go back to school, which was important to you. Now, you've been recalled for duty to your family. Does that make you happy?"

"I fail to connect—"

"Does it?"

Markus studied her like a rare specimen he couldn't decipher. "I don't know. I guess I'm indifferent. Yeah, I gave up the comfort of home, and likely traded it for a heavy dose of crazy, but Aunt C needs me, so I'm here. Katja will benefit from having me here. I can still take my classes. The net effect on me is neutral."

"Huh?"

"I gained equal to my losses. Thus, I'm indifferent."

Lucia realized then why she had always been so drawn to Markus. He equated emotion with logic. He was cold without being unkind, and within that coldness she was safe from inspection. He didn't exhaust any time wondering about her feelings, desires... her dreams and goals. She had rarely dated within her race, for her own reasons, but the risk of being with a Child of Man was always their curiosity and attachment. Not so with Markus, one of the few she'd returned to, again and again. And while he'd never outright said it, Lucia guessed that was why he returned to her, too. Neither expected anything of the other. They could have discussions like this one, exacting and analytical, and they could mean nothing.

Tell me about your parents, Oz had said, to her great annoyance, though she eventually had told him. *What was it like growing up in Farjhem? Have you ever been in love? What types of games did you play? What was your happiest memory?*

Oz's questions had exhausted her, both in their relentlessness and how they made her consider her life within the confines of his inquiries, but also in the fact that he'd asked them to begin with. She had never allowed such prodding from any Child of Man, and she still couldn't understand what had caused her to let down that guard for Oz. The only thing that made sense was the inordinate amount of time and loneliness they had to contend with in their months together, locked up in a huge house, away from the world.

Thorvald's cold request. Markus' interested but unfeeling eyes. Oz's beseeching kindness. They read like a timeline, in descending order. Or were they a circle? From her commanding master to a young Child of Man not unlike him, then weakening for one whose heart was too large for his chest. Was the completion of the circle now to return to Thorvald, and to the resumption of who she was?

"Look, you've been here longer than you intended. You're comfortable, something you once told me you hated." Markus squeezed her shoulders in several tight bursts that she supposed were meant to seem supportive but only reminded her how impersonal their relationship was. "It will be a relief for you to go back to what you know. To not have to play nursemaid when you're used to being a warrior. I'm sure after months of Oz, you've had way more of Children of Men than you ever wanted." He laughed. "I try to picture the two of you co-existing, and it just doesn't compute."

Lucia's heart caved. She lost her breath.

"You all right?"

She nodded. "I need a shower."

"Right." Markus hopped out of the bed with a quick search for his clothes. "I could use a nap. You didn't let me sleep much."

His smile had a robotic quality, as if he felt no actual joy in the joke he'd made, but was making an effort for her sake. It occurred to her he probably never did that for anyone else; that this might be his attempt at genuine care, for as much as he was capable.

"Couldn't help myself," she joked back, anxious for him to leave so she could be alone with her confusion.

"Most can't," he said with another jerky smile and disappeared from the room.

Lucia rummaged through her desk drawer for the cell phone Oz had bought her when they first took over as temporary mistress and master. She saw no point in the technology, and was even, strangely, frightened by it, but it had served as their lifeline all those months. He'd call her when she was out for a run too long—"You worry too much, Dad"—and she did the same when his trips for groceries resulted in what she knew was him staring up and down the aisles, wondering what to buy—"This is your way of asking me to cook something from Farjhem again, isn't it?"

She tugged the phone from the charger and stared at her call screen. Oz. Oz. Oz. Oz. Oz.

What is wrong with you? Take the summons! Get far from this swampy hellhole and back to the action!

Lucia's toes curled. The hard ache in her chest burned. Wiping the new sweat from her brow, she hit the call button.

It went to his voicemail, as it had the last two dozen times she'd tried him. When they were together—living *together, not together, pull it together Lucia*—he'd never let it get past two rings. He was so fastidious, to a fault. Every detail of his life mattered, to the degree Lucia often felt herself examining her own.

Lucia dropped the phone on the bed and rose. Outside the heavy-paned plantation shutters, a whole world awaited. One she'd roamed with great delight, year after year, finding purpose in Thorvald's service. That gift lay on the bed, next to the cursed phone, half a page of the words she'd waited so long to hear.

"There's nothing here for me," she whispered aloud, praying the sound of her own voice speaking the words would give them bigger life.

The lost Brotherhood children had returned home. The assignment was over. She and Livia were to return to Spain at once. *Return to me, mi belleza. We now near that which we have both desired for so long.*

Lucia's eyes moved side to side. The letter. The phone. Back and forth.

42
ALEKSANDR

Aleksandr had never needed a friend more than now, when he had none he could turn to.

The incident at the lake still rattled him. It was more than Sebastian's usual antics, and something in Aleksandr's gut wouldn't allow him to let go of the feeling that his "friend" had really meant to hurt him.

Uncle Jacob was occupied with something far more important than Aleksandr's woes, and his parents were wrapped up in the same urgent matters. This was a small blessing, for their eyes turned to Amelia meant they weren't on him for once. If they stopped by, they'd see their son in unwashed clothes with dirty ramen bowls strewn across his mother's lovely apartment. They'd see a young man with heavy eyes and a heavy heart, and if they looked deeper, a lost soul. Then they'd call in the Deschanel cavalry and make things worse.

So far, his daily, if brief, texts had kept them from suspecting his slow spiral into depression, but their attentions would turn back to him sooner rather than later, once Aunt Amelia was on the mend.

Aleksandr's heart sank to think of Aunt Amelia's condition, for it seemed to ultimately confirm what everyone had been saying around him all along, about The Prophecy. She would have a child. It was useless pretending that child wouldn't be a girl, because she would. No one even doubted it. The family had taken to calling her *daughter* since the news hit. She even had a name, already: Moira.

This daughter, if The Prophecy came to fruition, would come to mean a great deal to him. Would he love her at first sight, with some inexplicable magnetic pull? Or maybe he would loathe her, like fated heroes in movies, and only through strange twists of circumstance would they come together. Moira. He rolled the name around in his head, practiced saying it. Moira. Would Moira be the name of the woman he would spend his life with? Carry his child?

He didn't have the faintest idea what to expect, and no one spouting knowledge of The Prophecy had known either. Until his aunt had actually fallen pregnant, the vague notion of Aleksandr's future had been so much easier to speak of, an abstract story far from his reach. If Fiona were here, she would reassure him that he had the strength to decide for himself how to manage his life, and his role as their savior. She would stand by him if he fell in love with the mysterious daughter and completed what most felt to be his duty. She'd be there when it was over.

Nothing felt right since Fiona's strange decision to abandon him. It wasn't only his heart hurting, but his sensibilities. He was all but certain there was more happening here, yet hours and days of trying to decipher the situation, without Fiona's own version of events, was a fool's errand.

But she said to leave her alone.

That, too, felt strange, like an important detail of the riddle she'd laid for him to solve, more so than an actual request to heed.

Aleksei, I feel sick about what happened. I borrowed this phone from my mother after I got rid of mine. It's our community phone, for emergencies, so don't reply. I want to explain to you what happened, but I don't have the words, and I don't believe the timing would benefit either of us. I never meant to hurt you. Please believe this. Never. No matter what you might hear later, or think, remember that, if nothing else.

Uncle Jacob said to reach out anyway. Write a letter, he'd suggested, so Aleksei had. Twelve of them. In the first, he'd poured his heart out to the extent even he couldn't re-read the words without tears. Then his heart turned to anger as he accused her of heartlessness and worse. Finally, he'd calmed enough to write one with rational thought, but that didn't seem to get across what he intended or needed.

There's a secret to this, though. To figuring out vague meaning and making it clear. Wanna know what it is?

Yes! Please!

Ye need to ask 'er.

Jacob might not be here, but his advice hadn't left. Aleksandr *did* need to ask her, but his desperation had grown so great that he didn't have time to wait for a letter to arrive, and to wonder if she might or might not respond to him.

His phone vibrated in his sweaty palm. Another text from Sebastian. *Dude, I'm sorry. Come on. Let's hang out. I'll bring the beer.*

Any other time, he might jump at the olive branch, but no, it wasn't right. Sebastian's apology was all wrong, like everything else in his world since Fiona's strange defection.

Aleksandr ignored it. Then he ignored the remaining nagging voices telling him why calling Fiona was a bad idea.

• • •

Fiona's mother, Nora, answered, breathless. "Yes?" she asked, and Aleksandr realized she was answering a phone that only rang in emergencies.

"Nora... it's Aleksei."

All he heard from the other end was Nora's heavy breaths and then, "Aleksei! My goodness, child, how are you? Is everything all right?"

"Sort of." *No, not really, not at all.* "I was actually hoping I could speak with Fiona, if that's all right. I can pay for the call if you don't have minutes."

"Goddess. Pay for the call." Nora tsked. "This line isn't really for chatter, but seeing as the foolish girl threw her own phone in the bin, I suppose it would be fine, just this once. Though, maybe first you might tell me why she flew all the way to New Orleans and back the same day?"

Nora's tone had a hint of accusation, and Aleksandr catalogued that for later, but for now, her actual words left him reeling.

She had come. She had come to New Orleans.

And then turned around and left.

"I don't actually know," Aleksandr said. "That's why I'm calling. I never saw her."

"You never... why, that makes no sense, Aleksei."

"That's why I'm calling."

Nora's flustered pants again filled the phone. At last she seemed to decide this was Fiona and Aleksandr's problem to work out and left to go find her daughter.

"Aleksei?" Fiona's voice on the other end had the small, tentative ring of a child. "I thought I said—"

"I know what you said. And maybe later you'll forgive me for calling anyway," Aleksandr answered. He mustered the whole of his courage not to cave at the sound of her soft voice.

Not before he had his answers. "But you owe me an explanation."

Fiona stopped breathing. When she started again, she was crying. "What did he tell you? Or has he?"

"What did who tell me?"

"Sebastian."

"Sebastian?" Aleksandr's free arm shot out and knocked a bowl to the carpet. He looked down, but didn't pick it up. "What are you talking about?"

"Oh, Aleksei." Fiona sobbed into the phone, great racking breathy exultations that desperately made him want to hold her.

She didn't say anything else for several moments. He listened to her cry, silent on his own end as well. And in the silence, a story began to unfold.

Sebastian's curiosity over Fiona.

Sebastian's desire to invalidate her in Aleksei's eyes.

Sebastian's cruelty.

Sebastian's apologies.

A great knot formed in the back of his throat, but he had to know, whatever it was. No matter the pain it caused. "Tell me." His voice cracked.

"I didn't know." Her sobs overcame her words. She could hardly breathe. "After... there were signs, but I was so happy to see you... and... I should have seen them, I know, but... I *didn't know*!"

"Then tell me what you didn't know."

Sebastian's incessant questions. His need to know all the details of Fiona's visit, down to the minute.

"Fiona, breathe. And tell me."

"I love you. Please tell me you know this. At least, please tell me you believe—"

"I believe you." Aleksandr bit his knuckle to stop the shaking, to keep his poise. He had to, he couldn't break down. Not yet. "But I need to know what you wouldn't tell me. I need to know why you came all the way here and then turned your back on me."

Powerful sniffles filled his ear, followed by more desperate sobs. Her voice sounded small and not her own. "He tricked me. I thought it was you, and... and my guard was down, because I was so *happy* to see you, and I didn't know to look for the cracks in the surface..."

"Cracks in the surface?" he repeated, but all he'd heard was *He tricked me. I thought it was you.... I was so happy to see you.*

"He's... Sebastian..." Fiona worked to compose herself again as the hyperventilation took over. "He's an illusionist of some kind. Aleksei, he was *you*. All I could see was you, your soft kind face, and I melted. I let everything I was trained to see slip away because it was *you* and you'd accepted my apology and that was all that mattered."

The knot in his throat doubled in size, pressing at his windpipe. "Tell me," he croaked. "Just tell me, Fiona, and don't draw it out because the past days have been..."

Fiona's story tumbled out in a mess of tears and regret as she began with how wide and open her heart had been at the sight of Aleksei. It then took a violent left turn and escalated into her pure terror when she realized she'd been tricked, and ultimately raped, by a man Aleksandr had come to know as his best friend.

Sebastian had done this to Fiona. Sebastian had calculatedly pretended to be his friend, when Aleksandr needed one. Sebastian then betrayed him in the worst possible way. Why? What sinister evil must live inside him for him to want to hurt Aleksandr and Fiona so terribly?

The rage ebbed and swelled up behind his eyes until he could hardly see for the throbbing.

"Aleksei?"

"It's okay..." He dropped the phone, then, fumbling, found it again, but his mind was beyond the conversation now. Somehow, some way, he had invited this in. He had allowed this man to earn his trust and then hurt the one dearest to his heart. "I'm going to make this right, Ona."

"No. You need to stay away from him, Aleksei. If he knows you know, he'll do something crazy. He'll hurt you. He's dangerous!"

"It's okay," he said again, looking around the room, searching for something clean to wear.

"Listen to me. I've had a lot of time to think about this. At first, I was so upset at what happened, I didn't stop to wonder why he'd gone to all that trouble, and I still don't have the answer, but whatever it is, it's not good. He's not a good person. His only intention is to hurt you. I talked to Flynn this morning, and he's reached out to the archdiocese in New Orleans to do some investigating into Sebastian and keep an eye on him, and you, and I think it's best—"

"Ona, don't worry." Aleksandr closed his eyes to block out the dark spots swimming into his vision. The sway from his rising blood pressure knocked him sideways into the couch, but it would pass. "What kind of man am I if I can't deal with my problems myself?"

"Please don't. No, I have a better idea. Wait for me." She shuffled some things in the background in a frenetic manner. "I'll go to Dublin and catch the next flight to the States, and we can figure this out together."

"He won't get away with what he did to you," Aleksandr said. His mother had a gun somewhere in the apartment, but he didn't have the patience to tear the place apart. He couldn't stay a moment longer. "I love you, Ona."

He heard Fiona's faraway cries of his name in desperate

fear as he pulled the phone from his ear and ended the call. Blinding tears of rage poured down his cheeks as he toggled to his text messages.

Finding Sebastian's name, he typed, *Meet me at the lake.*

Aleksandr didn't remember how he got out of the Quarter, or whether there was traffic merging onto I-10. When he hit the Lake Pontchartrain Causeway and started the twenty-four-mile drive across the lake, he realized he'd spent the preceding fifteen minutes in a daze.

A hard, driving rain eclipsed any view of the water. He could have been driving on air, into the oblivion. In some ways, he was. He hadn't found the gun, but he didn't need one. He knew who he was. What he was. And what he would do.

Sebastian was powerful, too, but was blinded by his own arrogance. He believed Aleksandr to be weak, because Aleksandr never wanted his friend to feel threatened by his own immense power. Such was his selflessness that he hid it, pretending Sebastian's gifts were so much greater than his own.

There was no more cause for pretense.

He parked the car but didn't get out right away. He didn't see Sebastian's Ferrari, but that could mean anything. Sebastian might not have seen the text immediately. But Aleksandr had no doubt he would come.

The rain was relentless. Aleksandr didn't have the keys to *Femme Forte*. Sebastian had always stolen them from Olivia, who used the home often enough to have her own set. The back porch, though, was covered, and there was also a gazebo at the end of the second dock.

He liked this option best. From the gazebo, he could see not only the whole property, but the entire long driveway laid out, all the way to the distant road at the end. When Sebastian did arrive, he would see him long before the traitor saw Aleksandr.

Aleksandr didn't have an umbrella, but there was a red hoodie in the backseat. It belonged to Sebastian, and the thought of even touching it made him cringe, but he only needed to protect himself from the rain for a hundred yards or so. Then he could throw the cursed thing in the lake.

He slipped on the gravel outside. A river of water traveled downward from the drive to the lake. To the left, flash flooding pooled in the center of the lawn, and around the trees. *Maybe I should call Ashley and see if he can stop this storm long enough for me to settle my score.*

The gazebo was drenched at the outer bench but dry in the center. He ripped the water-logged sweatshirt off his head and heaved it into the lake with pained satisfaction. All around him, the rain thundered from the heavens. It was all he could hear except the thud of his angry heartbeat.

Fifteen minutes passed, and Aleksandr began to wonder if Sebastian was coming, after all. His thoughts, which he'd kept squarely compartmentalized since the phone call, inadvertently traveled back to Fiona, and the parts of the conversation where he'd begun to tune out, focused instead on his vengeance. Had she really said she wanted to come back to New Orleans? He tried to remember her exact words, but they were fuzzy, like piecing together specifics during a hangover.

Aleksandr turned his attention to the lake. A hundred thousand needles of rain pierced the surface, stretching for miles, far beyond where his vision could reach. He wanted to rewind the clock to his father's birthday, when he'd found out Forbia awaited him on the lake. He wished he were there now, listening to his father patiently instruct him on how to navigate the ungainly ship. He wished even more that Fiona was by his side.

But he was naïve. Too kind, and too trusting, because he could not imagine in others a deception of which he himself was not capable. Fiona liked to say he had the wisdom of the ancients, but not the experience and he'd never understood more what she meant than in this moment when his lack of experience had paved the way for this Greek tragedy.

Aleksandr turned at the sound of crunching gravel. He strained to see through the rain and fog, but there was nothing visibly apparent. He stepped outside the gazebo and put both hands over his eyes, looking for a break in the storm.

"Sebastian?" he called, though his voice died feet before him, trapped by the onslaught of the late fall storm. "Is that you?"

Nothing sounded in response, but the air near him changed. Not a wind, but a subtle shift in the atmosphere, one he pondered for a second too long before turning.

A heavy fabric came over his head and something sharp stung his arm. As he swayed in the muddy gravel, grasping for understanding, flailing for purchase, Aleksandr understood he'd miscalculated everything in his wrath.

There would be no confronting Sebastian, because Sebastian had calculated everything about their friendship, including this very moment.

Aleksandr was exactly where Sebastian wanted him.

43
VICTOR

Victor lay in the bed next to Olivia, eyes wide in the darkness. His mind was restless. He could not let go of what he had seen and heard with the boy, Sebastian.

Since his original discovery of Sebastian's "oddness," he'd kept his eyes and ears open for any signs that might be useful as leverage when he went to Colleen. He was certain she did not know what Sebastian was up to. The kid would not be allowed to run around unshackled if she did.

Mama, Sebastian is talking to the bad woman again, Victor heard Rory spill to Olivia just that morning.

Just go play, sweetie. Doesn't Thomas have an important date with Percy? Olivia's face had not matched her playful words. She'd gone dead pale.

But, Mama—

Rory, go play, please. And if your great auntie Colleen comes over, or anyone else comes over, we don't talk about the bad woman. Okay?

Pushing the matter with Olivia by asking his own questions would be a line Victor might not be able to cross back over. The way she sank into the carpet as she watched her son run off, her hands curled tight into fists, told him they weren't yet close enough for this conversation.

That was fine. He suspected she didn't know as much as she thought she did, and he could learn more by doing his own investigation.

Sebastian's talks with the woman named Margarethe, who he seemed to believe was his mother or had his own reasons for using the sobriquet, had escalated in intensity. Victor could only gauge the nature of Margarethe through Sebastian's responses to her, since she remained invisible to Victor, but his read on the situation was that Margarethe was violently angry with Sebastian, and Sebastian was doing all in his power to correct this. Back and forth, this went on and on, Sebastian begging his "mother" to continue believing in him.

The conversation from that night, though...

I know, Mother Margarethe. I have a plan.

Silence.

I know I said Aleksei was ignoring me, but that's changed now.

Silence.

I'm not blaming you, Mother. Please forgive me. I thought you wanted me to cut him down, and I went overboard, is all.

Silence.

But this time, he *messaged* me. *He wants to see me. He did exactly what you said he would do all along. It's almost too easy.*

Silence.

No one will know! His parents are too busy and they're not riding his ass for once. It's brilliant. He asked me to meet him somewhere private. He's going to walk right into this.

Silence.

I'll make sure no one follows me. I'm not an idiot, you know.

Silence.

Sorry, Mother.

Silence.

I said I got it.

Silence.

Fine, you want me to repeat it back? I'm to take him to the old Shoe Factory warehouse off River Road in Baton Rouge, past the refineries. Your contact will pick us both up there. But then what?

Silence.

You never tell me anything.

Silence.

Of course I trust you. I've done everything you asked, Mother. You can't even tell me now where they're taking us? After all I've done?

Silence.

Overseas is pretty damn general. And I don't even have a passport.

Silence.

What does she want with Aleksei anyway?

Silence.

I figured you wouldn't tell me. I hope one day you'll finally see I've earned your trust, Mother.

Silence.

I know he's waiting. I'm leaving now. Once we get him where the woman wants him, can I come back to you? Will I still be able to talk to you, where I'm going?

Mother?

Mother?

Sebastian sped off in his Ferrari minutes later. This was hours ago, and he hadn't returned.

Victor did not need to know the precise nature of Margarethe's words to piece together the important parts of what had happened. She had ordered Sebastian to kidnap Aleksandr and take him... somewhere. Overseas. Wherever—and whomever—the kid was going to, it wasn't a holiday.

While Victor had never seen Margarethe with his own eyes, he had undoubtedly *felt* her malevolence in the house, all along. At first, subtle, and then intensifying as her orders to Sebastian grew in urgency.

From the first, Aleksandr had played a key role in the discussions between Sebastian and Margarethe. Victor had listened, patiently, building his case against Colleen, dreaming of the moment she would have no choice but to help him see his beloved Ophélie again. All the questions he would ask! His apology, this time, would reach her. He knew it. No matter how their lives had veered, at heart they still were and always would be Cianán and Cerridwen, locked together by fate.

As his store of information had grown, though, matters had intensified, and now, as he lay there, contemplating, the young Aleksandr was in grave danger. With every moment that passed, the likelihood of preventing that danger waned.

Victor turned away from Olivia. Well, what was Aleksandr to him? The child of two people he'd never even met? A cousin of his Amelia? His own blood, he supposed, though a tenuous connection.

No, I am Cianán. My one and only goal was to see The Prophecy fulfilled. Aleksandr is one half of that prophecy, and without him, all is lost.

Did he still believe this? Even now, when he was no longer human, no longer Cianán, no longer anything but a creature relegated to the periphery?

You did this. You understood they meant Aleksandr harm and continued in silence to build your case, not caring what happened to the child as long as it met your aims.

Victor couldn't deny this. He could claim he didn't know what Margarethe's intentions were for Aleksandr, but it would be a weak defense, for it was clear, all along, that she had used

Sebastian toward a single goal. He didn't need to know what that goal was to act.

I would be giving away all my leverage, if I take forward what I know. Colleen will never help me. Olivia might never forgive me. I will be back where I started. I may never, ever find Ophélie.

Aye, said the other voice, the voice of Cianán. *But your soul will remain intact.*

Victor let his eyes fall on Olivia's bare shoulder for several, longing seconds and then quietly pulled himself out of bed.

44
ORIANA

Oriana made no apologies for her occasional escapes to The Menagerie. Her quiet retreat down the hall in silence, the long breath in as her lungs filled with roses of all scents and colors, as her ears took in the trill of parrots and roar of lions.

She had never wanted the throne of Farjhem. It sat on her shoulders, a tremendous burden, and she, Atlas. But she could not shrug it off until such time as she could place a strong leader on the throne, one who would, above all, protect Oriana's right to her beloved kingdom under the ground.

Oriana had yet to identify this leader. It could not be either of her siblings, which would cause strife amongst the Empyrean population, for the right of blood succession was an important tradition. Agripin and Nerys were her enemies, though, and life as she knew it would cease to be under their leadership. Agripin might have left her alone before, but he would never now. And Nerys would always do what she felt was right, a beacon of disgusting purity.

The search for more of her father's children produced no

results. Royal bastards were a Children of Men phenomenon, not something that happened amongst Empyreans... not when every birth had to be sanctioned by the Eldre Senetat.

Oriana considered having her own child and leaving him or her on the throne. But all those with strong bloodlines had fled Farjhem after the destruction, and those left were not fit to father her child.

She had put the search out for an appropriate mate, but she wasn't holding her breath.

For now, her only option was to lead Farjhem herself, and to do that, to preserve her sanity, she fled to the soothing cocoon of The Menagerie eagerly and often.

CYLER SLOUCHED ON THE IVORY SOFA IN HER PRIVATE CHAMBERS. HIS shocking red hair was a flame in a room filled with an absence of color. A blank canvas, in intentional contrast to the thousands of colors within the heart of The Menagerie, just beyond. Here, she was only herself. Pure.

She lowered her jeweled hand to Cyler. He barely hid a disgusted look as he kissed it. *I should make him lick my cunt. That would wipe the look from his face,* Oriana mused with a laugh. Cyler winced.

"Fortune has smiled our way, Vakkar," Oriana purred, using his old nickname. He loathed it, for it reminded him of a time where he was even less in control of himself than he was in Agripin's service. "I come to share news I've not shared with anyone."

"What about your Council?"

Oriana rolled her eyes. Her braid fell over her bare shoulder. "Don't be daft. I have no one I can trust. My Council is a band of yeomen and sellswords culled from The Menagerie.

They are no statesmen. They have never been privy to the way this world works, and what it takes to sustain it."

Cyler went rigid in his seat as she relaxed into hers. "Why would you trust me?"

"Ahh, Vakkar." She slipped off a shoe and stretched her painted toes, covered in liquid gold, toward his face. Her big toe tickled his lips. "Mark or no Mark, you are mine. I've watched you struggle with yourself to find an individual purpose, but there is none, not for you. Not without the service to another. You will serve Agripin, or me, or both, but never neither. Do not forget, you yourself orchestrated your surrender to me. You did not have to join your master, and I daresay you've hardly seen him at all since returning to Farjhem. You could have left and did not. And so..." Oriana slipped her toe between his lips. His eyes expanded to saucers with bewilderment and then, like an obedient puppy, he began to suckle. As she knew he would. As he always would. "I know you are mine."

Oriana dropped her foot and slithered across the couch. Her white gown hitched around her waist as she settled her thighs on either side of his. She said nothing. Waited.

Every last drop of color faded from Cyler's cheeks. His breath faltered. She imagined all variety of objections running through his head. She was wet at the sight of this creature, who had only ever loved men, thinking of ways to avoid fucking her.

At last, amidst the strange silence of their power struggle, Cyler unbuckled his pants, and his zipper came down. Oriana did not reach for his cock, but instead, waited for him to offer it. Cyler released an uneasy breath and withdrew his sex.

Oriana's face spread into a slow smile as she eased herself down over him. In spite of himself and his own innate desires, Cyler's eyes rolled back. He had been so desperate for the touch of another that even hers would send him into a temporary bliss.

She flexed her thighs as she began her slow strides. "Now that I have your attention. I've determined we've been going about our problems all wrong. The big picture was lost, somehow, but now, ah, now it is laid out before me."

Cyler's hands flew out and gripped her thighs, guiding her. She witnessed in his eyes a hatred for himself, but it was not greater than his desire. Good. She slowed her pace to taunt him into submission, making him ever more hers.

"All of our ills began many eons ago." She dropped one of her nipples into his mouth, and he sucked, hungrily. "When we aligned with the wretched Tuatha de Danann. Breaking that alliance was even worse than making it to begin with, and we were all cursed, evermore. But that curse has allowed for many of us to thrive in ways we never imagined. The Menagerie, The Senetat. These would have never been possible in the old world. And so, this curse has been our greatest blessing."

Cyler tried to speak, but instead, cut his teeth around her nipple, sending a wave of pleasure through them both as he squeezed.

"There are those in that Brotherhood and among the ruins of the Quinlans, who would end that curse, and thus, end what we enjoy about our lives. The Prophecy, they call it." Oriana licked the perimeter of Cyler's lips, then reached her hand down his back, scratching a slow trail. Her finger slipped down under him, finding the spot of his greatest pleasure. He bucked as she slid two fingers in.

"There are two who would fulfill this prophecy and end everything as we know it. By some reversal of fortune, Vakkar, one of those two has landed in my lap."

Cyler returned to himself for a brief flash. "What? Who? How?"

Oriana slid a third finger in, and he released a long moan. "Aleksandr, the son of Anasofiya. He will be mine. He's already on his way. If he sits in the prisons of Farsengel, he cannot mate with the other heir, and then cannot fulfill this prophecy."

"How, though?" Cyler gritted his teeth, straining against his pleasure for answers.

"By the strangest of ways!" Oriana laughed and shoved her tongue in his mouth, kissing him in a way she knew her brother never had. A trail of spittle followed her as she pulled back from a dazed Cyler. "A restless spirit, of all things. An ancestor of the Deschanels, who has spent centuries, if you can believe it, searching for the perfect necromancer to adhere to and thus return to a physical form. She believes the right vessel will even grant her immortality!"

Oriana quickened her pace, bringing Cyler closer to her, further from himself. He groaned and throbbed inside her. "One of my scouts discovered her, and she came to me ready to make a bargain. She can bring me Aleksandr in exchange for me helping her find a vessel. Through the Deschanels, she somehow learned about my brother offering Anasofiya and Finnegan the Sveising, granting them eternal life. I am to find her a body and give her this boon, and then we are equal."

"And will you?" Cyler managed. His head fell back.

"Will I help her? Only Emyr knows. But Aleksandr is en route to me now, and with him, nothing can stop us. Nothing can stop me."

Oriana leaned in and whispered in Cyler's ear, "Come for me, Vakkar. Show me you are mine, now and always."

A tear slid from Cyler's eye as he shuddered and spasmed beneath, releasing deep within her, his seed and will alike.

45
ANASOFIYA

The last time Anasofiya had seen such a gathering of healing forces within the Deschanels was during a time of her life she hardly remembered, when she'd been hit by a car as a little girl and had broken dozens of bones in her body. She had healed herself, at her father's gentle urging, enough to come home from the hospital, but then had been too exhausted to complete the process on her own. She was only a little girl. And her aunts and cousins had swept in with their soft hands and finished the rest.

Many of the same faces were here now who were there then. Other family healers, cousins from more distant branches, had also shown up to offer their service. Colleen seemed to know each one's complete family history. Ana wondered how she kept it all straight.

Yet, what not one of the Deschanel healers was capable of healing was what Amelia might need most: her mind. Children of Men, even ones as strong as Deschanels, were not meant to carry children of such rapid development. And while Finn and Aidrik had done their utmost to keep Ana's body fit and sound for the delivery, they had been able to do nothing to assuage her mind. Only now, when Anasofiya understood her darkness, her Wraith, had been an integral part of her psyche, did she understand that same darkness had kept her from losing herself to a greater void.

Amelia had no such equivalent. Anasofiya had already asked Wraith if she could help... if they could send Wraith in toward the same service... but Wraith could only ever serve the one who created her.

Ana stepped out onto the porch into the chilled night, hands shoved in her jacket pockets. As she exhaled, her breath furled into a white cloud before her. She grinned. How often did they get a night cold enough in Louisiana for frosted breath?

Across the street, Oz's house lay in darkness. No one knew where he was and when he was coming back, and without him, access to Amelia's fragile mind in her imperilment would stay blocked.

Ana eased into the swinging bench and closed her eyes, taking in the cool air. These small, stolen moments were all any of them would have until Moira was born, and though she wouldn't have been anywhere else in the world right now, the fleeting escape gave her a comfort not even Finn or Aleksei could.

Finn was upstairs, hands on Amelia, mind singularly focused on keeping her well. And Aleksei... well, she feared she had stifled him lately, treating him more like the child he seemed in her head than the adult he was in reality. He was probably enjoying the much needed break from his over-bearing parents, especially in light of his grief for Fiona. This was one ill they couldn't mend, and letting him find his own way was one of the hardest things she'd ever done. Harder for Finn, she knew. Once they'd confirmed with Nora that Fiona was safe, they understood there was no mystery to solve. Fiona had made herself clear.

Aye, Kjære. This is Aleksandr's battle now.

Aidrik, I really need some time to myself.

Wraith was next. *I told him this, Anasofiya. He wouldn't listen.*

Maybe the both of you can argue it out in silence, yeah?

"Can I join you?"

Ana jumped, sending the bench swinging. She looked up with a startled laugh. Cameron Sullivan stood in his long wool coat, watching her.

"Yeah. Sure. Sit down." She made to move further to her right, but she was already at the corner. There was plenty of room. The bench could sit three comfortably.

"If you wanted to be alone, I can go for a walk instead."

Ana waved him away. "I only needed the air. Sit. You're fine."

Cameron lifted the tails of his jacket and sat at the far end, leaving respectful distance between them. "So, you probably don't remember me from high school..."

"I remember you," Ana replied, pulling her knees up and under her as she settled into her corner of the chair. "You were a freshman the year I graduated. Oz was one of my best friends, so I knew who most of the Sullivans were. Plus, I dated your brother, Clancy, for that short bit."

"Uncle Colin thought you and Oz would get married. That's what he told my dad anyway. Dad, of course, was hoping you might marry Clancy. I don't know what it is with Sullivans and their fixation on wanting their sons to marry Deschanels."

Ana laughed with a wistful look. "We were kids. High school relationships almost never last for a reason."

Cameron raised a brow and looked away.

"Oh," Ana said quickly. "I forgot, you married Cassidy Weatherly, right?"

Cameron didn't meet her eyes. "She was in your class, I think."

"She was an early fall birthday, and just on the verge of the cutoff to be put in the next class down. She used to go around telling everyone she had youth on her side and would age better than the rest of us."

Cameron tried to laugh, but it fell more into a soft grunt. "Sounds like Cass. She's always felt her beauty was her greatest advantage."

Ana puzzled over the way he spoke of his wife. Her own opinion of Cassidy had never been very high, but Cameron was the one who had married her. "You have kids?"

Cameron beamed. "Two daughters, three and two. Ainsley and Willow. Wanna see pictures?"

Ana nodded and leaned in as he pulled a photo, fraying at the edges, of two little girls with bouncy blond curls. "They're beautiful. And they both have the Sullivan chin."

Cameron shook his head. "We can't escape it. It's like a curse." He pressed the photo back into his wallet and tucked it into his inner jacket pocket. "They're both pretty, like their mama."

Ana offered a polite smile as she wondered how much Cameron knew about his wife's indiscretions, which were legend around New Orleans. Cassidy Weatherly had always sought her validations in the arms of men, and that didn't stop, or even slow, when she got married.

"You can stop wondering. I know what you're thinking," Cameron said.

Ana froze. She hadn't let her guard down in this house of mind readers. "Sorry?"

"I'm not in your head," he explained. "I just know what *everyone* thinks when Cassidy comes up in discussion."

"Look, Cameron..."

To her great surprise, Cameron Sullivan burst into laughter. "I'm not a fool. I know what she does, and I know, for the most part, who she does it with. I take that back–I *am* a fool, for marrying her in the first place. But you're not a guy, so you couldn't possibly understand the hold Cassidy has on you. She makes you feel like you're the only man in the world when she's with you, even though you know she's made every other man she's been with feel that way."

Ana didn't know what to think of this admission. "You don't have to tell me this."

"I can stop, if it makes you uncomfortable."

She put out her hands. "If you need to get it off your chest, talk away. But you don't owe me any explanation for your decisions."

"Sometimes I feel I owe all of New Orleans an explanation," Cameron said with a heavy sigh. "Everyone I meet, the way they look at me... I can tell they're assessing me, wondering how much I know, how much I care. Thing is, I'm a Sullivan. We take on an obligation, we see it through."

"The Sullivan stubbornness, you mean," Ana said lightly. "I know all about that."

"I've heard it called that. I won't disagree that we can be stubborn, but it goes beyond that. We built our reputation on being good on our word, and we're pillars of this community. No matter what Cassidy does, I made a vow to look after her."

"That's very noble," Ana offered carefully. This was Cameron's confession, not a solicitation of her opinion.

He laughed at her. "And there's that Deschanel caginess. It's not noble, it's foolish. What other man would let his wife treat him like that with no consequences? She's never loved me. I was just the only man who would have her. What does that say, that not even her money is enough to make her a good match? Even my dad, who lives and dies by his honor, says I should leave her."

"You must stay for a reason, then. Your girls?"

Cameron looked down at his folded hands. "She's no mother to them, but whenever she thinks I'm considering walking, she turns it on, acting like I'm never there. She would use her father's money to take them from me, just to spite me. She doesn't want them. They'd spend their days and nights with a nanny, like they do now when I'm working. Cassidy has me right where she wants me, and I've let her do it."

"I'm sorry, Cameron. I don't know what to say."

"Thanks for listening, anyway. Clancy always said you were so easy to talk to. I find that's true of all the Deschanels I've gotten to know."

Ana reached over and squeezed his shoulder. "If it's your girls you're most worried about, I know Aunt Colleen would put the funds of the Deschanel Trust behind helping you. Both you and your daughters have Deschanel blood running in their veins. You're all entitled to the same protections the rest of us enjoy. We'd never let Cassidy take your girls from you. Trust me when I say, not even a Weatherly would go up against a Deschanel."

Cameron brightened, then exhaled a long breath. "Something to think about, I guess." He glanced down at his watch and shot forward. "We need to go in. Colleen has an announcement for all the healers in two minutes."

"What is it, do you think?" Ana tensed. She didn't have a good feeling at all.

He shrugged. "Your guess is as good as mine."

. . .

Colleen gathered them all in the dining room. Her somber expression didn't do anything to warm Ana's heart. Whatever she brought them together to say would require their strength once more.

Finn appeared beside her and slid his hand into hers. Jacob was nowhere to be seen, and Ana thought he'd probably stayed with Amelia. He rarely left her side and ignored the idea of healing shifts.

"For days, I have had our best researchers in the Collective looking for answers. Anything at all that might help us protect Amelia from herself. The last time she was imperiled, we came up empty, and only through Oz Sullivan's dreamwalking did we ultimately protect and save her. As Oz is nowhere to be found, and we know no other dreamwalkers, this is not an option for us this time around."

Colleen held her hands over her torso. The dim light from the dining room lit her lined, worn face, and Ana understood then that her aunt, the backbone of this family, had reached near the end of her own strength.

"All is not lost. An hour ago, our scribe called with news that gives me hope, and I pray it gives the same to all of you. While we cannot pull Amelia from her imperilment with any magic known to us, we can surround her with a greater magic. Think of it as a cocoon. The effect of this healing blanket will be to suspend her imperilment and trap it, if you will, within the cocoon. This should keep her safe until her daughter is born."

"That's great news!" Llewellyn cried. "So why do you have that look like someone's died?"

Colleen closed her eyes. She took several moments to compose herself before looking again at the gathered healers. "We have never done anything like this before. And we've certainly never tried it on an empath who is already imperiled.

The cocoon is a deep form of magic, the type that is often easier to apply than to remove."

"Cousin Colleen, are you suggesting that we might be sentencing Miss Amelia to a lifetime in this cocoon?" asked little Maybelle Guidry.

"What I am suggesting is that I am wary of unknown magic. Many of you know that, as your Magistrate, I always seek out new forms of knowledge. I never want us to stagnate, or drop behind our peers. Think of this in a more real world application, if you will. In the field of medicine, we do not begin practical application of any treatment until it has been tested repeatedly and over time in clinical trials and peer reviews, and proven to be an effective method. This magical cocoon is, effectively, still in clinical trials. It has worked on some and failed on others."

"Failure is not an option here," Luther affirmed. "Leena, we cannot fail and so we will not."

"My strength, Luther," Colleen whispered. Her eyes glistened with fresh tears. "No, we cannot fail. And as Deschanels, we have always prevailed when we *believed* we would. So I beseech all of you, here and now, to only enter that room with me if you *believe.* There is no place for doubt when Amelia's life is on the line. I won't have it.

"If you can offer me your faith, then I ask you to follow me now and help me place my daughter somewhere safer. And, when the time comes, I am going to call on you again to help me bring her out of it.

"But if you find you cannot enter that room without doubt, I ask you to leave us now."

Colleen nodded and started up the stairs. Everyone gathered followed in silence.

46

NICOLAS

A snowstorm off the Siskiyou Mountains had grounded them in Ashland, Oregon. Leander grudgingly trekked to an auto parts store to buy some chains, but the man there suggested they wait it out another day or two. Their rear-wheel drive car wouldn't fare well, chains or no, and landslides on I-5 had temporarily closed the highway. *Don't you worry,* he assured a horrified Leander, who looked equally horrified retelling the experience to Nicolas and Lauren. *Temps are warming up in a day or so.*

Lauren's already loosely frayed temper was close to becoming unhinged, and Nicolas knew he was largely responsible. He couldn't say why baiting her was such a delicious temptation, any more than he had been able to explain why he often did the same thing to Oz growing up. He would tell himself, *stop, you're going too far,* only to push forward another inch.

Where Oz would get exasperated and give him exactly the reaction Nicolas expected, Lauren brushed him off as an annoyance. She wasn't charmed or amused, and there was no "makeup" period like he had with Oz, where Oz, relieved Nicolas wasn't picking on him anymore, would be uncharacteristically playful and fun. Lauren recognized Nicolas was exactly who he was, and had no designs on changing him, something Oz had unwittingly spent his entire life attempting. As she said that morning when he boldly asked what she thought of him, "You're an asshole. The end." The words might have been easier on the ears had she not destroyed the last of his cognac stash, the nearest liquor store way too far to walk in the biting cold.

The end, Nicolas thought. Those words had underscored so much of his life. When he was younger, he blamed the universe, but as the years went on, he could only fault himself. He saw himself this way when he'd ventured to remain sober, for Mercy. The mirror he held up wasn't pleasant, but it was real, and he wanted to be a man ready to face it. In the end, the alcohol proved easier; his reflection, rosier.

Now, two days sober, the man in the mirror looking back bore a face painted with his long list of sins.

What he'd done to Oz was unconscionable. Not only in recent days, but throughout their long-suffering friendship. He had held Anasofiya's heart hostage, unable to give her what she needed, unwilling to let her find it elsewhere. He'd abandoned Adrienne with his self-fulfilling prophecy that he was "bad at being a brother." He'd let Aunt Colleen and the entire Council down, leaning on the excuse it was what they expected anyway, knowing deep down they were happy to see the positive changes within him.

And Mercy... he had hurt her in the beginning, but in the end, she was the one who turned all his sins back on him, her cold defection proving to him once and for all that he was either being divinely punished for all his prior wrongs, or was meant to be alone all along. The end result was the same.

He ached for Mercy. He loathed even the sound of her name as it rolled around inside his head. He was too good for her. He was no good for her. If she called him and asked him to come, he would drop everything to be at her side. If she called him, he would hang up the phone.

The alcohol had dulled these competing emotions, obscuring them, blending them together. To be forced to think through them and puzzle them out... to understand and come to terms with them... was worse than the pain of losing her.

"You're drooling," Lauren barked from the chair across the room. She leaned back in the armchair, reading *The Oregonian.*

Nicolas snapped himself alert. He wiped one hand over the back of his mouth and confirmed, yes, he had been drooling. "I knew you couldn't take your eyes off me."

"Hard not to notice a grown man with spit hanging off his mouth, staring into nothing," she murmured without taking her eyes off the newspaper.

Nicolas didn't even have the energy to spar with her. When he wasn't warring with himself, Oz's last words plagued him. He recalled them verbatim, that was the nature of his memory, only bringing forth clear images of the things he most wished to forget. *I'm done, Nic. Done. How many years have I catered to your ego? How many years have I let you walk all over me, claiming to be my friend?*

And Nicolas, even knowing Oz's desperation was real this time, that if he left he wasn't coming back, pushed. One more inch. Then two. Then twelve. He couldn't help himself. He couldn't stop. It was as much of a compulsion as his alcoholism.

He had to call Oz. Even if his friend wouldn't speak to him, he had to say these things burning on his heart before he got home and retreated once more to a world of drunken comfort.

Lauren's attention was fully back to whatever she was

reading. He needed privacy, but if he tried to leave, she'd tail him like a neurotic babysitter. He had to get her out of the room for a few minutes.

"I'm hungry," he declared.

"How nice." Lauren flipped the page on the paper.

"I didn't finish my breakfast."

"And whose fault is that, Prince Nicolas? I regret to inform you the royal kitchens are closed for inclement weather." She flipped another page.

"I'm not asking you to go get it. I can—"

Lauren shot forward, dropping the paper to her lap. "So you can find a place to sell you more liquor and then continue to make my life miserable? Yeah, I don't think so." She stood, stretching in her matching baby blue sweats. "Are you actually hungry? Or are you screwing with me again?"

I'm completely *screwing with you, but this time it's for a good cause!* "I'm actually hungry. The cheese grits were terrible, and an insult to Southern mamas everywhere." This much was true. They *were* terrible. "There's a McDonald's two blocks from here. I can walk that far without a chaperone."

"I can walk that far for you. What do you want?"

Nicolas reluctantly rattled off his order, realizing at once that he had not thought through his plan, seeing as he hated fast food. But he would be forced to eat it or risk her ire.

And, for whatever reason, he also didn't want her to think he was messing with her this time.

Lauren pulled on her heavy coat, slipping it over her sweats. She slid her feet into her boots. "I'm going to check and see if Leander wants anything, and then I'll be back in ten minutes. No funny business."

"Hey, I'm a funny guy," Nicolas said with a tired grin.

"I'm serious," she warned. A blast of cold air filled the room as she flung the door open, and then closed again. She was gone.

Nicolas peeked out the blinds. He waited until she emerged from Leander's room and was across the parking lot before pulling out his phone.

Oz's number went straight to voicemail, so he tried texting. *Please, Ozzy. Let's talk.* He tapped his foot, waiting for the response, knowing Oz was the type to respond in seconds, so when none came, he had to make a decision. Looking out the window again, he saw Lauren in the parking lot of the McDonald's. He had only a few minutes.

Nicolas held his breath and dialed again. Voicemail. He tried again, and this time it went to his box on the first ring, which meant Oz *was* there and was choosing to ignore him.

He didn't have time to keep at this. A message wasn't the way he wanted to make his speech, but it was that, or nothing.

When Oz's voicemail again picked up, he closed his eyes and said the words he needed to say.

"I'm the biggest dick on the planet. Not in a good porno way, either. I've done things I'm not proud of. I've said even worse. I'm awful, Ozzy. I'm really terrible, and I know this." Lauren popped out of the McDonald's. Nicolas' heart raced. He had to be quick. "I love you, Ozzy. I love even the things I always gave you shit for, like your hero complex, and your love of lost causes. After all, I'm one of those lost causes too, right? You deserve so much better than me, and you never let me feel that way, even when you had every right to. I'm not going to ask you to forgive me this time, because I knew how conflicted you were about Lucia, and I did it to hurt you. There, I've said it, the words are out. I wanted to hurt you. I wanted to hurt you the way I was hurting, so we could hurt together. That's not what a good friend does. It's what a shitty friend does. I'm sorry. As much as I can regret something, I regret hurting you more than anyone else. So, wherever you are, whatever you're doing, whatever you decide to do with this message, I hope you believe, at least, that I would take it all back if I could." Lauren's boots sounded outside as she shook off the snow. "I'm sorry, Oz."

The door flew open. Lauren's flushed face bore a puzzled look, directed at him. "Who were you talking to?"

Nicolas blinked away the threatening tears. He forced his best ironic grin. "Just your mom."

Lauren threw the bag at him. "My mom's dead, you asshole."

His smile faded. "Casper the friendly ghost?"

"Eat your food."

Lauren pulled the top comforter from her bed and pulled it around her, curling into a ball in the chair. Her red face peeked up from around the edges. Her pale blond hair flooded around the trim. Where he had thought she always looked perpetually exhausted around him, now he saw a deeply anchored sadness.

"I didn't mean that about your mom," Nicolas said, forcing down a bite of cheeseburger.

"We should be able to get out of here tomorrow. Until then, maybe you can try not to talk?"

Lauren disappeared further into her cocoon of blanket, cutting off any response.

Nicolas finished his food, every last bite.

47
VICTOR

Colleen wasn't at The Gardens. He tried to pull her whereabouts from her head of the household staff, Aria, but the woman had evidently been trained to block. He didn't have a chance to think of another extraction method. She offered the info he needed willingly.

"I'm to instruct any and all Deschanels that Mrs. Deschanel is at Magnolia Grace tending to her daughter for the foreseeable future. Any Council business should be directed to Jasper Broussard and he'll see it gets where it needs to go," Aria recited. He gleaned from her robotic delivery, not for the first time.

He found the news curious. When he had last found himself looking after Amelia, Colleen had been there too, and she hadn't been alone. She'd had a whole cavalry of Deschanels at her side, and he'd been too busy being kicked out to find out why. For Colleen to be there still—the foreseeable future had a cannily foreboding ring—then something was amiss. Jacob's strange behavior at his wife's bedside on the last visit seemed further confirmation.

Something *was* amiss with Amelia, and it hadn't improved.

Victor didn't bother with a taxi. He needed the eight-block walk to think about how he would approach Colleen, and help Amelia, without being thrown out of the city.

Two men stood on the columned porch, huddled together in intimate conversation. Victor recognized one as Luther Fontenot, whom his family had done recent business with, and who had been party to tossing him out of the house on his last visit. The other, a younger man, was unfamiliar.

Luther flung his hand out against the younger man's chest when they noticed Victor. Victor puzzled at the young man's quick anger toward him. They couldn't possibly know one another.

"What are you doing here?" Luther demanded. His arm relaxed as the man behind it did. "Colleen was clear. You're not welcome."

"I have news for Colleen," Victor declared. The young man's eyes narrowed. "First, can we clarify the animosity coming off the young one?"

"I know who are you," he said. "Jacob is like a brother to me. He has my back. I have his."

"And you are?" Victor asked, but he knew. He had not been idle in Olivia's arms. This must be Finnegan St. Andrews, one of the four heirs to The Prophecy.

Finn glared at him in steeled, obstinate silence.

"What news?" Luther clarified. He stepped forward.

"Don't listen to a word he says. He's a con man," Finn insisted.

"I know he's a con man," Luther said coolly. "Even con men occasionally come bearing news."

"My news is for Colleen only." Victor stepped closer, laying his hand on the wrought iron gate. "The news is urgent, and of the nature that, should she find you turned me away before I could deliver it, she would not ever forgive you."

"He's lying," Finn said. "He wants at Amelia."

"Friend, if I wanted at Amelia, it would be nothing to set you both aside, with little energy expended on my part," Victor replied with a level gaze on the hot-headed blond man contemplating his options. "Instead, I come offering a gift that becomes less valuable and more dire as the clock ticks down. I suggest you summon Colleen and let her decide what to do with me."

Luther was calmer but looked equally menacing as he regarded Victor, sizing up his worthiness, how far to trust him. The air was thick with his judgment. Victor saw before him the makings of a formidable ally.

Luther nodded at Finn. "It's fine. Go get her. If he's toying with us, you'll enjoy watching Colleen tear him limb from limb."

Finn paused. He let his gaze linger over Victor, an unspoken threat. Then he disappeared into the house.

"Tell me of Amelia. Is she unwell?"

Luther cleared his throat with a glare.

Victor gave a light bow. "As you wish."

Colleen broke through the front door. Her flushed face was framed by a flurry of matted hair. "You dare you show up here!"

He took a step forward, but a blur of panicked thoughts swarmed his way. Victor looked up and met the eyes of his adversary, and a stark, painful realization came upon him.

In her fury, Colleen had let her guard down.

"No," Victor whispered. His knees went weak. "Amelia. It cannot be."

Colleen froze. She backed away, Luther's hands shooting

out to steady her. “Leave us. You’ve done enough harm to my daughter. I won’t have you doing more when she’s vulnerable.”

“Imperiled... how did this happen? How could you allow this to happen?”

“I would never allow anything to happen to my daughter!” Colleen cried. She sagged. Luther held her tighter. “I have done everything, always, to protect her!”

“Leena,” Luther whispered. “Go inside. Be with Amelia. I’ll deal with this.”

Colleen tossed him off and marched down the stairs. Her hair fell out of what was left of her loose bun as she stormed toward him, mascara streaked down her face, the remnants of yesterday’s lipstick spidering out from her lips.

Her hands flew out before her, inches from her face. Victor thought for a moment she meant to cast a spell upon him.

“*You* did this to her. You, as much as anyone, as much as anything! Amelia is not fragile, but her weakness is the goodness of her heart. You took advantage and left a mark upon her that she cannot shake off.” Colleen pressed her fingertips to his chest and shoved. “You! You are an abomination, to this bloodline, to this world! To your heritage!”

Victor’s arms shot out and he gripped her upper arms in his hands. “Colleen, listen to me. I can help her.”

She tried to break loose, but his hold was too strong.

“Do you hear me? I can help her. I am to assume you have no dreamwalker among you?”

Colleen gaped at him, in rage, in wonder.

Victor dropped his arms and smiled. “I, dear one, am a dreamwalker. Not an amateur, as you settled for the last time she was in this predicament. But a practiced one. I have brought many empaths from imperilment, both within this family and without, and, if you’ll allow it, I know I can do the same for Amelia now.”

"You're a practiced liar, Victor de Blanchefort. A cunning man who knows all the right words, at the right time, and uses them to his advantage."

"I won't try and deny it," Victor replied. "Yet your opinion of me aside, you know my care for Amelia is genuine. I would not offer myself if I believed it would cause her further harm. I would move the earth to save her. If you believe nothing else of me, you know this, at least, is true."

Colleen's shoulders shook. Her tearless eyes bored holes in him as she deliberated whether to make a deal with this particular devil in order to save her daughter.

Her voice quaked when she replied. "If your interference causes even one cell's worth of harm to my daughter... if your influence causes her to question her love for her husband... if she comes back as *anyone* other than who she was when she went in... I will unleash a power beyond anything you have ever known in all your long days upon this earth."

VICTOR WAS ESCORTED TO THE TOP OF THE STAIRS WITH ALL THE ceremony of a prisoner. First flanked by Colleen, Luther, and Finn, and then others, as they peeled off from where they stood around the house.

When they reached Amelia's bedroom, Colleen stopped him. "Remember my words, creature. Mark them. Hear them in these next moments, as you construct your course of action." The venom faded. Her throat ebbed as she swallowed. "She is also with child. Whatever happens, nothing must be allowed to happen to Amelia's daughter."

Victor bowed. "I believe you'll find them both safe in my capable hands."

Finn grunted. Luther reached forward and opened the door.

Victor took in the scene. A handful of Deschanels pitched forward over the perimeter of Amelia's bed, as if in prayer, Amelia lying as still as glass, hands folded unnaturally over her sternum. Her white hair was a halo, completing the image he would not soon forget: Amelia as an angel of God Himself.

Jacob leapt forward in a shot. Colleen stepped around Victor and pressed her hands to his face. "Do what I could not moments ago, and be calm, Jacob. Victor is a dreamwalker. One more practiced than Oz. I don't rejoice dancing with our enemies any more than you do, but there is one truth I can't help but believe, and that is that Victor does not desire to see any harm come to Amelia. I think you believe that, too."

Jacob's granite face stared past her, past Victor. His lips were a hard line separating the two halves of his expression.

"This won't happen without your permission," Colleen pressed. "I promised you and myself this after I made the decision to allow Oz access."

The sound that emerged from Jacob's throat was scratched, like a man suffering from a grave illness. "Has it come to this? Really?"

Colleen dropped her eyes. "You know my fears. I haven't kept them from anyone."

"And if we refuse him?"

"Then," Colleen said, lowering her hands to his shoulders, "we live with whatever the uncertainty brings us."

Jacob looked past her, at Victor. "I know what you are. And I know what you think you can do, to me, to anyone, who looks at you wrong. But you have underestimated me at every step, and it will not take much, not at all, for you to realize that."

Victor took a single step forward, a sign, he hoped, of both acceptance and respect of Jacob's boundaries. "You have my word that I will see her out of her turmoil, and back to you, in the condition you left her. But you are wrong about me, Lord

Donnelly. I do know your capabilities. I have always seen you for who you are, because, in ways even you cannot deny, you are me, and I am you. My care for your wife is not of the nature that should threaten you."

Llewellyn wrinkled his nose at his brother and whispered, "Lord Donnelly?"

Luther shrugged as if to say, *is that really the strangest thing you've seen or heard in this family?*

"It doesn't threaten me. It pisses me off," Jacob replied.

"You and Amelia, the two of you alone, know where my heart lies. And, though I love Amelia, it does not lie with her," Victor said with some hesitance. He did not want to bring his battle for Ophélie here. If he was to help Amelia, he could not take along any of his life's baggage.

Maybelle stepped forward, adjusting her frilled dress with both hands as she approached Victor. "You heard his warnings, sir." She put one hand in the other and tried to crack her knuckles, but nothing happened. With a light frown, she shoved both hands to her hips instead. "Cousin Jacob isn't the only one who is a force to be reckoned with."

Alton put a hand on her shoulder. "We're not leaving the room, is what she's trying to say. And we will be watching."

Victor didn't need to assess the motley crew huddled in the room, waiting for an excuse to take him out back and make good on their threats. They would soon see his intentions here were as pure as theirs. Had they trusted him, instead of throwing him out, he could have helped her sooner. Perhaps even prevented her imperilment to begin with.

He could fix it now, and that was what mattered.

Victor looked at Jacob. "I know your worries. I know what happened with the Sullivan bloke. I can bring you with me, if you like."

Jacob regarded him with hard skepticism. "What? You mean, into her head?"

Victor nodded. "Oz did not know the breadth of his capabilities, or he could have done the same. I make this offer as a friend, even if the sentiment is not returned."

Jacob looked at Colleen. Her lips parted, but she offered him no words of advice. She hardly possessed the strength to stand upright.

"Okay. Take me with you," Jacob said.

Victor's eyes opened to a field of the most effervescent, exotically hued flowers he had seen in all his days. Marigold and poppy elevated to three dimensions, the color dripping from the petals like a separate, breathing entity with intentions and desires of its own. Magenta and turquoise assaulted his senses, the colors so stark and vivid that they were also somehow *loud,* screaming at him.

At his side, Jacob stumbled. Victor reached out to steady him.

"What's happening?" Jacob asked. His hands flew out before him like a blind man searching for purchase.

"The mind of an empath is an augment of their reality. None of what you're seeing is real, but it is based on a reality that matters to Amelia. Do you recognize where you are?"

Jacob squinted against the onslaught of color. A sharp whistle passed through his teeth, as if he'd been struck. "I do know this place. Sort of."

Forest green vines with the depth and texture of a sculptor's clay wound over the ground like waves. The effect was dizzying, and Victor once again caught Jacob before he went down. "Don't attempt to make sense of it. This is her creation, not yours. We are outlanders here, and none knows this more than the landscape we stand upon. A man could go mad in the deciphering."

"It looks like Monet had an acid trip at Giverny and threw up the results." Jacob squeezed his eyes closed. His lips counted off. He blinked away his uncertainty and looked at Victor. "Now what?"

"Now we find the center. We find the center, we find Amelia."

"How do we do that? How big is this place?"

"It is as big or as small as her subconscious desires," Victor explained. "As for the how... look at the foliage. Beware of losing yourself to it, but carefully observe. Do you see that all flowers tilt in a similar direction? That the waves of the vines crest the same way?"

Jacob looked around and slowly nodded. "West. Toward the back of the property."

"I'll lead. Don't dally long with any step. This is her creation, but make no mistake, it is also a weapon against anything that would harm her."

"We're obviously not here to harm her."

"When an empath is imperiled, all foreign sources have the potential to create harm. Her mind does not know the difference between a source of love and a source of destruction."

Jacob gestured. "After you, then, I guess."

As they followed the navigation provided by the flora, the depth of the colors escalated, as did the distortions that revealed them for the falsities they were. Puddles of color lay at the stem of every flower. The air grew thicker, and a light haze stretched the reality, bending the atmosphere.

Jacob was the one to spot the destination. "There. That gazebo. Oz said that's where she was last time."

"Good eye," Victor said. The form of the gazebo lay in the distance, but he could see nothing beyond the outline. Pollen and abandoned color whipped through the air, creating a dense fog of smashed pigment.

Pushing on, closer, the vines now whipped around their ankles in silent threat, whispering their warnings. *No further. Go back, interlopers. This is not for you.*

The stark white gazebo contrasted so heavily with its surroundings that it expanded into a pool of white, blinding them from seeing the contents. In the final stretch, Jacob broke into a sprint and began crying out her name.

"*Blanca*! Amelia!"

Victor slowed his advancement when he heard Amelia call out in response. He stopped altogether when he saw them embrace amidst their desperate tears. This moment was not meant for him.

Yet they could not remain in her mind prison for long, and if Victor was to protect her from herself, he could not dither.

Amelia's arctic eyes burned Victor with her judgment as he approached. He tried to smile, but found he had none to offer her.

Questions, many of them, sat on her lips. Jacob kissed them away, and whispered, "He's a dreamwalker. I know he shouldn't be here, but he knows how to save you. How to save Moira."

More tears spilled from her lids as she watched her husband. "Do you trust him?"

Jacob pressed his forehead to hers. "In this, yes. I'm here because of him."

Victor ascended the gazebo steps tentatively. "Listen to me carefully, Amelia. We do not have long, and the instructions I have for you are ones that can only be carried out by you. You alone. For this is your world, not ours."

"Last time I felt threatened by everything outside these walls," Amelia said. Both hands wiped away her tears. Her spine lengthened as if physically shrugging off the weight of her loneliness. "This time, I know what's outside of here is a threat, but it isn't coming in, and I can't figure out why."

"That's the cocoon of magic your mother and cousins wrapped around you," Victor said. "The magic is doing its job to keep you stable. What it will not do for you is bring you out of this state."

"And you know what will?"

"The flora remains a threat as long as you can see it. It keeps you bound to your gazebo in fear, unable to act, unable to leave. The gazebo is not your prison; what lies outside is. Do you understand?"

Amelia looked at Jacob. He shrugged.

"What you must do is completely remove yourself from this threat," Victor went on. He reached out to touch the soft, unmarked wood of the gazebo. "You created this as much as you created the garden beyond. *You.* And if you created it, you can amend it."

"But how? And what kind of amendment?"

"From a gazebo must be born a fortress," he replied. He reached forward and tugged her hands into his. Jacob tensed, but let it play out. "You are under siege, my darling. But your forces are weak. You won't outlast your enemy."

"Walls," Jacob said. "You want her to build walls."

At this, Victor found his smile. "Yes! Walls. Amelia, you must focus on closing the gaps of your gazebo. In turning the wood to stone. You asked me how, but only you know the answer, because this world is yours. A weaker empath would have died from her imperilment, overwhelmed by the forces seeking to destroy her. Not you. You found a protection. *You.*"

Amelia let go of his hands and pressed them both to her swollen belly. "And if I can't?"

"Those are simply the foolish words borne of fear. You are greater than your fears. You always have been."

"And when she does, she will wake up? She'll be out of her imperilment?" Jacob asked.

"Out of her imperilment, but still swaddled in the loving magic her mother wrapped around her. And I believe this is where she should stay, until Moira is ready to make her entrance."

Jacob didn't like the answer, but he didn't fight it. "I take it we can't help her build these walls."

"No," Victor affirmed. "In fact, we must leave her before she can begin her work in earnest."

"How will we know it worked?"

"You will know."

Amelia lifted one hand and pressed it into the gazebo created from her own mind. Jacob slid his head down toward her belly with a soft sigh.

"I don't think I have as long as Ana did, when she carried Aleksei. Moira is going to be unlike any other child born before her, breaking all the rules." She dropped her hand to Jacob's head. "I'll see you much sooner than you think, Donnelly. We both will."

"I'll give you two a moment," Victor said. "And then we must leave you to your work."

He descended the staircase and entered the malevolent garden, sagging under the weight of his exhaustion. Dreamwalking, for him, had always been effective, but it came at the cost of his energy. He needed rest.

But first, blood. Renewing, refreshing blood.

48
ALEKSANDR

Aleksandr's world offered so much darkness before even a sliver of light. Days of swimming in and out of awareness, but only given glimpses of his new truth.

Nothing had been clear to him from the moment the hood had come over his head. Whatever Sebastian had done to him had rendered him first woozy and then unable to stay alert no matter how hard he fought the surrender.

The method of his transport had shifted over the course of his journey. He started in a car, then moved to another motor vehicle. From there, a train, then, what he guessed was a plane, though he'd never been on one. Another car, and then, at last a cart. Perhaps a carriage. Whatever it was, his final stretch had been the roughest of all, and he was bruised and battered from limb to limb.

He slept through most of the voyage, not of his own choice, but his captors'. Sebastian was there, he felt him, but now there were others, who spoke in a language that felt familiar, but he did not uanderstand.

The last words he heard on his journey were, "We're approaching the gap," in English, perhaps for the sake of Sebastian. Then Aleksandr was again forced into a deep sleep.

WHEN HE AWOKE, HE GASPED AT THE COLD STONE AGAINST HIS CHEEK. His eyes flew open, then slammed shut again at the first light he'd beheld in days.

He heard no voices. Was he alone? He knew better than to hope for this, but until he could get his bearings it wouldn't matter anyway.

Aleksandr forced himself to open his eyes again. They strained against the brightness of the room, but he fought it, straining for focus.

He saw nothing but white. White, everywhere. The marble upon which his head rested was white. A lounger in the distance was covered in a white velvet cloth. Even the chandelier hanging above him held ivory sconces, held in place by a pigment-less base.

Was he in Heaven?

"He wakes." The voice was unmistakably feminine. Chocolate brandy, he thought his father would have said, both smooth and laced with a kick. The click of glass on marble sounded until it was close enough to be right outside his ear. "Do you know where you are?"

Aleksandr pressed his mouth tight. He didn't know, he had no inkling whatsoever, but what he *did* know was he had no intention of satisfying his captors. Not Sebastian or his conspirators. Not this woman with the oddly soothing voice and glass heels.

"Stubborn and proud, like your mother," the woman cooed. Amusement tinged every one of her words, as if she alone possessed a knowledge beyond them. "I have not the patience of my brother, nor of your fathers'. So I will tell you, Aleksandr Nicolas St. Andrews Deschanel. I am Oriana, Grand Empress of Farjhem, and architect of your fate, for whatever remains of it. You are mine now. You belong to me, for however long I choose to allow you to exist as a living, breathing creature upon the earth. I am not known for my mercy and begging will only incite my ire. Now. Do you know *why* you're here?"

Aleksandr's head spun. Farjhem. He was in Farjhem. Sebastian had conspired to get him here, but why? This was precisely the question the despot was throwing at him now, but he didn't have the answer. Why? Why Sebastian would hurt him wasn't the question, but why... how... he had come to work with their mortal enemy.

He was so far from home. So very far from anyone who loved him and would come forward to save him. He liked to tell his parents how he was capable of taking care of himself and didn't need anyone, but that wasn't true, not then or now. Aleksandr had the sharp urge to curl into a ball and sob like a child, as he had only months before when he was still shorter than his mother and playing games by the lakes and castles in Wales.

"Your Quinlan goddess possesses a sense of humor, aye? Though I suppose intelligence was never required to fill her supposed prophecy." Oriana's laugh cut through the guard around his heart. "You are here because of who you were born to be. It is not your fault, any more than it is mine to be born into royalty, but nevertheless, we can't escape our duty. We are who we are. I must run this realm. You must fulfill an ancient prophecy. Unless..."

Her heels clicked toward his face and her glass slippers settled before his eyes. The crimson polish on her toes was the color of fresh blood. "Unless your fulfillment of that prophecy keeps me from doing my own duty," she finished. "In your case, this is an undisputed truth. Without chaos, there can be no color. There can be no conflict, and thus, no secrecy. No need for a world like mine, an escape from said chaos. And I, like all creatures, am most interested in self-preservation. Naturally, you are too. In your silence, you search for ways to kill me, or at least neutralize me. I can't fault you for that. But I won't allow you the opportunity."

She knelt down. Her light cream dress pooled at the marble, as her head dropped down, and a crown of flaming red braids filled his vision. Jewels, in her hair, along her arms, at her neck, sparkled, dazzling. "Welcome home for the last time."

He next awoke in a room no bigger, or smaller, than their study back home. On the dirt floor, animal skins were scattered throughout, the singular sign of comfort. He scanned again. A latrine in the corner. A table in another.

And in the final corner, a man.

No, not a man.

"I've been wondering how long it would take my sister to figure you for her greatest weapon," said the creature, the Empyrean with the glorious red gold hair and a bare chest full of scars, trailing down to the tattered crimson leather lappets of a Roman soldier.

"Agripin?" It was a guess, but it was the only guess, given all he had come to know.

The fallen prince gave a half, disjointed bow from where he lay propped on a polar bear pelt, slumped against the wall. "At your service."

"So it's true. I really am in Farjhem. This isn't some joke."

"Not unless Empyrean humor is far removed from your own," Agripin replied. His fingers glided low on the air, as if conducting a song only he could hear. "I'm not surprised to see you, but I am surprised to see you alive. And sharing a cell, when there are so many to be had?" He laughed, a joke with himself. "Oh, Oriana. She threw you in the cell with the creature who killed your father. Does her subtlety know no bounds?"

Aleksandr swallowed. He forced his expression blank. He knew little of Agripin, only that he had been behind his father Aidrik's execution, a sin he had vowed to avenge one day. Even with Agripin clearly fallen from his prior glory, he was still his enemy, and he would not let him see his fear the way he'd been unable to prevent Oriana drinking it in. "Why are you here?"

"My sins are legion," Agripin said, bored, adding a nonchalant wave. "Well documented, not that it will matter to you where you're going. What I can't quite comprehend, though, is how they managed to pull you from the grips of your mother and father?" When Aleksandr remained a stone wall, Agripin grinned. "And how is my empress these days?"

"She's not your empress," Aleksandr said through gritted teeth. "She isn't your anything."

"Most Empyreans would rather see me back on the throne, with your mother at my side, than my vagabond sister ruling from her den of hedonism. If most knew I was here, they would organize a coup to set me free, and if and when that does happen, I will need my mate back. This is not complicated strategy, Aleksandr."

"You'll die in here." Aleksandr backed into the farthest corner, as far as he could find himself from the man who had killed his father. "You'll die in here because no one is loyal to you, not like you think. Because you've never been loyal to anyone yourself. And so no one is coming for you."

"Aye?" Agripin reached behind him for a bottle of whiskey. He broke the seal and tipped the neck at Aleksandr. "Then, you see, we do have something in common."

THE WRECKAGE

"The world breaks everyone and afterward many are strong at the broken places."

Ernest Hemmingway

49
MAXIMA

The prison of Farsengel, situated into the side of one of the two major glaciers marking the landscape of Farjhem, was said to stretch so far into the bowels of the volcanic base that the bottom tickled the top of the mines of Farskilt. No one could say for certain how many cells the prison contained, as there had never been a time in history when they'd filled them all. Hundreds. Thousands. More. At any given time, the average number of inhabitants was under a dozen. Most laughed it off as the Senetat's persistent desire to stay over prepared to a fault. Others thought they were built as an eventual final resting place of the rebellion.

Maxima, who for the first time found herself behind the bars rather than looking in, understood the vast number of cells in Farsengel were not intended as a planning measure, but a warning. An unspoken threat to those considering disobedience. *We could lock away every last one of you and it would be nothing to do it.*

There were, of course, differing wings for different types of prisoners, as in any royal prison. Just as Anne Boleyn had enjoyed some comforts in the Tower of London, while others in the same prison languished in hay and filth, those Empyreans of royal blood or royal purpose, no matter their crimes, were afforded a certain degree of respect.

The piles of Nordic furs couldn't hold a candle to her lavish apartments in the Sanctuary, but she reminded herself, over and over, until it became a sort of chant, that *it could be so, so much worse.*

Agripin had been moved to Farsengel the afternoon prior, a shocking move considering his status. No one had told her this, nor had she seen him. But his boastful insubordinate cries echoed across the hundreds—thousands?—of empty cells lining the cylindrical prison. The architecture here would end up being her most reliable bearer of news.

Agripin kept her company, though he likely never knew it. He belted drinking songs at the top of his lungs, for an audience of guards who had long ago learned to tune him out. She listened to him as she tore at the hunk of cold reindeer thrown into her cell without even a plate—so much for decorum—searching for a strange hope in his warbled cries. But if the emperor himself could not see his way out of this problem, how could she ever hope to?

Maxima, having spent the last two thousand years styling herself after the roman patrician class, had thus done much studying on what it was to be on the wrong side of power. Many chose their alliances on moral standing, like Cicero and his powerful speeches against the inevitable rise of Caesar as emperor. Others looked to how their alignment propped them up, like Pompey, who allied with Caesar in the First Triumvirate and later turned against him, creating civil war. In the end, both Cicero and Pompey died for their choices to defy the one wielding the most power.

She fancied herself more Cicero than Pompey, for she had

stuck to her deep-seated belief in the Brotherhood's cause, no matter the risk to her. And even though she'd failed in the end and been captured, she had no regrets of her involvement. She only wished she'd been more clever.

Like Cicero, she expected to find herself executed for her strong beliefs. Her last curiosity remaining was how long it would take for them to see to the task, or whether they'd leave her to languish in the darkness for centuries to come.

Later the same evening, the guards stirred once again with a captive. This one did not cry out, or make any sound at all, save the shuffling of feet dragged across the stone.

Agripin addressed the new prisoner with amused familiarity. Maxima strained to hear. Whoever it was, it seemed they were in adjacent cells, or perhaps, even the same cell, which made the situation even curiouser.

Then she heard: "Oh, Oriana. She put you in the cell with the creature who killed your father. Does her subtlety know no bounds?"

Who... but no. Oriana could not have possibly... could she?

The rest of the conversation reverberated across the empty stone, streaming to her in painful pieces.

Maxima collapsed in a heap of furs, her breath caught in a tight ball at the center of her throat.

Her efforts had been in vain. She could have borne her own fate if it meant their cause prevailed.

But it had not, and now, never would.

They had failed.

Sleep found her, mercifully. Her dreams were less forgiving.

. . .

Eyes. All she could see was eyes. Two of them, large as the orbs of Emyr in the sculpture at the Royal Palace.

Maxima closed her eyes to reset what must be a cross-over from her dream world, which had been a vivid but distorted recollection of her greatest failures.

"Maxima! Wake!" A hushed voice hissed at her, and this time, she did.

With a start, she rolled back, falling off the pile of furs and landing in a flume of dust. She coughed, clearing the air with her hand. A figure crouched before where she'd just lain, but she couldn't discern who it was.

She crawled forward, clearing a visual path through the dust. Hand after hand, she inched closer, not the least bit afraid of whoever had come to assail her. She would meet him, eyes wide-open, not cowering like a startled animal in the dark.

Maxima rolled back on her legs, as she unfurled herself, the new arrival coming into view. "Cyler?"

"We don't have much time, so it would be fantastic if you'd avoid the long list of questions about why I'm here," he barked, jumping to his feet. He peered out the open door—open! Wide-open!—and rushed back over. "Up!"

Her instinct started in on the same questions he'd asked her to withhold, but she had to know, at least one. "Why?"

"You'll probably come at the answer faster than I will," Cyler said. His top lip curled up in a light sneer. "It's not a trap. They have the youth, Aleksei, and this charade is nearly done. Oriana is set to win. Maybe you'll reach the Brotherhood in time to save him, maybe you won't. But those guards will emerge from their confusion any minute now, and if you and I aren't both far from the scene of your break-out, our care in the matter will be over in very short order."

Maxima rose, pulling at her skirts. Her hair had come loose

from the dozen interwoven braids, but her affrighted countenance was the last thing she needed to worry about now. "She will kill you."

"Only if she knows. Only if you fuck this up by standing around asking more questions!"

He was right, she had no time. Whatever hold he'd cast on the guards, Cyler had never been strong in his magic, and it would not hold long. Yet Cyler had never been allied with the Brotherhood. Had, in fact, brought Agripin back to Farjhem in chains himself.

"I'm not your enemy!" he pushed through a clenched jaw, shoving her out the door. "But I will kill you myself and claim you tried to escape if you don't get out of here *right this minute!*"

Maxima's pulse surged. All her fears, her worries, her cautions, they could hold her back or send her forward. She would die in this cell, or she could die out there, but out there, she would die on her own terms.

She let her gaze rest on Cyler for another second, then, with a brief shoulder squeeze, she rushed past him, down the long stone corridor, toward the secret entrance to the stairs leading to the Scryer's Temple, where she would, Emyr willing, call on one final favor from Scryer Naaron.

Outside the east passage of Farjhem, Maxima collapsed to her knees in two feet of snow. Her eyes scanned the area immediately around her. No one had followed her. She hoped Cyler made it back to the palace unscathed. She would puzzle over his strange decision to help her later. For now, she had but one single goal.

She removed the amulet from under her tattered gown and turned her thoughts to opening the channel, praying to Emyr it had not closed to her forever when word of her capture reached Birger and Astrid.

Above, the splendid blues and greens of the Aurora Borealis burst into a show of light, dancing on the surface of the snow. She very nearly cried at the beauty, a sight blocked to her in Farjhem, a sight that now meant freedom, even if she could not define freedom in any tangible way beyond the snow seeping in through her thin shift.

A new light appeared, expanding into the shape of a broad circle.

A portail.

Shaking, Maxima stepped through.

She emerged into the arms of Birger, who caught her as she collapsed. He carried her to a divan amidst the warm scents of salt water and sand. Astrid appeared at his side. Stian heaved his relief in the background as the portail closed.

"They have him!" Maxima cried. Sweat poured from her brow, and she didn't know why it was there, for she was not hot, not cold, not anything, only... was it the magic of the Senetat?

Was she dying?

"Who?" Her saviors asked in tandem, looking over her with grave concern.

"The heir," she whispered before succumbing to her exhaustion.

50
JACOB

The color returned to Amelia's cheeks. The rigidity of her limbs eased over time. A brief smile even passed across her face, though it happened so quick he had been the only one to see it. *Are your walls up now,* Blanca*? Is that what this means?*

Jacob certainly couldn't deny she *looked* much better. If he hadn't known better, he would have said she was taking an afternoon nap.

The problem was, Jacob didn't trust Victor. Although it was evident his intervention had helped Amelia, his motivations remained suspect, which put the whole thing into question. Jacob racked his brain trying to piece together why Victor would go to such lengths to help Amelia, a woman he claimed not to be pursuing romantically; a woman who had refused to help him and kicked him out of her house.

Jacob believed, all the way to his core, that Victor de Blanchefort was a creature who never did anything benevolent unless there was great benefit to be had for himself.

He found some comfort in the limited time Victor had

spent in her head, and that he had, this time, been there to witness the interaction. Oz's months in Amelia's head would always remain a blind spot for Jacob, one he would deny still bothered him, but that denial would be a lie. He would never know how Oz and his wife had fallen in love, and even if that love had been a false conflation of the magic involved in saving her, and the intervention of a well-intended cousin, Jacob would not ever forget the look in Amelia's eyes when she'd awoken and searched, like a cornered animal, not for him, but for Oz.

For now, Jacob's world had stopped spinning so wildly off course. Amelia was again stable. Moira, from Colleen's examinations and the ultrasound machine she'd permanently parked in the room, was entirely healthy. And even Colleen had improved—her hair again coiffed, makeup within the lines and perfectly drawn—something Jacob did not realize how badly he'd needed until he saw in hindsight how it had unsettled him. Colleen truly bore the weight of the emotional compass of her family.

Jacob laid his head down alongside his wife's, stretching his arms across her belly as he returned his focus, with the rest of her healing cousins, to keeping the cocoon whole.

"Did y'all know Cousin Colleen hired men with guns?" Maybelle stood in the doorway with an indignant and slightly excited scowl.

"To keep out the wrong sort of folks," Alton explained. He stood to stretch, then uncapped his bottle of water. "Like the de Blanchefort man."

Maybelle's scowl deepened. "Didn't that man just save Cousin Amelia?"

"Yeah... well... it's complicated." Alton seemed perpetually in swing between patience and complete fluster with her innocent but on-the-mark questions.

"Lots of things are complicated. Our disappearing coastline, for one, or the effects of fracking on the environment and why we ignore it because ain't nobody in this room not drawing a paycheck from the industry someway, somehow." She dropped her hands to her sides. "A man saving a woman, then being kicked out for it? That's not so complicated."

"It's better this way," Jacob said. "For him and for us. But you're right, Maybelle. He did save her. We won't forget that." *Which is probably exactly what he wants.*

"Some opinions are best kept to yourself, young lady," Llewellyn chastised, looking up from his vigil. "You're too young to understand."

"I understand y'all are a bit xenophobic. Is he not from around here? He dresses funny, I suppose. What don't you like about that nice man?"

"That's a big word for a little girl," Alton said in the voice adults use to talk to toddlers.

Llewellyn ignored him. "Watch it now, Maybelle, or I'll call your daddy. He didn't send you over here to give us a smart mouth."

"Rex?" Maybelle's laugh was a challenge. "No one sent me, Cousin Llewellyn. I came here because I wanted to help Cousin Amelia. If you say that man is a bad one, I won't keep arguing like my mama says I like to do. If you want me to kill him, I brought Daddy's brass knuckles. Like I said, I came here to help."

Jacob couldn't stop from laughing. "You really have brass knuckles?"

The look he got back suggested his question was far more illogical than her claim. "That's what I said."

"Do you know how to use them?"

Hands shot back to her hips like a magnet. "Do *you*?"

"Actually," Jacob replied. "I do."

"Don't encourage her," Alton said, but patted Maybelle on the head with soft affection. "Her imagination is already too big for that head of hers."

She scrunched up her face and looked up. "Heyyy!"

While they bickered, Markus arrived, followed by Anne and Jon. Markus only stood patiently as the cousins fawned over him, asking how long he was in town, remarking on how much he'd grown up, arguing in return that he'd seen most of them not even two months ago.

He answered their many questions in a single sentence. "Staying at *Ophélie* until Nicolas gets home, then going to surprise Katja and help her with Stella, and yeah, I'm taking my classes online."

"But Stella..." Alton said.

"Watch. They'll find her."

Markus stepped past them and moved to swallow Jacob in a half-embrace. "How are you holding up?"

Jacob nodded. "You know me."

The younger man grinned. "So you've been spending your evenings in underground fight clubs getting your ass kicked by meathead Russians?"

Jacob laughed. "Not this time. I'm okay. As long as Amelia is okay, I'll stay okay."

"She's got the Krewe of Deschanel all up in her business. She's not going anywhere."

"Neither are they. If she were awake, she'd be freaking out about all these people around her."

"And you? You need some air? We can walk. It's a nice night."

Jacob shook his head. "I stay calmer when I'm near her."

"Up to you."

Anne and Jon hovered by the door in an uncomfortable huddle. The polite thing would be to call them over and make conversation, but Jacob didn't have it in him.

All conversation stopped when Finn rushed to the door, breathless. "Where's Ana?"

Ana stepped out of the master bathroom, where she'd been cleaning the washcloths they'd been cycling over Amelia's forehead. "I'm here. What's wrong?"

"Have you talked to Aleksei today? Or yesterday? Or at all in the past few days?"

"Yes, I..." Ana dropped the cloth to her side. "Actually, what day is today? We were texting, but the days have been running together. I think it's been a day, maybe two. Let me look."

Finn ran his hands up his sweaty face and through his hair. "I'm going to guess it's been at least two days. Maybe three. He's not answering his phone, either, and I called him at least a dozen times. That's not like him at all."

Every eye in the room turned to Ana. Jacob realized they were conditioned now to expect tragedy. Her expression disappeared. "We need to go by. Maybe his phone died and he forgot to charge it... maybe..."

"I tried to land line we connected, too, Ana. He's not answering that, either. Also, I checked with the college. He hasn't been to class at all this week."

"Maybe..." The word hovered in the quiet room as she dropped her eyes to the corner. "Did you go over to the apartment?"

"I'm going now," Finn said. "Stay here in case."

Ana looked up, at him, past him, through him. "In case?"

Finn seemed to notice for the first time the gathered crowd, listening attentively. He dropped his voice, but it did no good. "I already told your aunt Colleen. I know, I should have come to you first, but if he doesn't answer, then I need to know she's already on it."

Ana slowly nodded, her thoughts elsewhere. "You did right."

"If I go over there, and he doesn't answer." Finn pressed his mouth together to throttle his emotion. "And I call you..."

"I know. Be quick."

WHEN HE WAS GONE, THOSE GATHERED IN THE ROOM SAT IN DAZED silence.

"I'm sure he's just sleeping. You know how the young ones are..." Llewellyn began, but even he seemed to realize the words were unhelpful.

Jacob pulled himself from the bed and went to Ana. "You don't have to stay here. You've done so much already. You should go with him, Ana."

"No," she said, breaking herself from her stupor. She wrapped both his hands within hers and looked him square in the eye. "Finn will know what to do. And we have to protect *both* our children right now."

51
NICOLAS

Nicolas had never been more ready to leave a place than Ashland. The town would forever remind him of where he scratched his emotional rock bottom and found he lacked the character to buoy his way back to the surface.

Two stops left. Only two, Lauren said often. Those words seemed to keep her from jumping off her own cliff, and while he took a fair share of blame in the creation of that cliff, he understood the man at the end of their journey, God willing, played a part as well.

As did her father, her sister, and any other man or woman who had caused Lauren to feel as if who she was wasn't enough.

Nicolas wanted better than that for Lauren. The first time the thoughts appeared in his head, he didn't know where the hell they'd come from, but they didn't leave. *I want her to be happy. She deserves to be happy.*

"Well, so do I," he'd muttered, dry-mouthed, searching as

much for a stinging retort as a drink. *Yes, but not the way she does.*

They hit the coast around ten that morning and wound their way north along Highway 101. The cresting waves of the ice-cold Pacific called to him, the way his father's gun once had. These would not be the warm waters off the Gulf at Deschanel Island. This would be ice to the marrow, a shock straight to the core of him where he might feel *something* other than despair for his soul.

The lead in Gold Beach was as dead as his current liquor stash. Lauren's mood improved slightly as her chant changed to *One stop left. Only one!* And then a call from Ashley bumped them back to two.

"I know your last stop was supposed to be Chehalis, Washington, but Rockaway Beach is along the way. An old shaman dropped us a call today that sounds promising. Anyway, you're on that side of the country, and best to check it out."

Nicolas could hear the words from the receiver all the way in the backseat, just as he could hear the wind melt from Lauren's sails.

Leander seemed to think it was a good idea to slip a hand over her knee as a means to soothe her. She recoiled and raised her hand so fast Leander jumped back and hit his head against the window.

Nicolas could have told him how that was going to end.

Rockaway Beach, population 1312, was a cozy seaside town nestled along the 101, which bisected the two-mile stretch of kite shops and pizza parlors.

Nicolas could have gone for some pizza, but Lauren was definitely not in the mood.

She made an abrupt turn on 3rd, and then a quick right on Pacific Street. The Silver Sands motel looked, to Nicolas, like a great place to meet a serial killer, but the parking lot was filled with families and young couples. At the beach beyond, the sky was a sea of kites of all color.

Lauren eased the car into a spot in the middle of the lot. As she corrected the wheel, Leander sprang bolt upright, and then tugged at the door handle.

"Calm down, sheesh!"

"Let me out. Now. Let me out."

"It locks when I drive. You know that," Lauren said, sighing, releasing the button.

Leander didn't hear her or didn't care. Once the door clicked unlocked, he flew from the still-moving vehicle, screaming at the top of his lungs. Lauren glanced at Nicolas in the rearview. He shrugged.

"Estella," Lauren whispered, reaching blindly for her own door as her eyes followed Leander flailing down the walk. "It's Estella. Oh my God, it's Estella!"

Lauren bolted from the car without stopping to close her door. She sprinted after Leander, who moved with the fluid speed of a track star. Lauren strained to catch up, but it was not Leander she was trying to catch.

Nicolas watched the scene from the backseat. He saw little point in joining them. If Estella was truly the person at the end of their chase, they'd apprehend her and go home. If it wasn't her, they'd carry on to Chehalis. Either way, like Lauren, he was glad to be going home. Colleen and Ashley could go fly a kite with their advice next time.

Then he saw her: the flaxen blond debutante frozen in place, holding an ice bucket half-tilted. A small pile of ice pooled on the cement at her feet. He could almost read her thoughts: an animal, cornered, learning for the first time that her fight or flight is set to... freeze. She seemed neither capable of running nor confronting her brother and Lauren, who had come to a winded stop on either side of her, effectively blocking her exit. Leander fell forward on his knees, wheezing. Nicolas laughed to think about the regret he would feel later for his sudden burst of athleticism.

Nicolas slipped out of the car and went to join the welcoming party.

Quillan first tried to block the door. When that didn't work, he yelled at Stella to run down to the beach, to the place he told her to go if things ever got bad. But Stella cried back that she would never leave him or Estella for anything in the world, and his attempt to reason with her was what eventually let his guard down enough for the three to push their way in.

Estella rushed forward, panicked and scared. "I didn't see them. I don't know what happened. I don't know. Quillan, what do we do?"

Quillan glowered at her with all the kindness of a mercenary, then swiveled his attention to Lauren, Leander, and Nicolas. "We can't go back."

"Quillan, we aren't your enemies." Lauren held her hands out like the heroine in a movie sent to reason with the madman. "We didn't come to drag you back, kicking and screaming. We're here because Stella is in danger, and we want to help."

He threw his head back and laughed. Stella glided across the floor and came up behind him, protectively, though with her stiff, self-assured gait, it was unclear who was protecting who. "You think you know."

"We know it's stupid to do this by yourself," Leander jumped in. "Dude, come on. Do you really think you and that bitch who shares my blood can protect her from a centuries old ghost forever?"

Estella glared at him, but the prevailing look on her face remained shell-shocked.

"And you can?" Quillan pressed his hand back against

Stella, nudging her toward the bed. "It's okay, Stella. They're not here to hurt us."

Stella smiled at him, but made no move to back away.

"Jesus. How the hell did you find us, anyway? Stella had a ward over the area."

"Not a very good one, apparently," Nicolas quipped. "Someone around here spotted you and called in a tip. And the girl's not a mystic. I am. Her ward is garbage against someone who can create a real one."

"Go ahead, then," Stella challenged, shifting into a defensive stance behind Quillan. "Create a real one. Show me."

Nicolas wasn't expecting that. He flashed a winning smile at Stella. "You can't afford a show like that."

"The ward worked." Leander sighed. "None of the telepaths could find you. But you can't stop someone who is already here from seeing you. Wards don't make you invisible, they just turn off magic detection."

Stella and Nicolas squared off in silence.

"It doesn't matter," Leander continued. "We found you. And it's a good thing we did, because shit is hitting the fan back home and we need to get Stella back to Colleen, where she's safe. And you need to get back to work. And Estella... who knows what the hell *she* does, but, Quillan, you have a life. And it's not here in this motel on the side of the highway."

"Colleen?" Quillan repeated. He choked out a clipped laugh. "Why didn't Colleen protect Stella before things got ugly? Where was she when it mattered?"

"No one can *really* help Stella," Estella said. "I don't even know if we can, so you can cut the self-righteous bullshit, Lee. Stella was very nearly killed, right under the nose of Colleen and all the Deschanels! And now she wants Stella and she sends... you?" She wrinkled her pinched nose, then looked down on Lauren. "And you?" Then at Nicolas with a sneer. "Ah, yes, the JV II squad that never makes it off the bench because their games keep getting cancelled. Excuse me if I fail to see how much importance Colleen places on Stella's safety."

"We volunteered," Lauren countered. "While everyone else had given up on you, and on Quillan, we didn't." She stepped forward, inching closer to Estella. "But I'm not here for you. I wouldn't have given up my life to do anything for *you*, not even after what you've done for Stella."

Estella laughed through her tight smile. "That's right, you're here because you're still the same sad sack who pined after Quillan, knowing he was in love with someone else."

"Stop it, Estella," Quillan warned.

Lauren didn't shrink from Estella's venom. She moved closer. "We all make foolish choices. Quillan was one of mine."

Nicolas glanced at Quillan, who had the good sense to look ashamed.

"I know I can do better. I *will* do better. But that's not why I'm here. I came because my pride is not bigger than my human decency, and I can separate my feelings for Quillan, which thankfully no longer exist, from my gratitude to his father and my sense of duty toward someone who I considered a friend, even if that loyalty was never quite returned. I don't need him to return it any more than I need validation from you. I'm more concerned with sleeping at night. It's called a conscience. I suggest looking the word up sometime."

Everyone in the room went silent after Lauren's speech. Even Estella. Nicolas' respect for Lauren, which had been developing in the background of his thoughts, rose a few more notches. Not many women had the confidence to face a woman as intimidating as Estella Broussard, and he rather enjoyed the look of shocked indignation on his cousin's face.

"Anyway," Leander said, with a roll of his brows, "Colleen

said we were to ask you a question. And that the answer to that question should help you get your head on straight."

Quillan held his arms out. "Okay?"

Leander looked past Quillan, to the reedy Stella, with the long legs, pink cheeks; the girl with the body of a woman, and the eyes of a curious child. "Is your brother pushing harder now? Are you finding it harder to block him out?"

"That's two questions," Quillan muttered, but turned to hear her response.

Stella dropped her eyes. Her arms hung low, her hands twisted in knots. "I don't know what else to do. I don't know if I'm strong enough to fight him."

"Stella!" Estella cried. "Why on earth haven't you told us?"

"I knew," Quillan admitted. His voice was so low, Nicolas strained to hear. "Stella and I have tried to find ways for her to evade him, but hell, I don't know. I have no idea how to help her."

"Quillan," hissed Estella. "You kept this from me?"

"Don't pretend you're here because I give a damn about you. We're not partners. We're not even friends. Remember?" he snapped. "Lee, what can Colleen offer us? That's what it comes down to, right?"

Nicolas felt out of place in this conversation, the same way he'd been on the trip all along. If he could offer one thing to this group, it was his experience on the Council. Now, he had a chance to be useful. "The full power of the Deschanel Magi Collective will be put to work to protect Stella. I know you're new to this, being a Sullivan, but ask Oz if you don't believe me. There's nothing we can't do. You ain't seen shit until you've seen a room full of Deschanels coming together for a common cause. Right, Lee?"

Leander nodded. He looked as surprised as Lauren to hear Nicolas sound rational.

"Look, guys, you ask why Colleen didn't help before? It's simple. She didn't know. Yeah, she knew about the strange growth spurts and shit, but she had no clue what was happening under the surface with the crazy ancestor and all that starlight awakening bullshit. No one did, until Estella turned kidnapper and threw everything into a tailspin. She knows now. And when Colleen knows something, the woman is a bulldog. A goddamned magical bulldog."

"My family is a joke," Estella pouted. She wrapped her fingers around Quillan's arm. He broke away. "We can protect her, Quillan. We've done fine so far on our own."

"Have we?" Quillan ran his hands over his unshaven face. Tiny red lines dotted his eyes. "It's not our decision. Stella..." He took her arms in his hands. "You tell me, what do you want to do? Stick it out here? Go back to New Orleans? You told me I would know when the time comes...is this it? Is this the sign? I'm not going to pretend anymore that I know what's best. I don't. Estella sure as hell doesn't. Only you know how much more you can take."

Stella's eyes swam with tears. They fell down her face in silent agony, and Nicolas wondered how long she had been waiting to feel the permission to spill them. "You're right. You can't protect me anymore. I don't know if Colleen can, if anyone can, but I am so tired, Quillan. I can't sleep anymore. I can't close my eyes. I don't think I have much fight left."

Estella threw her hands up in exasperation. "So, these losers show up and suddenly everything we've been doing isn't good enough?"

"It never was, you stupid girl!" Quillan cried. He released Stella and rushed at Estella. "Don't you get that? You showed up on my doorstep, don't forget. I was running away from *you.* And I did the best I could for Stella, under the circumstances, but it was never going to last because we are so far out of our league it's not even remotely funny. Look at her, Estella." When Estella rolled her eyes, he gripped her shoulders and spun her toward the girl. "Look at her! She's not well. How much longer are you willing to pretend she is so you can play surrogate mommy to a child who needs more than what two self-centered assholes were ever going to be able to give her?"

"I want to go," Stella said, barely above a whisper. "Please take me."

"You know your brother is there, in New Orleans?" Estella cried. "You're walking right into his hands!"

Stella shook her head. Her blond ringlets pooled around her bowed face. "He's not there anymore. He went... somewhere else. He's been quiet. Too quiet. I know he didn't stop wanting to find me. Never that. Take me home while he's still quiet. Please."

Quillan pulled Stella into his arms. "This has always been your show. The day you came, everything changed to you. If you want to go home, we'll go home."

Estella fled the room in disgust. The door slammed behind her. Leander let out a bemused whistle, to which Lauren smacked his arm.

He rubbed his arm. "This is unbelievable. The princess is fighting awfully hard to live like white trash with a man she hated a few months ago."

"We have three cars here now," Lauren declared. A change came over her. She stood straighter, and her voice was again steady, as it had been the day Nicolas met her at The Gardens. "It's not a good idea to drive them all back. I'll arrange with Colleen to have one shipped home to New Orleans, but we will have to drive two, as my car will only accommodate two additional, and we have three."

"I can drive Stella," Quillan said.

"No," Lauren replied. "You're coming with us. So is Stella.

Nicolas is the strongest here, for whatever the hell that means, and she needs to be surrounded by strength until we get her to Colleen. And you, Quillan, we came here for you. So you and Stella will ride with us."

Leander snorted. "You really trust Estella to drive home on her own?"

"I don't care much what Estella does," Lauren said. "But Colleen promised your father we would bring her home. And since she's your sister, you get the honor of riding home with her."

"You've got to be kidding."

"When I'm kidding, you'll know it."

Leander mumbled a whatever under his breath and stormed out after his sister. It was Nicolas' turn to offer the awkward look to those remaining. "Sullivan, how about you pack your stuff, and the kid's stuff, so we can get this show on the road."

Quillan nodded. He nudged Stella. "Five minutes?"

Stella sniffled. "Okay."

When they were gone, Lauren sighed so deeply her whole body arced. She sank into the bed nearby. "I can't believe it. I can't... we actually found them."

"I'm sure Colleen will have a nice reward in it for you when you get home," Nicolas offered. He was on a roll with being helpful.

"I don't need a reward."

"I know you don't."

Lauren looked up. "Quillan seemed to listen to you, when you talked. He dismissed Leander, and he's never treated me the way he should. But you... anyway, thanks."

Nicolas shrugged. "I don't even know him. I only told the truth, about the Deschanels. There's no way some beachside motel is going to be better protection for Stella than the hundreds of us back home."

"Well, it was enough. And enough was all we needed."

"I'm glad I could offer more to this trip than my rapier wit."

Her head shook through her exhausted, choppy laugh. "You also aged me about ten years, so, there's that."

52
FINNEGAN

Finn's grip on the wheel was so tight that when he turned the car and let off pressure momentarily, the blood rushed back into his fingers and a sharp pain settled in. He ignored the throbbing. Squeezed tighter. Drove faster.

What he hadn't told Ana... not then, not in a room full of her family where she would have to react for an audience... was what his empath senses were telling *him.* He was still new to this side of himself and reading his ability wasn't an exact science. Days earlier, he'd started to feel a tickle, but he explained it away as their concern for Amelia's condition. As it worsened, he continued rationalizing. Amelia had gotten worse. She'd become imperiled. Everyone in the family was an emotional mess. Of course he would be, too.

Finn and Ana had spent Aleksei's entire life protecting him, because the dangers to him—simply for existing, an abomination to the Senetat and all they believed in—were persistent, and very, very real. Aleksei had worn their protective vise with sweet patience, until he couldn't anymore. Fiona's strange behavior had been the fray in the wire that forced the issue. And, oh, how Finn had tried to respect it.

His relationship with his own father had been so different. Andrew St. Andrews raised his sons to be strong men and leaders in their own right, but he had never nurtured within them the facets of their human nature that made them the men they would become. Jon's sense of chivalry got squashed amongst massive medical tomes and in-home operations. Finn's empathy was dismissed as softness, a trait no man ever embraced willingly. A desire to connect with others turned into an aloofness so detached that it had taken someone very much like him, a cool, withdrawn redhead from New Orleans to resurface it.

He'd overcorrected with Aleksei. He could see it now, his soft handling of his son, praying nightly that he would learn to love whoever he was, whoever that was. This affection had stifled Aleksei, but how could Finn have known that? He'd been a father for a year! And his son was as tall as he was, with a face his own age. No one really understood the emotional development of a boy who had grown to a man in weeks. There was no precedent for this. No handbook. No one to guide him and show him how to do it right. Aidrik had tried, but Aidrik was gone, and he was not coming back. The ancient sword dangling in Finn's closet, bowing the rod, was evidence enough of that absence.

Finn didn't know how to be a father. He didn't know where the swing of the pendulum should land in order to find the balance between raising a strong man and raising a true one. He'd blamed himself for Aleksei's inability to shoulder his heartbreak and when Aleksei asked Finn and Ana to leave... he saw that as his penance. For not knowing. For not being the father Aleksei needed most.

And in that space, Aleksei had fallen into a danger far

worse than Finn's confused attempts at being a father. The tests of fatherhood had never stopped, and he'd utterly failed this one.

"Stop," he whispered, tapping his hand on the wheel as the light frustratingly stayed red. "This isn't helping. Overthinking never leads to anything good. You know this. Pull it together."

He tried to clear his thoughts for the remainder of the drive through the busy Quarter. This was not a skill he had to dig deep to find. For most of his life, he had used it to block out anything that might contribute to his "softness." Attachments to the girls he courted, concerns for Jon's growing desire for life as a hermit, the loneliness of living on an island with less than two hundred living inhabitants, all of which he knew with an intimacy he wished he could turn off.

Jon had rushed after him, leaning inside the car window with a look Finn hadn't seen since he'd had his terrible boating accident as a teenager. *I can come. No, I want to come.*

Why had Finn said no? Because he preferred the solitude in case what he found wasn't good news? Because he still wanted to punish Jon? Both seemed viable reasons. They weren't there yet. He was closer to Jacob after a few weeks than his own brother of almost three decades.

Finn swung past tourist pedestrians yelling at him for his carelessness and peeled onto Chartres. The road was closed for a street fair, except to local traffic, which was lucky. It turned a twenty-minute drive down that street into two.

He threw the car into park once he had it firmly wedged into Ana's dedicated spot. Outside the car, he stopped. He needed to prepare himself, and in doing so, channel Summer Island Finn, who could meet any situation without losing his cool. Finn had tried his soft youthfulness, and it came with losing his edge, and more importantly, his innate senses of the world around him. Possibly what Aleksei had always needed was a combination of both Finns, but he would worry about that later, once his son was safe.

When he didn't get an answer after four knocks, he didn't panic. He hadn't really expected Aleksei to answer. If he wasn't picking up his home phone, then it was unlikely he would swing the door open, smiling. *Logical. Stay logical.*

Finn slipped his copy of the key in the lock and turned. The door opened without problem, which meant the chain lock had not been placed. Ana's rare paranoia always surfaced when it came to crime in the French Quarter, and Aleksei had promised her he would always throw the lock. *Logic tells me he isn't home. He wouldn't lie to his mother.*

Still, Finn stepped carefully inside to examine the apartment for any signs of his son. The same dirty ramen bowls decorated end tables and couch cushions, but now the noodles inside were crusted. Finn lifted a glass of milk to his nose and snorted as the sour smell filled his nostrils. He set the glass back down. *Logic dictates it's been days, possibly a week or more, since he's bothered to clean.*

Finn eased down the hall, continuing his inspection, starting with both bathrooms, finishing with the two bedrooms. His bed was unmade—another strange detail, as Finn's militaristic upbringing had driven home in him a neurotic need for rigor in certain daily tasks, something he'd passed down to his son—and Fiona's picture lay on the bed. Finn imagined his son clutching the frame before disappearing. *Logic tells me she, or the memory of her, has something to do with where he's gone.*

Aleksandr's phone rested beside the picture. Finn noted tracing his location, the simplest solution, would now be out of the question.

When he was certain Aleksandr was not anywhere in the

apartment, Finn calmly pulled out his phone and clicked on the last number he had dialed.

“Colleen, hi, it’s Finn. I’m going to need you to please call in the forces. Aleksei is definitely missing.”

“I worried that might be your findings. I’ve already assigned Ashley to get the trackers on it.” Pause. “I’m sure he’s fine, Finnegan.”

“False reassurances aren’t what I need right now,” Finn replied, without the edge to his voice that his words implied. *Calm. Logical. Cool as a cucumber.* “Something is wrong with my son. He’s not out for a walk.”

“You’re right,” Colleen replied on the other end, stretching her words into the sigh of a matriarch that had handled one too many disasters. “Something is most certainly not right. And we will treat this with exactly the gravity it deserves.”

Finn shoved his phone, and his shaking hand, in his pocket and forced himself, one foot after the other, to return to his car.

53
TRISTAN

Maxima's arrival had done more than stir the Brotherhood back into action. It had sent through those gathered a current of urgency that had been lacking thus far. A central unifying event to spur everyone involved toward a common cause.

Tristan marveled at how they could be complacent about the deaths of their own kind by the hundreds, but the kidnapping of one boy caused them to draw up their pitchforks and torches.

"We're not so very different," Harriett said, looking up from the last letters she would write home before their departure to Farjhem. Her skin, from face to hands, had taken on a swarthiness in the Mediterranean weather, eclipsing the girl he'd first met, drawn in paleness and fear. Harriett had returned to life in his protection, but she had blossomed in this setting so far from home.

"How do you figure?"

"When hundreds of people die in the Middle East, we shake our heads and lament the state of the world, but we go about our business." She stopped her pen. "But God forbid someone kidnaps an adorable white girl from a middle class neighborhood."

"I guess I can't argue with you there." Tristan clasped his gladiator sandals for what he thought would likely be the last time. They would be of no use in cold Farjhem, and he'd slowly begun stripping thoughts of home from his internal monologues. If he gave it too much careful consideration he would go mad, so he didn't dig too far beneath the surface.

Harriett licked the last envelope in her stack. She gazed at the pile longingly, as if channeling her goodbye to the family through her last words. Tristan had done all he could to convince her not to follow him into Farjhem, but there wasn't anything to be said. Harriett's rebuttals weren't overly emotional, which made them hard to counter.

Simply, she had not started living until Tristan rescued her. And she was not interested in living in this world without him.

Tristan took in the soft, salty breeze from the open window with a wave of nostalgia for a place he'd only known a short time. If they survived, maybe he would bring her back here, and they could make a life of it. Maybe...

Tristan straightened his spine. Enough of that.

"Ready?"

Harriett dropped her letters in the basket for the servant and smiled before following him.

Everyone huddled in the elaborate meeting area, which Tristan had come to think of as Thorvald's Magical Cave. Most faces were now familiar to him, unlike the first night. He'd laughed with some, played around with others. Listened to their stories of the ancient days. And as he took in all their faces, and with them, their histories, he couldn't help envisioning them all dead upon the field of battle, casualties of a cause born of their shared desire. This image brought him more despair than even the ideation of his own death.

Tristan realized *this* was the danger in sitting still when you were at war.

"Time is not ours to waste any longer," Birger intoned, bringing the rush of voices to a din. "By now, all know the situation. Oriana has one of the heirs, and we should bear no illusion that she will leave him alive for long. He is worth little to her alive. His death ends all hope for any lasting, meaningful peace. We will remain perpetually in flux, perpetually in fear, searching for pockets of victories to tide us until the next conflict. Oriana... the Senetat... they want this. They thrive in conflict and would fade to obscurity in a time of peace."

Nods rippled through the cave. Beside him, Harriett bowed her head.

"The time is now," Birger continued. "We have enjoyed our solace in this hillside alcazar, but if we do not push forth to Farjhem, it will be our last solace."

"How will we get to him?" Trygve asked. "It has been millennia since I've set foot in Farjhem, but Farsengel is not so easily accessed."

"We will first have to deal with Oriana," Astrid answered. Her hefty braid had been thrown into a wreath of smaller plaits gathered around her head. She held her bow at the ready. "And the Senetat. We cannot enter Farjhem without detection, even with the power of cloaking we have in this group. We have to assume they will know we are there, before we make it where we need to be. A diversion that distracts Oriana with a single intruder long enough for many to trickle in."

Anders tapped Tristan on the shoulder. "Tristan and Tarek will go in. Maybe they can serve two purposes. Their ability to breach a telepathic block is stronger than anyone here, and they can locate both Oriana and Aleksandr before they're apprehended."

Nerys stepped forward from the shadows. "No, Anders. Tristan and Tarek's work cannot be risked. I will enter Farjhem, and while the guards are busy with me, they can sneak in and start the search. The guards will inevitably take me to my sister, as they have no other choice. Once they do, I can bide my time with her while the rest of you assemble."

"That is not an option," Thorvald boomed.

"And why not?"

"This plan places too great a risk on your life, Nerys. There is a high probability it will be you upon that throne when Oriana is unseated."

Her life is too great to risk, but mine is table scraps? I've been downgraded to red shirt status. Tristan sent to Harriett. She grinned back.

Nerys trained her cool gaze on the ancient one. "Any one of us could end up on that throne. But I am the only one Oriana would not have killed on sight. Her actions to me spell out her fears. She does not want this duty, but she understands she must preserve it, and killing me would place her own standing in great jeopardy. The Empyreans in Farjhem would not allow royal blood to be spilled. This is why Agripin rots in a cell, instead of wearing his head on a pike."

Murmurs from all over bounced off the cave walls. "What if you are wrong?" Thorvald answered.

"Then I am wrong," Nerys said with a slow smile. "But I am not."

Nora Quinlan appeared at Tristan's side. He was surprised to see her, as she had left days ago to return to her tribe in Ireland. She spoke directly to him, but her voice carried. "Can you hear him? Aleksei?"

Tristan had the urge to crush her in his arms, the distress was painted so clearly on her face.

"Can you search for him now?"

Tristan hung his head. "Farjhem is warded too tightly. I can't reach anyone in there until I'm in, according to Anders."

Nora looked at Anders. "There's no other way? What if she's killed him?"

"It's true," Birger said from the front. "He may already be dead. But our future has always been in the dream of taking back Farjhem, and we will do it no matter what we find."

The light in Nora's eyes was hope, and it was so close to blinking out. "Is it possible she hasn't done it? Could he be alive?"

Nerys answered, "Yes, it's possible. My sister is not politically minded. A pot of gold landed in her lap, and she knows, at least, that much. Oriana is most probably weighing her options. Once she orders him executed, she can't ever go back. Sitting in a cell, he is removed from our grasp and we are neutralized. What we can't know is how long she will deliberate. But we must not lose hope."

"She put him in a cell with Agripin," Maxima yelled from the back. "Thousands of cells in Farsengel and she puts them together? What could that mean?"

"Torture," Astrid said with a sad look. "She wants to drive the boy mad. Agripin ordered the death of Aidrik the Wise. What could be worse than being shut in a cell with the creature who killed one of your fathers?"

"Our plans, then," Thorvald said. "Lay them out. If we have no time to waste, then let us not waste what we do have."

Tristan lay next to Harriett under the soft cotton of the quilt that had proffered such comfort to them in their time of limbo. This would be their final night of freedom. One last evening to contemplate the meaning of life and run down the list of his sins and accomplishments.

At dawn, Stian would open a portail. One by one they would enter and find themselves in a safe house outside Trondheim, half a day from Farjhem. There, they would await the reinforcements from the leaders, but they would not wait long. By night, they would open a second portail, to Farjhem, with whoever they had.

The east Asian contingent had sealed their alliance. Other tribes remained uncertain. Tarek, though himself committed, had been unable to gain more than a handful of recruits from the African Empyreans.

As Birger had said, they would go with what they had, for better or worse.

Tristan and Tarek would enter via a secret—or not so secret, as Maxima had been captured there—entrance through a blacksmith shop no longer in use. There, they would immediately begin work searching telepathically first for Aleksandr, to confirm his status, and then Oriana. If they had time, they had a list of other names... Senetat, Scryers... but no one believed they would have that much time. Harriet would be at his side offering her silent support. Tristan had given up attempting to dissuade her.

Moments after his and Tarek's entrance, Nerys would follow her contribution to the plan. The others would wait a reasonable amount of time before entering Farjhem, not together, but spread out across all ingresses. Many would assemble where Tristan did his work, which offered him a small twinge of hope that he might survive, after all. He tried not to hold on too hard to it.

Some would be tasked with sweeping the village and recruiting others to join the cause. Others, to evaluate the

Scryers on the hill, determining who was on their side and who would need guard until the work was done.

Divide and conquer was the plan. The more who showed up, the greater their chance of success. It was not an arms race, like the wars of the Children of Men, but they were up against the uncertainty of where the civilians in Farjhem stood in this battle. A miscalculation could result in their failure from a loyal citizen uprising.

Anders had told him, *don't think about the rest of the plan. Focus only on what you're responsible for, because it's all that matters in the end.* Tristan wanted to retort that he'd read way too much fantasy and played far too many video games to ever be so tunnel-visioned.

Harriett pressed her soft lips to his. Her breath filled his mouth and passed over the surface of his skin, sending chills through him. "Sleep, Tristan. You'll need it."

"I can't turn off my thoughts." He slipped his hand up into her sun-kissed hair and pulled her in for a deeper kiss. "I don't really want to die tomorrow."

Harriet eased down beside him again and rested her head down into the crook where his shoulder met his neck. "I don't want you to die, either."

"I hear a 'but' in there somewhere."

She nuzzled her face into his skin, exhaling more of her hot breaths against his flesh. "But we came here for a reason. We left New Orleans knowing we might never see it again, and it was okay then, so it has to be okay now." Her hand traveled across his belly, and then up, settling over his heart. "I don't think how long we live matters, but how we spend the time. And the months we've spent together have been the only ones of my life that have ever mattered. If we don't make it out tomorrow, I'll know I left this world happier than I came into it."

"Dang, Harriett, you're going to make me cry."

"Will that help you sleep?"

Something else certainly would, but to lie with her the night before a task so important had a tawdry feeling he couldn't shake. It also seemed to seal the finality of their fate, and he couldn't go into Farjhem tomorrow believing they would die. They very well might, but he would not lose the last drop of his hope in his final moments. Harriett would die happy. Tristan would die with a sense of purpose.

"Thank you for loving me," he whispered and wound her tiny body into his lanky arms, wondering how two strange souls had found and healed one another. Wherever they went after breathing their last breaths, he prayed they would be able to go there together.

54
ALEKSANDR

At first, Aleksandr couldn't decide what he was seeing.

Agripin's smug lackey, Cyler, whom he recognized from when Cyler came to the Quinlan lands bearing news of Aleksandr's mother. And a woman he had never seen before, fleeing past their cell, flush-faced and carrying the body language of the guilty.

Agripin tensed at the sight of his lover, but this quickly faded to fury once he was out of sight.

"The bastard helped her escape." Agripin pulled in a breath. "He helped her escape and left us to rot."

"Who?" Aleksandr asked before he could consider that asking might connect him to the monster sharing his cell. They had no common ground; Aleksandr could never find common ground with the creature responsible for his second father's death.

"Maxima." Agripin watched him in the darkness.

Aleksandr guessed he was hoping he might ask who Maxima was, hooking him further into easy submission, but this time, he resisted and stared back.

Agripin explained anyway. "Formerly of the Eldre Senetat until your mother ripped them to shreds. She was the only one who survived, though that can hardly be credited a miracle since she knew about the mayhem about to go down. How, you ask? Because she's also a spy for the Brotherhood. Fancy that, eh? Until Oriana caught her and threw her in prison."

"I didn't know you and Cyler were a part of the Brotherhood," Aleksandr said, hoping his underlying message, *I didn't think you capable of this type of honor,* would be received.

Agripin snorted. "Because we are not! Who knows what deviant business Cyler has got himself into? He isn't my concern any longer. Not since he deposited me here at my sister's mercy."

Aleksandr glared, though he could hardly see him to ensure it was even aimed in the right direction. The moonlight had passed over the thin grate at the top of Farsengel, casting them in perpetual darkness. The only thing left to provide them with direction was the steady patter of rain falling down into the center of the circular prison. "To answer for your crimes."

Agripin's laugh echoed off the stone walls. Hay crunched as he rolled. "Not for the crime you concern yourself with, I assure you. Oriana would have seen Aidrik dead quicker than me. My 'crime' spared the life of your mother, but do I receive your gratitude for *that*?"

"You'll never hear anything resembling gratitude from me, monster. And I don't care what they charge you with, as long as you pay."

"How bold is the child who sits behind the same bars," Agripin said. He clicked his tongue. "You do know why you're here, don't you? I don't mean sharing a cell with me, we've already been over that."

Aleksandr didn't reply. He knew. And Agripin surely knew

as well. But he was tired of the creature's continued enjoyment of his pain.

He has taken everything from you. Fiona's voice, a blend of her advice and his own thoughts. *What will you take from him?*

"You won't leave here alive, Halfling. There's no outcome where you continue to draw breath for much longer. You only do now because my sister is not enough of a politician to know how to best deal with you. But she will come to her conclusion soon enough. What, then?"

Aleksandr pressed himself into the cold stone. He pulled himself taller, imagining stretching his spine as he uncoiled into a great leviathan, towering over the villain in the corner. "Then I guess your sister will find out what I can do." Could Agripin hear his voice shake? Could he see his wringing hands?

The smile died from Agripin's haughty voice. "Oh? And what is that?"

“Why would I tell you?”

“And what else have you to do with such information? Die with it?”

“I'd rather die with it than give you the satisfaction.”

Agripin laughed. “You get your sharp tongue from your father. Your first father, that is. Your second father knew when to hold his peace.”

Aleksandr's heart ached at the mention of Finn, and the idea that he'd inherited part of a man he might never see again. But Finn would live. He would continue on, long after Aleksandr was bones in the cold ground.

It hurt even more to be locked away in a room with the creature who had killed his other father. Aidrik would not go on. His time was done.

“You killed my father.” Aleksandr spoke the words clearly, from his gut, from his heart. “You killed my father for your own gain, and now you will answer to your own maker for that crime."

Aleksandr didn't see coming the ringing laughter from the other side of the cell. The sound of more hay crunching as Agripin doubled over with the weight of whatever could possibly be funny about something so terrible.

"Oh, Halfling. Didn't your mother tell you?"

"Tell me what?" Aleksandr spat.

"Aidrik? Your father?" More hay snapped beneath the fallen duke as he craned forward in the dark cell. "He's not so dead anymore."

55
VICTOR

Victor did not need blood to survive. Dhampir were not like other vampires. Blood was a novelty; a dessert, to some, an infusion of power to others. The vampires of gothic literature feared for their survival without a steady supply of red-blooded humans, but a dhampir sought one out when their own blood was running hot. After a fight, as a means to quell a fear, or, if they were fortunate enough to come across one of the magic persuasion, to temporarily absorb an ability for their own.

He did not particularly love the taste of blood. Nor did he enjoy the process of extricating it. To take blood either required the victim's permission or the victim's life, as they had no means of wiping their memory clean after the drink. He had to make use of a sharp object, as he had no protracted fangs with which to call upon, and there was no such thing as relaxing a victim into submission. Often it required great struggle. Humans, by nature, were self-preservative and did not go down easily. Keeping them down while draining their blood was even more challenging.

Victor's father, Marius, used to man his house with willing human slaves. They didn't know what Marius and his brood *actually* were, they just thought they worked for humans with peculiar tastes. This was not so unusual in South Louisiana, where vampire lore was fresher than ever.

But Marius ceased this practice years ago when he feared he was losing control over the loose lips of his employees. His father, Etienne, commanded they cease the practice altogether when one spilled the whole story in a bar. Without a steady stream of blood, those de Blancheforts bearing the mark of the dhampir were cautioned to drink only sparingly, and to practice the utmost care in disposal. *We only take from the depraved,* Marius liked to say, but not everyone in the family shared that moral code.

Victor possessed no such predilections about the lifestyles of his victims, but he did respect the underlying caution behind them: pick someone who will not be missed.

He varied up his routes so as not to give the police any patterns to chase. New Orleans was off-limits, a family rule, unless he could choose a dark alley or corner where no witnesses could tell a tale later. He had favorite spots, but was careful not to visit the same spot more than once a year, to throw off the scent of similarity.

Basin Street, sight of the beating center of the once-thriving Storyville District, was perhaps his most favorite of all, and fortune smiled upon him after his trip into Amelia's head, for it had been almost exactly a year since his last visit.

The balding redhead in the tattered mink stole and black wash jean shorts didn't leave him inspired, but she did take the edge off.

• • •

With a clear head and a burst of adrenaline, Victor understood what he needed to do. The clarity was overwhelming, like seeing distinct edges of everything within his vision.

In his fear for Amelia, he'd completely forgotten his reason for venturing to Magnolia Grace to begin with. This oversight could end up costing the young Aleksandr his life, if it hadn't already.

A strange contradiction. Taking one life with impunity, while seeking to save another.

His wife, Elisabeth, had once asked him how he could reconcile his strange proclivities. How he could stand up for a convicted felon's rights, or seek to protect the slaves on his plantation from the pain of family separation, but would then sneak into the swamps at midnight to take a life.

Victor tried to explain that it came down to the difference between a visceral need and a powerful one. He needed blood. He also needed to see his slaves cared for. Those needs came from different places.

Both required satisfaction.

He found himself once again at the gate in front of the massive Magnolia Grace, staring into the eyes, this time, of Alton Guidry.

The sting of fight was gone from this man, and Victor guessed he would find the same in the other relatives. He had earned some parity with them for saving Amelia's life, even if they didn't trust him.

Alton nodded without a word and disappeared inside. Colleen exited a minute later, with Finn in tow.

"I thank you for what you did for Amelia," she said amenably, each of her words carefully chosen. "But I think it's best we keep the home limited to healers."

"I'm not here for Amelia," Victor said. A tingle surged through his bloodstream. He had the urge to jog around the block a few times and come back. "I have news of Aleksandr, and I don't believe time is on our side of this issue."

Colleen stepped forward and narrowed her eyes, just as Finn's widened. "Is this why you were here earlier?"

"What do you know about my son?" Finn demanded. He pressed past Colleen and down the steps. "Do you know where he is?"

Victor tossed his hands in the air to signal his submission. "I don't know where he is, but I know whom he is with."

"Who?" Colleen and Finn both asked.

"The young Sebastian," Victor said, and Finn relaxed slightly. "This young man is not your son's friend."

"What are you talking about?" Finn asked. "What do you mean, he's not his friend?"

"Let him talk," Colleen cautioned, resting her hand on his back.

"I have passed enough time with Olivia to have witnessed, for myself, Sebastian's strange behaviors," Victor went on. Colleen and Finn watched him, skeptical, but patient. For now. "He is in communication with a creature, one only he can see, by the name of Margarethe."

"Heaven help us," Colleen moaned. "Are you certain? This was the name he spoke?"

"I am certain he is speaking with someone he calls both Mother and Margarethe, yes. I am also certain this being has instructed him to take Aleksandr and offer him up to a third party. Someone in Baton Rouge, in an abandoned factory along River Road. From there, they are headed overseas, but I don't know the destination. This is where my knowledge on the matter stops."

"What... no..." Finn dropped his eyes into the distance,

puzzling out what he knew versus what Victor had told him. "You're sure *Sebastian* did this?"

"I only know he disappeared following these orders and has not returned. And nor has Aleksandr, I assume?"

"Do you have an address?" Colleen's cool, collective self had returned, with her daughter stable. "Surely, Sebastian must have reiterated one?"

"Only what I've told you."

"When?" Finn came out of his daze and marched forward. "When did you hear this happen? When?"

Victor suspected what would come after the words were said. "Days ago."

He was not wrong. Finn was on top of him in a burst, Colleen yelling at them both.

"They could be anywhere by now!" Finn cried. His hand was at Victor's neck, securing him to the ground. "You knew this *days* ago, and you said nothing? Nothing at all, when you could have saved him?"

"We can use this information, Finnegan!" Colleen cried behind them. "Don't waste your time on anger."

"It was not my business," Victor managed through his crushed windpipe.

"That hasn't stopped you with Amelia! Or Olivia." Finn eased up and rocked back on his heels. "I don't believe you. You kept this information to yourself for a reason, and now you're telling us for a reason. And I want to know why."

"I can guess," Colleen said. "He had hoped to use it as leverage. Is that right, Victor?"

Finn threw a glance over his shoulder. "Leverage for *what?*"

"Ophélie. You thought I would trade this news for Ophélie," Colleen went on. Her heels clicked on the cobblestones. She knelt next to Finn. "And yet, here you are, having given up your leverage. I echo Finn's question. Why?"

Finn released him at Colleen's urging. Victor fell back and pulled himself up with the wrought iron gate. "When I stand before Ophélie, the day I stand before my love, I will do so with a clean conscience. I promised her I would not wrong her again after the ultimate wrong I forced upon her. Keeping the news of Aleksandr close to my breast was a pox on that promise. She would not want me to further slander myself to aid her."

Finn stumbled back and into the porch. His hands were knotted in his curls. "Colleen... he could be anywhere. He could literally be... oh my God. My God. I have to tell Ana. How do I tell her this? How..."

"We need to determine why Margarethe has any interest in Aleksei," Colleen said. She'd turned away from Victor. "It makes no sense. Stella is her target, and Stella is finally on her way home to us. What use could Aleksei be? He isn't a necromancer."

"He is an heir," Victor added. "I do not know why that would matter to Margarethe, but it matters to many others."

Finn ambled up the stairs and into the house. He used his fist to guide the way.

"I will not help you find Ophélie," Colleen said, half-turned toward him, one protective eye still on Finn. "But I will help you in another way, if you leave here now and never return."

"How else could you help me? There is nothing more I want from you."

"Olivia," Colleen replied. She met his eyes. "I suspect you've developed more than passing feelings for her. Perhaps you even care for her."

Victor looked away.

"I *will* put an end to her dalliance with you, but I can either do so with a full dose of the truth—of who you are and what you wanted with her—or I can find a way to let her down without tarnishing your image in her eyes. You disappear from her life, and she remembers you as someone who helped her through a difficult time. Do you understand?"

He wanted to reach his hands across the flagstones and choke the life from the self-righteous woman. What if he had decided he loved Olivia and wanted more from their so-called "dalliance?" Who did that harm? Who was Colleen to make this decision for him? For Olivia?

Yet Victor understood, also, that he could not stop her.

"Why not just tell her everything?" Victor demanded. "That's more your style, Colleen Deschanel, wielder of knowledge."

"I do this and we are even," Colleen said. "There is no unsettled debt between us."

Colleen pivoted and followed Finn into the house without another word, without waiting for Victor's response.

She didn't need his answer. She already knew what Victor would want, and his anger at this wasn't greater than whatever he now felt for Olivia. She won, this time.

But Victor vowed he would one day kill Colleen for this arrogance.

56
NICOLAS

Nicolas had been upgraded to the front seat with Leander having been relegated to sister duty in the other car. Quillan and Stella said next to nothing in the backseat, the young girl curled into Quillan with such vulnerability that Nicolas envied the trust between them.

Who had ever trusted him so much? Ana? Oz? He'd ruined that dynamic with both of them. Oz would never speak to him again—this time, for real. Ana and he were on amenable terms now, but there was an arm's length between them that might never narrow. Now that she was married and a mother, maybe that was for the best.

They swung down through Nevada, into Arizona and New Mexico. Mountains made way for red rocks and volcanic hills. Around Flagstaff, when the night was pitch-black, Nicolas asked if they were calling it for the day. But Lauren was determined to drive straight-through and make it to Colleen by the next afternoon, despite her bloodshot eyes and regular interval yawns.

"Let me drive. You should sleep for a bit," he said.

She glanced at him from her peripheral, taking size of him and his words. Through his errant behavior, he had trained her to question everything he said for the potential of an underlying ulterior motive. He had none this time, but assurances alone would do nothing.

Lauren ended her assessment with a smirk. "Do you even know how to drive? I thought you had valets who took you everywhere."

"I won't deny that," Nicolas replied. "But I actually prefer to drive myself sometimes."

"When you're in the mood to slum it with the plebs?" Lauren goaded.

He shrugged. "You said it."

She was apparently too tired to suppress her sleepy grin. The tightness that had been trapped in his chest since they arrived in Ashland faded to a flutter at the sight of it. Then it was gone.

Lauren glanced in the rearview at Quillan and Stella, both dead to the world. "If I let you drive, you won't send us careening off a cliff?"

"I can't promise that. What if the cliff has a sweet jump calling my name?"

"You're not inspiring confidence."

"Sleep, Lauren." Nicolas pointed to the exit sign as her headlights washed over the words. "I can manage to keep us alive at least for a few hours."

LAUREN WAS ASLEEP BEFORE HE HAD EVEN NAVIGATED BACK ON THE highway. Her breath fogged the window as her light snores became the ambient background noise of his driving.

Nicolas had embellished his driving skills a bit. He did like to drive, but often his need for a driver came in tandem with his need to drink, and no matter how faded he was, he refused to get behind the wheel drunk. Deep down, he had always believed the accident that took his parents and sisters involved alcohol, but even if he was wrong, it was proof a split second could change everything, forever.

His life had been a series of moments like this. A single decision splitting his life in two, forcing him to choose which side of the fork in the path to take, often without understanding what would happen when he did. Forgive Ana, or push her away. Follow Mercy, or follow his gut. Hurt Oz to wake him up to his complacency, or allow him to get there on his own and preserve a lifelong friendship. He had chosen so horribly wrong on each count, ticking off his list of sins in a trail of failed relationships.

No wonder someone as cool and polished as Lauren would see him as a spoiled child. "Prince Nicolas" she called him, without the least bit of playfulness. She wasn't wrong. He had cultivated this image for himself, through his desires, his behaviors... his choices. As she had said, he didn't exactly inspire confidence.

Nicolas still couldn't pinpoint why he'd come on this trip, other than a spontaneous whim following Aunt Colleen's harsh advice. But he'd done nothing to help and everything to make things harder than they needed to be. Hopping on a plane home would have been the most useful decision he could have made, but he'd stuck it out, stubborn and determined, and with a glance at the tow-headed blonde curled up in the passenger seat, his subconscious reasons were beginning to reveal themselves.

He might never know why, but it was important to him that Lauren Weatherly see him for the man he could be, rather than the man he was.

Nicolas had been his own worst enemy throughout,

staying as drunk as possible. As difficult as possible. Only when the bottle had no longer been an option had the hazy glasses slipped away, and the vision of his past, present, and future lay before him, did the full weight of his remorse set in.

Who was she to him? A lawyer from a good family, pretty by most standards, though not necessarily a match for his exotic desires. *By all accounts a catch, but utterly unremarkable,* was how he might have described her to Oz, but then he would have flinched as the last word left his lips. For Lauren might not have excellent breasts, or an ass he wanted to bury his face in, but her composure and quickness to call him on his bullshit was so unreservedly refreshing that he began to crave it the same way he salivated over the last few drips in his empty bottle of cognac.

The night before, he had a dream about Lauren. He had held out his hand to her. It hovered in the air, in the space between them, as they regarded one another with the same tension that had marked their short relationship. And then, in the ultimate show of vulnerable trust, Lauren had dropped her face into his outstretched hand. Her soft face cheeks were a hot rush of reality against his palm. Even in his dream, he understood there could be no greater intimacy than this. Nothing sexual could come close.

There they remained for time inestimable, until he awoke, trembling.

Nicolas found himself praying for more leads to follow, only to later question why on earth he would want to be on the road longer than they needed to. Then, as Lauren eased the car from the lot in Rockaway Beach and aimed it toward home, he saw clearly the end of whatever he was feeling.

Lauren's world and his would not cross back home. Only through this rescue mission had they found common ground, and he knew she couldn't wait to be home and rid of him. In her shoes, he would feel no differently.

But Nicolas had only ever walked in his own shoes. Only he could make sense of his twisted, conflicting thoughts. How he was indifferent toward her, yet craved more interactions with her. How he could want all this, and yet his desire for her was not acutely sexual, as it had been with Mercy and nearly every single one of his past conquests. Instead, it was a need to stay up late into the night and spar with her. Him, playing the perfect asshole. Her, the perfect foil.

Dawn broke as he crossed into Texas. Lauren yawned against the window and broke into a haphazard stretch.

He wanted to tell her to go back to sleep, but he didn't. He wanted to talk to her more.

Dried spit curled at the corner of her mouth. Her hair, pressed against the glass all night, stood up so high she looked like the girls in the eighties hair band videos.

"Well, aren't you the image of radiant beauty," Nicolas joked as she squinted into the visor mirror.

"I know it's tough, but please try to keep your hands to yourself," she said drily, with a side-grin.

"Lucky for you our lives are at stake or you'd be in some trouble."

Lauren laughed. Nicolas counted that as the fifth one since Rockaway Beach, paired with ten smiles. He didn't flatter himself as having anything to do with either. Her mood gradually improved the closer they got to home... and away from spending her time with him.

In the back, Quillan and Stella still slept. They'd been conscious only sporadically on the trip home, and never for long. Nicolas wondered what the hell had happened back in Rockaway Beach. Maybe he didn't want to know.

"Ready for me to take over?" Lauren asked. She'd pulled her

short bob into a tiny ponytail, having given up on controlling it in any other way.

Nicolas maneuvered the car off the highway and into the parking lot of a roadside diner. Leander and Estella pulled in beside them like clockwork.

Lauren suggested they grab a quick bite before beginning the homestretch. She had a glow in her cheeks as she talked about home.

What if I could put a glow like that in her cheeks?

The question stayed on Nicolas' mind the entire rest of the journey back to New Orleans.

57
COLLEEN

Colleen ignored the black stars dancing before her eyes. She swallowed down the emptiness that had come to consume her fears and make them darker, more hollow, less accessible. Some would have called this strength, but she knew the cost at which her strength had always come with.

Blanche's ominous words had, at last, become clear, and the revelation, too late. Sebastian had always been Blanche's backup plan, as she must have seen a weakness in Estella even as a girl. Because they'd been unable to solve this, Sebastian had fulfilled Margarethe's expectations. But it was not Stella he had come after.

How Victor had known this before anyone else was a blow Colleen would always take as a personal failure. Especially knowing that her distracted delay in handling his dalliance with Olivia was what had allowed him to learn this valuable information. There were few people she would rather be indebted to less than Victor de Blanchefort.

Olivia sat across from her in an emerald grandfather chair.

Her hands gripped the arms. Somewhere, Rory played with Aria. His giggles reverberated in the distance, bouncing across the marble.

Katja had parked her wheelchair on the other side of the room, observing them both with hawkish eyes.

Colleen didn't relish being the bearer of this news. Should she start with the good? End with it? The gain of one child would not blunt the loss of another. A happy ending seemed worlds away.

"I have news to share with you both. Initially, it was only one thing, but now it is two, and we have very little time," Colleen began.

"If it's what I think it is, just blurt it out," Olivia said. She shook one of her hands, which had gone white from her iron grip on the chair. "Katja and I have waited this long."

"Skip the foreplay, is what she's saying," Katja gruffed.

Colleen watched them both. The eager anticipation in their eyes, embedded in fearful skepticism. She would give them the good news first. For the bad news was so terrible, they would need some of their hope to digest it.

"Stella is coming," Colleen said. Her smile was genuine. Whatever other horrors lay ahead, one of their own had been found, and she was coming home. An ending to a story that could have gone in another direction entirely. "She will be here tonight."

Olivia's gasp rocked her body forward in a heaving sob. She doubled over in the chair, murmuring exclamations of happiness, her words unintelligible.

Katja grinned into her palms. A single tear slid down her cheek. "And she's okay?"

"She's perfectly fine, according to Lauren, though I will, of course, perform a thorough examination of my own when she returns," Colleen said. "She's grown into her adult form, like S

—" She didn't stop herself so much as the word caught in her throat, like a curse. "Sebastian."

"Where on earth was she?" Olivia cried, as she pulled herself back against the chair in an effort to regain her composure.

"As we suspected, Estella sought out Quillan. She found him in a small coastal town in Oregon. There's much yet we don't know, such as why Quillan went to Oregon, how Estella found him when we could not, and what happened during their tenure at the motel they called home. I would advise you both not to overwhelm Stella with these questions, as we have no idea what she has been through. And I would also ask that you consider your words to Estella. As misguided though she was, she was trying to protect Stella.

"But these things are not as important as having her home, and I am very happy to say they've already crossed the Louisiana border from Texas and will be here before we know it."

"Heavens to Betsy, I can hardly believe it," Olivia said. She pressed her hand to her mouth to suppress another sob. "Praise God!"

"That's so soon," Katja mused with a growing smile. "Do you think Sebastian will be back from his camping trip by then, Liv? It would be awesome if he could be here when she arrives."

Colleen folded her hands, drawing in as much breath as she could without putting too much attention on the gesture. "That's what I wanted to talk to you about."

Footfalls sounded in the corridor. They all looked back to see Ashley standing in the doorway.

"Yes, dear?" she called over.

"What time did you want the Council meeting set for? You said you'd get back when you had a time, but it's already dinner. I could set it for the Witching Hour, like the last few?"

"Meeting?" Olivia asked. "What for?"

"Later, darling," Colleen said, avoiding Olivia's eyes. "After Stella arrives would be best. Call Lauren and she can give you an estimate."

"All the Collective, or Council only?"

Colleen nodded. The women in the room burned holes in the back of her. "Council only."

"Aunt Colleen, what the hell is going on?" Olivia's eyes narrowed.

"I know of no other way to say this, so I will tell you what I know, which is less than I'd like," Colleen started. She set her spine straight, kept her head raised. They had followed her, all of them, all these years, and so much of that came down to posture. "Sebastian's communications with Margarethe did not come to an end, as we once believed."

"What? No," Katja said. She wheeled closer. "That's not possible. I would know. Liv would know. There are *four* of us in that house." She wrinkled her nose. "Five with Liv's new boyfriend."

"Sebastian keeps to himself so much, but..." Olivia either didn't know, or didn't want to finish.

"I regret to tell you this part of my news is not up for debate, ladies. And he is not only in contact with her, he is also doing her bidding. Information I would not have known if your lover, Olivia, had not come forward to share it."

Olivia's eyes flew wide. "How do you know about that?"

"Are you really so surprised when you did so little to keep it a secret? Your indiscretions were not hard to uncover when they were already half un-raveled." Colleen shot her a knowing glance. "Your relationship with Victor de Blanchefort is over, by the way. He has left New Orleans to return to his own family. Nothing more will come of this affair."

Olivia collapsed back in her chair, bewildered but chastened.

"Are you sure, Aunt C? Really, truly sure?" Katja pressed.

Colleen nodded. "I wish that I were not, Kat, but I won't lie to you. There's more."

"He's done something terrible, hasn't he?" Katja sounded like a little girl.

"He's taken Ana's son. Aleksandr. This kidnapping was apparently done at the request of Margarethe, whose motivations are unclear, but they are undoubtedly not for his good." Colleen drew a sip from her tea for a quick reset of her senses. "We know they went first to Baton Rouge, but we have no indicator at all of where they went next except for the vague notion of 'overseas.' Their supposed rendezvous in Baton Rouge was set for days ago. They could truly be anywhere."

"No," Olivia whispered. "How could he? How could *we?*"

"His behavior is not your fault—" Colleen attempted.

"How could we not *know*?" Olivia shrieked in response. "Two of us. He had two women mothering him and it took a man sharing my bed to figure this out?"

Katja stared dazedly into the wall.

"Often we miss what is right in front of us," Colleen soothed. She reached for her niece, but Olivia withdrew, rolling from her chair to a standing position.

"No, I missed it because I was falling in love with a man I knew nothing about! I need to go to Ana. I need to offer my help. Her son is in danger, and it's *my* fault..."

"We can evaluate our individual culpability later, Olivia," Colleen said. "I could blame myself for not paying enough attention to Sebastian's behavior, knowing his history of seeking to please Margarethe. But this is not the time. What *it is* time for, is to prepare for the return of our Stella, and to ensure her safety by all means necessary. I want to propose she stays here."

"Why the hell would she stay here? She's my daughter!" Katja strained in her chair. Colleen wondered once again when her niece would acknowledge she no longer needed it.

"At the risk of being insensitive, I would remind you that your son proved not to be safe under your roof," Colleen said as calmly as she could. "That is not a failing of you. You were simply not prepared. But I am. The Gardens is a veritable fortress. I have guards all hours of the day, and the mansion itself is built to withstand an act of war. It is soundproof, and the windows are not glass. Stella is safe here. Safe not only from others, but from herself, and from the prying words of Margarethe, should she discover she's here and attempt to make contact."

"What do we do then? Go home and pray Sebastian comes home, while we twiddle our thumbs?" Olivia demanded.

"You are welcome to stay here. All three of you. I have room and then some, and my home is yours." Colleen rose. "And no, you don't twiddle your thumbs. You spend time in self-reflection. You get involved with the Collective. You open your eyes to the world around you. Any one of those things would be better than nothing. Because we must prepare ourselves for the possibility Sebastian has done something irreversible. Aleksandr is an heir to a prophecy that is important to many across this world, and there are those who pray for its failure as much as its fulfillment. If Margarethe has found herself in bed with one of those in the failure camp, and Sebastian has been party to delivering one of our own into enemy hands, there is little I can or will do to protect him."

Olivia's mouth quivered as she searched for words. Katja hung her head low.

"The Council meeting is tonight. We will commission resources toward Aleksandr's safe rescue." She again folded her hands over her torso. She must look them both in the eyes for this part. She owed them that. "Our hope is to also bring Sebastian home safe. But should we be in a position to choose between the two, I need you both to know that our choice will be Aleksei."

58
ANASOFIYA

Ana had never experienced such a vast sense of helplessness. She'd taken Finn to Amelia's home for a reprieve, to clear their thoughts, formulate a plan, neither of which had happened to any useful degree.

Her husband, the man she had pledged her life to and never looked back, not once, sat at the other end of the oak dining table, face buried in the palms of his calloused hands.

He could be anywhere, Ana. Anywhere in this world. Absolutely anywhere.

Finn's words burned a hole in her chest, where the answer should be, but wasn't. Finn was right. Aleksandr could be anywhere at all.

Anasofiya, it is time.

She flinched at Aidrik's voice. At her request, both Wraith and Aidrik had remained patiently silent over the past weeks, to the extent she had nearly forgotten they existed. So much had happened to take her away from the woman who first discovered these beings lived within her.

Aidrik, I'm at a loss. We know nothing at all. Nothing! How are we supposed to work with that?

You know in your heart where our son was taken. Your acceptance of this will lead to a stronger plan.

Aunt Colleen has the meeting later, but I saw the look in her eye when she left for The Gardens. She can't save us this time.

Did you hear my words, Kjære?

Maybe. I don't know. I don't know anything at all right now.

Anasofiya, your skill at remaining collected in trying times has always been your greatest strength. Do not forsake it now in your greatest hour of need. You must listen now to your instincts. You know where Aleksandr is. There is only one place he could be. One person who would want him this much.

Tell me, then, instead of speaking in riddles! You know I hate it!

But she knew. Before the letters fell together to form the name, Anasofiya knew exactly who had wanted her son. And now she had him.

I can help. Bring me forth, Anasofiya, and let me help you save our son.

"Oriana," she whispered as Aidrik sounded the same name within her.

Finn looked up. "What?"

"I know where Aleksei is," Ana said. She tugged at her braid, one of her many nervous habits since childhood. She had good reason to be nervous now, but those same nerves would get her through the next few minutes. "What did the Quinlans tell us before we left? Do you remember? They said all those opposing the Brotherhood would do anything to get their hands on him, because without him, their hope of a better future is lost."

Finn's mouth parted in a daze. His eyes stayed on the table, his fingers wrapped around a candelabra.

"Finn, there's something else I need to tell you."

He swayed in his grief, gripping tighter.

"Finnegan. Look at me."

Her husband looked up. His bloodshot eyes bored directly into hers, and she had never wanted to erase a look or an emotion more.

"I have a secret," Ana went on. Within her Aidrik held tight to her heart in silence, for strength. Wraith stirred and whispered encouragement. "I know we promised no secrets, but I kept this one from you for good reason. Because I didn't understand it, and I couldn't tell you until I was sure."

Finn's response was raspy. "Sure?"

"I told you about my Wraith," she went on, ignoring her fears. She had to get this out before the meeting. "But it turns out I can construct more than just a manifestation of my darkness."

"Ana... I don't have a clue what you're talking about, or why it matters right now."

"It hasn't ever mattered more than it does right now." Ana pushed her chair back from the table and stood. "What I'm about to show you is real. As real as you or me. I know your rational mind will look for ways to discredit it, as mine did, but I know now that, impossible as it might be, this *is* real."

Finn gave her an exhausted look but didn't break his eyes away as she whispered from within and conjured Aidrik forth from deep within her.

One moment there was two, and then there was three.

Finn choked out a startled sound. His chair skipped back across the cypress flooring, then toppled altogether as he stumbled to his feet, tripping over himself. He fell back into the china hutch.

"Hello, Brother." Aidrik's voice rang crystal clear.

"Jesus Christ," Finn whispered. "Jesus Tap-dancing Christ."

"Not Jesus," Aidrik answered amenably.

"You died. Ana saw you die. Everyone in Farjhem saw you die."

"Die I did," Aidrik replied. "If my evigbond was any other than an etheric summoner, I would have remained so."

"This doesn't make any sense!" He whipped his head toward his wife. "Ana, what the *fuck*?"

Aidrik took another step. "It does if you open your mind. Our bond fused me to Anasofiya in a way that took hold and grew new life. For months, I stayed within her, growing stronger, for her. For you, Finnegan. For Aleksandr."

"No." Finn's head flung back and forth. He backed away, crashing into another table. "This isn't possible. This isn't real."

"Finn, please trust me." Ana held her hand out to Aidrik, who took it. "He's real. He started as a voice and grew into someone who can live and breathe on his own, like any of us. He's returned to who he was."

"How long have you kept this from me?" Finn demanded. "All those talks, late into the night... our confessions... and you said *nothing*?"

"She said nothing for fear of her own erroneous interpretation of facts," Aidrik said. "I came to her first in Finland and helped her find her strength to defeat Agripin. Even then, she struggled to believe in me. When you returned to New Orleans, she stuffed me far away. She pretended my existence had been a figment of her imagination, and meanwhile, I grew even stronger."

"So, what, we're supposed to just accept at face value that someone we all knew to be dead... someone I *felt* die, deep within me... is back?" Finn eyed them both with dark suspicion. "Ana, why?"

Ana took one step forward, and then another. She held her

hand linked with Aidrik ahead of her. Finn recoiled, but his back was flat against the wall. His face whipped to the side, as if he could shrink into the wallpaper with enough will.

Aidrik's hand left Ana's. He stretched it out toward Finn and let it hover in the air. Finn regarded it with abject horror, but as it drew closer, inches from his face, Finn's eyes squeezed closed. Aidrik's hand pressed into the softness of Finn's cheeks. His knees buckled at the moment of connection. Aidrik rushed forth and wrapped him in his arms, as they rose together.

Finn sobbed into his brother's chest. He ran his hands over Aidrik's face, tugging at his hair, ripping at his shirt. Aidrik took Finn's face in both hands and pressed his lips tight to Finn's.

Ana watched in wonder as Aidrik slipped his tongue into Finn's mouth and kissed him with a passion born of fear and love, of hope and promise. Finn returned the kiss with unexpected fervor. He ran his hands under Aidrik's shirt, over his smooth flesh.

With a force that made Aidrik cry out, Finn flipped him and pressed him against the china hutch, one hand pinned to the back of his neck. "Fuck you," he whispered, spittle flying from his mouth. "Fuck you, fuck you, fuck you."

Finn's free hand fumbled with the buckle on his trousers. Aidrik remained in place, despite that his physical strength was greater than Finn's. Finn struggled through his tears to pull his zipper down as Ana watched, wordless. Aidrik's hand reached behind him; his fingers wrapped around Finn's hardness and then released again. A permission Finn didn't need.

Finn thrust into Aidrik from behind, hand still braced against his neck. Tears streamed down his cheeks as he cried out with each violent drive, a sound that traveled from deep within him, somewhere animal, visceral. Somewhere depraved. A place where he could never be satisfied and never abandoned. Aidrik closed his eyes and braced himself against the oak at the loving assault.

Finn's grunts came to an abrupt end as he stumbled away, breathless, pants pooled at his ankles. He looked at Aidrik. At Ana. Back. Forth.

Without a word of acknowledgement of what had transpired, Finn quietly pulled his trousers back up and buckled them. He ran his hands over his face, and when he looked at them again, he was visibly composed, a different man entirely from the one who had taken Aidrik against the hutch moments before.

"Is this..." Finn choked up. "Lasting? Will you always be here?"

"As long as Anasofiya draws breath, as will I. I am an extension of her, though I am now strong enough for singular existence. But if she dies, my tether to this earth dies with her."

Finn looked at Ana, but she gave him a light shrug. "He knows more about it than I do. If he says he's here to stay, we have to believe it. I want to believe it, so badly."

"Me too." Finn wiped the last of his tears away and shook off his grief. His shoulders squared. "I have your sword, Brother."

"Your sword," Aidrik corrected. "My gifting of Ulfberht was not conditional with my death."

"It's in the closet. I haven't felt right wearing it."

"Retrieve it now," Aidrik said. "For you will need it when we march on Farjhem."

THEY WERE DUE AT COLLEEN'S COUNCIL MEETING, INVITED AS SPECIAL guests. But they did not intend to go and receive direction. They would go and give it.

Aidrik and Finn declared they would go to Farjhem. Jacob

arrived and vowed to go with them, on the condition Ana stay with Amelia and see her through the birth of their daughter.

Ana once told Aidrik she wasn't raised to stay behind while the men handled business. Yet now, with all at stake, she understood it was not one but both children who needed saving. Ana was the only one with the knowledge of what Amelia could expect when her time came. She could better serve everyone by staying, and she trusted Aidrik to look after both husbands and see to their safety... but most importantly, the safe extraction of their son.

"Don't be afraid," Jacob said, hanging behind with Ana when the others went to the car so they could make their way to the meeting.

"Why?"

Jacob kissed her cheek. "Because I'm not. Amelia couldn't be in better hands. And from everything you both have told me about Aidrik, the Galactic Empire could show up in all their glory and we would still blow up that Death Star."

"Finn loves *Star Wars*," Ana said. She blinked away her tears. "Tell him that joke when he's missing home."

"I'll tell it so damn much he'll start missing home for other reasons."

59
LUCIA

Lucia hesitated before knocking. His car was out front, but that didn't mean he was home. He once told her he enjoyed the streetcar more than driving. But it was late, and he would have no reason to be on the streetcar in the evening, so that rationalization seemed less and less possible the more she stood outside in the cold considering it.

The door swung open. Oz stood before her in his pajamas, an indecipherable look plastered across his face.

"Why are you here?" he asked.

"I left the plantation. Nicolas is home, and I decided I didn't want to be there when he returned."

Oz rolled his eyes. "Your actions would indicate otherwise."

"Something I regret," Lucia insisted. "I would take it back if I could."

"What does that have to do with me?"

"Can I come in?"

Oz looked around. "How did you get here?"

"I walked."

He gaped at her. "You walked? From Vacherie? That's an hour by *car*!"

"So, can I come in?"

Oz stepped back from the door. "I'm guessing you won't leave until I say yes."

For as well as Lucia felt she knew Oz Sullivan, she had never before stepped foot in his house. The cottage was lovely and cozy simultaneously, with both modern accoutrements and antiques mixed together in seamless synergy. Not a speck of visible dust to be seen, and when she stepped inside, he gave her feet a pointed glance until she slipped off her boots.

"Where are Na and Chris?"

"Still with my mother until tomorrow morning."

"Why were they with your mother?"

"Because I was gone for a while."

"Gone. Where?"

"Away."

Lucia crossed her arms. "Is this how it's going to be?"

"You're the one who came to my house, uninvited."

"You're acting like Naomi when Christian takes her favorite toy," Lucia accused. She snaked out her arm and took Oz's chin in her hand, turning his head back and forth. "Dirt in your pores." She lifted one of his hands. "And under your nails. Were you on an archaeological dig?"

"Yes, because that's the most rational conclusion to come to when you see dirt on a city boy." Oz shook his head but smiled to the side.

Lucia grinned. "In the absence of a true story, I'll always make one up that's far more interesting. You should know that by now."

"You do have a flair for the drama," he said drily.

Lucia flopped down in an armchair across from a row of

bookshelves. With a sigh, Oz took a seat on the couch. "Where were you really?"

"What does it matter?"

"We could sit here in painful silence as an alternative."

"I mean, why do you care? Why are you even here?"

The pain in his eyes was her fault. She didn't fully understand it, but she knew this, nonetheless, as she knew he would rather be alone than admit he didn't want to be.

"I just do. Okay?" Lucia folded one leg over the other, the top one bouncing with her nerves. "Can't that be enough?"

Oz didn't answer. He only stared.

She turned her gaze to the books, reading the spines, searching for a way to break the awkwardness, when his voice cut through the silence. "I went to Abbeville."

"Abbeville?" She turned back to him. "Isn't that where Adrienne went when she was missing?"

Oz pushed himself off the couch and shuffled into the kitchen. "It is."

"What were you hoping to find?"

Oz returned with two beers. She took hers, even though she hated beer. She took a long sip, watching him over the top of the bottle.

"I found him. Jesse."

"Wasn't he...."

"Yes," Oz said. "He was. He loved her when I couldn't. I needed to talk to him. To hear how he spoke of her and saw her, and what their life was like." He tilted the neck of the bottle between his index and middle finger and sipped. "I know what you're thinking."

"What am I thinking?" Lucia herself didn't know the answer. Her mind was open.

"*He* invited *me*," Oz replied. "He sent a card when Adrienne passed. Inside was a letter, and he said if I was ever in a mind to talk about things, his door was open."

"That can't have been easy for you," Lucia said. His free hand tapped his knee with an increasing rhythm, and she had the impulse to reach out and lay her hand over it. "Did it help?"

"You mean did it make me forget her?"

"Emyr, no, Oz! I would never sug—"

"It didn't help me get over her any more than you fucking my best friend did," Oz spat. He finished his beer and slammed it on the end table. "Not that you cared enough to have any motivation for it other than fulfilling your own needs."

"If you want the truth, I didn't think of you at all when it happened." She wouldn't lie to him, but speaking the facts set a heavy stillness in the room that was louder than her pounding pulse.

"You're right, that's *so* much better."

Lucia shot to her feet. "Because we're friends, Oz! You made it clear from the very beginning that you and I weren't happening, and once that was established, I took you at your word. You're important to me, but I know what our boundaries are. Or I thought I did."

Oz watched her hulking before him, cheeks aflame, breaths heaving her frame forward. He pressed his lips together and gestured toward her chair. "Doesn't matter. Maybe it's your fault, maybe it's mine. I can't hold you to one standard out loud, and another in my heart."

Your heart? "What are you saying?"

"I'm saying I'm tired. Exhausted. Head to toe, body and soul. And quibbling over who shot first isn't worth the energy anymore."

"I miss you," Lucia blurted. She pulled her knees to her chest and hugged them. "You asked why I came? That's why. I missed you, and Naomi, and Christian, and... us. I missed what we all were together."

This pulled a smile from Oz. "Dysfunctional?"

"I was going to say a family."

Oz tensed, but seemed to fight against whatever his instincts pressed him to say. "Where will you go?"

"Thorvald wants me. Something big is happening."

He nodded. "That's what you always wanted. To go back to him."

"It's what I thought I wanted."

"You mean you don't?"

Lucia laughed. "I might be as confused as you are right now, Oz. I thought I knew a lot of things, but everything I believed in has been thrown into question. I don't know if I'll answer his summons, or ignore it. Maybe I'll go work in a coffee shop in Bywater."

"I'd like to see that!"

Lucia twisted her lips. "As if I would ever settle into a life of an average Child of Man."

"The blasphemy of such an idea." He pointed to her barely touched beer. "Sorry, I forgot."

"I'll finish it. I'm a finisher."

Oz raised a brow.

"I have no idea what I meant by that. None at all."

"Where's Livia, then?" Oz asked.

"I sent her back to Thorvald, where she belongs. She was his charge."

He nodded. "Where are you headed? Not long-term, but tonight?"

"Hotel, I guess. Any recommendations?"

Oz thumbed toward the stairs. "Take Naomi's room. She's not using it."

Lucia cocked her head to the side. "Are you sure?"

"I said Naomi's bed, Luc, not mine."

"I know, but..."

Oz stood and stretched. "I'm exhausted. The room is just up the stairs. You can't miss all the unicorns."

"I like unicorns," she offered feebly, looking for a better response but coming up empty.

"You're a lot like peeling back an onion," he said and shook his head. "Good night, Lucia."

Lucia watched him disappear into the back of the house. "Good night, Oz," she whispered, unsure of whether his offer to stay was an extension of their old friendship or an invitation to a new one altogether.

Whatever he was offering, she would never again take it for granted.

60
SEBASTIAN

Sebastian lay upon the pile of furs with an eye on his new mistress. The empress moved with the fluid grace of an exotic feline, which felt perfectly in place with everything he had seen so far in The Menagerie.

He was their darling. Oriana's. Margarethe's. His final test had arrived, and he had passed with flying colors. He, the boy who hated school! Some credit should be given to Aleksandr, though, because he made it so easy. Almost too easy.

Margarethe's form came to life in this land of magic. It wavered like a failing projection, pieces of her fading in and out, but Sebastian could watch her flickering body all day. He was finally beholding his true mother. This, and this alone, would have been enough payment for his loyalty.

Oriana drank a blood-red substance from a crystal goblet. Some ran down her chin, and a spot landed on her lily white dress. Margarethe cackled.

"How does it feel to be so close to everything you've ever wanted?" Oriana asked, paying no mind to the bloodstain taking over her dress.

"Glorious. Redeeming," Margarethe answered. Her unruly red hair flowed around her like a crude halo. "And you will help me retrieve Stella? As promised?"

"I will send whatever assistance you need to see it done. But I believe the destruction of the foul prophecy will turn all of our lucks, witch. Long has it allowed rebellions to rise and hope to thrive. But no more! Without an heir, there is no hope."

"You mean Aleksei?" Sebastian asked.

Oriana's laugh sounded more like the trill of a macaw. "You really have kept your acolyte in the dark, haven't you, witch?"

Margarethe stiffened. Her form flashed perfectly clear. "I've shared what he needs to know. His focus on the friendship with your hostage was more than enough."

"Are you going to tell me now? I've done what you asked," Sebastian replied, on the verge of a pout.

"Allow me," Oriana purred, ignoring Margarethe's indignant look. "Your 'friend,' if one can call someone a friend once they have betrayed them, is one half of an ancient prophecy that predicts the cessation of war and advent of peace between both Empyreans and Quinlans. Entire rebellions have risen on the hope of this prophecy, and they have continued on, spurred by this deep belief." Her dress swished across the marble as she moved. "How do we annihilate a belief?"

Sebastian stared in reverent silence.

"You cut off the source," Oriana said. "The other heir is destined to be born. And now, she is destined to fade into obscurity. A promise of what might have been."

"Aleksei is important?" Sebastian said.

Margarethe shook her head. His stomach dropped at what he perceived was her disappointment.

"Alive, he is everything. Dead, he will be nothing," Oriana answered. "And I have you to thank, darling Sebastian." She ran her jeweled fingers over his chin, then knelt low. "I will reward you in my own way later. Yet perhaps there is another way to thank you for this priceless gift."

Sebastian's body was a river of chills as this exquisite creature ran her hands over his face.

"Would you like to do the honors when the time comes?"

He swallowed back his horror at again not understanding. He didn't care as much what this creature thought of him, but Margarethe's disapproval was a shot to the heart. To his great relief, Oriana didn't wait for his response before continuing.

"When I give the order for execution, it should be you, Sebastian. You've earned the right to wield the sword that takes his head." She turned to Margarethe. "That does seem fair, does it not?"

Margarethe shrugged.

"It's no matter to me. I have headsmen and magic fiends alike who are up to the task. But why reward them when they were not the ones doing the hard work when it counted?" She pressed her lips to Sebastian's nose, then shocked him when she bit down. He jumped back, inciting a giggle from her. "This is my gift to you, should you choose to accept."

They were going to kill Aleksandr? Sebastian smiled to stall for time, to understand the situation he'd brought them both into. Margarethe had said *nothing* about hurting him, only that someone important desired him. But that was a foolish excuse, because did he really believe they wanted him for cake and ice cream? Hadn't he, deep down, known all along this would be the end of the road for his friend?

Friend. From the beginning, his relationship with Aleksandr had been a contrivance from Margarethe's mouth to his ears. Every conversation, every laugh, every bit of playfulness. At some point, playing the role had become easier and easier for Sebastian, who had never had anyone else he felt this level of comfort with outside of Margarethe. But his relationship with her was cold and formal, beneath it the promise of something greater and more powerful if he could hold on to his patience.

With Aleksandr, he had someone who could enjoy with him both the mundane and the exciting. Aleksandr laughed at his jokes but also called him on his behavior when he was out of line. He was there within minutes of a phone call and taught him to do some of the things he might have learned himself had his father not died: fishing, hunting, skipping rocks. He'd pretended to be bored by all of these things, but he had absorbed it with a keen ache for what might have been, had his life not been destined for more.

"Of course I want to do it," he said, because they were both staring at him in anticipation and he needed them to look somewhere else, even for a moment. Not at him, anyway, not where his heart, which had always been a peculiar organ, was beating on his sleeve, its contents bared.

"Brilliant," Oriana declared. Gold clattered as she slapped her hands together. "Now, it's time to make plans. I believe we should do it soon, and public. There must be no question that he is gone, so a private execution is out." She recited through her stream of thoughts, running down her options. Margarethe nodded but bore the look of someone who had made a pact with the devil.

Sebastian thought of his birth mother, Katja. He was cruel to her, for reasons he understood and reasons that might never be totally clear to him. She had brought him into this world, but he had never felt a part of it. Never needed to, once Margarethe appeared and showed him what his life *would* be. But every night, she popped her head into his door once she thought he was asleep, and whispered, *Good night, sweet prince.* And even though she couldn't cook, breakfast awaited him each morning, no matter what time he woke, long after Olivia had gone on to work at her flower shop.

Sebastian's chest hurt. Was he missing her? Her youth and brokenness? Her crude anger at the world and how her decisions had turned on her, but more, her moments of softness when she smiled at the simple things that made the day? She reminded him, constantly, that she was his mother, and he replied, in equal constancy, that he had no mother. He couldn't tell her about Margarethe, not after Stella slipping off into the night. She and Olivia would never let their eyes off him.

As he looked around at the purple and gold tigers, the flora of magenta and turquoise, the explosion of everything that could never be the way it was without outside interference, Sebastian realized why he had not relaxed even a moment in this strange world.

Normalcy is overrated, he had told Aleksandr, all the while failing to realize how much he himself had adapted to it and needed it.

As Oriana rattled on, Margarethe's intense gaze fell on Sebastian. She seemed to be searching within him for an explanation of what he wore on his face.

Hold not to what feels good, my child. Her voice appeared in his head, for the two of them only. *As Christ's followers are tempted by sin, you are tempted by goodness. By the trappings of a comfortable life. But you must rise above these trite desires and look at a future that is more glorious than what you could ever see before you. More glorious, even, than what your mortal mind can conceive.*

Yes, Mother.

We have aligned ourselves with the right supporter this time, Sebastian. Oriana has the means to see this done for us. With Stella back, you can take her life and her power within you, and you will grow strong! So strong! Strong enough to hold my soul and yours for eternity, where we will rule with a power unlike anything the world has seen!

Sebastian nodded. He looked away. For the first time in his life, he closed his mind to the only woman he had ever called mother, wondering where his real mother was, and whether she missed him.

61
VICTOR

In Victor's many, many wandering years, he had formed very few attachments. This might seem strange to anyone who knew his family had taken the immortal blood, for how could there be any greater attachment than one which surpassed a lifetime? But while Victor would have given his life for any one of his family, in many ways they simply existed as furniture to his vagabond life.

His quest for Ophélie had spurred within him a purpose that guided him forward the way nothing else ever had. She was his Dark Tower, a single-minded quest that would bring him... well, what would it bring him? At some point he had lost sight of why he had followed her at all.

As he sat upon the bench at Audubon Park, Victor could not think of a single place to go, nor a place where he belonged.

After he had shared the news about Sebastian, his one and only instinct was to go to Olivia and comfort her. To give his apologies for keeping things from her, and then offer her even more of himself. He didn't know how this neurotic, passionate woman had grabbed tight to his heart, but she had, and he couldn't conceive of his decisions causing the loss of her.

Victor might never know if they had. If Colleen hadn't gotten to Olivia yet, she would in short order. Olivia might be on shaky ground with her aunt, but she would believe her over a man who had shared almost nothing about himself. Immortality had given him the wisdom to know when he was beaten.

He nevertheless found himself outside Olivia's house, talking himself out of digging the hole deeper. He might have, had he not discovered her husband had returned. Was this, too, Colleen's doing?

Victor's first, acute instinct was to drain the blood from the cowardly man and deposit him somewhere he'd never be found. His own blood boiled at the thought of Greg Claiborne with his arms around Olivia, after he'd abandoned her to his own weakness.

But Greg was her husband, and Victor... now, he was nothing to her. A means to an end, no longer useful.

So Victor left, because what else could he do? He loved her. In his quest for another love, he had found this one, and the loss hit him harder and deeper than waking up to Ophélie gone. But, like Ophélie, to love Olivia was to respect her wishes. He had no calls from her on his phone—this wretched technology tether he'd bought only to communicate with her—and the absence was all the clarity he needed.

He liked to imagine Ophélie was not so far away after all. That she'd followed him, perching on the edge of buildings like a gargoyle as he moved through his adventures intended to bring him closer to her, never realizing she was there all along. If she was watching now, what would she think? Would she laugh at how his voyage had completed a full circle, finding him back in the dredges of his own self-loathing? Did she instead wear a sympathetic look, praying silently for him to find his way again?

What advice would Ophélie, ever pragmatic, give him now?

Clean up your own messes and be gone.

Even now, a century and a half later, her voice was as clear as the first time he'd heard it.

He could go to Colleen and offer his aid, but she would turn him into the night, if she didn't try to kill him first. Olivia no longer needed him. And Amelia... Amelia...

He had his answer.

He could no more sit at her bedside than he could sit at Colleen's on the Council, but he would watch. Like Ophélie, his imaginary but ever-present gargoyle, lurking in the shadows.

Victor would look after Amelia until her child was born. That she would never know would be the greatest gift he could give her, or himself, in this quest for absolution.

62
NICOLAS

Nicolas hid his shaking hands under the table. The alcohol withdrawals were stronger now than they had been on the road. It would have been so easy to fill his flask before he left *Ophélie*. He would have been entirely better equipped to take in the news as he met with his fellow Collective Council members.

Yet whenever he envisioned the relief from taking a drink, it was Lauren's face that appeared instead.

He wondered where she was now. After delivering Stella and news of their travels to Colleen, the group had dispersed to go their separate ways. Patrick swallowed his son, Quillan, in his big bear arms in the most uncomfortable hug Nicolas had ever seen. Jasper sobbed at the sight of Estella, who remained poised like a rock until her father melted. Then, she, too, let down the façade and allowed her father to take her home. Lauren slipped out in the middle of the teary welcomes, before Nicolas could say goodbye. Or thank her.

Hours later, he and his peers sat in the Council chambers, faced with a new and terrible dilemma. They had invited in

Ana, Finn, and Jacob, as they were the most directly affected and had a right to be a part of the solution. And a fourth, too... Aidrik. *He's supposed to be dead,* thought Nicolas, but was that really the weirdest thing he'd seen or heard lately? The rest of the room gawked at Aidrik's unexpected presence, full of questions, but Ana and the rest never offered any.

"I won't call this meeting to order with the usual formalities," Colleen said. She pressed her hands to the table and rose. The rest of the room rose with her, except Ana and Finn. Finn's arms wrapped around his wife as the two stared stoically into the bookcase ahead. "Time is not on our side. We all know what our challenges are, and they must all be given equal gravity.

"First and foremost, Stella is safe at The Gardens. I've increased the guards and have placed calls to those within our ranks willing to come help. She will remain there until Sebastian and Margarethe have been neutralized."

"Neutralized." Imogen Broussard made a sour face. "Do we mean to hurt this child? Really? One of ours?"

"One of ours?" Ana repeated, peeling herself from Finn's embrace. "At what point do we throw down the loyalty? What will it take? He kidnapped my son and took him to what could be his death. But you're worried about the delinquent demon, Imogen?"

"I only meant... sorry, Ana."

Even a year ago, Nicolas would have been at Ana's side, her most fierce protector. But she had a husband now, and Finn could provide far more than Nicolas ever could, an admission that should have hurt, but only left him numb and helpless.

Colleen gestured for everyone to take a seat. "Our goal is not to harm Sebastian, but Ana is right. Our first priority is Aleksandr, and if Sebastian proves to be the obstacle in doing so, then we find ourselves in a dilemma that I won't long toil over. Sebastian made his choice." She folded her hands and waited with exaggerated patience for Jasper to light the sacred candelabra. Jasper grinned and took his seat. Nicolas wondered how the man ever functioned in the mundane, like paying bills and doing dishes.

"Stella, then, is safe. Aleksandr is not, and we must act with haste. Ana believes he may be in Farjhem, and that Sebastian and Margarethe operated under orders from the acting empress, Oriana. Given Aleksandr's importance to all involved, this seems to me a very likely possibility, and Finn and Jacob have agreed to leave at once."

"Just the two of them?" Luther asked. "Against the strength of all of Farjhem?"

"We're trying to reach one of our Quinlan contacts. They will know how to find the Brotherhood, who will help us," Jacob explained. "And we will keep trying, but if we get to Farjhem without reaching them, then we go in on our own."

"That seems incredibly foolish," Jasper agreed. "We should send others with you."

"If you want," Finn said. He had pressed Ana's face to his shoulder, one hand running the length of her hair. "But we leave tonight. After this meeting. We're not waiting for help."

"Who is 'we'?" Pansy Guidry asked. "Y'all three and that strange warrior fellow in the corner?"

Aidrik nodded.

"Jacob and I, and Aidrik," Finn replied. "Ana is staying with Amelia and the healers."

"Don't let us hold you back," Colleen said. "But Jasper is right. We will send reinforcements behind you. We would never send you into such a volatile situation alone."

"I'll get the burner phones," Imogen said. "So we can coordinate location and send help to the right place."

"I'll go," Nicolas announced, jumping to his feet. Ana gave

him a strange look, as if noticing his presence for the first time in a very long time.

Colleen guided him back into his seat. "You will not. We have enough problems with our heir also in danger. And yes, I know you've named Aleksandr your heir, but his current status is tenuous, and we can't have yours be as well."

Nicolas held his tongue. His argument, *I've changed, I want to help those I love. I want to be useful*—would be ill-timed. This was not the place for revealing his road trip epiphanies.

Besides, he feared they had come too late to matter.

"I'll activate the phone tree as soon as we adjourn," Imogen said.

"Thank you." Colleen nodded. "Lastly, we have Amelia and her unborn daughter to think of. In light of Aleksandr's kidnapping, I've increased security at Magnolia Grace, and if the need arises, we can move her here as well. The healers remain on regular rotation, and Ana will be at her side as chief supporter during the delivery, which I will supervise alongside two other doctors in our family. Anne also has experience as a midwife and has temporarily moved in at the house."

The conversation stretched on another twenty minutes. Plans were made, and concerns raised. Nicolas wanted to be a part of both, but found his voice wasn't his own, and his thoughts were elsewhere.

I shouldn't be here. I should just abdicate for Ashley. I've done nothing to help.

Colleen nodded as others spoke, but her peripheral gaze fell on Nicolas. His face flushed at the way she looked at him, like she was seeing straight through to the center of him. Could she read his thoughts?

"One last thing," Evangeline said from the video conference in the center of the table. "I received final word from the Sullivans on our offer. They're in."

. . .

Nicolas pulled his coat on as the others engaged in small talk in the foyer. Ana and her men had already fled, and only the Council remained. Imogen retired to the office to make her calls, but the others lingered, chatting about the health of their children and the storm on the horizon.

Colleen's hand fell on his shoulder. "You're changed," she said.

He slipped his gloves on. "Or I'm just confused and dying for a drink."

She smiled. "No, nephew. You *are* changed. And I think that change may have a name."

Nicolas looked at her.

"Call her. You can't be of use to us until you have learned to be of use to yourself."

Lauren picked up on the second ring. "I was just getting ready for bed. Everything okay with Stella?"

"It's not Stella..." Nicolas pressed his hand to his mouth. He was afraid of his words. Their potential.

The shuffling on Lauren's end ceased. "Where are you, Nicolas?"

"The Gardens."

"Okay." Lauren sighed. "Okay. I can be there in ten. Can you hold it together that long?"

Nicolas nodded, not realizing she wasn't there to see it.

"Nicolas?"

"Yes. I can."

. . .

Lauren pulled up in eight minutes. She threw the passenger door open, and Nicolas stumbled in.

"Where do you want me to take you? Home?"

He shook his head.

"Somewhere else? Is there anywhere you can go that doesn't have a steady supply of alcohol waiting for you?"

He feared looking at her and seeing only annoyance.

But then he did, and all he witnessed in her eyes was concern.

"What happened in there?"

"It isn't what happened in there," Nicolas said. When had she become the one he could turn to in his greatest need? Had there been a realization for either of them, or was it so organic that the end of their animosity and the start of their friendship blended into an unrecognizable blur?

He handed her an envelope. "I got this today."

Lauren watched him with increasing disquiet before she turned the envelope over and opened it.

"Dearest Nicolas... I was wrong. I cannot fathom what allowed me to let you walk away. Change your mind. Come back to me. You know where I am. Love, Mercy."

Lauren let the letter drop to her lap. "Wow. That's heavy."

"I know."

"What are you going to do?"

"What do you think I should do?"

Lauren blew out a breath. She folded the letter again and slipped it back in the envelope, handing it to Nicolas. "I can't answer that for you. You love her. I know that much from spending way too much time in a personal space with you. But I don't know her, and I don't know your relationship. So I can't know what you're thinking, or feeling."

Nicolas dropped the letter into his inner jacket pocket. "You wanna know what I'm feeling? I'm fucking pissed. I'm so angry I'm past the point of needing a drink, I want all the drinks!" He pivoted in his seat to face her. "How *dare* she? I would have followed her anywhere, and she leaves me for some pipe dream about having a child. She literally left me in the middle of a highland forest, with my heart in my fucking hands."

Lauren offered a tight smile of sympathy. "Maybe you need to tell her this."

Nicolas laughed. "No one tells Mercy anything. She's more stubborn than anyone I've ever known. She wants me back, but look at what she said. She hasn't changed, Lauren, she's hoping I have."

"Well," Lauren said. "Maybe you have."

"If I've changed, it's into a man who knows the difference between when I've done wrong and when someone has wronged me."

"I wish I knew—"

Nicolas cut off her words with a kiss. He gripped her face in his hands and choked back the tears fighting inside, channeling it instead into this moment with the most unusual woman he had ever desired.

Lauren's hands came upon his forearms and she gently pushed him away, extricating herself. "No. I'm not that girl, Nicolas."

"I know you're not. Lauren! That's why I can't stop thinking about you, why I can't stop—"

She pressed her hand to his chest. "You have to stop. It does, okay, it hurts me to see you like this, but all I can offer you is my friendship."

Nicolas leaned his head back into the space between the seat and the window. "I deserve that. You'll only ever see me as the man who drinks to solve his problems."

"I know that's not all you are," Lauren said gently. "But I

deserve someone who looks at me as more than a way out of those problems."

"That's not true. I see you as so much more."

"Do you?" Lauren's smile was sad. She fixed her gaze to the distance. "Well, I don't want to spend my time wondering whether that's true. I'm happy to be your friend, which is more than I thought possible last time we were at The Gardens together. There are a thousand girls who would be more than willing to answer this call. But not me."

Nicolas buried his face in his hands. "I don't want to be who I am anymore."

Lauren squeezed his shoulder. "Then don't. Instead, be who you could be."

He pulled in a deep breath and blew it out. "I think I know where I want to go."

"Yeah? Where?"

"Take me to Magnolia Grace so I can help Amelia."

63
ALEKSANDR

Aleksandr was rolling. Rolling, rolling down a hill of tall emerald grass, amongst a sea of heather and briars. His mora chased after him, calling out her warning about the briars, giggling with him each time he made an oomph as one stuck and flew off him.

His mora caught up and ran alongside him, her hair-like-fire free-flowing in the breeze. Her face was peeled back in radiant joy, and Aleksandr thought he could roll forever if she stayed like this just as long.

In an instant, her happiness faded to horror. She screamed his name, and then sprinted ahead of him, her playfulness now a part of the past.

As he rolled, his eyes came upon the source of her fear: a large boulder. His momentum was too great. He couldn't stop.

And then his mora knelt before the boulder and the last thing he saw before he thudded into her was her loving arms, held open, telling him everything was going to be all right...

Aleksandr awoke in a sweat. His feet had slipped from the blanket and now lay against the cold stone, frozen stiff. He yanked them back into the pile of fur and hay, but it was no use. The shock pulled him all the way back into consciousness.

The creature who killed his father watched him in the dark. That this would be the last and kindest face he saw before the hour of his death left him questioning what terrible things he must have done and not realized.

It was only a matter of time now. There was no scaffold in the center of Farsengel, but Agripin had mused they would want a spectacle such as this, the death of the heir, to be as public as possible. *You cannot kill a dream if hope yet exists.*

Aleksandr had tried to hold tight to his own hope, but there was nothing anymore for it to latch on to. No mora waiting at the end to catch him from certain doom.

"My prediction is today," Agripin called. His hollow voice hidden in darkness had become an unusual comfort to Aleksandr, who had never enjoyed being alone. That it came from the killer of his father stripped that same comfort away, leaving him empty.

"A mercy, if so." Aleksandr's voice cracked. He ran his hands over his unshaven face, hearing Fiona's sweet voice. *I love a little scruff on my man.*

"Have you not found a way to hold them off, then?"

"Should I have been looking?"

"How can you not?"

Aleksandr lifted his eyes to the blackness of the ceiling above. He wondered who occupied the cell there, but he already knew. No one. This prison was for show, not for function. With Maxima gone, they were utterly alone.

"Aleksandr, are you not your mother's son? Your father's son? The blood of Aidrik the Wise?" Agripin sounded offended.

"What are you on about now?"

"All these hours you've lain here in silence, and you *haven't* been spending them looking for a way out?"

Aleksandr's laughter echoed across the stone. "I'm sorry, do *you* know of a way out? I'm not Superman. I can't just activate my eye lasers and burn through those bars. And even if I got out, how would I ever get out of Farjhem alive? Why would you even ask me this?"

"What I know is that the son of Aidrik wouldn't wait obediently for the guards to escort him to the square."

"You don't know a whole lot if you still ended up here."

"Ahh, but I am not here to die. I am here to be neutralized."

"That's better?"

Aleksandr turned over in his makeshift bed, staring out the slats of the prison cell. He craved interaction, but he loathed Agripin, and so he continued to find himself sparring with the creature, and then aching with remorse at his weakness.

When Agripin spoke again, something in his voice had shifted. "Maxima got out. This means others must know you are here."

Aleksandr looked over his shoulder. "So now you're playing my friend?"

"I have no friends," Agripin replied. "Only facts."

"No one is coming to get us. There's a fact for you."

"Halfling, you may be worth more to Oriana dead in the pyre, but you have a thousand soldiers who would die to prevent that. Have you truly never considered your worth?"

His worth was the long and short of the problem. It was all of the problem. If he had been given a normal childhood, a normal life, he would not be locked freezing and lost in a cell in a magical land. He never had a first tooth; they had all come in at once, and it was a full adult set, so he never went through a phase of believing, and then denying, the Tooth Fairy. He went from a crawl to walk in days, from a walk to run in hours. His awkward phase came and went so quickly they never had time to laugh at it. He was a genetic and spiritual anomaly, and the hope of thousands to boot.

Whether he died on the pyre in Farjhem, or miraculously lived on to fulfill his destiny, his life was not his own. It never had been.

"The end is still the future until it is here," Agripin said.

Footsteps sounded in the corridor outside, growing closer. They looked at one another.

"Welcome to the future," Aleksandr said in a near-whisper, pulling his head high, determined to face his fate with the courage of his mother, the tenacity of his father, and the wisdom of Aidrik.

64
TRISTAN

Tristan thought about his time away from home with a degree of irony. He had seen so many amazing, beautiful places. Morocco. Thailand. Spain. He had dreamed his whole life of being able to travel the world, and now he had, but the circumstances had hardly allowed him to enjoy it.

No more had that been true than when he stood outside Farjhem on the eve of the Third Runean War, with a Brotherhood army of five hundred strong, on Norwegian soil, on the precipice of his potential death.

Only the Quinlans and Children of Men shivered in the deep snow. The Empyreans, born of fire, stood tall and erect, some in skin-baring tunics, others in flowing robes. All faced forward, to where Birger, Astrid, and Nerys stood upon a large boulder.

"This is not our first turn at insurrection," Astrid cried. They were so close to Farjhem. If not for the draoi and mystics among them, creating a powerful ward against detection, the soldiers of Oriana would have already descended upon them.

"But it is," she went on, "the one in which we will prevail!"

A cheer roared over the sea of red-haired warriors of Emyr. Harriett smiled at Tristan's side and squeezed his hand.

"You all know the task assigned to you," Birger called. "Whether you are aiding those in the villages to flee to safety, or in the den of evil itself, facing off with Oriana, your role matters! We must protect our heir, no matter the cost. To do so, we must provide enough distraction for Tristan and Tarek to locate him."

Tristan looked at his feet, buried in snow to his shins. What if he failed? Not just died, which he expected to do no matter the outcome, but outright fell down on the job? He'd never had to practice his telepathic skill under any real pressure. Anders' demanding nature didn't count, because there were no real stakes.

"We do this in the name of the Brotherhood. Of our sister, Runa, and all who fell with her!" Birger cried. "Most of all, we do it for Emyr, Our Father, whose vision of our people went so terribly awry when the Senetat rose to power."

Calls of "here here!" and "Our Father!" sounded through the encapsulated silence of the snow. It was so quiet, in fact, Tristan was lulled into a strange sense of peacefulness. It was as if war didn't wait for him, moments away.

"We have but two goals!" Nerys' strong voice now sounded over the gathered warriors. "Safely retrieve our heir and take back our city. We must not lose ourselves in this battle, friends. We must not take life where it is not necessary to do so. All life matters in the eyes of Our Father, and we must act in His name, always."

More nods.

"Yet, we cannot afford to fail. Not this time. Not today," she went on. "So pray for your strength, for your courage, for you will need it. Your power to discern friend from foe. You may only get a single second to make this decision, and pray Emyr steers your aim true."

Birger, Astrid, and Nerys continued to take turns rousing the gathered warriors. Tristan pitched forward when a voice from behind startled him.

Anders stood at his side, cheeks flushed with excitement. "Are you ready for this?"

Tristan looked at Harriett first, who watched him with the patient love she always wore. He slowly returned his focus to his mentor. "What if I fail?"

"You can't."

"Oh, I can, trust me, we both know—"

Both hands clapped down on Tristan's shoulders. "No, Tristan. When I say you can't, you can't. I know this pressure is eating at you, but you are the only one who can do this. Your skill is greater than Tarek's, though the creature would be ashamed if he knew this. If you do not find a way through, we have no hope. We fail. We lose everything we've hoped for, worked for. Died for. Do you understand?"

Harriett narrowed her eyes. "You think that's helping him?"

"I think Tristan is a man grown who deserves to be spoken to in the manner of the same," Anders returned. "We aren't playing with child's toys. We are looking to you, a Halfling, to provide the tool and means to our salvation. This is no small thing… in fact, I can think of no greater thing. If I don't leave you with the full gravity of this task, then you very well might fail. If you fail, Aleksandr dies. If you fail, many of us will find ourselves on the pyre as well. If you fail, all hope fails with you."

"No pressure," Tristan muttered, but he had heard the words. Not that Anders needed to say them. He'd said them to himself, over and over, where they burned through his sleep, his dreams, his every moment of wakefulness.

"If fortune is smiling upon us, you will never again know such pressure," Anders said, and Tristan knew this was the closest he would ever come to positive reinforcement with his mentor.

"Will you come with me?" Tristan asked.

"To the Blacksmith shop?"

Tristan nodded. He loathed this feeling, that he was a little boy again, searching for affirmation from a distant mother and an always working father. He wondered if he would search the rest of his life, never finding what he needed. Then he realized the rest of his life could potentially be measured in minutes.

Anders rubbed his hands together. "I can't ask anything of you that I wouldn't do myself," he said after a pause. "I would be honored to join you."

They all turned to look as the crowd bustled into action amongst whoops and roars. Anders' eyes went wide and he grinned. "It's time. Follow me. I know the way."

Anders bounded off with the same nervous excitement Tristan always imagined soldiers bore in ancient Rome, or any battle before technology made hand-to-hand combat obsolete. This one had even come with a motivational speech.

Tristan turned to Harriett. "Whatever happens..."

Harriett silenced his words with a kiss. He tasted the salt of her tears. "I know."

65
ANASOFIYA

What started with the healers would end with the clan.

Ana lay next to Amelia as she slept, whispering reassurances. Telling her the story of when she first laid eyes on Aleksandr, and how everything within her clicked into place. Finn and Aidrik each helped fill out the puzzle of her convoluted life, but Aleksandr had completed it with a single look.

The healers were in their trance, only half-present. Sometimes she hardly noticed them at all. They'd become part of the background of the vigil Ana kept, as she diverted all her focus to Amelia, and not to her fears that her whole life was in flux. She knew better than to dwell on all the possible outcomes, but her pragmatism kept all of these in the back of her mind, especially the one where none of them came home to her.

Her pragmatism also plainly reminded her that, given the odds, this outcome was the most likely.

"Moira is such a beautiful name," Ana said. She dropped her face to Amelia's neck and draped one hand under her belly.

"It just came to you, didn't it? It was like that with Aleksei, but I had known for some time I wanted to honor my mother's family, the way she had when she named me Anasofiya Aleksandrovna. Anasofiya for her lost sister, and Aleksandrovna to represent so many of the men in the Vasilyev family. I had hoped to find them one day and take Aleksei to meet them." Ana closed her eyes. "I won't talk like they're not coming back to me. They are. They *have* to."

Olivia was the first to arrive. Ana hadn't spoken to her cousin beyond basic pleasantries in many years, so she didn't know what to say now.

She settled on hello.

Olivia's face crumbled into a wrinkle of distress and tears. "I'm so sorry, Ana. From the bottom of my heart, and all my soul."

"Sorry?" There were so many things going on that she didn't know where to focus Olivia's apology.

"Sebastian. I saw how… how good Aleksandr was for him, and I backed off to let him breathe a little, because he was always so *angry* at me for stifling him—"

Ana went to her cousin and pulled her in for a tight hug. "Sebastian made his own choices," she said as Olivia sobbed in her arms. It would be so easy to cast fault, a convenient place to direct her anger and fears so they would stop threatening to take over. But her life had been a series of events both fortunate and unfortunate, and to blame others for the bad would be to relinquish her credit for the good. "I don't blame you for this, Liv."

Olivia separated from the embrace. She wiped her tears on the back of her wool sleeves. "How can I help? I asked Greg to look after Rory, because I can't sit at home wondering. I'll go mad."

Ana looked around at all the healers, focused, oblivious to

them. "Well, you can grab a chair from downstairs and keep me company. Catch up on life."

Olivia smiled through her tears. "I would like that."

NEXT CAME ANNE WITH A VALISE OF HER THINGS. SHE WOULD STAY IN one of the guest rooms until Moira was born, and then for some time after. She told them Jonathan had gone with the men to Farjhem. Ana took this news in with a mix of feelings. Finn needed the strength of his brother, but if the worst happened, Ana would lose even more. For Jon, despite the darkness between them, was her brother, too.

Ashley showed up with Noah, and Colleen wasn't far behind. More chairs appeared from the dining room. When they ran out, Colleen called for more.

Then came Augustus. He sat in silence next to Ana, but not before he said, "Deschanels have always been stronger together. I'm here, Ana."

Lauren and Nicolas showed up next, together. Ana didn't know what to make of Lauren's tentative smile or the way Nicolas looked at her when she didn't know he was, but something about the two of them put a part of her at ease. Worrying about Nicolas had been a significant part of her life for so long, just as the reverse had been true for him. It would be easier to let go of that old habit if she knew he had the steadying presence of someone else.

More and more Deschanels arrived. Guidrys, Fontenots, Broussards, and more. When they had to open the bedroom window to cut through the dense heat of so many bodies, newcomers spilled into the hallway, into other rooms, into the dining room. On the street, cars wrapped around the corner.

Idle chatter faded to silence within a couple of hours. Ana fell back into her position with Amelia, curled at her side on the bed. She looked past the many heads between her and the fogged windowpane. Was that... no.... it couldn't...

"It's snowing," Maybelle cried out. For once, she resembled the little girl she was supposed to be. "Snowing!"

The conversations roared to life, as everyone mused over the unlikeliness of snow this time of year, or in Louisiana at all. They argued over the year of the last snow, and where they'd been. The oldest in the room proudly declared that *they* had been alive to witness the best snow events, while the younger ones reminded them that the Christmas Eve storm of 2004 was the biggest since 1899, so unless they were alive then...

Ana smiled and drowned them out. Her father was right: Deschanels were stronger together. Even their presence was a boon, and a physical reminder of what they were capable of when they joined in a common cause.

I sense peace in you, Anasofiya. Odd.

Ah, hello Wraith. No longer respecting my wishes?

I assumed, naturally, that you might need me now that your other confidantes are gone.

Ana didn't argue that point. Wraith was right, but not for the reason she thought she was. Wraith was part of her, and thus, part of the Deschanels. Ana would take every last one of them. *And odd. Why odd?*

Forgive me. You know I am direct. Everyone you love is in danger. How can you be at peace?

Not everyone. Look around me. Can you see the world through my eyes?

When it suits you.

Do it now, then.

You forget, Anasofiya, I have been a passenger to your soul since the time of your birth.

And?

You spent your years pushing this family away. And now they give you comfort?

Wraith, this is where you and I will never find common ground. Humanity is not a set point. It's what makes us capable of change and looking for ways to better ourselves. You have always been the part of me that holds me back.

How thoughtful you are with your words, Anasofiya.

I don't mean it as awful as it sounds. You are one thing, one part of me, but you are not my humanity. My humanity is fluid, and you are fixed, like an anchor. All ships need an anchor, but they also need the sea. Do you understand what I mean?

And you always chide me for my use of riddles.

It's not a riddle, it's a metaphor. When any of us become incapable of change, we cease to be the very best of ourselves. You've shown me what my power is as a sorceress. But my discovery that I am capable of love has shown me my power as a member of this family, and of the human race.

A peculiar family. They've been on about snow for an hour.

Not everything in life has to be intrigue and action. Sometimes the small moments are the ones that make you appreciate the bigger ones.

This all sounds especially droll.

Because you aren't here to cultivate my humanity. You were born of my darkness, and my darkness you remain.

Sigh.

And, Wraith, I may be clinging to my humanity now, but there will come a time, as there always comes a time, when I need you more. And when that time comes, I know you will be ready.

Aye, Anasofiya. The darkness awaits.

EPILOGUE: FINNEGAN

They arrived at the Deschanel safe house in South Carolina at daybreak. Their flight would depart from Atlanta and change through Amsterdam. From there, directly to Trondheim, which would put them not very far from the hidden entrance to Farjhem.

Nora had left word with Flynn of the plans, anticipating that Finn and others would be in contact once news of Aleksandr reached their ears. The Brotherhood were marching on Farjhem. They might very well be engaged this moment, or perhaps they already had, and news hadn't reached the Quinlans of the results. Finn had no idea if they would arrive on time, or too late. But in the absence of knowing, he focused on what he did know.

Aleksandr was alive. He could feel it. He would know if that were no longer the case. Aidrik, too, was alive. He had explained the how, but that no longer mattered. He was here. Finn's brother was back. Anasofiya awaited him at home. The only woman he had ever loved, and the only woman he ever would. Finn understood it had taken greater strength for her to stay back than it had taken for him to come. She held vigil while her whole world raced off into the unknown.

Finn would have done anything to leave her with the promise of his return. Of Aidrik's. Of Aleksandr's.

In the end, all he had been able to leave her with was the vow of his fidelity and a gift of the conjoined crosses of their mothers he'd worn around his neck since the moment he realized he was hopelessly in love with her.

The four men sat on the back deck of the house, eyes fixed on the sea. They had thirty minutes until they would leave for the airport. They should rest. But there was momentum in their racing thoughts, and it would not be stopped.

"This could be our last sunrise," Jonathan remarked, lacking the sentiment the words commanded. His empty expression betrayed the numbness within.

"It could," Finn agreed. He took a swig from the warm beer. "Thankfully, it's a hell of a pretty sunrise."

"Yeah, not like those ugly sunrises," Jacob agreed with a shiver. "Who has time for those?"

They all smiled. None had the energy of spirit for a laugh.

"I will never understand Children of Men," Aidrik declared. "Not wholly. But I concur. This is indeed a worthy sunrise."

They didn't talk about what they had left behind, or what lay ahead. The four men instead drew their strength from each other, their unified silence amidst a storm of thoughts, and the ethereal beauty of what might be their last sunrise.

This is the end.
This is the beginning.
The stage is set. The players, ready.

The House and Crimson & Clover comes to a startling conclusion in ***House of Dusk, House of Dawn.***

What are your predictions? Ready to find out? Download ***House of Dusk, House of Dawn*** today.

WANT A TEASE FIRST? READ FURTHER FOR AN EXCERPT.

HOUSE OF DUSK, HOUSE OF DAWN EXCERPT

Tristan gave one last searching glance at the monolithic glacier towering above them, a frozen wall stretching clear to the sky. Though inanimate, the iced fortification pulsed with the life of what lay beyond. The steam of pure cold rising from the ice was as clear a reminder as ever that he was as far from home as the earth allowed.

Anders was not wrong: the magic cloaking Farjhem was infallible. Marveling at this sheet of ice so massive it was seemingly unscalable, one would never guess it foreshadowed an entire world beyond. Only the subtle undercurrent of beating power rising with the steam betrayed this glacier was more than it seemed.

Harriett bundled in tighter. Her mind was as silent as her mouth and Tristan did nothing to challenge that. Even if he had felt talkative, he had nothing to say. The danger they headed into was immeasurable next to anything they'd done in their lives so far. Words would be as inadequate as they were useless at this juncture.

Tarek nodded at Anders. "Are we going to admire the view or get this done?"

The words snapped Anders back to his regimented self. "Follow me." He started off into the mounds of snow, but halted, turning to face them. His shouted response was hardly a whisper among the interminable blanket of eternal winter. "Say nothing when we get inside. Not until I've determined we are alone."

He trekked forth without awaiting a response. Tristan, Harriett, and Tarek dutifully followed.

Tristan was in the seventh grade when the first *Harry Potter* book released. He'd clamored and begged his mother to stand in line with him outside the Garden District Book shop, hours before it opened, sweating in the late summer heat. A boy wizard is sent to a magical boarding school, where he learns cool spells, makes lifelong friends, and triumphs over evil sorcerers? What's not to love?

He never told Elizabeth, not after the first book, or the second, or even the fourth, that he knew deep in his marrow his own life would have turned out for the better had he been sent away to learn more about who he was instead of spending his youth minding the emotional state of his mother.

Now, he would give anything to go back to those old days, to ease her from a panic attack, or reassure her of his love. He would take all the bad and uncomfortable just to have her back.

Both Elizabeth and Connor were on his mind as the stalwart group moved achingly through the blinding snow. He focused on lifting one boot with great effort and thrusting it back down with powerful inertia. Over and over. They were not going far, but a yard was a mile in snow this deep. *Mind your body temperature,* his mother cooed from the back of his mind somewhere. *If you begin to sweat, you must slow down. It won't do to have the sweat freeze against your skin.* His father had words for him as well. *Don't think about how far you have to go, son. Instead, think of how far you've come.*

Tristan slammed to a stop when he hit a wall. No, not a wall, Tarek. The snow muffled Tarek's grumbles. Harriett fell against his back as she caught up to the traffic accident.

"We're here!" Anders yelled.

Where? Tristan wanted to ask. The view hadn't changed in an agonizing long while. Snow and ice as far as his gaze could span. White upon white upon more white.

Anders looked up, along the ice shelf, toward the sky. With a brief glance back, he nodded and moved forward. He disappeared into the glacier.

Harriett gasped behind him. Tristan felt the same shock. But Tarek didn't falter in his lagged steps, and then, he too disappeared. They were both gone, with no instruction and no explanation. Just... gone.

It's like that book of yours, Tristan. You know. The one about the wizard.

Harry Potter, *Mom. And it's not just one book.*

Yes, whatever it's called. I remember you telling me the little wizard walked right into a wall and it took him somewhere magical. In my day, we called an experience like that a 'good trip.'

Platform 9 ¾. Not LSD. No one cares about your drug stories, Mom.

Well, whatever, Tristan. You know what to do.

Yes, he knew what to do.

He reached for Harriett's gloved hand in the blizzard and squeezed through the thick fabric.

Tristan closed his eyes as he approached the glacier and took a leap of faith.

There was nothing at all to it. No flip-flopping of his unsteady stomach, no strange gust of air. Arriving through Farjhem's secret, forgotten entrance was as easy as walking through any regular old door in Tristan's world.

The consistency of the air changed dramatically in an instant. The choking, bitter cold of outside was replaced by a new but equally repressive must that filled their lungs and produced immediate bouts of coughing from all but Anders. The creature had no pressure points, Tristan thought. His construction was pure blood and steel.

Plumes of dust fell from the dark sky. Anders' refusal to bring in light meant Tristan was left to guess at the contents of the sediment, and his mind immediately went to the crumbling, ancient bones of his Empyrean ancestors.

A shudder passed through him. Harriett shook her head.

Don't tell me you didn't think the same thing. He broke their shared silence.

If I had but one last wish, Tristan, it would be to visit all the places your imagination goes to and see the world through your eyes.

Tristan didn't know how to respond to that, and meanwhile, Anders had progressed forward and disappeared from his limited view. He struggled to catch up, and Harriett fell into pace behind him.

He had so many questions. He should have asked more before the start of the mission, should have quelled his swiftly beating heart and budding adrenaline and stopped long enough to understand the practicalities. How long was the tunnel once inside? How big was the Blacksmith shop? What the heck was the crap that would fall on them from the sky like old death?

And how would they know when the rest of the Brotherhood's army made it into Farjhem and put their plan into motion? Anders and Tarek intimated *they* would know, but would they share?

Ahead, Anders' heavy steps stilled. Tarek as well came to a stop, and soon, Tristan could see why. They had entered a clearing that seemed to be some kind of room, if you could call it that. More like an enclave, and a somewhat tidier version of the dark and dusty cave they'd just emerged from.

The room had some natural light, though Tristan could not determine the source. All around them, extraordinary steel languished in rotting wooden cases. Sword upon sword, the likes of which Tristan had only seen in movies and read in books. But these weren't decent props; before him lay a graveyard of perhaps the most impressive sword collection existing upon the earth.

Moths and spiders ate away at the corners of the Blacksmith shop. Two massive steel anvils flanked a cobwebbed forge whose better days were long behind it. Termites, or some other parasite, had long consumed most of the wood in the room, and the cases listed to this side or that, barely held aloft by their foundations. Some had long ago given up the ghost and lay in tattered heaps on the dirt floor, their steel contents in a messy pile. Weapons that would sell for more than his father's car in a free trade market just *lying* there, as if they no longer had a purpose in this world.

Tristan had a strong urge to ask more about the place, but his better sense—which was a new, surprising part of himself he was only beginning to come into—kicked in before he could make the error. The time for his questions had passed, and that time may never come again. He was not a child anymore, expecting placating by all the adults cultivating his natural curiosities. The dependencies of adult intervention in his life were his greatest struggles in achieving grown-up independence. Now, for the first time in his life, he made the switch from child to adult without much effort.

He looked at Anders. Anders closed his eyes. Listened. For what, Tristan didn't know, and once again, knew better than to ask.

When his eyes flashed open, Anders had a peace about him that calmed Tristan enough for him to release his long-held breath.

"We are alone. For now." Anders' voice reached barely above a careful whisper. "I do not expect this will last long. I have nothing else to tell you, Tristan and Tarek, that you don't already know. The clock here will tick faster than any you've ever encountered. Harriett and I will pace the perimeter for as long as we need to, or until our safety has been breached. Are you ready?"

Tarek nodded. Tristan paused long enough for Anders to say,

"You have no choice. The clock starts now. Be swift!"

Tristan felt the quick, soft squeeze of Harriett's hand, her one brief reassurance before she disappeared to help Anders. He looked to his left at Tarek, but the creature's lids were closed, the eyes beneath them fluttering like the onset of R.E.M. sleep.

Tristan drew in one final breath, cleared his mind, and his eyes, too, closed.

Aleksandr. Show yourself.

ALSO BY SARAH M. CRADIT

KINGDOM OF THE WHITE SEA

Kingdom of the White Sea Trilogy

The Kingless Crown

The Broken Realm

The Hidden Kingdom

The Book of All Things

The Raven and the Rush

The Sylvan and the Sand

The Altruist and the Assassin

The Melody and the Master

The Claw and the Crowned

THE SAGA OF CRIMSON & CLOVER

The House of Crimson and Clover Series

The Storm and the Darkness

Shattered

The Illusions of Eventide

Bound

Midnight Dynasty

Asunder

Empire of Shadows

Myths of Midwinter

The Hinterland Veil

The Secrets Amongst the Cypress

Within the Garden of Twilight

House of Dusk, House of Dawn

Midnight Dynasty Series

A Tempest of Discovery

A Storm of Revelations

A Torrent of Deceit

The Seven Series

1970

1972

1973

1974

1975

1976

1980

Vampires of the Merovingi Series

The Island

and more

The Dusk Trilogy

St. Charles at Dusk: The Story of Oz and Adrienne

Flourish: The Story of Anne Fontaine

Banshee: The Story of Giselle Deschanel

Crimson & Clover Stories

Surrender: The Story of Oz and Ana

Shame: The Story of Jonathan St. Andrews

Fire & Ice: The Story of Remy & Fleur

Dark Blessing: The Landry Triplets

Pandora's Box: The Story of Jasper & Pandora

The Menagerie: Oriana's Den of Iniquities

A Band of Heather: The Story of Colleen and Noah

The Ephemeral: The Story of Autumn & Gabriel

Bayou's Edge: The Landry Triplets

For more information, and exciting bonus material, visit www.sarahmcradit.com

EMPYREAN & QUINLAN

ENCYCLOPEDIA

Aanya: A kind and beautiful Empyrean Agripin once loved, but was forbidden from claiming as his duchess her due to her lack of lineage.

Aidrik (Also: Aidrik the Wise): Once a well-respected member of the Eldre Senetat. After Aidrik discovered their true nature, he sliced the Mark of Emyr from his face, freeing him from the Senetat's tethers. He met and saved Anasofiya from death, becoming her evigbond. Lived in a triad with Anasofiya, and her husband Finn, until his death, at the hands of the Senetat.

Aleksandr: Empyrean son of Anasofiya, Finn, and Aidrik. Shy, introspective. Named heir of the Deschanels by Nicolas. A mystic, and time shaper, whose abilities are still surfacing.

Anders: An Empyrean Mercy co-habitated with for a short period of time. She believed him Ascended, but he was, actually, a scout for the Brotherhood, under the direction of Thorvald. His most recent assignment brought him to *Ophélie*, where he is tasked with training and protecting the Brotherhood children.

Arborkinetic: A form of telekinesis involving flora. A strong arborkinetic can command plant life to do their bidding, and some can communicate with plants. Anne Fontaine Deschanel and Duchess Nerys are both arborkinetics.

Ascension (Also: Grand Ascension): The ultimate death and rebirth all Empyreans are promised. It is tied to Emyr's Mark, which is said to come alive when their time is near. Once active, the mark is then supposed to usher them through death and rebirth, into the arms of Emyr. The truth is the mark is simply an infusion of dark magic administered by the Eldre Senetat, from which they control the activation and subsequent death of Empyreans.

Astrid: Brotherhood leader of Ireland and the British Isles, alongside her evigbond, Birger. Birger and Astrid are in the minority in their decision to make peace with Quinlans. They also co-exist peacefully with humans in the nearby villages where they live in a tribe of other similar-minded Empyreans. Many look to them as the moral compass of the Brotherhood. They have one child, Eydis.

Baldur: A sadistic scout for the Senetat who captures Amelia and Jacob, torturing them for information. Is killed by Jacob.

Bestiakinetic: One who can commune with animals. Finnegan becomes a bestiakinetic after being given the Sveising. Yiva and Jorun are also bestiakinetics.

Birger: Brotherhood leader of Ireland and the British Isles, alongside his evigbond, Astrid. Birger and Astrid are in the minority in their decision to make peace with Quinlans. They also co-exist peacefully with humans in the nearby villages where they live in a tribe of other like-minded Empyreans. Many look to them as the moral compass of the Brotherhood. They have one child, Eydis.

Blacksmith: Forger of Ulfberht, and creator of Empyrean Steel.

Bodhran: Goatskin drum used in Quinlan ceremonies.

Brotherhood: See "Dragon Brotherhood, The."

Brother of Emyr (Also: Sister of Emyr): Another way to reference a halfling (or, someone who has both human and Empyrean blood).

Brynja: One of the oldest, original Empyreans. Together with her partner, Einar, they are Brotherhood leaders, residing in Russia. Part of Runa's rebels who escaped after her execution, they are often called, by Runeans, "Adam and Eve."

Child of Man/Men: What Empyreans call humans.

Christiane de Laurent: Aidrik's original evigbond. Human. Lived at the end of the 16th century, as a courtesan of the French court. Wife of Marquise Deschanel, and mother of Claude.

Cianán (Also: Jacob Donnelly): One fourth of the prophecy, descended from the Tuathan tribe of Gorias. He has been reincarnated over thousands of years, with his lover, Cerridwen. Their journey evolves in each lifetime, with the ultimate test being their love bringing them together in their final lifetime, when they have no memory of former lives, thus fulfilling the prophecy. Their child is meant to join with the descendant of Falias and Murias. Jacob is the reincarnated soul of Cianán.

Cerridwen (Also: Amelia Donnelly): One fourth of the prophecy, descended from the Tuathan tribe of Findias. She has been reincarnated over thousands of years, with her lover, Cianán. Their journey evolves in each lifetime, with the ultimate test being their love bringing them together in their final lifetime, thus fulfilling the prophecy. Their child is meant to join with the descendant of Falias and Murias. Amelia is the reincarnated soul of Cerridwen.

Claude Deschanel (Also: Viscount Deschanel): The first halfling Deschanel, being both human and Empyrean. Child of Christiane and Aidrik.

***Crann bethadh*:** Also known as the "Tree of Life," and the center of the Quinlan tribe. It gives life to the tribe, by providing everything they need, from food to shelter. Also a portal between worlds, and the spiritual link to the goddesses.

Crimson Guard: The official guard of the Farjhem, under command of the Senetat. Their uniform consists of blood-red robes.

Cumdach: A lavishly ornamented shrine used in Quinlan ceremonies.

Cyler: Agripin's young, brash second-in-command, and lover. Often shirks orders and goes his own route, though he is known for being excellent with strategy. Is a frequent visitor to Oriana's Menagerie.

Dagr: 7,000 years old. Born without Senetat knowledge, and is one of the Brotherhood leaders, residing in Morocco.

Daughter of Emyr (Also: Son of Emyr): Referencing pure-blooded Empyrean women.

Deschanel Magi Collective: A secret, ancient society, created with the intention of cataloguing all the family's abilities, as well as protecting and preserving the family. Each generation has a Magistrate, the current one being Colleen Deschanel.

Dragon Brotherhood, The: Secret organization of Empyrean rebels. There is no central leader, but instead regional leaders across the world. Some leaders are ready for battle, others content to live in peace.

Dragon Empire, The (Also: Dragon Brotherhood, The): Another name for the wider Dragon Brotherhood.

Draoi: Male Quinlan. It is said these males are sacred, as their occurrence usually portends something important, and prophetic. Draoi are often quite powerful, able to spin wards and time dance. To birth a draoi is to be considered blessed. Male druids often come into their powers when they reach sexual maturity. Attempting to draw from them earlier can sometimes lead to disastrous results. Jacob, Finnegan, Padraig, and Father O'Connor are all draoi.

Drekar: A term of familiarity amongst the Brotherhood. Translates roughly to "dragon."

Duchess Nerys: Nomadic daughter of Grand Emperor Aeron, and sister to Agripin and Oriana. Known for her love of all creatures, and her call to traveling. A bestiakinetic, with loyalties to no one and nothing except peace. Joins forces with the Brotherhood, as she believes they are most likely to achieve that.

Duchess Oriana: Beautiful, wayward daughter of Grand Emperor Aeron, sister to Agripin and Nerys. Known for having a menagerie of human pets, and for her cruelty toward defectors. Is loyal to the Senetat.

Einar: One of the oldest, original Empyreans. Together with his partner, Brynja, they are Brotherhood leaders, residing in Russia. Part of Runa's rebels who escaped after her execution, they are often called, by Runeans, "Adam and Eve."

Eldre Aeslius: One of the nine members of the Eldre Senetat. Following the events at Aidrik's execution, his fate is currently unknown.

Eldre Brutus: Was originally a member of Emperor Elof's privy council, but when he discovered Elof was plotting with rebels, Brutus betrayed and exposed him. The Senetat "Ascended" Elof, giving the crown to his son Aeron. Following the events at Aidrik's execution, his fate is currently unknown.

Eldre Cassian: One of the nine members of the Eldre Senetat. Following the events at Aidrik's execution, his fate is currently unknown.

Eldre Felix: One of the nine members of the Eldre Senetat. Following the events at Aidrik's execution, his fate is currently unknown.

Eldre Lucrecia: One of the nine members of the Eldre Senetat. Following the events at Aidrik's execution, her fate is currently unknown.

Eldre Maxima: One of the nine members of the Eldre Senetat. Has been a secret sympathizer of the Brotherhood for many years, and officially joined their cause following the events at Aidrik's execution.

Eldre Tacita: One of the nine members of the Eldre Senetat. Following the events at Aidrik's execution, her fate is currently unknown.

Eldre Valerius: One of the nine members of the Eldre Senetat. Right hand of Grand Eldre Servius. Following the events at Aidrik's execution, his fate is currently unknown.

Eldre Senetat, The: The ruling government over the Empyrean race. Established many millennia ago, they claim to be blessed by Emyr, and charged with doing His will through enacting and protecting laws. The Senetat grew corrupt with this power, and unknown to most Empyreans, are controlling the fates of all citizens. The creation and installation of Emyr's Mark is the vehicle by which they exact their control.

Empath: The ability to sense feelings, emotions, or sensations in others. There are varying degrees of empaths. Amelia Deschanel is considered the strongest empath in the family. Lucia and Livia are also empaths.

Empyrean (Also: Farværdig): Also known as the Farværdig ("Father's Chosen"), Empyreans are as old as man, and similar genetically, but with several key differences. Where some DNA is dormant in humans, the entire strand is active in Empyreans, giving them special, paranormal abilities, including greater strength and speed, and immortality via perfect cell replication. Their home is Farjhem, in the northern expanses of Norway, but most Empyreans live scattered throughout the world, blending in with men. All Empyreans are born with red hair (which fades to a chromatic silver as they age), and are exceptionally tall. They are also primarily solitary, not subscribing to traditions such as a nuclear family, marriage, or commitment. The exception to this is evigbond. In their early days, they enjoyed a strategic alliance with Quinlans, but, once broken, both races were thrust into strife.

Empyrean Laws: Mandates set by the Eldre Senetat. include regulations around childbirth, mating with humans, and other fundamental freedoms.

Empyrean Steel (Also: Crucible Steel): A rare steel with high carbon content, smelted in a small furnace, and cooled slowly. In swords, it was both strong, and flexible. The technology was not used anywhere else in the world, and was considered better than Damascus Steel, which is the closest point of comparison.

Empyrean traits: Born of fire. Elevated body temperature. Red hair (the redder the strands, the more pure the blood) that takes on silver chromatic hues as they age. When emotions are heightened, they are said to emit an orange glow. Most have pale, smooth skin, and are very tall. All have special telepathic/telekinetic abilities, with some stronger than others. Average lifespan is two thousand years, though it is believed without the mark, an Empyrean could be functionally immortal.

Emyr (Also: Our Father): God, to Empyreans. He is represented by a phoenix, rising from the ashes.

Erikr: Brotherhood resistance leader who led one of the only semi-successful rebel revolutions after Runa's. Was executed in a block of ice. Leader of the Second Runean War, and considered the father of the Dragon Brotherhood, which was formed with the help of Ptolemy I.

Etheric Summoning (Also: Etheric Summoner): More rare than a mystic, an etheric summoner can draw from their greatest weakness and manifest it into a physical strength. Also known as a wraith. Anasofiya is an etheric summoner.

Evigbond: The physical and chemical bonding process that occurs when an Empyrean meets their permanent mate. It is irreversible, and only severed by death. An evigbond between Empyrean and humans is especially potent. Aidrik's first evigbond was Christiane, and his current is Anasofiya. Mercy experienced evigbond with Nicolas, until her "death." Evigbond can occur in two different ways. The first is an uncontrolled, chemical reaction. The second is through consummation.

Eydis: Fifty-year-old daughter of Brotherhood leaders Birger and Astrid. She is halfway to maturity, and emotionally equivalent to a young girl of around nineteen. Wide-eyed, rebellious, but kind-hearted. She sees how in love her parents are because of their evigbond, and is determined to find hers. Her birth accompanied a year of great prosperity for crops in Ireland. Is an illusionist with a specialty in influencing.

Falias: One of the four tribes of the Tuatha Dé Danann. All Quinlans descend from one of these four tribes. The tribe of Falias is mentioned in The Prophecy as such: *A male Quinlan, pure of heart, and a special affinity for animals.* It is not yet known who the subject of this reference is.

Far: Empyrean word for father. Can be used by a child speaking to a parent, or in reference to Our Father, Emyr.

Fardag (Also: Father's Day): Annual Farjhem celebration held in homage to Emyr.

Farjhem: The homeland of the Empyreans. Translated to "Father's Home." Located between two glaciers in northern

Norway, it is not accessible by anyone except Empyreans, or those with Empyrean blood.

Farsengel: The place of law and order in Farjhem, where suspected criminals are sentenced and detained awaiting further punishment. Many stories high, the outside edges contain hundreds of cells, and the inside of the arena has a large stage.

Farskilt: Deep in the bowels of Farjhem, beneath a volcano. "Separated from father." Empyreans are sentenced here for "rehabilitation" when they commit spiritual offenses. Citizens are told that offenders are "reunited with Emyr" and the end of their rehabilitation results in guaranteed Ascension. The reality is they are labor mines, and Empyreans work there until their inevitable starvation and death. The Empyrean equivalent of a prison camp.

Farvann River: (Also: River Farvann): The river flowing through the fjord and glaciers of Farjhem.

Farværdig (Also: Empyrean): See "Empyrean."

Father O'Connor: A draoi descended from the tribe of Gorias, and the man who saved Jacob from tragedy as a youth, sending him to New Orleans. Brother to the tribe elder, Seara. Great-uncle of Amelia.

Feast of Officium Maximus: Once every hundred years, the Scholars graduate their group of fledgling Empyreans into the world. This ceremony, for which many return home, is accompanied by a great celebration.

Findias: One of the four tribes of the Tuatha Dé Danann. All Quinlans descend from one of these four tribes. The tribe of Findias is mentioned in The Prophecy as such: *A female Quinlan, and halfling Empyrean, reincarnated over two-thousand years, originally Cerridwen. Lover of Cianán.* Amelia Jameson Donnelly is the subject of this reference.

First Father: When an Empyrean child has multiple

fathers (via Sveising), the initial father, at conception, is referred to as First Father.

First Runean War: Resistance to the creation of the Eldre Senetat, led by Runa, a warrior who represented the opinions of many Empyreans. Despite her strong supporters, the rebels were destroyed, and Runa publicly executed. Their stunning defeat weakened the resolve of many Empyreans who believed in her cause (henceforth dubbed Runeans by the Senetat), and most went into hiding.

Fledglings: What the Empyrean youth are referred to when they reach the age of spiritual maturity and are released into the wider world.

Forbia: An abandoned Hudson Bay wolf pup discovered and adopted by Finnegan. She becomes his familiar, and he names her Forbia, after his beloved ship he left in Maine.

Galon: A kinsman of Aidrik who was forced into Ascension by the Senetat after he angered them.

Goddess Danu: The goddess and leader of the Tuatha Dé Danann.

Goddess Morrigan: The goddess of divination, and one of the surviving Tuatha, foretold one day that four individuals—one descendant from each original clan—would unite the Empyreans and Quinlans once again. This prophecy was delivered to both a Quinlan and an Empyrean, and said that they would go through nearly two millennia of war and strife before finding peace.

Gorias: One of the four tribes of the Tuatha Dé Danann. All Quinlans descend from one of these four tribes. The tribe of Gorias is mentioned in The Prophecy as such: *A male Quinlan, known as Cianán (little ancient one), reincarnated with Cerridwen.* Jacob Donnelly is the subject of this reference.

Grand Eldre Servius: The ruling grand eldre of the Senetat for several millennia. Was lesser-ranked at the time of Aidrik's service. Was known for his "scorched earth" policy and for taking the restrictive laws of the Empyrean race to the far extreme. Killed by Anasofiya at the execution of Aidrik.

Grand Emperor Aeron: The last ruling Grand Emperor of Farjhem, and the Empyrean race. Had a reputation for being kind, and benign, but showed no interest in meaningful involvement with his people. Was activated when Agripin spread false rumor of his treason. Agripin then succeeded him as grand emperor.

Grand Emperor Agripin: The current ruling Grand Emperor of Farjhem, and the Empyrean race. Previously Grand Duke Agripin. The only son and oldest child of Aeron and Theda, both deceased. Fought in the Second Runean War, where his distaste for the Senetat was born. Over the years, his love of easy living kept him from taking action, but his partnership with the Brotherhood grew over time. He used Aidrik and Anasofiya as part of his campaign, which results in the burning of Farjhem. Is currently in Trondheim with the rest of the Brotherhood, plotting their next move.

Grand Emperor Elof: Father of Aeron, who succeeded him when he was "activated" for suspected trafficking with the rebels. Betrayed by Eldre Brutus, who was his closest confidante.

Grand Emperor Seti: Ruling emperor of Farjhem at the time the Senetat was created. Supported the Senetat's inception, as he was not interested in being the upholder of laws.

Grand Empress Anasofiya: Born a halfling of the Deschanel clan in New Orleans. Aidrik gave her the Sveising to save her life, which gifted her with more potent versions of her existing abilities, as well as suspected immortality. Married to Finnegan, but evigbond to Aidrik, which created an unorthodox polyamorous triad between them. Mother to Aleksandr, who is the son of both men. Her skill as a resurrection shaman pales in comparison to her most potent ability of all, etheric summoning. She is currently magic-bound by Agripin following the execution of Aidrik, where she destroyed hundreds of Empyreans.

Grand Empress Theda: Mate of Aeron and mother of Agripin. Deceased.

Great Cleansing: Following the creation of the Senetat, Empyreans who refused the mark were sought out and executed. Those who survived were branded Runeans.

Great Commitment (Also: Officium Maximus): The graduation ceremony, once every hundred years, when Empyreans reach their age of maturity and are released from the Scholars' tutelage, out into the world. This ceremony includes the installation of Emyr's Mark, a magical brand in the shape of a phoenix that is said to include a part of Emyr Himself. In reality, it is a device of the Eldre Senetat, as a means to control the Empyreans once they leave Farjhem.

Hakon: Still a fledgling, son of Emperor Aeron through a tryst he had with Hakon's mother. The mother escaped from Farjhem, and she died after birthing Hakon. Trygve took him in, under his wing, in Mongolia. Is a bestiakinetic.

Halfling: Humans with some amount of Empyrean blood/ancestry. A human is considered a halfling even if their Empyrean blood is many generations back.

Holger: Kind and helpful scout of Birger and Astrid, sent to look after Jacob and Amelia.

Illusionist: One who can manipulate the reality of others. Some do this by changing the physical interpretation. Others do this through influence. Markus is an illusionist who can change his appearance. Eydis can influence people to do her bidding.

Inner Voice: Empyreans believe in the concept of an "Inner Voice" guiding them toward their destiny. For Mercy, the Inner

Voice was an illusion crafted by Aidrik, who was guiding her toward safety.

Isabella Deschanel: Daughter of Margarethe and the necromancer. Was the first starlight awakener in the family, raised in secrecy due to her rapid growth. Her life, and eventual burning at the stake for witchcraft, was chronicled in the propaganda pamphlet, *La Sorcière de Villeneuve*. The current Deschanel line descends through her.

Jorun: The Brotherhood leader over South America. Quiet and reclusive, she relates better to creatures on four feet, as a bestiakinetic. Lives apart from the other Empyreans of the region, but looks after them from afar.

Killianshire: A small village in southern Ireland, where Jacob was born and raised. Father O'Connor presides over the cathedral here. The village is Quinlan-friendly.

Kjære: Aidrik's term of endearment for Ana. Translates roughly to "my dear" or "my dearest" in Empyrean.

Leif: The Brotherhood leader over the Caribbean region. Was once a member of the Senetat, but over time grew weary of their hypocrisy. He escaped and became a critical leader amongst the Brotherhood. Can bind the magic of others.

Livia: Born in Spain to an Empyrean mother and human father. Her father had dark olive skin, and her darker skin tone puts her in danger, as no purebred Empyrean has these tones. Is closely guarded under the wing of Thorvald, and has a special bond with Lucia. Empath.

Lucia: Escaped the Scholars when she was still a student, leaving Farjhem without a plan other than the idea of her freedom. Thorvald found her and took her under his wing in Spain, dubbing her *mi belleza*, and fostering her great loyalty. He makes her a scout, and pairs her with Anders. Her most recent assignment took her to *Ophélie* to help train and protect the children of the Brotherhood. Is an empath who can absorb the pain of others without impact to herself.

Margarethe Deschanel: Granddaughter of Claude Deschanel and, therefore, a great-granddaughter of Aidrik. Refused to accept death was the end, and married a famed necromancer, learning his secrets. Upon her death, she was determined to come back, immortal, through a starlight awakener. She pushed her daughter, Isabella, to instruct the family in maintaining pure bloodlines, to increase the chances of a starlight awakener being born into the family. Her attempts to come through non-necromancers and necromancers alike led to many Deschanel deaths over the centuries, which was falsely attributed to the Deschanel Curse. When at last starlight awakeners are born, in the form of Stella and Sebastian, she is prevented from coming through. It is believed she has not given up.

Mark of Emyr (Also: mark, Emyr's Mark): A magical infusion, in the shape of a phoenix, given to all Empyreans at their Great Commitment. The mark is about two inches in diameter, and can be placed anywhere on the body, a choice made by the Empyrean receiving the mark. Empyreans are told the mark includes a part of Emyr Himself, and that when it is time for their Grand Ascension, the mark will call them home to Emyr. In reality, the mark is a sinister plot by the Eldre Senetat, created as a means to control the Empyreans and destroy them.

Marquise Deschanel: Husband of Christiane de Laurent (Aidrik's first human evigbond). He was the First Father of Claude Deschanel, the first Deschanel born with Empyrean blood.

Mercy (Also: Clementyn): Lived three thousand years as an Empyrean who believed in the illusion of Grand Ascension. Piety drove all of her life decisions, often to the point of folly. In her youth, she spent many years with Aidrik, and they did not part on good terms. She found herself crossing paths with Nicolas Deschanel, and when her mark activated, she died but was resurrected by Anasofiya, then becoming human. She currently resides with Nicolas at *Ophélie.*

Mora: Empyrean word for mother.

Murias: One of the four tribes of the Tuatha Dé Danann. All Quinlans descend from one of these four tribes. The tribe of Murias is mentioned in The Prophecy as such: *A female Quinlan, born halfling Empyrean but given far more at maturity.* It is not yet known who the subject of this reference is.

Mystic: Most powerful of all magi, among Empyreans and halflings. Mystics manifest their abilities in different ways. Some are strong healers, others can engage in nested visions, dream suggestion, wards, and other unique traits. All are strong telepaths. Aidrik, Nicolas, Agripin, and Aleksandr are mystics.

Necromancers: Can speak with the dead, though limited to those who have not "crossed over." Quillan is a necromancer.

Nested Vision: A nested vision is an ability only accessible by mystics, wherein the mystic can travel into the mind of another and observe the world through their eyes. The most powerful mystics not only observe, but also control the host. Nicolas Deschanel has newly discovered he is a mystic who can engage in nested visions.

Old Aita: Believed to be the oldest living Empyrean, she is shamed for not having experienced her Grand Ascension. Scholars use her as an example of how not to end up, and as a means of driving fear amongst the fledglings. She is said to have pure white hair.

Ophélie: A plantation on the west bank of the River Road in Louisiana, about an hour from New Orleans. *Ophélie* has been the family seat of the Deschanels for over 200 years, and is passed down through the oldest male in each generation. Nicolas Deschanel, the current heir, has lived there his whole life.

Our Father (Also: Emyr, Our Father of Light, Our Father of Fire): Additional names for Emyr.

Portail: A portal created by a terrakinetic that can send travelers to any point in space.

Quinlans: An ancient line of druidic women, descendants of the Tuatha Dé Danann, and more recently, the Goddess Morrigan. All Quinlans descend from one of the four Tuatha tribes: Findias, Gorias, Falias, and Murias. They believe nature is unconditionally sacred, and that everything is interconnected, and balanced. Their powers are all drawn from nature. They live in secrecy, in protected groves and simplistic structures, all centering around their *crann bethadh*. In their early days, they had a strong alliance with the Empyreans, but that alliance was broken and both races have suffered the consequences. While the Quinlan genetics are passed through the females, in rare cases the male will also manifest. These males are known as draoi, and are more power than the females of the tribe. Most Quinlans keep the Quinlan surname.

Quinlan, Deirdre: Daughter of Seara. Mother of Noah, Nora, Nevina, and Niamh. Grandmother of Amelia. Is the youngest, and so has never taken a strong position of leadership. More of a free spirit, even for a druid. Married Kellan Jameson, a human. Kellan did not know what she was, until after Noah (her youngest) was born. When he threatened to leave, she secreted her daughters away to the tribe. Upon return to fetch her son, she learned Kellan had taken him to New Orleans.

Quinlan, Fiona: Only daughter of Nora. Is young—25—as Nora did not have her until later in life.

Quinlan, Meara: Middle child of Seara, sister of Deirdre and Philomena. Always happy, joyous, but simple-minded. The rest of the tribe closely protects her. Childless, she is not capable of a mutual relationship.

Quinlan, Nevina: Middle daughter of Deirdre, sibling to Nora, Niamh, and Noah. Does not travel outside the tribe. Is worried Jacob and Amelia are too "modern" for the job, and that the goddess waited too long to manifest the prophecy,

Quinlan, Niamh: Youngest daughter of Deirdre, sibling to Nora, Nevina, and Noah. Kind-hearted, and powerful, but often quiet, and whimsical.

Quinlan, Nora: Oldest daughter of Deirdre, sibling to Nevina, Niamh, and Noah. Tapped to take over as leader when the current one passes. Her practical nature makes her a competent leader.

Quinlan, Padraig: A draoi, and husband to Regan. He descends from another tribe of Falias. Trains Jacob, who has newly come into his draoi nature.

Quinlan, Philomena: Oldest child of Seara, sibling to Meara and Deirdre. Bitter to not be her mother's choice as successor. Strong-willed and often quick-tempered, especially now in her old age, which is why Seara did not choose her. Had one son in her youth, and gave him away when he was not a draoi.

Quinlan, Regan: Daughter of Nevina, sister to Kieran. Married to Padraig.

Quinlan, Rosemary: Mother of Enid, and grandmother of Jacob. A member of a tribe of Gorias, she has traveled to Seara's tribe to help with the prophecy.

Quinlan, Seara: Current leader of her tribe. Mother to Philomena, Meara, and Deirdre. Great-grandmother to Amelia. Sister to Flynn. All three of her children were intentionally conceived by men she picked herself, and planned a one-night stand. Has the essence of an oracle, who sees all (the prophecy was passed to her by the last leader). Knows her time is near, and is training her granddaughter, Nora, to take over.

Resurrection Shaman: A healer who is able to resurrect the recently deceased. Resurrection shamans are incredibly rare, and the ability is often volatile. Rarely do subjects come back exactly as they were before death. Anasofiya Deschanel discovers she is a resurrection shaman after Aidrik infuses her with Sveising.

Royal Palace of Farjhem: Residence of the royal family of Farjhem.

Runa: Leader of the minority opposition who rose up when the Senetat was created. Her execution is a symbol of strength for her followers, Runeans. She is often deified amongst her most devout followers. Her uprising is known as the First Runean War.

Runeans: Rebels. Those who oppose the Eldre Senetat are generally lumped together as Runeans (followers of Runa). Secretly, they have organized as the Dragon Brotherhood. Some in the Brotherhood are bloodthirsty and feel a call to action. Others are content to live quietly, off the grid of Empyrean society.

Scholar Saxon: The philosophy Scholar who carried out the execution of Mercy's parents after they were accused of heresy.

Scholars: A group of instructors selected by the Eldre Senetat to oversee the education of all Empyrean children. Their teachings often include propaganda-style support of the Senetat, and a fear-based deterrence of breaking rules. The Scholars spend a hundred years with Empyrean children.

Scholars' Temple: Place of instruction in Farjhem.

Second Runean War: Led by Erikr, the Runeans came together once more, in the spirit of Runa's beliefs, to overthrow the Senetat. As with the first uprising, they were squelched, and Erikr encased in a block of ice. This was the last large uprising of the rebels, who are now scattered and in hiding.

Senetat Sanctuary: Meeting place of the Senetat in Farjhem. Known for being sterile and devoid of any color excepting the crimson of their robes.

Shaman (Also: Healer): Another word for healer. There are varying degrees of shaman in the Deschanel family. Colleen Deschanel is said to be the strongest.

Sindre: Hails from the same Irish village as Birger, Astrid, and Eydis. A young elementalist who can conjure both fire and water, and often employs this skill to the hazard of others.

Skadi (Also: Skadi the Ruthless): The Brotherhood leader of Eastern Europe, residing in Bulgaria. She is known to be ruthless, cutthroat, and volatile to approach. She is remiss in her duties as a leader, in comparison to her peers, but is fiercely protective of her region.

St. Andrews, Finnegan: Husband of Anasofiya, father of Aleksandr. Born and raised in Maine to a normal, magic-free life. At his wedding, he accepted Aidrik's gift of Sveising, to grant him longer life and keener abilities. Recently learned he is descended from the Quinlans, and is a draoi, through this mother's side. Through his father, he is also descended from strong magic. Is a bestiakinetic.

St. Andrews, Ennis: Grandfather of Finnegan, father of Andrew, husband of Fiona. Lives in a protected, secluded clearing in the Scottish Highlands with his wife, who he keeps alive and young through potent magic.

St. Andrews, Fiona: Grandmother of Finnegan, mother of Andrew, wife of Ennis. Lives in a protected, secluded clearing in the Scottish Highlands with Ennis and is kept alive and young through his magic.

Starlight Awakener: An exceptionally rare form of necromancers said to "awaken the starlight," and employ the power of the heavens to occupy the living, and achieve immortality. Margarethe bred the family for centuries in search of a starlight awakener to come back through. Stella and Sebastian are starlight awakeners. Before them, the only known starlight awakener was Isabella.

Stian: A Brotherhood leader who chose Africa as his region because of the strife. He never stays anywhere for long, and is always moving around, helping where he can. As a terrakinetic, he can create a rift in the Earth, allowing a man to leave one place and appear in another, called a portail.

Sveising: DNA fusion unique to Empyreans. It is the process that allows multiple fathers for offspring, as well as the means by which Aidrik is able to save Anasofiya. Sveising can occur through sexual consummation (in the case of creating multiple fathers), but a mystic can also do it without consummation.

Telepath: One who can read the thoughts of others. Rare telepaths can read thoughts over long distances. Very few telepaths can also break a telepathic block. Tristan is a telepath who can reach across long distances and breach blocks.

Telepathic Block: A block employed my magic users to keep telepaths out of their head.

Terrakinetic: The ability to manipulate the spatial elements of Earth to your advantage. Example: a portail. Stian is a terrakinetic.

Thorvald: Brotherhood leader of Spain. He resides in the *Costa del Sol*, where he trains warriors and scouts in preparation for the inevitable war against the Senetat. Also one of the ancients, or earliest Empyreans.

Time Dancing (Also: Time Dancer): A skill unique to draoi. The time dancer can "dance" through time, a form of time traveling, but cannot change the past. Jacob is a time dancer.

Time Shaping (Also Time Shaper): An Empyrean skill that allows the individual to stop time and "reshape" it. The effect can be catastrophic if the caster is untrained, or if time stops for too long. Aleksandr is a time shaper.

Tribe: A group of Quinlans, usually descended from the same Tuatha tribe. All tribes have an elder, and a scribe.

Trygve: A Brotherhood leader, over Mongolia. One of the oldest Empyreans, having also been from the time of Runa, Brynja, and Einar, and has the markings of the ancients: exceptional height, dark red hair. Has one of the larger followings of the leaders. Known to be fair and loyal, but also quick to action and swift to justice.

Tuatha Dé Danann: Descended from Goddess Danu, early deities in Gaelic history, originating in Norway and later settling in Erin (Ireland). Ruled Ireland from 1897-1700 B.C. Many of the tales of faeries stem from their legends. There are four major tribes of Tuatha, each with a unique talisman of power. They hid in *Tir Non Og*, the otherworld, after Milesians drove them out of their lands. They believe strongly in reincarnation. Tuatha were the original druids, though modern day druidism became its own unique thing. The Quinlans descend from the four tribes of the Tuatha.

Ulfberht: A Viking sword produced between 800 and 1000 AD, made from Empyrean Steel (known to Man as Crucible Steel), known for its unusual combination of strength and flexibility. Though man believes this sword was crafted for Vikings, it was, in fact, created by Blacksmith, an ancient Empyrean metallurgist. The technology used to make Ulfberht baffles scientists to this day. Aidrik wielded one of the last of the originals, but gave it to Finnegan prior to his death.

Ward: A magical protection with unclear barriers, most

potent at its center. The ability to create wards came as a result of the alliance between Empyrean and Quinlan, and it was set forth that only an Empyrean (mystic) may create a ward, and only a Quinlan (draoi) can adhere it. Aidrik's ward is one such example, the center of it cast over *Ophélie* where it is most potent, with effects radiating out to protect other relatives. The protection diminishes the further out you go.

Yiva: Brotherhood leader of Southeast Asia, specifically residing in Thailand. Yields a body-length spear and is a powerful bestiakinetic. Known as the "she wolf."

ABOUT THE AUTHOR

Sarah is the USA Today and International Bestselling Author of over forty contemporary and epic fantasy stories, and the creator of the Kingdom of the White Sea and Saga of Crimson & Clover universes.

Born a geek, Sarah spends her time crafting rich and multilayered worlds, obsessing over history, playing her retribution paladin (and sometimes destruction warlock), and settling provocative Tolkien debates, such as why the Great Eagles are not Gandalf's personal taxi service. Passionate about travel, she's been to over twenty countries collecting sparks of inspiration, and is always planning her next adventure.

Sarah and her husband live in a beautiful corner of SE Pennsylvania with their three tiny benevolent pug dictators.

www.sarahmcradit.com

www.ingramcontent.com/pod-product-compliance
Lightning Source LLC
Chambersburg PA
CBHW020344310726
48979CB00015B/2498/J

* 9 7 8 1 9 5 8 7 4 4 1 0 9 *